The Bird's Child

The Bird's Child

SANDRA LEIGH PRICE

FOURTH ESTATE
An Imprint of HarperCollins*Publishers*

Fourth Estate
An imprint of HarperCollins*Publishers*

First published in Australia in 2015
by HarperCollinsPublishers Australia Pty Limited
ABN 36 009 913 517
harpercollins.com.au

HarperCollins*Publishers*
Level 13, 201 Elizabeth Street, Sydney, NSW 2000, Australia
Unit D1, 63 Apollo Drive, Rosedale, Auckland 0632, New Zealand
A 53, Sector 57, Noida, UP, India
1 London Bridge Street, London, SE1 9GF, United Kingdom
2 Bloor Street East, 20th floor, Toronto, Ontario M4W 1A8, Canada
195 Broadway, New York, NY 10007, USA

National Library of Australia Cataloguing-in-Publication data:

Price, Sandra Leigh, author.
The bird's child / Sandra Leigh Price.
ISBN: 978 1 4607 5000 1 (paperback)
ISBN: 978 1 4607 0420 2 (ebook)
Magic – Australia – Fiction.
A823.4

Cover design by Matt Stanton, HarperCollins Design Studio
Cover images by shutterstock.com
Author photograph by Joern Harris
Typeset in Sabon LT Roman by Kirby Jones

Dedicated with love to:
my Mother and Father
and
my Little Jackie Winter,
my little familiar

PART ONE

1929
In Full View

ONE

Billy

This window is my eye. From my room I can see everyone, including my neighbour, the girl who lives in the room next to mine, hobbling down the street in her new shoes, a pair made of silvery leather with a strap that buckles delightfully across her ankle.

From the moment I laid eyes on her that morning in the street I knew she was my shining light. I made sure she didn't see me reflected in the shop windows along King Street, nor when I followed as she turned into a leafy avenue. She ran up the front stairs of a house and my eyes tracked the hem of her trousers – just like a man's. I hadn't seen anything like that since France, when a lady ambulance driver delivered her wounded to the hospital and we all gawped from our beds at her legs.

The girl vanished through the front door and I saw there was a *ROOM TO LET* sign in the window of a grand old house, with three tiers like a cake. A cat like spilled marmalade filled the sandstone groove worn into the stair and seemed disinclined to move, so I took the steps two at a time. Looking up at the cast-iron lace on the balcony, ornate as a petticoat, I knocked and waited, hoping to catch another glimpse. Deep in the house the wireless made tinny sounds like a pocket full of thruppences. Still I waited. On the side of the house was a pompous plaque, *LEDA*, it said, as if a house could not do with a number alone.

Leda. Was the girl seduced by a swan or the swan seduced by a girl? I could never remember. There on the stoop, I could feel the heat coming off the building, the sun captured in the stone, the house like a living thing.

The door opened and the landlady appeared, her fine bleached hair scooped to the top of her head and held with a pencil. She took one look at me and my box of retrieved things, which had come so close to oblivion, and led the way to a room at the top of the stairs. Strangely, the vacant room had been painted pupil-black, but that was not enough to deter me. I followed her back down the stairs to the sitting room and waited on the velvet settee while she bustled around the kitchen.

A large carved sideboard crowded with photos caught my attention. I craned my neck in hope her face glittered back at me from their frames. Instead a door opened in the house and with it a draught brushed against my legs, followed by the reward of her, moving in the mantle mirror down the stairs. She shone. Her face was translucent, lips painted, pressed petals from the pages of a book, only in want of my kisses. The silver sparks of her shoes caught the light. I wanted to follow to see where she was going, I wanted to know all – what her breath was like upon my face, how her voice sounded close to my ear, how she looked first thing in the morning, her eyelids dewy with sleep. My curiosity was like an itch. The front door slammed with the assistance of the breeze, making all the oriental bibelots dance, and she was gone.

'What line of work are you in dear?' the landlady's voice sallied out from the kitchen. My thoughts spun. How many jobs had I had? More than could be counted on a caterpillar's toes, I'd keep them a week or month and move along, pocketing whatever coins I could jingle. I had been many things: a child scavenger, a gravedigger's assistant, a boy soldier, a rabbitoh, a shearer, a knife thrower, an apothecary's assistant, a hypnotic apprentice. But never again a dupe and a fool.

'I am …' I paused for effect, and the kettle began to hiss as if it knew a liar, 'an artist.' Of sorts.

'An artist! Oh you will fit in here quite perfectly, monsieur.' Why had she spoken to me in French? All I had ever seen of France was the arse end of a trench.

'Rent is paid in advance, I'm sure you understand,' she called out.

'Perfectly,' I replied, cutting her off, in want of no pity. 'I start tomorrow at the box office of the theatre down the road. I'll be good for the rent. I can pay my own way.' The first job I had stumbled upon I took; I would be beholden to no one, never again.

The reassuring weight of my wooden box pressed on my lap, my old cradle, my beer crate. I was keen to check all had been preserved just as I had left it and stole a glimpse of all I had in the world. But I lowered the lid as she swept into the room, a clattering tray clutched in her hands. There would be time enough for me to do a proper inventory once I was alone, in my new room.

'Of course, of course, *mon chéri.* Your room gets very fine light. It was my father's study once and he could spend all day in there with his nose pressed to the print of a book and never notice it. Really the ancient world that he studied seemed more solid than the room he sat in. God bless him, Mr …'

'Little. William Little after my father, but people just call me plain Billy.' My father, the sly old bastard, would have to rely on what he had reaped in this life for his rewards in the next, for there would be no blessings from me.

'Oh fortuitous heavens, it must be a sign! My father's name was William too. You shall fit in here just so,' she went on like a pork chop in a synagogue.

'All these rooms – where do you sleep?' I asked as politely as I could muster, imagining her rattling on through the night regardless of who was there to listen.

'Oh, I have taken the space in the attic. So you'll be sharing the house with me and a young woman, her room is next to yours.'

When I closed the door behind me I placed my box upon the bed and curled myself beside it, the dark walls comforting like a womb. Sleep dragged at my eyelids and I woke with a start, not recalling where I was, listening to the house settle around me. My head ached as I stood upright and leaned against the wall to watch the quiet street with only the gathering of the clouds for company. Hanging from my shirt sleeve was a gossamer thread of hair, a heartstring. The hair of my silver-heeled girl? I stretched it taut and plucked it and listened for a bewitching music, but I had not earned the ears to hear. Her hair the colour of a spider's web. So very different from the first girl I thought I loved.

Her name was Golden Fortune and her hair was as black as rain falling in the darkness. There was something of the doll about her – she was around five foot two inches, dressed in the calico pyjamas that her people wore, a simple backdrop for the fuchsia flare of her cheek, and on her feet black velvet slippers with tiny gold embroidery. In her hair were stones twisted in golden twine, just a comb, but in the slick of her dark tresses it was a crown. Golden Fortune worked for her father, a wily old oriental who ran his own opium den down at the Rocks, right under the noses of the police. It was Golden Fortune's job to make sure the customers remained comfortable, their heads resting on worn cushions from the first blissful inhalation of smoke, and to float like a golden koi though their hazy fancies and shuffle her fingers though their pockets and the treasures therein.

I do not know where it was that my father developed a taste for opium, whether it had been while he worked the docks or during his travels at sea, but it was a taste he would never forget. We were living in a room above a pub in the Rocks so he could be closer to the boats and the fresh gambling companions he would cheat out of their wages. Where or who my mother was was as much a mystery to him as it was to me, or so I thought. My father claimed in one of his floating moments that someone had left me on his doorstep with nothing but a piece of paper, the words *Ha ha* scrawled upon it. But I could never glean the truth. My father treated me with carefree negligence, as if the heavens had made me and therefore were responsible for my mothering. When I was an infant he had procured an Aboriginal barmaid as my wet nurse and it was she who had wiped my tiny arse and rocked me close to her heartbeat when I cried. She sang to me songs in her own language, songs of brolgas and emus and magpies, until, as an older child, I couldn't get to sleep without rocking myself with their melody, just as my father couldn't seem to sleep without his daily lullaby in the poppy's embrace.

The opium den my father favoured was hidden by an innocuous wall made from bales of wool, hidden in plain sight at the back of a warehouse. The wool bales were stamped with black-inked names of farms all across New South Wales, some stamped with the image of the proud merino's spiralled horns. According to my father, opium was a legitimate import like wool was an export. Had the sickly stink of opium penetrated through the bales and into the wool itself? Would it be spun into wool or smoke?

Golden Fortune's father dabbled in more than one line of business, but he knew she was his biggest asset. He often called out her praises from his small black lacquer desk down the back of the den, hung with curtains made from the old hessian stamped in a language I didn't understand, more like naughts and crosses than words. While the opium smokers gazed only at the calligraphy or rising smoke, I watched Golden Fortune, her eyes the only glittering thing moving in the half-light. From the pockets of the regular dreamers she took only a tithe. In the case of the customer just passing through, she would rummage a little deeper, the tax for being a stranger. In my presence, she only skimmed my father's pocket, and if I was lucky, she'd slip me a shilling of the plunder.

Sometimes Golden Fortune would try to teach me to play mahjong, not that I ever mastered the game, for I would only ever win when she let me, if I had pleased her. I was in the habit of bringing her gifts: a blue wren's egg, a boiled sweet, a perfect glass marble – anything to see her reaction. She was the only friend of my childhood.

I remember one day my father was, as usual, lying on his back, the pipe still lolling in his fingers, soon to be abandoned on the floor. The smoke was sickly strong in the air, as the rain polka-dotted the window. Golden Fortune greeted me with her usual disinterest, the comb in her ebony hair luminous in the gloomy light. The comb's twisted gold held a world in itself: turquoise crickets, bloodstone dragonflies, quartz shimmering koi, the milky green jade of butterfly wings, all interlinked with delicate knots of seed pearl and coral.

Her father was working out the back and only nodded to acknowledge my presence. When Golden Fortune bent down over my father, the comb clattered to the floor, and a swathe of her hair fell over her shoulder, revealing the skin of her neck, so pale that I shivered. I wanted nothing more than to put my dirty thumb prints all over it. None of the dreamers stirred. She snatched the comb back up and wound her hair into its teeth before she got back to the task at hand inside my father's coat pocket. She hesitated and I watched her gold-flecked eyes grow large with curiosity. What had her dexterous fingers plucked? The buds of her chest rose and fell under her calico sheath. She reeled it out: there between her slender and stealthy fingers was a golden pocket watch I had never seen before.

Golden Fortune held the watch aloft by the chain and it spun by itself in the air. I held my hand out for it, but the beauty of the thing fixed it to her hand and she would not give it up. The watch spun in the air between us – its golden back was engraved with something, but it was spinning too fast for me to decipher the words. My father stirred. Golden Fortune hesitated. Her doubt was the signal for my action. I reached out and grabbed it and she acquiesced without a sound, knowing in her little thief's heart that it would be a more fitting thing to be seen in my possession than hers.

My father settled back down and I clicked the catch and watched it spring open. On one side was the fine stark face of the watch and on the other was a photo of a woman who could have been my twin. Did I have a sister and not know it? I wanted to kick my father in the ribs right then and there, but I didn't. Not because I wasn't brave enough, nor fired with enough rage, but because if I was going to do it, I wanted him to be awake, aware of where the bruises came from. I was trembling and Golden Fortune gently took the watch from my hand, holding it close, her fingers running over the engraving. I knew she was tempted not to put it back and it was then that I knew everything was in my favour.

The steady rhythm of her father's fingers upon the abacus stopped abruptly. As he brushed past the curtain I saw the beads were still spinning, his count forgotten as he rushed out of his office, his pigtail streaming behind him like a kite's tail. His emergency was my opportunity. He turned the key in the lock and left us alone with the smoke and the sleepers.

'What do you want for it?' she said bluntly, loudly, not her usual whisper at all. Her audacity caught me unawares.

What could I ask for in exchange for the watch; what couldn't I ask for? Surely five minutes passed with all the possibilities and everything in between, till Golden Fortune interpreted my unspoken request and slid her shoulders out of her calico pyjamas, her hips shimmying out of the cloth. She stood before me naked, her narrow sloped shoulders and the slight flare of her hips reminding me of a fish out of water. I reached and pulled out the precious comb from her hair and placed it on the floor. Her hair untwisted itself slowly as if unwinding underwater. The only sound between us was the ticking of my father's watch.

Golden Fortune was the first living female I had seen in the flesh. I had seen my father's collection of French postcards, tucked under his mattress, but they were nothing compared to this.

If my father's drug was opium, mine was surely to be skin. The texture of Golden Fortune's skin surprised me: the most supple silk draped upon her bones, her hip and collarbone ivory points pressing against it. I looked at all the opium sleepers, some eyelids leaden to the world, some fluttering like poppy petals in a breeze. When my hand touched her, her eyes widened. I could have done anything, but all I wanted was to touch every inch of her golden skin. I ran my fingers down her arms to her fingers, a gust of goose flesh blowing like pollen across her shoulders. I ran my fingertips around the aureole of her nipples, watching them blush and grow harder. I tracked both sides of her ribs and encircled her waist, cupping the twin moons of her bottom. I crouched down, my hands swirling over her belly, down the flank of her thighs, tracing the mons veneris of her nest. I demanded she turn around, her straight hair like a horse's mane twitched down to her hips. I flicked her hair back over her shoulder, whipping it back like a rein, her neck shining for my touch. And so I did, with my fingers, my lips, my tongue. She shivered without restraint, before dropping to the floor, gathering her calico garments and making for her father's office, leaving her comb and my father's watch abandoned on the floor.

Without thinking I gathered up the comb and shoved it in my pocket. I heard her father's key in the lock, so I plucked the watch off the ground and flicked the glass plate off with my thumbnail and took the photograph before she returned.

By the time Golden Fortune's father was in the doorway, I had tucked the watch in her mahjong box, roused my father from his stupor and led him out the door. When he sobered up and came down from his heaven, he reached into his pocket and let out an almighty howl, but refused to tell me what he was missing. After the watch was gone he vowed to give up the poppy altogether and instead fell into the world at the end of a bottle.

With her silvery hair still twisted around my finger, turning my skin as pale as hers, my vigilance was rewarded. She appeared in the street below, a newspaper tucked under her arm. *How beautiful were her feet with shoes.* Geisha steps. The late afternoon sun painted her all over golden, an idol, though she was white as white can be. She stood out from all around her, the world made silhouette by her light. Her skin was incandescent and had the waxy quality of a candle. She leaned down as if she had dropped something, but no, she was easing off her shoes, wincing, her stockings ruined by two little peepholes of flesh where blisters flared against her heels. Ahead of her, men had started to trickle past, their shapeless coats tugged at by the breeze. Were they half the gentleman I was, their coats would be off, a bridge for her feet to walk upon.

The light in my room turned a stark yellow as the approaching storm squeezed the last of the sunlight from the sky. I looked out the window again. A man's skullcap was lifted and tossed away on the fingers of a gust like a coin in a magic trick, right over to the dainty instep of my little neighbour. She stopped it with her toe, and plucked it up with her spare hand, her shoes clasped beneath her elbow with the newspaper. She returned it to its owner, then the sound of the thunder made her start and do a quick foxtrot on the road. Her feet moved quicker as the first raindrops splashed and the branches of the trees overlapped like waves on a violent sea.

Her newspaper flapped only once before it fluttered up into the air, a suspended flock of black and white pages, her mouth cooing for them to return. One obscured the windscreen of a car as it tore around the corner. If the car had so much as sprayed her with gravel, I would have tracked it down and made a pretty pattern across the paintwork with my blade and turned its rubber tyres to ribbons. Pages blew towards a bicycle, flickering in the spiralling spokes. The bike stopped, but the rider continued, his jacket billowing until his limbs seemed to fold in on themselves and he fell twisted at her feet. She crumpled to her knees. Was she injured? Her mouth moved but no sound reached my ears from behind the glass. If he had made her bleed, I would have him bleed in recompense, an eye for an eye.

She put the cloth of her blouse to his temple, the faintest smear of red swelled onto the white. His fingers clutched at her and I wanted at once to pull the window up and shout. How I wished I had been able to calculate the exact moment when my little neighbour would be at the mercy of the elements. It could have been me cycling by, it could have been me leaning on her tender arm, subject to her gentle ministrations. But it was his hand on her arm, not mine. I looked away for a moment as I pulled the lid off my box and retrieved the mother-of-pearl opera glasses, which I was relieved to find had not been pawned. My fingers twirled at the focus wheel. Had a bruise suddenly formed on her flesh? No, it was just a blot on my eye. Lucky for him I could blink it away.

I steadied my hands as I had seen the snipers do in France. I could see a strange marking on his hand, a smudge no blinking could make clear. I rubbed the lenses of the opera glasses, one after the other, with my shirt tail. Yet still the illegible mark was on his hand. Perhaps some headline had released its ink with his sweat. I knew that when you bought pork from the butcher, the pink flesh displayed all yesterday's news backwards. I fiddled with the focus; the letters jumbled and rearranged themselves before my eyes. It was a tattoo running along the middle finger of his left hand, from the top of the nail to the base of his wrist. I cupped my hand against the light. It was one long word. I tried to make it out, sounding out each letter to see if it would make sense.

I was about to give up, when the word was suddenly clear, sprung like a lock, the letters obvious, their meaning obscure.

Abracadabra.

Had I timed it perfectly I might have counted the steps she would take until she neared the house. I could have descended the stairs just as she ascended them. Instead I delayed, observing from the top of the stairs as she entered the front door. She was undamaged, but one could not say the same for the newspaper clutched beneath her arm, tattered like a drunk's blanket. The rain had set her hair a-frizz, her cheeks suddenly rouged, and there was something about the way her lips parted, the breath panting out of her, her teeth small like pearls. I caught my breath.

She sat down on the settee in the living room, the newspaper pages falling around her like a nest as she searched them until she found the one she wanted. She discarded the rest to the fireplace, perched with kindling and waiting to be lit. I'd already read them all – debt, repatriation agreements, the decline of the price of wool. Tentatively I took another step down as she rested her chin in her hands, the employment page spread over her legs. She circled the possibilities with a reluctant swirl, hardly leaving a mark at all. I couldn't believe my luck, she was just sitting there awaiting my introduction. She lifted her face toward me as I approached, and blinked, her hand coming up to shield her eyes. I stepped forward out of the glare of the chandelier and extended my hand, observing all the delicacy of her features, the curious absence of her eyebrows, the blonde fringe of her eyelashes over her dark eyes, and the transparent pink lips free of their paint. In that moment I imagined her in the gold braided theatre uniform and felt the little flare of her torch shine into the darkened corners, wishing it would shine into me.

'There is a position going where I work, in the theatre, for an usherette, if you are interested? Billy Little at your service,' I said, sweeping into a bow. I had just secured a position at the box office myself. Usherettes came and went, a feminine procession every day of the week, I was sure of it.

She smiled. 'Sounds better than this lot,' she said warily. 'Better than my last job.'

'Which was?' There was so much I wanted to know, but she just looked down at her newspaper.

'Anything to pay the rent.' As much as I wanted to pry it all out of her, I let her be, lest she shut up completely.

'Would you be interested then, Miss ...?'

'You can call me Lily,' she answered, looking me squarely in the eye, so I knew she was lying, but still she had given me a name: a little victory.

'I can introduce you to the boss tomorrow after breakfast if you like, Lily.' Her name on my lips made me smile and she smiled back. I'd give her my own job if they couldn't find her one.

'Thank you, Mr Little, I appreciate it.' She extended her hand and it rested briefly in mine, a bird's handshake before fluttering away, our little bargain. I watched her walk up the stairs, the way the trousers cinched and draped her all at once, before waiting a respectful time to follow on her heels and return to my room. There I realised that my thumb was still encircled with her hair, the tip livid with blood.

The rain splattered the window. I had the comb tucked safely away and I was tempted to take it from its hiding place. But I didn't need to see it to imagine what it would be like to slide it into the halo of Lily's pale hair. The creatures made of jade and quartz would come to life. Would she ever let me?

TWO

Ari

The rain fell in the darkness, tiny fists a tantrum upon the tin roof. Miss du Maurier had been kind enough to let me use a little space where once the horses had been stabled and now was just a shed, somewhere I could practise on my own, without interruption, a place close to home. There were two stalls and an open space where the old trap would have been housed, and a small fireplace. I furnished it with a tattered armchair reclaimed from the lane. I kept my books and my Houdini scrapbook in a milk crate, and on the floor was an old kangaroo skin I had found rolled up under one of the saddles. A kerosene lantern hung from above, giving off a greasy metallic smell.

Since her father passed away, Miss du Maurier had decided to rent out rooms, more for company than for money. To get the house ready, I had helped her paint each room a different colour. We had painted one of the upstairs rooms black; I wasn't sure that anyone would want to sleep in a room like that – it would be like sleeping in a tomb – but Miss du Maurier had insisted, a dramatic gesture, a room made memorial to her father. She had offered to help me paint the shed, but I preferred it as it was, the abandoned paint tins stacked in the neighbouring stall.

I had waited all day to come across the road and see how my precious cargo had fared. The day had all but disappeared between work at the Red Rose and my uncle's errands – reading the newspaper for an elderly Jewish lady, teaching the violin to a congregant's son, cleaning the synagogue windows up a ladder. My uncle kept me as busy as he could, leaning on my indecision, which he thought a weak spot. But for me this made a safe distance between his expectations and my dreams. With the evening meal over I had slipped the shackles of my uncle's glare and returned to the shed, hesitant to lift the covering cloth from the box. The creature was still in shock, its yellow-lidded eyes not yet opening to the light. Just like mine the first day off the boat when I was a small child.

My aunt held me close that day, even though I had just met her, while my uncle barely let his eyes alight on me. The city rose up out of the dust, the buildings themselves made of sand. The sky seemed vaulted and never-ending, though it was the beginning of evening and the weeks at sea made the horizon tilt at every bump. Sharing the road with our cart were black shining motorcars, while on the footpath people walked dressed in light summer clothes. I was still wearing my winter coat. We turned into a large boulevard flanked by green grounds which seemed to house a castle. My aunt leaned down to me and whispered in Yiddish, '*Universitet.*' University. My uncle clicked his tongue, which I thought was a signal to the horse, but my aunt and uncle shared a glance that even the horse sensed and twitched his ears at. We trailed onto a different street, L'Avenue. The foundations of the synagogue were rising brick stumps in the dry mud, growing from my uncle's ambition. Next door, in a building that had once been a peanut factory, was a hall where services were held in the meantime. My aunt and uncle lived in a flat above it.

Walking down the path came Mr du Maurier, as rigid as a piece of chalk in his grey suit, his cane tapping instructions to the ground. Clasped to his arm was his daughter, her hair shorn shockingly short for the time, her sheer dress whipping around her legs. I later found out that she was a dancer at the Tivoli, at which my aunt and uncle exchanged another glance and said no more, grateful for the friendship of her father all the same. My uncle spoke a greeting and they called out something in the language I was yet to understand. They stopped by the side of the cart and shook hands and Miss du Maurier put her hand up to my face and smiled as if I had done something clever. Her fingers were cool on my hot skin.

The parrot lifted his eyelid and looked up at me now with a world-weary eye. I dipped my finger in a glass of water and let the drop fall into his beak, his almond-rough tongue reaching out for it. Poor little thing. He was a little miracle of colour: Eden-green feathers, chalkier on the breast, a black band like a velvet choker around his little throat – created by G_d with the other birds on the fifth day according to the Torah.

The parrot's tongue searched for the tip of my finger, while the pincer-sharp beak pressed close to enough to draw blood. I did not pull away. When I was a boy I had read in the newspaper that Harry Houdini had a pet parrot, an African grey, he had taught to pick locks and say, 'Hip hip hooray.' I had foolishly read these words aloud to my aunt and uncle.

Straightaway my uncle had snatched the paper from my hands, ripped out the offending article and thrown it into the hot mouth of the stove.

'Hip hip hurrah! The disgrace of it! *Hip! Hip!* is the abbreviation for *Hiierosolyma Est Perdita,* Latin for 'Jerusalem is destroyed', coined by the Romans under Titus's destruction of the Temple. The *Hurrah* was added by German Knights in the Middle Ages while they were crusading in the Holy Land. It is Slavonic for 'to Paradise'. They shouted it while killing our people. Let me hear no more of it!'

When Houdini died, I had later learned, the parrot went to live at a boarding house as Mrs Houdini couldn't bear to hear her husband's voice coming from the mouth of the bird. It escaped one day, turning a key left in a lock, deft as its master.

The green parrot looked up at me, a slow filmy blink. What would my uncle make of it?

I pulled my collar up around my neck, nestled the parrot in the front of my shirt and made a dash outside. Perhaps there was something in the kitchen I could feed him with. Some oats in milk or breadcrumbs? Miss du Maurier left the back door unlocked and I was free to come and go as I pleased. After my shift at the Red Rose I'd spend some time trying to learn my tricks in the shed, poring over the instructions, until they were tangled in my head. Sometimes if Miss du Maurier was still up, she'd call me in and we'd share a pot of tea, or she'd ask me to play some of her old Tivoli songs on the piano for old times' sake, her slippered feet remembering half-forgotten steps. But as I approached the house, I could see the door was already wide open and the girl sat on the stoop, hands under her chin as she watched the rain fall, the water drawing vertical lines against a backdrop of darkness.

When I had crashed into her with my bike I had only seen a blur, but now I could see her clearly, sitting on the back stairs, lost in her thoughts. She appeared amidst the raindrops to be stitched from the light and I hesitated unsure if she would fade from my sight, a figment made solely by my eyes, the afterimage of the extinguished lamp. I stepped forward, but the rain was too loud on the tin roof for her to hear my footsteps. When she saw me she skittered sidewise before her eyes adjusted. Her hand fluttered up to her chest.

'Sorry to frighten you,' I said, the water dripping off my elbows and into puddles at either side of my feet.

'I just got a shock, that's all,' she said, rising to her feet and dusting off the back of her trousers. I had never seen such a thing, a woman in trousers, and tried not to stare. 'I am so sorry about yesterday ...' With the rain falling about her in the darkness, she was as white and silvery as a sapling birch.

'I should have watched where I was going.'

The water from my wet hair started down my face and travelled the ridge of my nose, but she didn't seem to notice. She resumed her seat in the doorway, shuffling over so I could pass if I chose to. But I didn't choose to. I shrugged off my wet jacket, trying to release myself of the tight grip of the wet wool, carefully cradling the parrot with one hand beneath my clothes. As I attempted to peel off the coat I became entangled. The parrot dug his beak into my skin – an accident or in protest – and I winced. Then her hand was on my shoulder, pulling at the coat until it slid free and she draped it over the back of an old beach chair that was sheltered from the rain. I was glad that my uncle was across the road, deep in his dreams – touch between unmarried men and women was strictly forbidden.

'What is in your shirt?' she wondered, wrapping her arms around herself.

I sat in the gap she had made for me, our bodies close, our shoulders nearly touching. Somewhere out in the night a plover made its ghostly echoing call and the rain pelted even harder in response. Sheet lightning flared up in the sky and seed pods fell to the ground from the plane tree. The parrot attempted to stretch his wings, his claws trying to find traction in the few hairs that gathered on my chest, until his green head sprouted over the top of my shirt.

'Oh, he's beautiful!' she burst out. 'Where did you find him?'

'I found him crouched in the gutter, just before I started work,' I replied, pulling him free. 'I put him in a darkened box hoping he would recover.'

She reached over and took him, the tips of her fingers brushing mine, before she cradled him in the crook of her arm. His eye rolled up at me in bliss. When he was calm she pulled out each wing like a Spanish fan and the bird shivered beneath her touch. She handed him back to me and picked up seed pods the rain had shaken from the trees, placing one spiky ball between her teeth and plucking out the seeds within before offering them to the parrot. His beak opened ravenously.

'How did you know he would eat that?' I asked.

'At home flocks of parrots hang off the plane tree for hours, stripping them seed by seed. When there are no leaves left on the trees, the birds hang like jewels.' She smiled at me. Her face gleamed as if she had been caught in a photographer's flash and the glare would not leave her skin.

I passed the bird back to her and tried to release the seeds from the pod myself with my teeth, but nothing came free in my mouth. Her laughter tumbled out of her.

'How long have you boarded with Miss du Maurier?' I asked. The first I'd seen of her was when we collided on the street.

'I escaped here almost a week ago,' she said, scouting around for another seed pod to crack. 'You? I thought you lived across the road.'

'I do, but I've been coming over here since I was a little child. Escaped also,' I replied, running my hand through the wet bramble of my hair, trying to make light, yet not wanting to elaborate to a stranger, no matter how friendly. I did not want to make her the bearer of my burden.

'Well, aren't we a bunch of escapees,' she said, breaking apart another pod and sorting the seeds in the palm of her hand. 'Yes, real escape artists, that's for sure.' The rain seemed to slow, rivulets carving their way through the couch grass.

'When I enquired about the room, Miss du Maurier mentioned that there was a young man who used the shed for his magical aspirations. I knew then I had to take the room. I am assuming this young man is you? Would it be rude of me to ask what those aspirations are? You see, once my curiosity has been piqued, then there is no end to it.' Her face was as open as a book.

'You took the room because of me?' I asked in disbelief, feeling my face grow hot.

She blushed in reply, her voice flustered. 'It felt like a sign. Superstitious nonsense, I know, but my father loved magic, it made me think of him.'

'I have an interest in magic, just for myself, for my own amusement,' I said cautiously. 'It's nothing really, a silly hobby. Miss du Maurier thinks everyone has stars in their eyes.' Self-consciously I tugged my sleeve over my hand, letting the wool conceal my tattoo. The parrot stepped up my forearm to find better purchase, his eyes wide and blinking in the darkness. I looked at the green feathers graduating to pink in his tail, rather than see her expression, wishing I had kept my foolishness to myself.

'Yes?' she said breathlessly, and I took courage to look at her. She didn't blink. She didn't look away. She was waiting for me to say more, her eyes were on my lips. What did I have to say that was worth her hearing? I looked away and heard her sigh. I could have fallen into that silence and never spoken again.

'My father had a magic trick he taught me once. It was famous in our household, especially at Christmas,' she said wistfully. She pulled out her trouser pockets, 'Do you have a coin on you? I can show it to you if you like.' A woman in trousers. Suddenly it came to me: Houdini had made Bess wear a type of trousers upon the stage when they first started out. It was in the book my aunt had given me. Plunging my hands in my pockets, I rummaged for the coin she requested, but all I could find was a handkerchief and scraps of paper.

'Sorry, no luck,' I said. Whatever I earned at the Red Rose I handed over to my uncle. It was I who was curious now. 'Tell me how it is done.'

'Well, that would be telling, a magician doesn't reveal her secrets,' she said, blinking, her milk-coloured hair cascading into her eyes. As she brushed it away, she looked straight at me, a slight tremor in her eyes. I was still waiting for an answer. 'It involves a coin disappearing into skin, a lot of rubbing and a lot of misdirection. Something to impress a five-year-old, it would be nothing to Houdini.'

My heart pounded, *Hou-din-i, Hou-din-i,* his name my private incantation. How many times had I said it over and over in my head to block out the past? Everyone knew who Houdini was, but I always thought of him as mine, my own, my phantom father. To hear his name spoken by her laid me bare. Who was she?

Without warning the parrot spread his wings and fluttered upward. I was concerned he would fly into the window and pound against the glass, unable to see it. But I needn't have worried, for the parrot alighted with a start upon the platinum waves of the girl's hair, as a wild and gleeful gasp escaped from her lips. I would have left him there, just to see the delight in her face, but she coaxed him onto her hand as he chattered and cocked his head, showing as much curiosity in her as I. Even when she handed me the parrot again, he was reluctant to step that short bridge between our fingers. Our hands hovered, waiting. The mark on my hand looked like a dirty smudge in this light and I was made self-conscious by it, until she clicked her tongue between her teeth and the parrot shuffled his feet back in my direction.

'Night then,' she announced, standing up, and I hurried to stand with her. She tipped the remaining seed from her hand and trickled it into my palm.

The following morning a bird sang out out in the rain like a slow bell silenced when the postman came through the gate. My Uncle Israel liked to be the first to scoop the mail into his eager hands, always looking for letters that never arrived. His consolation was to sit at the breakfast table, scouring the newspaper for stories of anywhere near home. I pulled on my clothes and leaped out of the bedroom; it didn't pay to be late.

Aunt Hephzibah looked up at me as she turned the valve of the samovar, the steam swirling around the top of the cup. She had beaten my uncle, the newspaper and post gathered close to her chest, no envelopes at all. We took our places at the table. My uncle led a short prayer, and then unfolded the newspaper in front of him, his glasses fogging up from the steamy tea. Something caught his eye and he spluttered.

'Israel, what is it?' Aunt Hephzibah asked.

'There is talk again, a possible reformation of the Jewish Territorialist Organisation. And another proposal to make a settlement in Uganda or South America or even here of all places. Unbelievable. They will fail again,' my uncle said, toast crumbs settling in his beard. My aunt refilled our cups from the samovar, the steam exhaled on her face. 'The Promised Land is the land we were promised, it's not something a committee can decide.'

The article would go in his ageing brown scrapbook. It was a rare evening that my uncle didn't have it spread out on his desk, rereading the past as if he could unravel the puzzle and prophesise the future. My uncle finished his breakfast and took the newspaper with him to his study, the crisp white printed sheets to be sacrificed to the flash of scissors. When he was finished he would return the discarded newspaper to the dining table, with all the gaps and windows and half-sentences he had made, censored as if we were at war.

The heavy rain of the night before had cleansed the road, the smell of eucalyptus enveloping the streets. On the footpath, the shredded leaves of trees, as if from random pruning. When I arrived at the Red Rose, Jandy was out the front sweeping the footpath. He was bent over the broom, his bald head catching the gleam of the sun. When he saw me, he looked up, his snaggled teeth revealed in a smile.

'Ari, Ari, what a storm!' he said with the relish of a connoisseur. 'How is the parrot? Is it ready to be stuffed and become a pirate prop next door?' He gestured to the theatre across the road as a motorcar drove by, blowing all the refuse of the storm back over our feet.

'Ai ai ai,' Jandy exclaimed, setting to the path again with renewed vigour.

I went in and started filling up the lolly jars, the smell treacle-sweet. Whilst I was wiping down the table tops, Jandy bustled in, the bell hitting against the door.

'You never did answer me about that parrot,' he said, starting to polish the chrome-topped coffee machine.

'He lives,' I said. My thoughts flew straight to the girl and how the parrot had taken the seed from her mouth as if the two of them were made of similar stuff – except where the parrot was coloured by a rainbow's touch, she was almost completely bereft of colour. Even her eyelashes were like paintbrushes dipped in milk wash, so fair they hardly made a shadow beneath her eyes. She was distinctly moon-like, moth-like and yet altogether familiar. She was a glimmering girl.

Miss du Maurier had given me a book for my birthday which my uncle frowned at every time he saw me reading it. It was a book of poems and one carouselled in my head unbidden:

And when white moths were on the wing,
And moth-like stars were flickering out,
I dropped the berry in a stream
And caught a little silver trout.

When I had laid it on the floor
I went to blow the fire aflame,
But something rustled on the floor,
And someone called me by my name:
It had become a glimmering girl
With apple blossom in her hair
Who called me by my name and ran
And faded through the brightening air.

Jandy polished his pate with his hand and then, with one happy flick of the switch, turned on his pride and joy, the soda fountain that slowly burbled to life. The shop doorbell sang out and in walked the first customer of the day: the Birdman, named for his uncanny ability to mimic any bird sound he heard. Jandy whipped out a frosted glass and filled it with milk and chocolate syrup and stuck in a spoon to stir it up, just the way the Birdman liked it. The Birdman. If he had another name, he never used it.

He sat down at the bar and offloaded his swag on the floor, taking his ease in the stool. The swag appeared to be made of some sort of blanket or coat, the russet-grey fur lush at the edges. You could not tell if he was young or old, his weather-beaten face was so covered in beard. Above it, his keen-eyed glare took in everything. He whistled as he swiped the stockman's hat from his head and placed it on the floor. He was always whistling. It made me think of a bird I once saw as a child in my grandmother's jewellery box, opening its red mouth, spinning around when the lid of the box opened.

'Been keeping well?' Jandy asked. It was a rare few weeks that the Birdman didn't make an appearance. 'We found a parrot the other day out on the footpath. The racket it made as Ari here scooped it up in a tea towel! Beak like a can opener.'

'Did you now?' He drank from the frosted glass and wiped the milk carefully from the corners of his mouth.

Jandy nodded in my direction. 'Our feathered friend is in Ari's care.'

The Birdman turned his bright eyes toward me. 'What did it look like?' I described the powdery green feathers tipped with pink, the black velvet choker of feathers around his throat. 'Hmmm, not a local then, by the sounds of things.'

None of us were, it seemed. We had all been shipwrecked by storms over which we had no control.

'One of my neighbours got him to eat some seed cracked out of a pod. Do you think I could train him?'

The Birdman's eyes twinkled. 'Parrots can be trained, that's for sure, but there are other birds that pose a more interesting challenge.' He puffed out his chest, swung his elbow over the back of his chair and held out his glass for a refill.

'Like what?' I asked.

'A lyrebird. That's what you need. If you could get hold of one. That bird is a true sign of God's hand at work.'

'What's a lyrebird?' I said. There were more birds in this country than could be imagined.

'A lyrebird, my boy, has the language of angels. Now there is something not many have seen nor have heard, but I have. A lyrebird in full possession of its instrument.

'What do you mean?'

'I was out in the bush a while back, tramping the road. The dust blew ferocious and I hoped to Hades that some car or other would come and let me hitch a ride to town. But it wasn't a car that started wending its way toward me, but a willy-willy.' The Birdman gave me a piercing look and took a deep breath. The hairs stood on the back of my neck. 'I took to the scrub like a wanted man. As the willy-willy roared closer, dust filled my nostrils and coated my tongue and I covered my face with my coat as best I could, hoping it would pass me by. But the willy-willy was in a rage. It was a *thing* hungry for throwing. A hailstorm of pebbles pummelled my back. Somewhere in the distance I heard the faraway sound of a car engine, it seemed to grow louder, approaching, coming in my direction. Could I make a run for it to see if I could hail a ride? But as soon as I lifted my head the car silenced.'

What was a willy-willy? Fear crawled from the corners of my mind; I had never escaped the terror of being chased. Even in the night I still woke with their footsteps pounding in my ears.

The Birdman paused and waited for my complete attention before he continued, and once he had it, spared a moment to let his eyes wander over the spectacle of sweets.

'Had the car broken down? Perhaps the wind had tricked me, with its voice like a bullroarer screaming in my ears. My Aboriginal grandmother had told me stories of Willy-Willies. They were not just furious air, they were wild and dangerous. Why, didn't the willy-willy once see a beautiful dancing girl and want her for himself, spinning her up into the air until she turned into a brolga? I didn't want to be caught in its maw, to become a thing of feathers and legend, struth no. The car sounded up again, the motor revving then ticking over. And then with one last whip of pebbles the willy-willy was gone.'

He paused for a sip of his milk and ran his hand through the shrubbery of his beard and I felt the breath return to my lungs. The willy-willy was just a spirit of the imagination. It had not the power of speech or hands to do violence; it hadn't the ability to steal life.

'I looked for that car, but there was none in sight. I turned and looked in the other direction, and almost passed out from fear. There before me were two giant horns, curled and gleaming in the dusty sunshine. I spat on my fingertips and wiped my dirt-caked eyelids. The horns were feathers; the sound of the car was the lyrebird's mimicking song.

'The bird turned and looked right at me with currant-black eyes and branded me in his stare. He then sang a song, not his own. I could hear a cockatoo, kookaburra and a flock of screeching rosellas, then, without blinking, he serenaded me with the whoosh and stir of the approach of the willy-willy. So realistic it was, I checked over my shoulder to see it hadn't returned to make more mischief. The lyrebird sang a symphony, followed by the wild scales of a piano. I didn't dare blink. I would have clapped, but for the fear that he would mimic the applause back at me. I would have spoken my thanks, but to hear a human voice out of the bird would have sent me off screaming further into the scrub, food for bunyips.'

'Bunyips?' I said. The Birdman didn't seem to hear me. There were more strange creatures in this country than I would ever be able to imagine.

'I was relieved to find a set of streaming bright headlights veer over the horizon. I bolted to the road and flagged down the driver, who surely thought he had seen a ghost, my face dusted with the remnants of the willy-willy's kiss.

'Thank you, Driver,' I said, feeling for my hat, but it was long gone down the windy gob of the willy-willy.

'Spot of bother?' he asked, as we set off down the road just as the dark began to settle.

'Just caught in a wind storm.'

'That all?' he said dismissively, sucking on a smouldering cigarette.

'Well no, as a matter of fact, there was a bird out there that scared the bejesus out of me. It sang like a car.'

'Well,' said the driver, 'ain't that an odd occurrence. He didn't happen to also sound like a flute by chance?' I shuddered in my seat, how could he know? 'My son found one of them lyrebirds as a chick and raised it till it was old enough and ugly enough to look after itself. The thing is, my son heard they were good mimics and spent hour after hour playing this chick classical music from the wireless in hope that his foundling would pick up the notes. One morning I was woken very early, my son had started his training with the wireless before sparrow's fart, even the chickens complained from their roosts. It was too early. I shouted for him to turn the radio off, but all I heard were my son's snores in reply. I looked out the window and on the verandah the bird was singing his pea-sized heart out – a symphony – as clear and as beautiful as if he were playing the instruments himself.'

The Birdman stood up from his chair and hoisted his swag upon his back, happy to have paid his debt of beverages with tales, but I wasn't finished listening, I could only hear the faintest strains of the lyrebird's mimicry in my own head. What else could it do, this magician of the birds?

'Is that true?' I wondered aloud.

'Every word God's truth,' he said, patting his hat upon his head, but he would say no more. I held the door open for the Birdman as he left, his tongue moistening his lips ready for the tune to come trilling out.

After my shift at the Red Rose I went back to the shed instead of going home, but there was no sign of the girl. The parrot rocked himself on one of the beams that strutted the roof, his tightly clenched claws acting like a swing.

Miss du Maurier popped her head around the door, a basket of dew-tipped washing under her arm. 'Saw the lantern on, thought you may have left it on by mistake,' she said before she spied the parrot, a green splash of colour in the dim shed.

'O my, Ari, what a beauty,' she cooed, and held her hand out to the parrot, her bangles clanking together. The parrot cocked a wary eye and rocked back and forth before ignoring her.

'Who's the new girl?' I asked, sounding surlier than I intended.

'Oh, I hope you don't mind me mentioning your endeavours, I know you are very private about them, my dear, in light of your uncle, but she is such a sweet thing. Lost her father in the war, seems a bit lost herself. Her name is Lily. And now we have another lodger, a Mr Little. We shall soon have a full house!'

When Miss du Maurier went back up to the house, I tried coaxing the parrot down myself, a seed in my palm, but he seemed disinterested, a full belly no doubt, by the look of the scattered seed. I reached out my hand and whistled and waited. The parrot tilted his head and I whistled again. Something in the tune spoke to him and he took wing, flapping through the updraught of air, and alighted on my head. It was a start. But could he speak? What if I could get the lyrebird the Birdman spoke of, a second bird, could it speak, could it sing? Would it be able to learn the old songs my mother used to sing? Could the two birds sing together? *One for sorrow. Two for joy.*

THREE

Billy

Miss du Maurier poured my tea in an extravagant stream, topping my cup up until my bladder was almost wrecked, but I didn't dare hop up and visit the lav, just in case Lily came down. Breakfast came and went and I was still seated amidst the mess and spill of dishes. So I wandered upstairs and leaned my ear to her door to listen for any movement, but not even the dust stirred. I went into my own room and closed the door with all the might of my frustration, the windows rattling their protest. The world was washed with sunlight, the rain had dissipated but she wasn't out in the street; no one of any importance was. I grabbed my hat. I descended the stairs two by two; I flew straight over them, heading for the door. But on the footpath, barring my way with her shopping, was the boy's aunt, who, prompted only by the lightest of questions from me, was all too eager to divulge certain things into my confidence before I was on my way.

In the park at the end of L'Avenue, a group of children had made a kite out of some of the recently fallen twigs and a sheet of stained butcher's paper and were trying to tempt the cold wind to take it up into its icy heights. A boy's running limbs tangled in the kite's string, sending him and their creation sprawling. And there sitting in the long grass, shivering in his shirtsleeves, was the neighbour Lily had knocked from his bike just days earlier. Ari Pearl. Miss du Maurier had told me his name when I had winkled her for information.

But Lily was there with him too. The Jew had made his jacket a fabric island for her exquisite bottom. How cosy they had become, their heads tilted together, his with its little cap, hers with its halo of hair. Last night at the theatre had been her first shift. Bedecked in her rouge usherette's uniform she had looked like a bellboy, a beautiful little soldier, with her red hat tilted to the side of her head. Her arm had brushed against mine in the foyer as she'd given me her thanks for helping her. She had given me such a smile, I longed to fall into it and never come back. She didn't know that the front-of-house manager had been more than happy to give her a job when I'd tipped him a fiver. If only a fiver would buy the Pearl boy off, so that I could sit next to her now.

Unexpectedly, the long tail of the kite draped itself over her body like a sash. The wind had annointed her, made her the world's queen. She removed it gently, so as not to tear the carefully twisted paper ribbons. The boys her humble subjects, with their scabby knees and dusty shoes all stood still as she took the kite from their hands and rolled up the string. Standing up slowly, she took hold of the string with one hand and, with the other, the crossed twigs in the middle of the kite, weighing the paper in her hands. And then she ran, the kite's tail arrow-straight behind her. With a flick of her wrist and a whoop from her mouth she let go of it. The kite took to the air, ducking and diving with the ease of a swallow, and her straw hat followed. It rolled in my direction with divine precision so that it was only natural that I retrieve it. Today the wind was *my* friend. She handed the kite back to one of the boys, who took it from her gingerly.

I fingered the straw in my hands, the roughness a delightful scratch. I held the crown up to my nose and inhaled the scent of her freshly washed hair. I was overcome with the need to bury my nose in the nape of her neck, but I was disturbed in my reveries by her very self, standing right in front of me.

'Why are you hiding behind my hat, Mr Little?'

I hadn't realised that I still held it up to my face like a man peek-a-booing at a baby.

'I fully intended to return it to you. I just didn't want to interrupt your little tête-à-tête.' The flush rose in her face. Lily stood in front of me, and I still held her hat. Would she lose her cool and snatch it? Even in the wintry sunshine she was turning pinker by the moment, the scalp at the parting of her hair turning pinkest of all. I was an idiot. Right before me I was letting that smooth lunar skin burn. Before my eyes I imagined the fine white living porcelain of her skin at the mercy of the fiery kiln. I blinked and handed her the hat and saw the immediate relief shade brought to her features.

'Would you like to meet Ari?' She nodded in the direction of the Jew, who seemed so swamped in the sea of long grass that he looked in need of a lifeboat.

'Another time, perhaps?' If he wasn't man enough to stand up and come and shake my hand, my feet would not step an inch in his direction. 'But do tell him his aunt is delightful.' Watching her face melt into curiosity was worth the price of admission. 'See you this evening then,' I said and bid her good day. Of course I would be in the right place at the right time to escort her to the theatre later. She returned to her perch on his jacket in the park, the grass folding in behind her to conceal them. What they talked about only the swallows pitching wildly around their heads knew, but I would find out soon enough.

The latch of her door gave way to my touch like heat to ice; she'd forgotten to lock it. Unsurprisingly, her room was different to mine. Her room glowed, the light bounding with a defiant joy off the white walls, so that it seemed larger. I thought the room would offer her up to me, scattered objects each with a little part of her soul wrapped up in them. There were several fine silver hairs on the hairbrush, a pillowcase scented with rosewater, two dresses in the cupboard, one a nondescript cream colour, the other the colour of midnight, a blue that would have made her face look like the benevolent moon, her hair a frizz of shooting stars. I opened the chest of drawers, so empty that it rattled. A baser pervert would have fondled her smalls with the greatest of pleasure – taking her stockings, putting his hand though them and imagining her flesh in the web of silk – but I just noted them and went on to the next drawer, which was completely empty. She had even fewer possessions than I. Where was the detritus of her life? Where was the address book, the framed photographs, the notes from loved ones? I had seen men in the ward in Paris with more, the remnants of their old life crowding around them, talismans and idols to prove that they still lived. But she had nothing much of anything.

Under the bed was her suitcase. I dragged it out, a single dust dolly rolling out with it. Inside was only a battered illustrated book on magic wrapped in an old scarf. The name *Matilda* was written in looping script on the flyleaf. I turned the next page and there was an inscription in an older hand. *To my darling wee girl, life is magic. Many happy returns, your loving Father.*

Around the suitcase edge the lining was coming away. I ran a finger along it, liberating the last remaining fibres like slitting an envelope. She had hidden it well. Curled like a snake, a long silken skein of her hair was tucked away. As I pulled it out, it cascaded down over my arm. She was on her own. Was she a self-made orphan? She had up and left whatever life she had to make a new one, I was sure of it. I brushed her braid across my cheek, feeling a cool delicious swish, a caress. Why had she shorn herself so? And kept the thing so hidden? It smelled of lavender water and something else, exquisite and not quite nameable, the essence of her. Her lack of possessions, her seeming disdain of *things*, made me doubt whether what I really wanted was a souvenir of the adventure we would have.

Perhaps this time the only souvenir I would settle for would be the girl herself.

'Why is it that you aren't married, Miss du Maurier? A handsome woman like yourself,' I said at the dinner table later that day. I knew very well that women of a certain age had had their pick of the male crop prematurely harvested, left with nothing but their yellowing trousseaus as keepsakes, but I also knew that flattery would help my case when I told her my rent would be late. Miss du Maurier went a little pale.

'Would you like a hand, Miss du Maurier?' Lily asked, but Miss du Maurier shook her head and retrieved her handkerchief from her brassiere strap and blew her nose.

'I'm fine, dear, we all lost someone we loved in the war,' she sniffed, before she walked back into the kitchen.

'Were you in the war, Mr Little?' Lily asked, her sincere face glowing back at me.

I nodded.

'So was my father,' she said. 'He never came home. He was in France.'

'I was in France, too.' I had to answer her, as much as I detested talking about the whole bloody thing. She looked at me, her eyes swilling with tears before she blinked them away. Her vulnerability arrested me. How was I to proceed? To comfort? Miss du Maurier swept in with three plates of grey meat and pale vegetables and my stomach wheeled. I wasn't sure if I even wanted to hit the full stride of my own cock-and-bull story, to drag it all up. Would she ask me to tell her more? I was unsure if I could ever refuse her anything.

'He was in the Holy Land, my soldier. We were to marry when the war was over. But it wasn't to be,' Miss du Maurier said, sitting down next to me, her hands neatly folded in her lap.

'Where was he killed?' Lily asked. Her knife and fork were gripped upright and motionless in her hands.

'Oh, I had a letter from someone, telling me my fiancé was dead, and I mourned. Until I saw him again when the war ended, arm in arm with another woman, a gold band on his finger. Hadn't the guts to call it off with me, the coward.'

To have Lily bend closer, I'd paint a heroic picture, one triumphant detail at a time, but I'd keep the truth to my grave – the sights of men dying, the smell of rotting flesh, my tortured frustration at leaving my mates to their battlefield fate without my heroics, the rain that made us human peas in a muddy soup, the sound of the gunfire pounding in our ears from dusk till dawn, dawn till dusk, the voices of the enemy, their guttural gibberish from across no-man's-land, sometimes their voices raised in song, the woodsy scent of their cigarettes filling our nostrils – but no, it was Miss du Maurier's broken heart that palpitated for us over dinner, Miss Havisham all over again in her rotting lace and pestilent perfume. Her voice whined on like a shell through the air. What did she know of it?

Out there in that infernal mud, I listened to the bloke next to me yack on about the smoothness of his girlfriend's thighs, a smoke dangling from his bottom lip, when *boom*, a shell landed somewhere above us. My mate's face was torn to ribbons, my face splattered with the red confetti of his blood. Aside from that I was fine – nothing was broke or bung, pierced or tattooed. My mate slithered to the ground, a red balloon expelled of all air.

Oh, I was all right for a bit, happy to take commands, shoot the odd round at Gerry, eat with gusto my ration from a can, kick the rats away at night and the odd brazen bugger in the day. But all the time my mind was ticking over at a hundred miles per hour as to how the hell I could get out of there. If I went AWOL it would almost be as bad as death; if I shot myself I would be branded a coward, something I was unsure my manly pride could survive. I would have to risk an accident.

So I took my life in my hands and took a jaunt into no-man's-land. Of course it was a stupid risk but I'd grown madder than a cut snake with each passing day, desperate to get home. I waited for Gerry's songs to grow more out of tune, when the schnapps might have blurred their vision, then made a mad dash under the dark of the moon. In my hand I held a grenade, aiming to chuck it over into the ditch if I ever got there. It is rude to be a guest and not bring something.

Those leaping strides I took seemed to take a lifetime, the detritus of the battlefield tripping me up in the darkness. I didn't dare look, as I had seen what was out there when I planned my course with binoculars – helmets, scraps of cloth with flesh still attached, mud made from men, men like me, who longed for a full belly, a warm dry bed and that friendly curve of feminine flesh beside them. Was it too much to ask for?

I felt the blood trickle down my leg before I actually felt the hot sharp pain of metal. At once I was afraid and grateful. All I had to do was run back, still within the sniper's sights. I turned and ran for dear life, my blood pumping out of my leg, the smell hot and metallic. I was not sure if I was running away from or into the mouth of hell. But I sent my note of gratitude, my grenade, pin free, tossed in my kind would-be assassin's direction. What a way to say thank you to the poor bastard, happy in his schnapps. He probably thought he was aiming at a rabbit. Oh well, *c'est la vie*, as my Frog allies would have said. I must have made it back over the edge at last: the beautiful bang I had set in motion, my thrown metal bouquet, was the last music to my conscious ears.

When I woke, I was in the army hospital, happy as a pig in muck, thinking my plan had succeeded, until a sour-faced doctor came to my bedside and told me my wound was superficial and they would return me to the front promptly once my scab healed over. So I had to settle for the kind faces of pretty nurses, with their sad-eyed smiles. To drown out the moans of the other men – amputees, shell-shockers and the general wounded – I took to reading the only book available, the Bible. I took to it like a drowning man, starting with the begetting, to the Song of Songs, until all I could think about were the Delilahs and Jezebels, all the whores of this Babylon who waited for me on the other side of the hospital walls.

I was taken back to the front with my leg bandaged. My mates in the trench had barely had time to miss me – I had been gone less than a week. So it took a different kind of cunning. Amidst the rumours I would be getting a medal for my previous 'act of bravery', I took it upon myself to be rid of that place. When the next mortar exploded in our bunker, I rolled around as if death were upon me. In my hand I held a cold piece of metal that I had doused in whisky, and in the confusion I shoved it with nary a blink into my thigh. It hurt like Hades but I was soon shipped out to Paris. It was to a hospital, of course, but it wasn't all that bad.

After I had recovered, the streets were mine, as was the certificate of leave. I was happy hobbling the boulevards, sipping coffee in the cafes, taking in the shows at the Folies Bergère and the Moulin Rouge, my time measured in the pink world of flesh and frills. One of these arbiters of entertainment was Josette, a delightful little strumpet who did a number in the revue, a tableau vivant, whose flesh was as smooth as ivory, but which I knew was as soft as butter. She had a thing for accents, though I didn't think I had one, calling me her *petit kangourou*. The delectable Josette would smuggle me past her half-blind concierge and up the flights of spiralling stairs, the steps only as wide as a child's foot, until we reached her tiny room – a bed, a dressing table and an old crate for a chair. The bathroom was shared and if a bloke wanted to have a bath, he had to cross the concierge's palm with silver to cover the cost of soap and a towel, though I knew one could be bought at the market down the street for a mere fraction.

All this aside, it was worth the ascent for the salty taste of her flesh, the taste she lathered up with every kick of her legs under the audience's steamy breath, the grease of makeup, the smoke of the lamps. A saltier woman I had never met, her skin fizzing on my tongue. If we ate apple tart or crepes suzette, the salt of her would turn a sweeter flavour, a sherbet if you will, to trip and dance upon my tongue. With every lick, my crepe Josette would prickle with goose flesh, until I thought she would dissolve. I could have spent an eternity there, my tongue hanging out, but it wasn't long before my marching orders came to return to Australia. I toyed with staying behind, but I knew I would soon have tired of my petite salt lick. I had already had all the sweetest flavour from her and I had begun to miss my mother tongue. I think poor Josette had plans for emigrating, a gold ring jammed on her finger, queen of the kangaroos, a castle made from gum trees, a crown woven from the red petals of waratahs. She departed for the matinee, all kisses and *mon amour*, and left me to pen my farewell and claim my memento.

I felt the satin of her underwear, like trailing my hand in cool water. Too predictable. I stretched the lengths of her stockings under my nose and enjoyed the salty smell of her dancing endeavours, but knew such trifles would be too paltry. Surely there was something more fitting, more enduring, for my collection of souvenirs. On her dressing table was an enormous bottle of fragrance, the shape of a grenade in cut glass, the hand pump like the loop in the pin. I picked it up and sprayed a series of puffs into air, the droplets of perfume falling on my face like light rain, settling on my tongue like the salt spray of the sea. It was the scent of the fresh lilacs that lined the boulevards. It made me care not two brass razoos whether there was a war on, for the taste of perfume was like Josette, my salty mermaid. I wrapped my glass treasure in my kitbag and slung it over my shoulder, hoping it wouldn't shatter.

Goodbye Paris, goodbye boulevards, goodbye Parisian minxes. Hello sunshine, hello blowflies, hello the stench of the harbour and my father's beery breath. Hello the mother tongue, hello my she'll-be-right-mate you-beaut vernacular. When I got back to Australia, it was a semi-paradise, there seemed to be five women for every man. I didn't spare a thought for the poor buggers back there, thick with footrot in the trenches or with worms beneath the ground. Pity the poor creatures stuck somewhere in between on a damp stretcher. But I was free of all that, the doctor at my physical determined that I had tangoed with one too many exploding artillery shells. It was my secret that I'd taken fate in my own hands, tapping that piece of metal into my thigh. The doctor wrote an address on a little piece of paper and sent me on my shaking way.

I followed the directions to the school of arts. When I got there it was devastating, all these virile men sitting around weaving baskets, chattering amongst themselves like old women about their aches and pains and the goddamned state of the weather. I would have walked out that door and never turned back if it hadn't been for the teacher lifting her head. It had been bowed like the rest of them over their handiwork, her long tapered fingers guiding those who shook as if the very Lord was entering them. I let her show me to my seat and lean over my shoulder, her breath sweet on my neck, her hands on mine as I purposely went limp, her fingers dexterously twining the willow of the basket through its frame. Her eyes were the colour of a splendid wren, a blue almost painful, and I felt all the other cripples' eyes burn into my back at her sudden attention to me, the newcomer who looked unscathed at first but became wounded at her touch. I, like them, knew a good thing when it presented itself. Some of these fellows wouldn't have even been that close to a woman *before* the war, let alone after it.

Her name was Marion, all crisp in her freshly starched shirt, her knees pressed together by the tightness of her skirt, but it was her neck that struck me, and no doubt the others. It was pale and long and if I said it was like a swan's I could be accused of cliché, but sometimes only a cliché will do. It was white, like the neck of a painted geisha – though there I suppose I was alone in knowing what a geisha was.

It wasn't long before I was weaving my fingers in the basket of her hair as she kneeled before me, her magic working wonders on the same thing the doctor had said would never work again. Or so I told her. A woman like Marion liked nothing more than a cause, a challenge, a chance to put something right, and so, in the storeroom before setting up for class, she set her lips to making it so. She was a potter by trade and I was clay to her healing touch. So one of her own pots, fluted like the petals of lilies, was my souvenir, its pale milky glazes like those pearls of mine on her tongue.

Miss du Maurier finished her tale and stole me away from my delicious reverie of clay and flesh. I recalled that I hadn't seen the pot in the box. It would look like Lily's skin against my room's black walls, like a creamy marble in a museum.

Miss du Maurier got up from the table and rummaged through a letter rack on the sideboard and produced an envelope. Lily's eyes opened wide, her cheeks turned pinker than fairy floss at the Easter show. I took a sideways look at the writing. It was addressed to a Mrs Someone or other, the script familiar. I had seen it in the book under her bed she had labelled with her real name, Matilda.

'Lily dear, I hope you don't mind, I found it on the stairwell, but I took the liberty of putting the return address on the back, you wouldn't want it getting lost in the post. I've been meaning to post it, but here, you have it and you can put it in tomorrow's post.' Miss du Maurier handed it to her as if it was nothing but the simplest of goodwill gestures – to write the name of the street, the number of the house, not ever dreaming that was the last thing Lily might have wanted. Lily's hand shook as she accepted it and quickly concealed it in her pocket.

'I must have dropped it the other day after I knocked Ari off his bike. Thank you for thinking of me, Miss du Maurier, it had slipped my mind. Full of old news now no doubt, time to write another,' she said, short-winded, her fingers touching the blunt edges of her self-inflicted bob.

'I couldn't help notice the address, dear. Beautiful country. We had a holiday there when I was a child, to see the snow.'

Lily was frozen for a moment and she looked at me bewildered, as if she was trying to find a reply. I held her gaze. My Lily of the Valley in the snow, flakes of ice swirling between us. Miss du Maurier was waiting for a reply, but there was none forthcoming. All the suspicions aroused when I had snooped in her room were confirmed: she had run away and I wanted to know why. In time she would open like a flower to me. Magic, the Jew boy and propriety all be damned. What made her run away would be the key to make her run to me.

FOUR

Ari

The parrot looked up at me when I entered the shed, wings outstretched like an invitation to an embrace. He was clutching the edge of the stall and the seeds I had left for him earlier were strewn across the floor in a neat circle, as if he had searched for the perfect one at the bottom of the tin. I filled the water bowl and he bobbed his head in it, letting the water trickle down the nub of his tongue. Again he raised his wings at me as if imploring me to release him, his beak reaching down to untie the cord until he gave up and decided to groom his wet bib of feathers.

'It won't be for long my *sheynkeyt,* my darling.' I ran my hands up and down the freshly preened feathers and got a nip for my unwanted caress, his beak carefully reordering the feathers.

I picked up a seed pod and released a seed, placing it upon my lip before gingerly letting the parrot do a nervous sidestep onto my finger like a green Charlie Chaplin. I held him up to my face, that beak like a can opener, so close that I almost lost my nerve. Lily had not been afraid of the parrot's kiss. Why should I be? I felt the tongue lightly tickle my lip before the seed vanished. I laughed in surprise, and the parrot, startled, flapped his wings in an immovable flight, his claws digging into the cushion of my palm.

'Steady now, my *grin hartse*,' I crooned as I tried another seed, this time controlling my surprise yet delighting in the touch. It was like a kiss had travelled between her and me, upon the beak of this bird. The parrot, as if hearing my thoughts, leaned down and nipped my thumb to wake me. Most men my age had danced close and held hands and kissed girls, but I had not. I observed *shomer negiah*, the law against touch, but my skin was curious. Even more so since Lily had sat down beside me in the park.

'What are you reading?' she had asked, leaning over and tilting the newspaper toward herself to read the headline, her hand near mine, the print rubbing off on our fingers. Amidst the news of falling stocks and job losses was the story that had made the hairs on my arm stand on end.

'*Houdini Speaks!*' I said. Her gasp was a magpie's song; I felt like I was flying high in the wind. She leaned closer.

'But what did he say? He's been dead for three years now,' she said, the curiosity in her voice mirroring my own.

'*Rosabelle, answer, tell, pray, answer, look, tell, answer, answer, tell* was the message given to Mrs Houdini by the medium at the séance.'

'What do you think it means? Could Harry really have talked to Bess from the other side?' Her cold fingers brushed mine as she released the newspaper.

'They had a code just between the two of them, a message just for her, if the time ever came that he went first. It's not common knowledge.' I felt the paper shaking in my grasp so I folded it back in on itself, my hands seeking the refuge of my pockets. 'One of their earlier acts was a medium show, messages from the dead for those left behind. He later went on to say it was hokum and was regretful he and Bess had misled people, but the Houdinis had their little code, just in case.'

'A code, just in case?' she repeated, her eyes a strange blue like glass. 'Do you think it's possible to receive a message from the other side?' The way she asked made me uneasy. How could I answer that? The other side was the World to Come, the province only of the angels.

'Well, if anyone could, I'm sure it would be Houdini,' I said.

'Houdini. I would have loved to have seen him, even if it was just a glimpse. He was due to come to my town once a long time ago.' She pulled up her knees under her chin and cocooned herself in her arms. 'It was strange, that nearly blank page in the newspaper when he died. Did you see it? A whole page bought just to have a few lines printed: *IN MEMORY Of My Beloved Husband HARRY HOUDINI Who Went Away October 31, 1926*. It was as if she was expecting him back any moment.'

I knew the page, it was arresting. I had removed it from the paper before my uncle had had the chance and folded it carefully away to keep. That such a page should be so quiet and blank amidst the jangled type from across the world was disquieting, as if a raucous band had halted midnote and not even an echo remained.

'They started out together,' I said, 'the two of them doing the Metamorphosis. They were hardly more than children, Bess and Harry. Most people don't ever think of Bess as a magician, but she was, in her way.'

As she looked at me, a strange slant of light moved across her eyes, so that she was nearly squinting. She held her hand up to shield her face from the sun. 'The Metamorphosis?' she asked.

'Where two magicians swap places, seemingly in an instant.' She blinked at me and I thought she was going to ask me the secret of how.

'Have you ever thought of starting an act?' she said instead. Her question startled me and my mind drained of thought. Before I could reply she was entangled in the ribboned string of a child's kite. She stood then, laughing and twisting out of its clutch, freeing herself, before breaking into a run and releasing it to the dip of the wind, her hat following close behind. A passing gent stopped it with his foot and as I watched Lily retrieve it, her question soared in my mind. There were so many reasons why I had stifled this dream, never admitting it to anyone. If not this now, then what? Was I only ever to live the dreams of others? I waited for her to return to my side.

'A magical act?' I said, not trusting my ears.

'Well, you already have the right tattoo,' she smiled, glancing down at my hand, and I resisted the urge to hide it. My face burned. I did not realise she had read the word written there. 'We could do it together.' The wind flirted with the brim of her hat, but she held it firm. 'Why not?'

'Why not?' I echoed, as all the reasons why not were being listed in my mind, in my uncle's voice. 'It's just something I do for my own amusement. I've hardly got anything to offer.' What could I tell her? My uncle detested anything to do with magic. All he wanted was for me to be a copy of himself, a rabbi with a congregation of my own.

'We could make an act. Train the parrot together.' Together. The word made me shiver. A black and white bird fanned its tail in the nearest tree, silently hopping up the branches in pursuit of a small lizard before catching it in a joyful gulp.

'What's that bird called?' I asked Lily, pointing. The air was full of their dipping song.

'It's a currawong,' she said. 'They like the rain.'

How hadn't I known its name? Until Lily told me, I had always thought it just some kind of magpie. I had been here most of my life and I still didn't know the name of the bird that sang me awake each morning. Lily looked down at my watch, the upside-down numbers unreadable, until with the slightest of touches she turned the clock face toward her. 'I still have a little time before I have to get to the theatre. Shall we try to catch one?'

'It can't be that simple, can it?' Did she seriously think she could just pluck one out of the leaves? Was she playing with me? The fig trees seemed alive with currawongs – their name, like their song, was strange, a wild trill of sound, so full of vowels. Lily walked beside me, her eyes following the black and white dip of wings, and I was unsure of what to say.

'Look for their nests, like a platter of twigs,' she said as we walked with both our heads craned to the copse of branches above us. L'Avenue was lined with towering fig and gum trees, crowned with leaves. 'There has to be one around here. See, right there.' How could she see? I could barely make it out until she leaned closer and I followed the direction of her gaze.

'Come on, give me a leg-up,' she said as she removed her shoes and placed them on the ground. I hesitated, unsure of what I should do. What if my uncle saw me?

The sun was low in the sky, the light a diffuse gold. All around us the chorus of the currawong. I bent my hands together and made a living step for her foot and for a moment she hovered, her weight borne by my arms, then she was gone, her arms circling the branches and her feet finding footholds in the bark, her shirt tails a sail. As she climbed up the tree, the leaves closed in behind her and hid her from view. She didn't plummet as I feared. As I waited time passed slowly, with the occasional glimpse of her limbs above me as she clambered upward. I should have offered to climb. I put my hands upon the smooth white bark of the ghost gum and noticed for the first time that it was like her skin. I pulled my hands off as if I had been burned.

'Do you need any help?' I called up, but the leaves muffled her reply and then a branch with leaves rained down upon me. There was a kerfuffle of wings and an angry currawong swooped low out of the tree, clipping close to my head, before alighting on the nearest cast-iron balcony, clacking its beak at her, its orange eye blazing. It dipped its tail like a chevron. Lily appeared amidst the lower branches.

'My father always said I had a way with birds, but obviously not today,' she smiled, running a hand over her mussed-up hair before she eased herself to the ground. I averted my eyes as her legs dangled near my face, but when she faltered, I quickly offered my hand to steady her, worried that she would fall. She was in my arms in an instant, my hands slipping up the hem of her shirt, and she slipped in my grasp to the ground. I stepped back and she dusted off her hands on her trousers.

'If you don't want to work together, I understand,' she said quietly. I had offended her, and I still hadn't given her an answer. The silence pressed at me; the feel of her skin was still ringing on my hands. 'I should be getting to work. I don't want to make a bad impression.' She stepped away tentatively.

'Lily,' I called out after her and she turned toward me. I offered her my hand. 'We can try, can't we? Let's shake on it.' She grinned at me then, and her milky fingers pressed mine. Her touch made the hairs on my neck stand on end. The first star of the evening blinked awake in the sky.

The secret plan blooming in my chest made me feel like a different man, different from the man my uncle wanted me to be. Why should I be just like him when I was marked apart? I already made my way in the world; why did I need to follow his exact steps? Yet how could I break away?

When I got home there was no sign of my uncle, and I was relieved, for he would have read my face as clearly as the scrolls of the Torah. His study door was open and as I peered in I was struck by the neatness of his desk. Usually it was a chaotic type of order, like a bird's nest, with random pieces of paper, pages marked with the silvery scrawl of pencil, slit envelopes of letters stacked perilously close to toppling, typewriter ribbon adorning the desk like streamers. My uncle in frustration pulled the ribbons out, for his preference was for the handwritten word. 'Moses didn't need a typewriter when God bid the commandments and neither do I,' was his reply when my aunt chided him for the wasted ribbons on the desk, which not even she was permitted to dust. But now the desk was tidy, the papers and ribbons cleared right away; not even the ring from his teacup remained. All that sat upon the surface was his scrapbook, closed to the world, and, surprisingly, my copy of the poems of Yeats. Why was he reading that? He detested it when I did. Had he been through my coat pockets?

I listened for his step in the hallway but the flat was quiet, the only sound the wind whipping the drying sheets. I leaned over to the scrapbook, the pages stiff beneath my hand. Some of the pages were neatly dated. Some of the articles from the newspaper were cut precisely with scissors, others ripped with a sense of rage, the torn words carefully pasted in, all dated with my uncle's precise hand.

Outside the wind whispered secrets to the leaves of the trees. I returned to the pages of my uncle's scrapbook, an entire page devoted to one word only:

Aliyah, Aliyah, Aliyah.

The scrapbook was a maze of his longing. His perfect copperplate script filled every line, even the margin. *Aliyah*, the return, the return to the homeland. The words flooded over me. I flicked to a random page, and there, page after page, articles on the pogroms across Europe. I tried to tear my eyes away, but I couldn't stop the words – rapes, massacres, mutilation, castration, evisceration in homes, businesses, streets, shops and the synagogue, village after village, date after date.

I slammed the book shut, an icy chill threading itself around my body, my heart shuddering in my chest so loud it hurt my still sore ribs. The memory of the utter silence nudged into my mind. The room wavered. The silence was a roar of nothing in my ears. Not even the clock on the wall ticked.

* * *

I remembered the silence of my grandmother's house. All I'd known as home. That night she suddenly became still, her ears straining, her hands paused between the rise and fall of a stitch. Where my mother was, I didn't know. Outside, a flap of pigeons, their wing beats animating my grandmother's fingers again. Her stitching resumed with the precision of a machine. A log in the fireplace spat and hissed from the snow falling from above.

'Why are you mending my coat, Bubbe?' I wanted to ask – there was nothing wrong with it, no holes I could see – but she had one ear on the clock, the other on the silence. She patted the stitching down and broke the thread with her teeth. She ushered me over and I knew by her solemn eyes I wasn't to speak. The room seemed different: the red Persian rug I would so often sprawl on with a storybook no longer seemed our rug; nothing in the room was familiar any more. The kitchen table and chair legs cast shadows like bars in the dim light. It was as if the silence had stolen everything that was ours, as if it had moved into our homes and we were nothing but ghosts, tiptoeing around it, afraid of letting a ripple of our voices disturb its peace.

My grandmother pulled the coat over my shoulders. The weight of it surprised me and I almost toppled backwards like a wooden skittle. She held me upright and slowly pushed the buttons through their holes. I noticed how old her fingers were, the knuckles puffy, pale. She pulled my collar close around my ears, her hands smoothing my flesh. Those hands running across my face will stay with me forever.

'Whatever happens, my beautiful *boychick*, do not take off this coat. Until *Aliyah*. Promise me.' I nodded, scared by the seriousness of her voice.

The back door opened and in burst my mother. She wordlessly scooped me up and pressed both of us into my grandmother's arms, a final embrace, before she ran back with me through the still open back door. Over her shoulder, I saw my grandmother sit back quietly in her chair and pick up some knitting from her sewing basket. But then she just sat there, the needles poised as if she couldn't remember what stitch she had last made. The red wool spilled from her lap to the floor.

I wore that coat for as long as I could until my Aunt Hephzibah pulled it off my stinking little body. The weight of it was a surprise even to her.

I put the scrapbook back on the newly ordered desk and wished my hands had not ventured to touch it, let alone open it. I left my book of Yeats where it was and was grateful to hear Aunt Hephzibah's familiar light footstep on the stairs.

'Ari dear, I met Mr Little today, one of Miss du Maurier's lodgers,' her cheery voice called to me. I stood straight and tried to breathe deeply. When her bright face appeared in the doorframe, my presence there was not lost on her, her eyes travelling over the newly cleaned desk.

'He works up at the Bridge Theatre. Maybe he could help you get some more work, maybe they pay more than the Red Rose?' Her words trailed off as her eyes roved over the newly ordered room; disquiet dawned across her face. She looked again at the order, the neatness, as if it conveyed a message neither of us could read.

My uncle mounted the *bimah* and announced the order of service, his voice ringing out in the quiet, the pages of everyone's *siddur* turning quickly. I breathed in the quiet. This was the synagogue of my uncle's longing, built from his endeavours and subscriptions. The building was simple and modest, just like him. He removed his black hat, and his grey hair was covered in the black velvet *kippah* embroidered in silver thread by my aunt's patient fingers, the corners of his mouth tugged downward, as if pulled by invisible string. 'It is the Sabbath, Ari, she is our bride, remember. Would you keep a bride waiting?' My uncle called out the next part of the service, and the pages turned in unison, but I seemed destined always to fall behind. I looked down at my own hands, the letters along my finger seeming green in this light – *abracadabra* ...

I remember receiving them into my skin, the white pain of the stylus going into the soft flesh of my finger, the small finger of a child. I remember the blood and the ink, my mother's warm hand on the back of my neck, reassuring me with each wave of pain. In the morning there was a blobby scab-shaped word trailing down the length of the middle finger of my left hand, as random as spilled jam. When eventually the scab fell off I was left with a newly minted word in my flesh. There was no explanation given that I could recall. I was too young in any case to understand.

It wasn't until my uncle and aunt stripped me down to bathe the thickened grit of long travel off my body that they noticed it. Already my uncle had lamented about my hair. My *upsherin*, my locks, had been cut before my seventh birthday, and he was keen to see that I had made my covenant with God as Moses' sons had, that a *mohel* had seven days after my birth ushered me into my birthright with a quick snip of a blade. In that he was reassured. Then he removed the gloves that I had worn halfway across the world.

When he saw the word he froze as if it were a message just for him. He spat on his fingers and rubbed it across my hand, thinking it would reveal more, like the child's game of writing in wax and revealing letters in lemon juice. When the word would not come off, he turned to my aunt. She took my hand gently in hers, as I stood quivering, my little body ready to dissolve in embarrassment, standing naked in front of strangers. Aunt Hephzibah let the warm water trickle over my shoulders. She carefully cleaned the grime from the whorls of my ears, soaped my hair and rinsed it clean, careful not to let the soap sting my eyes. My uncle stood silently watching, waiting for an explanation, hoping some message would sprout from my lips, but I was the message. A child.

'It is a tattoo, Israel,' my aunt replied calmly.

'But it is forbidden to alter the body. *Do not make gashes in your skin for the dead and do not put tattoos upon you. I am the Lord.* Leviticus 19:28. How could she?' I remembered the words sputtering out of him.

My aunt plucked me from the bath and pulled me into the warmth of a towel that had been dried crisp by the sun. She dabbed down my limbs with such delicacy that my skin was still damp. She had never bathed anyone other than herself before.

'He is lucky to have survived at all, Israel. If that is all that marks him, if that is his only scar, he is blessed. Why even the word, Israel, if my Hebrew doesn't fail me, means 'the blessing' *ha – brachah,* from 'the curse' *dabra.* How can you worry about a word when it is a child we have been given?'

Still he looked at my finger, shaking his head, and I wished the bath waters would rise as Moses could command them to and swallow me up. My aunt wrapped me closer to her. I could feel her heart pounding in her chest as my uncle approached, the yellow cake of soap held before him, sharp scented and slippery. My aunt's arms gripped tight around me. The soap won the battle with his hand – it ejected itself with all the force of a firecracker, bouncing several times on the black and white linoleum tiles of the floor. It was then that my uncle began to cry, his tears streaming out of him silently. My aunt and I watched him leave the room and listened to the slam of the study door. Then she quietly proceeded to rumple my hair until each curl was dry.

I rubbed the word printed across my finger, the ink now faded, the letters stretched but legible all the same. The service was over. I wanted nothing more than to slip across the road to the quiet of the shed and let my hands tickle the pale green feathers of the parrot's neck as Lily had done. I wanted to see if he would hop from finger to finger with my encouragement, wanted to give him words over and over to see if he could speak in a human voice. Instead my uncle and I walked up the stairs together and took our places at the table, the prayers from our lips nearly soundless.

'So Ari, have you given it thought?'

My uncle spoke as if this were a casual conversation. My aunt looked sharply at him, her hands suspended in mid-air, interrupted in the simple action of picking up a knife and fork. I sliced a piece of the chicken and put it in my mouth, my uncle's question leaching it of all flavour. I chewed it and chewed it until there was no meat left, not willing to open my mouth and meet his hope for an answer.

'I have written to a yeshiva in Europe on your behalf, Ari, in lieu of your answer. It is time to be a leader in your community, to become the rabbi you were born to be.'

'Israel.' My aunt lowered her hands and rested them in her lap.

'If you don't make decisions, Ari, they are made for you.'

I took a sip of water and considered saying something, but what could I say that would make him hear me? I wasn't going to return to Europe and I wasn't going to a yeshiva, no matter how many letters my uncle presumed to write on my behalf. My serviette fell to the floor when I stood up. I retrieved it, folded it quietly by my plate and left the room.

When I opened the back gate, a loud commotion was roaring within the house, Miss du Maurier's voice a pitch above it all. I burst through the back door and through the kitchen. In the sitting room, Miss du Maurier and Lily stood over the fireplace, while the new male lodger, who I assumed was Mr Little, was tipping a vase of water over the flames.

'Don't drown the poor mite,' Miss du Maurier shouted.

'Trust me, Miss du Maurier, I know what I'm doing,' he replied. 'Better a wet bird than a cooked bird. The smell of burning flesh is atrocious.'

Lily, a tea towel at the ready, leaned into the wet slushy ash and blackened wood and pulled out an animal, made of soot and sticks it appeared, before she folded her hand over its eyes so it couldn't see that it had survived the pyre. They were all so absorbed they didn't notice me.

'What happened?' I said and Lily turned around, a smudge of black on her chin.

'Damn bird nested on top of the chimney,' Mr Little said. 'Hand it over. I'll wring its neck and put it out of its misery.'

'Mr Little!' Miss du Maurier said, shocked at his language or the murder of the bird I wasn't sure. I knew she wouldn't tolerate either.

'It's more soot than burns, I'm sure of it,' Lily said. I could see she would not hand it over to the executioner. 'Come on, Ari,' she said and I followed her out to the shed, leaving Miss du Maurier bending over the hearth with a dustpan and brush, while Mr Little stared, his blackened hands slack at his sides.

The parrot swooped down to the bucket and watched inquisitively as Lily dipped a face washer into the water and ran it down the currawong's wings, until the water was black. The currawong had fallen into some kind of trance; the bird submitted to her ritual bathing without complaint, her orange eye focused on the middle distance.

'Oh,' Lily said as she ran her nail through the filberts of the bird's tail. 'She's lost the tip of her tail feathers. May affect her flying.'

The parrot dipped his beak into the sooty water and reclined back, gulping at the water, dip after dip. Finding no dry cloth to hand, Lily dried down the currawong with her shirt tails, while I looked around for a suitable box. The old bamboo birdcage that had once been a palace for canaries was an option, a temporary prison covered with an old towel, but there was no need. The currawong flew up onto the rafters, her tail a fan, and watched us below her quizzically as we watched her above.

'Well, that answers that then,' I said.

Lily sat down in the old armchair; there was a warm flush on her pale cheeks. Her face was like a lit lantern, a bright white. As if we were simply continuing our conversation in the park, the questions burst out of her, each one soaring dizzyingly, one after the other.

'Did Mrs Houdini confirm that the code was correct? The one Houdini supposedly delivered from the other side? If so, who is Rosabelle? Was it a nickname for Mrs Houdini? I thought her name was Bess,' she said expectantly.

She coaxed the parrot to perch upon her hand, his head bobbing up and down to a beat only he heard.

'Rosabelle is the name engraved in her wedding ring,' I said, 'from the song she sang when they met – *Rosabelle, sweet Rosabelle, I love you more than I can tell. Over me you cast a spell. I love you my sweet Rosabelle.*'

She looked from the parrot to me as if she could see my thoughts. Talking of love in the shed, alone but for the dozing ginger cat and the birds, was not permitted. She did not know that, I did, but I wasn't going to be the one to leave.

'And the rest? The pray, answer bit? I could make no sense of that at all.'

'*Answer, tell, pray, answer, look, tell, answer, answer* – it was the code for the Houdinis' mind-reading trick, it was in a book my aunt gave me, but it means more than that,' I said. The lamp turned her hair gold and the parrot gently ran his beak through the strands, already claiming her as his own.

'What does it mean?' she said, blinking against the glare.

'The first part is their old cipher, but the rest is their code alone, a magic word in their own private language. They had agreed that if there was life on the other side he would try to get a message through. *Believe* was that word.'

'Believe? Believe that the dead can talk? Houdini spoke?' Her voice caught in her throat.

'Houdini was obsessed with the idea of being able to talk to those on the other side. He spent half of his adult life trying to get a message from his parents who had passed over, and then for the rest of it he tried to debunk the whole thing and expose the mediums and their charlatan ways.'

'So you could say he had a bet each way? If Houdini was on the other side, why would he use a medium if he despised them so much? Surely he would pass the message directly to her? Do you think it is possible?'

'For the dead to talk to us? I don't know.'

Blotches of colour rose in her cheeks, tears pricked at her eyes. She blinked them away.

'So where do we start?' she said. Her voice was tight in her throat. The parrot started chattering to her as if he had the words to comfort her that I lacked. Lily encouraged the parrot to step onto her hand and we watched him do a sideways walk up her arm until he perched on her shoulder. She ruffled the short green feathers on his head with a fingertip and the parrot bobbed up and down, lost in his pleasure. 'How do we teach you to sing or talk or whatever it is we will get you to do?' she asked and the parrot screeched. We looked at each other. Lily grinned. 'Answer for everything, you have!'

'What about something like this?' I pulled my violin from its battered case, my fingers tentative upon the board, and played a short bar. But I stopped suddenly. Some other sound cut through the notes. The currawong swooped onto the opposite rafter, carving a draught through the cool air. In the violin's place came a strange otherworldly trill. Upon the rafter, the currawong hopped from one foot to the other, agitated. There was only one person who whistled that way.

'What is that?' Lily wondered aloud, as the ethereal song made the air prickle around us.

'How'd you feel about us expanding our menagerie?' The word *our* felt large in my mouth.

'With what?' she said excitedly.

'That most magical of all birds. I'll be back in a few minutes. Don't go anywhere,' I said.

The Birdman was nowhere to be seen, but his notes lingered in the air as if invisible staves hung there still. I hurried into the lane that ran along the back of the house and waited to hear it again. The whistling swelled, whether it was nearer or further away I couldn't tell for sure, but I tried to follow, ran in hope to the heart of it, stopping every few moments to listen again. Somewhere, someone smashed a bottle, and the splintering of glass echoed in the darkness and right into my mind. The sound flooded panic into my limbs. I had run like this before when I was a child; every footfall took me back to that night.

The clutch of my mother's hand was on mine, and black spots appeared behind my eyelids. I wanted to stop there and then in the dark cobbled streets, to curl into a ball and let the stones part and swallow me. My mother drew me onward, stopping in the shadows of the buildings when there was silence, nothing but our own ragged breaths in our ears. 'Ari, just a little further.' Her voice was a struggle between the calm and the quake, then our feet would find their wings again. The frost was already coating the cobbles and dampening our shoulders. Behind us was the shock of smashing glass, cries of people shoved from their beds, the splintering of doors, the solitary cry of a child winnowing out into the air like a wisp of smoke out of a chimney. This sound like no other made my mother's feet run faster, my legs barely able to keep up. She ran with me almost flying behind, a child-shaped kite catching the air, the corners of my coat whipping at the wind. I remembered glancing up and noticing the pinpricks of stars, looking oh so cold and far away.

The wind gusted through the gum trees. If I had closed my eyes I could have heard my mother's voice. A huge gust shook down a rain of gumnuts upon my head. I saw the Birdman up ahead stooping to stroke the ears of a dog, its tail going one hundred beats to the minute.

'What can I do you for?' He lowered his pack, a puff of dust exhaling off it as it hit the ground.

'I need a lyrebird.'

'A lyrebird, heh? A bit of my spiel rubbed off, I see.'

'Something like that,' I said, trying to conceal my annoyance that he was right. His grey hat veiled his eyes. In the tree behind him a raven watched us, her black feathers catching the sheen of the lamplight. Shouldn't all birds be asleep with the sunset?

'I know what you're wanting it for, but I can't just pluck one of God's creatures from the bush and see it live its poor songbird life in bondage.'

My heart sank. The Birdman had all the time in the world to dally; the world kept time for him by the seasons and tides and vagaries of the moon. He was free to wander at will, yet I had time always breathing down my neck, chasing me whether I ran or not.

'I'd be wanting to know he was going to a loving home, not to have strange rituals performed upon him. Why, he could be mistaken by someone for a chicken and get plucked and eaten. *One for sorrow.*'

I could see my uncle in my mind's eye, pacing back and forth, his feet testing the patience of the floorboards.

'It is for our act.' The raven swooped low and instinctively I ducked – her talons were outstretched, as if making for my face. The Birdman reached out his arm and the raven took roost. His hands ruffled her shaggy beard as if it was the most natural thing in the world for a man to do.

'*Our?* Is there a girl? There always has to be a girl. The world started with a man and a girl in the garden.'

'There is a girl.'

'Good, good. Walk with me. What sort of girl is she? *Three for a girl, eh, four for a boy.*'

How was I supposed to answer? Lily was not just a girl. She was the miraculous creature upon which my dreams now hung.

'Go on, mate, spit it out – *six for secrets never to be told.*' He had caught me by surprise, my feelings palpable in my chest.

'She is my neighbour, the one who helped me feed the parrot.'

'Oh, 'tis a good thing, a girl of the bush. Not that I don't trust you, mind, it would just be better that way. A woman's touch and all that, closer to the homeland, a native by default, I am sure you will understand. See this bird here, that tree, the possum who lives in that tree, the insects that the possum eats, the blossoms that the bees drink from – for all these things I am responsible. The lyrebird even more so, for my people believed that the lyrebird was family. So, if I am to get you this bird, I am entrusting you with my brother. It is only right that I should know he will be taken care of by someone who has at least a skerrick of wild knowledge, someone who will not keep him caged all the time, who will let him pluck and scratch at the ground for choice bugs, fan his tail and sing to his heart's content. Can you promise that, my friend?'

'Of course.' I had no more interest in keeping a creature of G_d's enslaved in cruelty than he did. The raven hopped from his shoulder and hovered in the air for a moment before I felt its claws sink into my shoulder. The magnificence of that sudden grip overwhelmed me.

'She likes you. Ravens don't go to just anyone.'

'How can you tell a crow from a raven?'

'Crow and raven – cut of the same jet feather.'

The moon was low on the horizon and my uncle would be wondering where I was, but I had no intention of running as if a riot were behind me now. Lily would be waiting, that I knew. My uncle, he could wait some more. And those jet-black raven's feathers were soft like the running of water against my skin.

FIVE

Billy

Miss du Maurier was practising her dance steps on the wooden floor. I had helped her roll up the moth-eaten Turkish rug and listened to her torturing the floorboards with the staccato beat of the Charleston. Lily had come back from her shift at the theatre and sat on the settee, her legs crossed, her foot waggling in time to the music as Miss du Maurier danced. Would she get up and join her? I waited with anticipation, imagining the lightness of her step, the swing of her freshly bobbed hair, then Lily started to cough and smoke puffed into the room.

'You really ought to get someone to clean your chimneys, Miss du Maurier,' I called out over the music. 'Wouldn't want the house to catch fire while we are all asleep.'

'Heaven forbid! You are absolutely right,' she said, her feet not missing a beat, old hoofer that she was.

It was then that the nest fell into the flames, followed close behind by the unfortunate bird, making enough racket, billowing smoke into the room. Lily was up on her feet and ready to plunge her delicate hands into the smouldering mess when I promptly intervened, plucking a bunch of flowers from a vase and tossing the water on the flames, saving those precious white fingers from the puckering blisters of a burn. That was when the Jew entered. But that still didn't stop Lily. She leaned closer, a tea towel open in her hands, and scooped the sludgy cooked bird into her arms as if it was her darling. And just like that they waltzed out together to the old stable. It is bad luck to have a bird in the house. If only I could have wrung its neck without her seeing.

The thought of him and her in the shed made my skin itch as if a mosquito had taken its drunken fill. I hurried to the top of the staircase, just as the flyscreen door swung back, and I scrambled to the end of the hall and the vacant bedroom that looked over the backyard. As I opened the door I was overwhelmed by the smell of attar of roses, as if the violet walls were painted with the scented oil. The culprit was a bowl of Miss du Maurier's potpourri sitting on the windowsill. The smell was so rich and thick it almost made me gag.

They walked through the backyard, happy strides to the old shed. The Jew pushed the door open with an almighty shove and they were swallowed by the darkness within. I raced back to my room and returned with my opera glasses. With a lamp lit within, their shadows appeared like two marionettes, my little neighbour and her accomplice. I twirled the focus and saw a leg and an arm but never the whole article from this height. Across my eyes a shadow as the curtain closed. Then nothing. Dark things can happen in sheds. The brass and mother of pearl was cool against my face, the inscription the coldest of all.

To Minnie on her 16th birthday from her loving Daddy.
All the World's Your Stage.

Minnie was the boss's daughter and I was his gardener. She would practise singing her scales day in and day out. It was the strangest thing I ever did hear, as if someone were torturing a cat with a violin bow.

I got the job by answering an advertisement in the newspaper. I knew when I saw the address of the place I wanted to work there; it had gardens big enough to lose oneself in. The boss had given me the job based on my own beautifully crafted copperplate references, with the odd floral phrase from the dictionary.

I had never used a pair of garden shears in my life, the unwieldy buggers were slippery in my hands, but while shaping the hedges I had a convenient view through the music room window: a dowager pianist sat hunched over the ivory keys as if she could barely tell which ones were black and which ones were white, while Minnie stood singing out her caterwauls. When she caught sight of me, instead of screeching at the sight of a stranger, her notes went flatly on. I didn't need to hear Melba to know how the notes should sound; any drunkard on City Road could tell you that. Either a note hurts or it doesn't. Minnie's were painful.

What Minnie lacked in the sound department she made up for in the anatomical. I knew that by my own very special powers of persuasion I could make her hit the note aright. I had read *Trilby*; I knew that all a pretty lass needs is encouragement of a particular kind, like a feather's gentle tickle of her tonsils.

Every day I cut grass, pulled out weeds, trimmed hedges, watered blossoms, sewed seeds, and every day I stood in the window as she practised, willing her to dare to lift the sash. Until the day she did, sticking her head out while the somnambulist pianist played on, her fingers hitting keys with as much passion as a train clicking over the same tracks again and again. Minnie's breath touched my face, my mouth on her ear. Her father's voice rang out in the halls and I leaped into the rose bushes beside the windows. I could just see his pink pig-anus mouth through the curtain's brief opening.

'For you, my darling Minnie. Happy sixteenth birthday.' He handed her a box of peach watermarked satin. The pianist tinkled on.

'Oh Papa!' she cried in delight, the lid open, the froth of tissue paper on the floor. She pulled out a pair of exquisite opera glasses, tiny mother of pearl tiles covering the surface.

'Read the inscription, darling,' her father said. '*All the World's Your Stage.*'

He squeezed his daughter so tight I thought her ribs might crack. She looped the baby-pink ribbon around her neck so that the opera glasses nestled close to her breasts, and continued with her practice. With every sound she made, they rose and fell, a brass breast-plate that concealed the flesh beneath. Her hand wandered up to them throughout her song – her fingers playing with the focus, caressing the nacre, brushing the inscription with her fingertips – so that I thought she would even be reluctant to remove them come time to bathe.

When her father exited I gently tapped at the window and whispered our rendezvous, insisting she bring her new acquisition with her.

The moon rose, a quiet observer, a drowsy eye not yet open, as I let myself into the hothouse. A wave of steam floated over me. The jungle blooms from distant shores, cultivated by Minnie's papa and pampered like his daughter with only the very best, exhaled their thick spicy perfumes. I waited, lighting a taper I had swiped from Saint Joseph's, filched from behind the priest's back, a warm glow-worm of light undetectable from the main house. I heard her coming from yards away, her footfalls cracking twigs and sticks. She fumbled for the latch of the hothouse door, rattling and shaking the knob until I was sure even her accompanist, truly deep in slumber now, would hear. She tumbled right into my open arms, nearly dropping her new opera glasses, her treasure soon to be mine. In my arms she smelled of soap and fresh linen and sixteen years of inexperience. I could have melted her into me in moments, peeled off her clothes and licked the perspiration from her clavicle. But I wanted to stretch my pleasure.

'Come, my dear,' I whispered to her, 'lift up your arms.'

She did as I gently commanded, and I gathered up the beautifully starched nightgown that fell about her ankles and lifted it up to her knees. It must have tickled, or she was overcome with nervousness, for she squealed and I stopped, waiting for the house to wake and rain its wrath upon me. I gave her a special glare and she froze, excitement and fear wrestling within her. My fingers brushed upwards toward her thighs, the nightgown swelling in my hands. I pulled it up over the jut of her hip, a nub trying to burst into the fulfilment of a curve. I released her from her gown but my little onion was wearing another layer, a pair of lace-trimmed knickers and camisole. A ripple of goose bumps travelled down her arms.

'Big deep breaths, my dear,' I said, soothing her with the treacle of my voice, lulling her nerves. She would sing better all right after I had given her the master lesson.

I put my finger on her mouth and pried open her quivering lips. I felt her pearly wet teeth and I knew that clay couldn't have been more malleable. The opera glasses she cherished still dangled in her hand. I tried to remove them, but her stubborn fingers held fast to the cord. I yanked them further till they came away in my hands while her teeth bit hard down upon my finger. She reached for her glasses but I just held them high. O, how her hair smelled damp and animal! I wanted to see how desperate she could become, to what levels of depravity she would fall in the attempt to retrieve her bauble. I held them even higher and in her reach for them, her nails scratched at my arm. Outside the wind blew across the gravel path, a tree branch went rat-a-tat-tat on the windowpane, and as Minnie's lips pressed against mine, the tenor of her body slapped against me, the sweetest pitch-perfect song of all.

I saw his face framed by the window. A fox doesn't need to be told when to run. I secured the opera glass cord around my wrist and made for the back entrance, not knowing that thorns had made their wild home in the abandoned seedling patch. I could hear her shrieks in my ears as I gathered pace, unable to tell if it was Minnie coming to her senses or her father beating them into her with the dried willow switches that were cut ready to be woven into a cottage garden fence. Yet in those shrieks were the perfect notes she had lacked in her lessons, sounding out clear and profound.

Inside the shed someone moved right up to the window and I pulled the opera glasses away from my eyes and blinked. I wiped the perspiration off my palms onto my trousers: the metal and shell had grown hot while I had watched for my little neighbour. Downstairs the gramophone was silent. Miss du Maurier called my name, for I had promised to come help roll the carpet back. I closed the door to the mauve room, leaving its cloying scent behind me. Lily had no father to protect her here. And she wasn't going anywhere.

Deep in the night I heard Lily call out in her sleep. I flicked off the bedclothes and cupped my ear to the flimsy wall. 'No!' she shouted suddenly, and I jumped back, thinking that she had seen me, but it was impossible. 'Stop!' she shouted again, and I grew afraid for her. I slipped out my door and into her room, half-expecting to see an intruder, but there was no one there except for ourselves and the invisible ghost of her fears. The street lamp bled beneath the curtain and showed her to me: she was sitting up, wild-eyed, cowering in the corner of her bed, looking for all the world like the Virgin rejecting her Annunciation. I stood back, not wanting to disturb her, but curious as to what she would do next. She stayed like that, frozen, so that I thought she had returned to sleep, when she very slowly covered her hands with her face and sobbed. My fingers tingled to comfort her, but I knew better than to disturb a dreamer. I'd learned that from the war: a dream was sometimes the only place one could take flight. Her tears subsided and she slumped back down on the bed, her back toward me, drawing her knees up to her chin. Cautiously I stepped over to the bed: the strap of the camisole fallen off her shoulder revealed a trail of silvery scars across the delicate skin of her back. Who could do such a thing to this precious girl? My fingers hovered over them, wanting to follow their dips and lines like a map of the constellations, to touch the stars, to discover her secrets. Instead, I carefully plucked the sheet and laid it over her bare shoulder, tucking her in like a baby.

In the morning, noise lapped up through the floorboards as I turned over, the sheets garrotting me as I tried to return to sleep. But the damage was done; dreams were a lost continent now. I threw back the covers and let my feet rest on the sun-warmed floorboards, my trousers cold as I pulled them up my legs. My shirt was so woefully thin in places, without a singlet you could see a flock of goose bumps across my back. The mirror showed my reflection, in need of a shave, but I couldn't wait, for the commotion below was going along without me.

I walked down the stairs ever so slowly. The sitting room had turned into a jumble sale run by a harem – cloths, carpets, dresses, feathers, veils, scarves hung from the chairs, furs draped over the back of the sofa like strange antimacassars. In the midst of it all crouched Lily and Miss du Maurier, rummaging through an enormous trunk. Then Lily stood up in the wave and swell of it, like Venus emerging from her shell. They hadn't heard my foot on the stair and I wanted to pause and absorb the scene a while, unnoticed. But I wasn't able to, for behind me on the stair loomed the Jew, a good foot taller than me with the steps' advantage, but caught in no-man's-land, unable to advance.

'Morning, ladies,' I said, taking the final few steps to the landing. There is nothing like a striking entrance, or so I thought. The Jew had come down behind me and it wasn't until he reached the floor as well, the light flooding around him, that I realised why the ladies were struck so silent. He was wearing a beautifully cut evening suit, which gave off the sharp smell of camphor. The trousers fell with an elegant drape, nipped in at his waist, the tails dipping at his knees. The silken shirt, yellowed with age, still had the benefit of the tailor's art, the cuffs' stitching holding their stiffness after all this time. Above the collar his shaggy hair curled. I had the sudden urge to shear him, pressed between my knees like an errant ewe.

'The hat, the hat!' Miss du Maurier screeched, her excitement at his visage uncontainable. Lily reached down amidst the froth of fabrics and props to a red and white striped box and pulled out the slickest satin topper I had ever seen. It was like a black cake, the sheen refracting light across the room and catching the reflection of our faces. The Jew walked forward and passed me, all eau de mothballs, and took the hat gingerly from her. He turned to face the old mirror over the mantle, his back to us, and positioned it on his head. From behind he glistened, the static coming off him, tall and dense with darkness. Satisfied with his reflection, he turned to face us again

'Oh my, I haven't seen anyone look so fine for the longest time,' Miss du Maurier sighed. 'My father was the last to wear that hat and I'm not sure he even wore it more than once.'

Lily just stood there speechless, her eyes taking in the dark height of him. The suit was beautiful, there was no doubt about it, and at another time I would have thought nothing of walking into a Zink and Sons with all the airs and graces I could muster, a nom de plume on my lips, to try on a suit and walk away with it swinging over my shoulder, knowing that some tight-arsed bastard in Vaucluse would open the bill and wonder when he ordered it, while I didn't even have one brass razoo to my name. But to see a suit like that on *him* invoked a fearsome rage within me.

'So what do you think?' he said, ignoring Miss du Maurier and me and directing his question straight to Lily.

She gazed at him, bedazzled, and then looked from Miss du Maurier to me as if we all waited for her appraisal, her pretty sea anemone mouth opening and closing, not sure which way the current was taking her.

'What do you think, Mr Little? Shall I call you Billy?' He extended his hand to me.

'Of course, Harry, be my guest.' I bloody well knew his name wasn't Harry, nor was he Houdini, but I wanted to test the waters to see if he would bite.

'Ari,' he corrected me. *La-di-da.*

I shook his hand and squeezed it as hard as I could muster and watched for a wince to spread across his features, but it never came.

'You look ...' I said, trying to hide any enthusiasm for the outfit, '... sharp.' It pained me to say and I watched his face keenly to see what effect my words had on him. He looked away.

'What are you going to wear, Lily?' Miss du Maurier asked.

Lily looked around at the old theatre costumes, headdresses and reams of fabric, then peered into the chest to see if there was anything else in there, her fingers absently fingering the plain stuff of her own dress.

'Come upstairs with me, darling, there are more things up there that may be more to your liking,' Miss du Maurier said, taking Lily by the arm.

Soon the Jew and I found ourselves alone, with the tapping of the ladies' footsteps upstairs our only conversation.

'Shall I pop the kettle on then?' I said brightly. I might be a paying guest, but it was still my home, and though he had a cubbyhouse like a termite nest out the back, he was still just a visitor. I padded into the kitchen and filled up the kettle. My movements were deliberately slow, so that I could think of something that would get the hair pricking the back of his collar. 'How is your act coming along?'

'Well, thank you,' the Jew said, still hesitating near the stairs. He was a little shy without the ladies to guide him.

'When is your audition?' I called out. All I could hear in reply was the rustle of desiccated tea leaves into the old chipped china pot. I could see him in the mantelpiece mirror shifting from one foot to the other.

'A week, Saturday morning,' he murmured, taking off the silken topper and fingering the polished sheen of the rim.

'You have been spending a lot of time with young Lily,' I said.

All he could manage was a nod of agreement, and the cloud of his silence thickened the air. There had to be something to make him rumble and spill. I carried the tea things in and plonked them on the table. The Jew moved a bit closer; by God he was a tall bastard.

'So what did you do before you started work at the Bridge Theatre, aside from being an impromptu member of the fire brigade?' The sound of his voice so near made me jump. I turned and there he was standing in the doorframe, his height almost blocking the space completely, his gaze direct and without the ruse of politeness.

He could sniff all he liked, for what could he possibly know of the likes of me? Snippets of hearsay from Lily, a general sketch from his aunt, an array of flattering details provided by Miss du Maurier.

'After the war, you mean?' The mention of the war made the Jew shift uncomfortably in the doorframe as if all of a sudden his skin didn't fit.

'After the war I did a lot of things – a bit of man-of-all-work, if you know what I mean.'

'Like what in particular?'

He was like a dog with a snake. If he was going to shake me so, beware my bite. Let my words stop up his questions and render him mute. Let the Jew be damned and him not know it.

'I was a shearer up north, hard and dirty work, but there is satisfaction in it. The wool is grimy on the outside, but part its greasy lushness and you find it clean and as pure as Snowy Mountain snow. My hands became soft as a baby's bum from all that lanolin, so smooth that not a line remained. Even my fingerprints softened and I am sure they would be illegible if I were ever required to press my inky finger upon the law's notepaper.'

The Jew thrust his hands into his pockets as if it was him that had blood on his hands. A lie written right there on his finger. A tattoo, pricked out with a needle until the blood and ink intermingled. A Jew with a tattoo: who ever heard of such a thing?

I was a shearer all right, but not for long. One day a carnival came straggling past the property where I was shearing. We all went to the neighbouring wool shed, a gander to ease the monotony of sheep in and sheep out, ready to throw pissy one-liners at their two-bit circus. The other blokes had all had a belly full of sherbet, the froth still tickling the hairs of their noses, their thirst nowhere near quenched. Me, I never touched the stuff. A greasy git presented himself before us and opened his coat to us with a flourish, and there in the lining was the flash and flare of his knives. Some blokes shifted uneasily in their seats: a man with thirteen knives in his coat grinning at us like an insane butcher bastard was not what we had been expecting. He stood there and pulled a knife out of his pocket and used it to comb his beard, dividing it until it was cleft in two. He called someone out of the audience to hold up a mirror for him. He took the knife and dragged it across the stubble of his cheek, as one would a cut-throat razor, the scraping sound making the men wince and long for soap. As if that was her cue, out stepped a girl in a mere bandage of a costume, barely covering her plump little body. He called for assistance to help secure the girl to a wooden wheel. Hands went up quicker than weeds after rain. Since I didn't put my hand up, he chose me, and I, being of a good nature, accepted.

Her flesh tingled beneath my touch; she was grateful no doubt for some warmth as the wind whistled from under the uneven floorboards. And I was gladdened to feel the velvet of a woman beneath my fingers. The ropes held firm her limbs and it seemed almost cruel to tie them so tight as to leave welts in her skin. As I returned to my seat the knife thrower tested my knots before giving the wheel a dramatic spin. The girl spun like water draining down the plug.

He threw the first blade and it flew with frightful accuracy, slamming into the wood above her spinning head. He did it with such ease and lack of showmanship, the knife could have been just a card being dealt in a game. He took the second one and threw it so fast it blurred before our eyes. It landed between her outspread knees. The third knife flew, as did the fourth, with dull thuds into the wood, the crowd unsure whether to cheer in case it distracted him from his aim. With the fifth knife, he paused, the blade waiting. He seemed unsure of the perfect moment to release it, the wheel slowing, the form of the girl returning from the spinning blur. He released the blade, but its arrival was strangely silent, muffled by the tender carving of the girl's flesh. The blood. Oh my, the blood. She screamed like a slit pig.

'And a little butchery, pigs mainly, not that you are familiar with them, begging my pardon.'

No pork for the likes of him. No bacon, no ham, no crackling, no sausage, no trotters or knuckles rendered down to stock. He looked at me then and his eyes narrowed. I had him rattled.

The Jew fiddled with his cuffs: he was in need of cufflinks. He twisted his wrists uncomfortably, trying to catch the buttonhole. 'Where were you in the war then? Lily mentioned …'

Ha, she had been talking about me; that was heartening. How had her voice sounded when she'd spoken of me? A hint of endearment? A little curiosity, her voice purring for me?

'The Holy Land and France.' I wasn't going to tell him that the only holy land I had found was between a woman's thighs, exploring Eliza, the knife thrower's girl, as we baptised each other in my canvas bed in the shearers' quarters, the galvanised-iron walls pinging from the heat and our sighs.

I had decided that I would take the disgraced knifeman's place in the routine. I needed a change from the sheep and their constant bleating; I was made for the finer things of the flesh. I had a steady hand and Eliza was docile as a lamb. She took a handful of balloons out of her bag and tied them at random points around the wheel where the knives should find their home. She cut a paper doll as large as herself and pinned it to where only days before she had bled. At first I hit everything, until gradually the newspaper girl flapped a sigh of relief in the wind, without a rip or tear.

It was a quiet evening when Eliza strapped herself to the wheel and trusted me to tie her bonds even tighter. She had taken to wearing the shirt with which I had staunched her wound, my best bloody shirt, but I didn't begrudge her for she had already well repaid the loan ...

'Lily?' the Jew said, his voice barely audible over the complaining scream of the boiling kettle.

Lily, Lily. Right behind him was a vision that made my mouth turn to paper. Lily stood there like an apparition in a yellowing wedding gown. Their reflections loomed in the mirror. With a trick of the light, she was the smoke, he was shadow.

'Lovely couple, don't you think?' Miss du Maurier piped from behind them. My voice had been extinguished.

Lily smoothed the satin with her palms. When she turned, my eyes tracked the ivory buttons snaking down her back and wondered what it would be like, one by one, to release them.

SIX

Ari

Miss du Maurier had offered me her father's morning suit, which she had retrieved from a cupboard under the stairs, a film of dust coating the surface of its box. She bustled me up the stairs.

'Where should I change?' I called out behind me.

'Use mine.' Lily called. 'Top of the stairs, first right.'

I swung open the door and was surprised to see how bare it was. There was her sunhat hanging on a hook behind the door, a couple of books sitting on the marble-lipped fireplace. I ran my fingers across the spines, feeling the compression of gold lettering. A pair of candle stubs sat fixed in old chipped saucers. Her silver hourglass-heeled shoes sat on the mantel, strangely disconcerting and fey, as if they had stepped through the glass themselves.

I tore off my jacket and kicked off my shoes, undid the buttons of my trousers, pulled my shirt from the back of my neck. I looked at the floor: my *tallit katan*, my *tzitzit,* the trappings of observant men, were crumpled together, the threads tangled like reeds around the dark puddle of the legs of my trousers, the one blue thread like a river. Each knot in the thread was a mitzvah, a commandment as given to Moses. They sat like an accusation on the floor. My uncle had showed me how to tie them, doing it for me until my small fingers had the dexterity to do it for myself, his hands guiding mine. I caught sight of my near naked self in the long cheval mirror and it made me uneasy. The lacy quilt of her bed stretched behind me, a sea.

As I lifted the suit out of the box, the camphor flew sharply to my nostrils and the tissue paper the suit was wrapped in fell away like a ribbon cut at an opening. I slipped the trousers on and buttoned up the shirt. A hint of cologne lingered for an instant and was gone. The coat skimmed my shoulders as if the suit had been cut to my measure. In the mirror it wasn't me that looked out, but a black and white image come to life in the silver shimmer of photographic paper. If my uncle looked out of my window would he be able to see me? Was someone always watching me? Billy Little always seemed to be somewhere nearby, a repeating shadow. Of course the man had a right to be wherever he wanted in his place of residence, but something didn't sit quite right. Was it his silhouette I had spied through the cobwebbed window when Lily and I had practised with the birds in the shed? Even when I was on my own, he would hover over the pegging of his freshly laundered shirts on the clothesline, and then sit watching them dry on the back steps, smoking his cigarette with an almost deliberate slowness. I was glad I'd hung up a curtain. I had read about the lengths magicians will stretch to filch others' secrets, sending spies and stealing notebooks. I wasn't fool enough to think we were at that point yet, but I didn't want to be sabotaged before we began.

I felt I had been preparing for this all my life. The line of letters on my hand was a compass pointing in the direction I should follow, my true north, but could I really fool myself into being a magician in borrowed clothes? In the last century, Robert-Houdin had first worn evening wear to match his audiences: the magic of theatres in fancier dress, a world away from the fairground. Houdini had worn Robert-Houdin's name. But whose name did I wear? I had left it behind with my mother, when she had been slain in the preposterous name of religion.

To my uncle, his beliefs were protection, a flaming sword to divine the way. For my aunt, it was the keeping of a home as you would the temple, immaculate. But I didn't know what I believed. All I understood was the magic in the old stories – Aaron writing his name upon a rod that grew into a blossoming tree, Moses parting the water with his staff, the desert well that appeared at Miriam's bidding. Miriam, as a girl, saved a baby by her cunning, with a basket, a river and a passerby. It was my mother who had first told these stories to me, the wonder in her shining face making me feel she had witnessed such acts with her own eyes. When I heard these stories, even in my uncle's commanding tone, I was in thrall to them, feeling that somehow they could drag the past into the present, and with them bring back the missing, the lost.

A button plucked itself from the shirt and spun on the floor, a mother-of-pearl coin seemingly conjured from nowhere. Had my father been a fairground master of such legerdemain, making coins dance through my mother's hair as if they were butterflies? Is that why she chose to mark me so? I picked up the button and slid it into a pocket of the tailcoat – inside I could feel the silk give way in my hands, thanks to the appetites of moths. In the pocket was a programme from a long-ago performance and I held its crumbling pages in my hands like a siddur and said a silent prayer for them all, my mother, my grandmother of blessed memory.

Back in my own clothes, after the strange thrill of seeing Lily and myself dressed for the stage, I headed out to the shed, passing through the kitchen, but there was no sign of Mr Little. When I opened the back door I was aware of music, a faint choir, a dawn chorus. There on the back step was a lyrebird, poked into a crate, its tail feathers sticking out like fingers. Carefully, slowly, I lifted the crate. The lyrebird stopped his song and stared at me with his ebony eye, distrustfully.

'Lily!' I shouted. The lyrebird, startled at my voice, curled deeper into the darkness but had nowhere to go. 'Lily!' Up from the highest window of the house, Miss du Maurier's face appeared, scissors in her hand and pins between her lips.

I grinned up at her. 'Could you please tell Lily we have had a delivery.'

I could barely wait to show Lily. I carried the lyrebird into the shed, out of the light, hoping that this might somehow soothe it, so it would sing. The parrot looked up from his perch. *Dabra*, he said as if it were my name. I placed the crate carefully on the floor and gently untwined the string. The currawong swooped low, nearly touching my ears with her wings, twisting her head at me as she observed the door of the crate as it fell open. A plume of dust filled the air as it hit the earthen floor. With one tentative claw the lyrebird took a slow, elegant step as if trying to avoid a puddle, before the other foot followed. Out he came. He shook his body vigorously, before searching the ground impassively with his beak. To my eye he looked not the least bit exotic, more like a tweedy pheasant, the grey, brown and russet of his feathers the disguise of autumn leaves. I waited for the famous song as if I was in the synagogue waiting the cantillation of the hazzan. His tail dragged along the floor. Where was the famous display the Birdman had talked about?

The lyrebird flicked his netted tail to the side and I felt the hairs stand up on end. What if the Birdman had picked up a hen? Then, without warning, it looked toward the door and it opened, flooding the floor with light. Lily stepped into the shed, bringing with her a light all her own, dressed in the pearly lustre of Miss du Maurier's wedding dress carefully cropped of its train to her knee, beneath it her lower legs again startlingly clothed in trousers. She carefully closed the door behind her, but the bird was alert to the subtle click of the latch. Trembling, the lyrebird's tail rose up like the rays of the sun, a glorious and fragile thing, a huge feathered gossamer web. His small throat throbbed, the sound bubbling upwards, the notes heading straight to the rafters as if ready to sit upon them as a note upon the stave. I reached for the bow with one hand and the mahogany shape of the violin with the other, without taking my eyes from the lyrebird. Lily looked at me, the surge of excitement flying between us like a spark. The parrot blustered down from the rafters, blowing Lily's hair into her face as he resumed a lookout on her shoulder.

Three notes I played, only three, the sound of them hanging in the silent air. The bird shifted his feathers, a swishing that commanded attention. The currawong's tail swivelled off the old horse stall, orange eye observant. The lyrebird waited to make sure all eyes were upon him. Even the cat that sat on the sill paused between moistened tongue and fur and peered through the smeary window, startled somewhat by the three perfect sounds that came from the bird, three exact notes, as if I had dragged my bow across his throat.

Lily stole a quick look at me and I at her, not quite able to believe our ears. 'Do it again,' she whispered, neither of us taking our eyes off the bird. I played the next sequence of notes and the lyrebird's throat bobbed and burbled long past my small sequence of notes. A whole other song filled the shed and sent a thrill up my spine. A rain of notes from a piano, the sound of human hands running across ivory and ebony, but coming from the deep recesses of a feathered breast. Lily reached out and brushed her hands gently across the frond of the lyrebird's tail, gently as if across a harp, but the lyrebird continued. Jealously, the parrot squawked from his place on Lily's shoulder, claws stamping up and down, nearly slipping on the silky satin of the dress. His neck stuck out, beak open, a green tantrum. It was then that the lyrebird stopped. He turned his head towards the parrot, one clockwork tilt, and blinked before he opened his beak and squawked louder than the parrot ever did. Lily and I dissolved in laughter.

Lily and I practised with the birds until the last available minute before she had to run to her shift at the theatre, but I remained behind playing songs to the birds, hoping that the lyrebird would sing his symphony for me again, but he went quiet, as if his love song was for Lily alone. It was dark by the time I finished, the birds' eyelids lowering, beaks ruffling under feathers as I turned off the light. Did birds dream? We dreamed of flying; did they dream of walking the earth?

My uncle would have begun prayers across the road, his book just waiting for the kiss of the pointer. The women in the gallery would be waiting, thoughts bent on the Shabbos meal that they had prepared earlier, hoping that no cockroaches had found their way beneath the gauze covers. Aunt Hephzibah always cried when she found one sampling the glaze of the challah bread, which was never to her satisfaction, as if the water or the flour contained something upside down in this topsy-turvy part of the world, something that prevented it cooking just right.

The challah in my grandmother's house was always cloud soft. I lived with my mother in my grandmother's house. Above the mantelpiece was a photographic portrait of my grandparents: my grandfather dressed in his best suit, his dark beard near obscuring his mouth, the curls I had inherited from him oiled down into subdued waves, the glare on his spectacles making him look like he had shekels for eyes. My grandmother wore her thick skein of hair in a swirl above her head. If you had looked only at my bubbe's eyes, you would have thought her the most earnest of women, but if you had looked lower, you would have been startled by the scampish smile above the froth of lace at her throat. My grandmother used to say to me that I was the spit from my mother's mouth. I carried the belief for a long while, that babies were formed from the spit of their mothers, until Aunt Hephzibah heard me say it, laughed gently and put me right. Below the portrait was the family menorah, a silver menagerie of birds and flowers that twisted out of the metal, which appeared forever tarnished from the smoke from the fire until the festival of lights, Chanukah, came, and then it was polished until its luminosity rivalled the moon's. Next to it were the Shabbat candlesticks in use weekly, never free of the spit and polish delivered every Friday by my grandmother's dexterous fingers before the candles were lit, prayers said, hands covering the eyes so as to sanctify the start of the Sabbath.

In the mornings my grandmother would sometimes go to the synagogue as my grandfather had once done. I sat with her in the ladies' gallery, watching the clouds of breath escape through the men's lips, my teeth clattering in my mouth from the cold.

'See those lions, Ari,' she said, pointing down to the lions rampant on the side of the ark. 'You, my Ari, are my lion.' My bubbe would lean over and tuck me close into her dark fur coat, russet-tipped, smelling of stale perfume. It was my bubbe who would wake me later, ready to brave the thick slough of snow until we reached the warmest place on earth, our little island, our home.

Once one of the women of the congregation came up to us as we stamped our feet on the footpath to warm them. She wanted to know how Bubbe's son, Israel, was doing in the wilderness. My grandmother was about to answer, but the other woman was pulled away by her husband, my grandmother not able to answer and sing the praises of her successful son. We were like the rocks the tide moves around, the people brushing past, their sleeves barely touching ours, as if we existed only as proof of the swell of their tide. I heard my mother's name floating in the snow-laden air and it sounded strange, they spat it out with the ice. *Zipporah.*

At night as a child I would call for my mother, the black wings of bad dreams brushing against my head. But it was my grandmother who would come, the faint sweet smell of peach schnapps on her breath, the crackle of the gramophone, the long sob of a cello. In the mornings my mother would be there, her eyes red, her hands ink-stained, in time for morning prayers, the *shacharit.*

We would all say the first part together: *Blessed are you, our G_d, King of the Universe who did not make me a slave.* But then the lengthy pause began, where no one spoke, even though the air ached for it. My grandmother's long sigh was the signal for the argument that would begin.

'You should let him say his part, Zipporah, he may be a boy, but one day he will be a man.' My mother blew upward at the escaping tendrils of her hair.

'There are no men here,' my mother said.

'Zipporah! Your father of blessed memory has passed, your brother is abroad, Ari's father ...'

'I will not have him say it,' she said, her voice steely. It wasn't until I arrived at my uncle's that I knew what it was they argued over. I was required to say: *Blessed are you, our G_d, King of the Universe who did not make me a woman.* This only confirmed for my uncle the godlessness of my mother.

The thought of my aunt's imperfect challah bread made me hungry, and the only food in the shed was birdseed. I hurried back home, knowing it was too late to attend the service, but I surely wasn't too late for the Sabbath meal surely. A fruit bat startled me, its shadow projected large onto a white wall of a house as it flew. The temple lights were on, but the doors were closed. There was no sound of prayer. I fumbled for the key to our flat and tried to fit it in the lock. But before it could find a snug fit, the door swung open.

My uncle stood before me, his face red to bursting with all the things he wanted to say. When he opened his mouth the colour drained slowly from his face. I waited for him to say his piece and let me pass, but no words came. The fruit bat flapped low over our heads, its screech in our ears. Aunt Hephzibah opened the window of my room above, as if somehow her benign presence could influence what was about to be said.

'Can I come in, Uncle Israel?' I asked, trying to hide the exasperation in my voice, but still a little trickled out. It only served to enflame him.

'Have you decided to commit yourself to the study of the Torah? Have you made your decision to study at yeshiva to become a rabbi? If the answer is no, you may not come in.'

I took a backward step on the footpath. This was the home I had grown to manhood in. My height was tracked in pencil measurements marked proudly on the wall. I had travelled across oceans to call this my home, not by choice but by destiny. On my schoolroom slate this was the house I chalked, the smoke puffing out in a childish swirl; these were my parents standing in front of it. I had another home once before in a dream, but it was long gone. If marked with a string, the way back would be worn thin with the constant fingering of memory, of longing, of wondering how to get back.

'I take your silence as a no. Consider this no longer your home.'

The door slammed closed. Before I could speak the key clicked in the lock. I looked up desperately at my aunt, but even she was speechless, my uncle's force creating a whirlwind that spun her madly back from the window and into the house as she heard his foot on the stair.

SEVEN

Billy

Miss du Maurier had filled the days before the audition with her recollections of the stage, until it had become unendurable. I had avoided her as best I could, loitering in my room until it was almost a relief the day of it came just to hear the end of it, for I couldn't bear another minute of the atmosphere in the house, nor my desire to know what it was had been going on in the shed. I arrived at the theatre earlier than my shift demanded. I would find work for my hands to do, even if it meant cleaning the privies. But she burned in my mind, the word made flesh. To drink her in was all I wanted. The house lights were on in the theatre; I had been hoping it would be as dark as a church so I could sit and dream the future with my prayers. A cleaner walked onto the stage with his bucket spilling rags, the mop a wood-and-cotton rifle over his shoulder.

The foyer was filled with hopeful flotsam ready to audition and I wondered what Mr Harry Clay would make of the two of them, the bride and groom with their pigeons. Then the boss man himself walked in, freshly pressed as if he had just stepped off an ironing board.

'You're here early, Little, not come to do some adjusting of the till, are you?' The faces of the would-be performers swivelled like owls in my direction. Who was *he* to call *me*

Little? I wanted to erase his face with my fists. I had to speak. The longer my silence, the more his joke became an accusation. Was I losing my nerve? Hadn't I always been flasher than a rat with a gold tooth?

'I wished, sir, to come a little early to make sure the bookings are in order. Last night some drongo overbooked and we had to turn folk away.'

He tipped his hat in my direction and turned to the sunflower faces watching him, their imposing sun. 'Which one of you wants to be first? The theatre's being cleaned and my office is being painted, so here will have to do.'

I tilted open the internal blinds of the box office, a secretive slant. A couple stood up and the fellow opened a box of knives. Clay looked warily at his baroque moulded walls. I thought of Eliza, my circus girl, my voodoo doll.

To impress Eliza I had nailed a circular piece of wood loosely to a tree and spun it as fast as I could, before dashing back to my spot, pulling down the blindfold and aiming like the billy-o in the right direction, satisfied only by the pop of balloons. The odd knife flew into the leafy branches, rousing the squawk of cockatoos. Before I returned to Eliza I sharpened the blades on the strap, thwacking them back and forth, lost in the rhythm, until the edges were precise, surgical and bright. I was eager to show Eliza the finesse of my skill.

When I walked into our room, Eliza was rolling about with another man. They were so distracted by their heavings that they never heard my entrance, let alone my retreat. This I was not prepared for. I had anointed her with my attention and made her anew in my image; it was not fair of her to rebel. Was I not giving her the world?

I was not nervous that first time upon the stage. Eliza was strapped in for the spin and I took close aim, grazing her flesh where I could. One by one my silver sickles sang. Spin she did, but she would not cry out. The applause at my acts of risk encouraged me, as my whistling blades shaved the finest of hairs from her skin. They did not know that every throw was accuracy in perfection. I wanted the trickle of the graze to spell out my name in her blood.

If I had been sharper, perhaps Lily wouldn't have turned to another. If my suit were made of gabardine or wool or tweed, if the trousers had pleats and pinstripes, my collar stiff as a stranger's groin, my cuffs snowy white. If my tie were made of silk, with polka dots and a matching handkerchief like a plume in the pocket; if my face smelled of citrus or sandalwood cologne. If my shoes were shiny as a beetle's back, clear enough to see my face in, if my socks weren't riddled with holes like a piece of cheese. If my hat were free of lint with a clean striped band of grosgrain ribbon, the brim at a cocky tilt. If my suit were as fine as the Jew's, then perhaps it would have been me who cast her off before she did me.

I opened and closed drawers to make myself sound busy. Upon the counter I could see the front-of-house book. Lily's name, the print shaky and etched into the page as if the bloke who was on the shift when she came had traced the original words over and over again. I ran my fingers over her name like braille. Lily del Mar, a silly but wonderful invention, the original I would pry out of her yet, as the oyster knife shucks the pearl. I hoped Clay's office would still be filled with brushes and turps by the time their audition came, for the foyer was my domain. I felt the knife I kept strapped to me, pointed as a guiding star. The handle was made of heavy wood, counterweighted so it could spin handle over blade when it skimmed the air.

Harry Clay was weighing up the idea of the act against his precious gilt lobby. 'Not bloody likely in here, sunshine,' he boomed. 'Come back next week.' The knifeman closed his case and the next clown stood up to grasp his moment. At that moment the pair of them arrived, birds swinging in their cages. Lily was flustered; I could see the harsh rouge of exertion in her cheeks. At that moment the cleaner came from the theatre into the foyer, clanking his sloshing bucket.

'About time,' muttered Clay and all the hopeful auditionees, my Lily of the Valley included, followed behind him, all a raggle-taggle-gypsy-o.

I tested the knife's weight in my hand and I felt its need. Who was I to hold it back? It flew through the room, my strange metal bird, happily planting its lethal beak in the wood of the box-office window frame, exactly as I had aimed it. Clay looked up from his meek disciples and over to the box office, but dismissed the evidence of his own ears. As they disappeared into the theatre, I walked over and pulled the knife from the grain and admired my calligraphy. With only a little more encouragement from the tip of the blade, snick-snick, two *L*s shone back at me upon the wall – *Lily Little* – for all the world to see if they were sharp enough.

I left my box-office cubby hole to peer into the theatre, to try to catch a glimpse. I didn't want to see his paws upon her; I wouldn't be responsible for what else my knife longed to say. The door silently opened an eye width. For weeks they had spent hours cloistered in that shed, resistant to my keen observations. Whenever I asked Lily for a clue she smiled and said a magician never shares her secrets. As I peered through the theatre door, I watched the Jew fiddle with his violin case as Lily freed the birds. The parrot fluttered up to the gantry above, until with a whistle it came to her outstretched arm, a green smear against her calico skin, while the currawong seemed reluctant to step out into the false light of the stage.

Lily squinted out into the darkness of the auditorium, waiting for her cue, and the Jew stood solemnly, his head bowed. Was he composing himself or had he lost his nerve? Out of its cage, the lyrebird took several dainty steps across the front of the stage before it found its imaginary mark and flicked its spectacular tail outward, a firework of feathers. Lily draped her arms around its throat, like Pavlova and her pet, and I gasped.

Clay barely looked over his shoulder, his cigarette glowing like a sniper's decoy in the dimness.

'Clear the theatre please, Mr Little,' he said, and I wished like hell I had a rifle on me.

Once the audition was over and her shift began, I tried to catch her eye again – oh, that red pillbox hat and the platinum ripple of her hair beneath – but she eluded me.

I balanced up the till at the end of my shift. Always a temptation, to line my pockets with a little pay rise, but mindful of my purpose not yet served, I abstained. My plan was still being knitted together.

With the theatre closing, I walked out into the night, wondering whether to linger for her. I looked upwards and saw the very stars arrange themselves to spell her name. The cold air braced my nerves and I roared it into my lungs, blowing smoke rings as I walked along the street. It was too early to go back to the boarding house to wait for her – there was the risk of being trapped by Miss du Maurier's tales. I saw the Red Rose was still open and I made my way in, not caring if the Jew sat there tinkling at the piano. I had my plans for him too, not yet, but soon. A good plan needs nurturing like a seedling – soil, water, sun and shit. He fortunately was not in sight. Though she would be. All I had to do was wait.

I ordered my cocoa and cupped it to warm my hands, sipped its dark sweetness, but declined the waitress's enticement of cake. I loathed cake. My stomach heaved at the thought of it. All the sweet I wanted was her, my little neighbour. She would be along soon; I knew her route as she walked the same way every time. I'd follow her at a respectful distance, keeping my careful eye upon her, along King Street, with its overswilling pubs, sly grog shops and the punters from the boxing matches with the smell of blood in their nostrils. The street was probably even busier in the night than the day, lit with round streetlights like a string of pearls. But as soon as you turned the corner, the light was extinguished. One couldn't be too careful around these narrow streets. I kept watch for her out in the darkness, luring her in with my mind.

A bone-handled bread knife had been left on the table, broad and flat and dim. I ran it across the lines in my palm; I could make a better future for myself, no matter what the lines said.

After Eliza's betrayal, I packed up my knives and laid them to rest for a time, letting the blades go dull and blunt. I had a few bob in my pocket, so I was not skint. There was only so much time one could spend bent over a beer like my father, holding up the bar with the soapy suction of the glass. The library seemed a natural refuge, a place to take stock. After all, it had been a book that had helped me block out the screams of amputee soldiers after I had sent my metal bouquet into Gerry's trench after I had delivered my own stigmata.

The library was quiet and warm, and when I had tired of reading I could nap behind the pages or have a gander at the female readers with their pursed expressions as they stumbled across difficult words. I favoured reading autobiographies such as Casanova's with his nifty invention of the lottery and his adventures with women, though he was obviously a flagrant liar who wouldn't know honesty if it was shoved up his arse as an enema.

Every day, the regulars showed up, until I became one myself. Another regular was the perfect professor, his tie a stiff fabric goitre beneath his chin. He always moved slowly, as if in a dream, never turning a page without a dab of moisture from a quick flick of his narrow cat-like tongue. Occasionally he would remove his spindle-rimmed glasses and wipe them clean, though they seemed impeccably clean already. It was as though even the dust would not dare settle on him. Our professor was smoother than a fake pearl.

I took to surreptitiously watching him from behind my book, the meticulous rhythm of his movements strangely alluring. I squinted at the authors he read – Mesmer, Charcot, Freud. Whoever they were, I wanted to know. But when I went to the shelves after him to find the volumes myself, they were not there. They had not been returned. I asked the librarian, but even she could not track them down and could only list them as lost or stolen. So when I next saw my portly professor, I watched him more closely.

He picked up a book, his tongue darting in and out of his mouth as if the words printed were cream, and tucked it under his arm as if it was already his. I quickly pulled my jacket on and put my book down, not taking my eyes off him for a second. His eye was fixed on the face of the librarian, who stood still before him as if caught in a snare. His spare hand waved twice, a strange gesture, and her hands fell down by her side as if they were no longer part of her body. He slipped past her, brazen as brass, but she just smiled and bid him good day, purloined book and all.

Not only was the book now his, the street was as well. If pedestrians came toward him on the footpath, it wasn't the professor who stepped aside, oh no, everyone was a mere rowboat to his warship, scuppered to make way. He walked past a fruit stand and reached for a pear shaped with the perfect flange of a woman's bottom, fondled it and put it back down, before grasping another and sinking his teeth right in. Perhaps it wasn't ripe enough or was too floury, for he put it back down, a deep gouge in its side. The fruit seller, a swarthy continental, just waved cheerily at him, not registering the ravaging of his property. My professor was golden, untouchable.

I quickened when he quickened, stopped to inspect the time when he did (though I had no watch myself). His beautiful gold fob watch, like the one I had traded with Golden Fortune, was yanked with indiscriminate attention. Maybe he thought he could just filch another one when the fancy took him. His steps slowed. He looked about him and for a moment I thought he caught my eye, his blank stare seeing right through me. He quickly spun on his heel and disappeared through the door of the nearest shop. I stepped back and read the sign on the awning.

APOTHECARY

Home of Professor Cuthbert Crisp's Elixir du Jour

The curiosity pounded in me, knocking my heart for six. I pushed the door open and it took me a moment to adjust blinkingly to the light. As I did, I almost wished I had never set foot across the threshold.

The professor was standing right in front of me, big as a brick shithouse, blocking my passage. My feet felt rooted to the spot. Who was this man? He would have filled the arse end of a trench without much ado. I had to crane my neck to take the bulk of him in. If he had bid me drink a foul concoction of Anzac soup I probably would have; I could not look away from his face, ugly prick that he was. He flexed his fingers into a fist and I felt my body brace for the blow, but I couldn't have moved even if I'd wanted. My body had become a standing carcass waiting to be pulverised by a butcher's fists. He didn't strike then though – for that he made me wait.

Instantly, I was in thrall to Professor Cuthbert Crisp, who was to become my teacher, the refiner of my talents. Though I would one day come to wish that it was I who could teach him the lesson of a lifetime, in the same way he had delivered mine.

As I finished draining my cup in the Red Rose, I caught sight of her ghost face in the doorway. She had spotted me before I had spotted her and she had paused on her way for me.

'Lily,' I called, thrilled, rising to my feet and ushering her in. 'Let me buy you a drink.' If I could have drawn her into my arms I would have, but it was too soon, too soon.

'It should be me buying you one,' she said as she sat down. 'I owe you, after all.'

That she did. Or perhaps I was in debt to her. It was a delight to see her in her usherette's uniform, the red suit with brass buttons and matching pillbox hat. She was like the Queen of Heaven, the way her face glowed back as she illuminated the aisle with her torch, a tender guide for latecomers. Would she be able to show me the way too, pale angel at my side? Would she drape her arms around my throat, as she had with the lyrebird? Could I hope for as tender a touch?'

'How'd the audition go?' I prodded her. 'Where did that lyrebird come from?' It had surprised me to see such a thing, a bit of the bush lit electric on the stage.

She looked at me with her mercurial eyes and blinked her pale lashes. When she opened them again, had her eyes changed colour?

'Well, I think it went well, but Clay had to dismiss a certain spy before we could begin.'

It was my turn to colour, blood rushing to my face.

'Forgive my curiosity, Lily. Every time you and your friend disappear into the shed, I can't help wonder what you've been up to.' Her eyes fell then to the table; my double-edged question had made its point. My aim was true.

'We have not quite perfected it all yet, you'll have to wait like all the rest to see,' she said bluntly. Her confidence was slipping from me, but I would kindle it yet. 'It will surprise you.'

'Will you still be an usherette?' I'd miss seeing her as my little usherette, my bold little soldier, her light blazing through my own no-man's-land.

'Maybe. It's too soon to tell. It's better than my last job, that's for sure,' she replied.

'Which was?' I pressed her again.

Agitatedly she fiddled with the bowl of sugar, dabbing up dropped granules on the table and plying them between her fingertips.

'Just helping a bit at the general store,' she lied. I could see it as she looked into my eyes; it was writ large in her irises. She would tell me one day, but for now I could only imagine. Feeding poddy lambs? Arranging flowers in a church? Teaching children Sunday school songs?

When her cocoa came, she held the cup close to her lips, blowing a cool wind on its steam, her mouth moist as a bitten cherry. I stared at her, drinking her in, her skin, her smell, until I looked solely at her eyes. Instilling my will in her with my eyes alone. Oh, I could dry her wet little lips with my own!

I kept my eye fixed upon her, just as I had been taught. She blinked several times, a helpless doll, her lashes fluttering to stay open. I reached out to her, my fingers coarse against the silk slip of her skin, her hand showing no resistance. That she submitted so easily to my strong eye, the timbre of my voice, my gentle stroking of her skin, all this delighted me. Her eyes shone with a darker light, her pupils swelling, spilled inkwells in her iris, and I had that thrill I had first felt long ago, when I had learned all from the master.

But Lily pulled her hand away from mine. My hand quivered from the shock of it. I had to contain myself, for I wanted to clutch at her and bring her back, her hand held close in mine as it should be.

'I have to be going,' she said, rising from the chair like mercury. She left the cocoa unsipped and disappeared through the door. The steam made question marks in the air that I was afraid to blow away in case they multiplied.

I thought she was receptive to the tenor of my touch, the hypnotic stroke. Had I lost my gift since Crisp, since Merle? She was still fallow, but I could wait, with a patience unsurpassable. She would have the full measure of me soon enough, and then it would be my name, only mine, that she would think of dawn through to night, not his. There would be no more questions, no hasty departures; she would be mine and mine alone.

EIGHT

Ari

My expulsion was a bitter pill to swallow and the judgement unclear. Was this to be just for one night, to teach me a lesson, or for good?

The shed was the one patch of earth that had afforded me my freedom, yet as the temperature dropped, my breath pearling on the windows, it felt like a cell. I wished I had worn my thickest jacket. The birds at least had feathers to nestle under, soft bodies forming their own little eiderdowns. I had the old kangaroo skin and was grateful for its warmth even though my toes were cold as hailstones.

Would I ever be welcomed back? In my ignorance I had assumed my uncle's constant reminders were just hopes, yeshiva an option, not something he insisted upon absolutely or else endure exile. I had foolishly thought he would come to understand my ambitions. I was not his son, though he had been all the father I had ever known. It was my Uncle Israel who had taught me to read – not just the *aleph* and *tav* of the Hebrew letters, but the English ones as well. His patience was limitless as he would go from the Russian to the Hebrew to the English, never once raising his voice if I got it wrong, encouraging me to try again. It was my Uncle Israel who had placed my stubby childhood fingers on the board of the violin, tattooed finger and all, and guided the bow in my hand across the strings. He had helped my eyes follow the black and white dance of notes in their parade between the fence of lines. It was my uncle who had tucked me into bed and told me the stories of the Torah and the Talmud, like the story of Noah.

Once, tucked around the corner of the kitchen door, I overheard my aunt and uncle discussing the name. At first I thought they were talking of the naming of a child not yet born, that perhaps my aunt was expecting and I would find myself with a cousin, to be just like a brother or sister. But I was wrong.

'Why couldn't she have called him Noah?' my uncle said. My aunt ignored him and carried on scrubbing the same dish in the sink. 'Noah is a righteous name.'

'So is Ari,' she said, and so I knew they were talking about me.

'Ari is the name of a beast. Noah is the name of the Venerable. A lion attacked Noah on the ark and crippled him. Samson fought a lion with his bare hands.' When I heard that, my name sat uneasy on my shoulders as if somehow it was not mine. 'If he were my son I would not have called him so. Nothing good can come of naming your child after an animal.' No father ever named me; my father had died before I was born.

My aunt paused, and in the silence I could hear the slow whisper of the suds subsiding in the sink. Then she spoke quietly so that I strained to hear her voice. 'He is our child but not our son.'

These words confused me and I wanted to call out and ask what they meant, but that would have exposed me as an eavesdropper, a disobedient child who had snuck out from under the covers when I had been told to stay in bed until morning.

'Zipporah was your sister, Israel. And even her name means "bird", have you forgotten this so soon? Whatever frustrations you feel about what happened, it is no fault of the boy's.'

'I cannot forget soon enough,' was all he said.

The next night, after I had said my prayers, my uncle tucked me in and was about to tell me the story of Samson and Delilah, when I interrupted and asked for the story of Noah. He shifted uneasily on the edge of my bed, pressing the springs to a squeak. Why was Noah's name better than mine?

'When G_d announced the flood and Noah built the ark, he took birds, including the Raven and the Dove. When the Raven resisted the order to find land, Noah declared that the world had no need of it and cursed the Raven and cast him out, not knowing that the Raven would return one day and rescue Elijah in the wilderness. If G_d could save Noah, why not my mother?

So Noah was forced to send the Dove. When she returned with a green sprig, Noah knew his ordeal was over, but still the loss of so much life weighed on him. He asked G_d why he had let the Flood happen and G_d chided him. "You knew you were going to be rescued, but yet you didn't care for others. If you had begged for clemency then and there, there wouldn't have been a flood at all."'

If I had known what was to happen to my grandmother, my mother and me, if I had begged for mercy, would G_d have stopped what happened? I curled more tightly under the kangaroo skin, as the parrot stretched his green wings in his sleep, iridescent in the gloom. Was speaking the words power enough?

I woke with a strange feeling upon me. Lily was leaning over me, silent as the moon, white and shining. She made no effort to move away, and waves of her silvery hair, the tips damp from the morning air, touched my face. But before I could say anything she stood upright. I could still feel the tickle of her hair on my cheek. The morning light filtered weakly through the window.

'Wake up, sleepyhead, we've work to do,' she said, resting her hip on the arm of the chair, tickling the parrot under his chin. 'Most people try a bed.'

'My uncle has thrown me out,' I said. It felt strange to say it so plainly. 'He's cast me out.'

'What for?'

What could I tell her about my uncle's decision when it was his silences that communicated more than his words?

'He has his own reasons. They are his alone. They are not something we share,' I said, sitting up on my elbow. I felt like I hadn't slept at all. I didn't want to think of my uncle any more. He had more pity for himself than any other living being.

She opened her mouth to ask another question, but I cut her off. 'But you know you've never told me of your home, Lily, where you've come from,' I said, desperate to deflect, to forget myself, to not be like him.

'It is not a pretty tale,' she said, looking away from me.

'Try me.' She looked up at me and held my gaze a moment, then looked away again. I could hear the quake in her voice as her words came out in a rush of breath.

'I worked at a petrol and service station. Did I tell you that before?'

I shook my head.

'I told my mother I was working at another shop. I'd worked at the general store, but the owners had to let me go when their son returned. He'd tried to make a go of it in Sydney after the war. But he'd beaten his wife in his sleep, gambled away the family home, his wounds all on the inside. The tremor in his hand the only tell. When he returned to town, they could hardly keep me on as well. So I got whatever job I could get. The war widow's pension only went so far. She would have hated that I worked at a petrol service station, not a proper job for a lady. Funnily enough she never asked which shop. She was too preoccupied.

'Every afternoon I left the house wearing a pair of my father's trousers under my dress, the legs rolled up under my hemline, until eventually I did away with the frock altogether.

It was better that way. No need for the spectacle of a girl in a dress pumping petrol reaching my mother's ears. It was on the outskirts of our town. One petrol pump and a bathroom and a meagre stand that stocked peanuts and soft drink.'

She paused, her eyes narrowed, and her face went pink from her cheeks to the tips of her ears. She pulled at the sleeves of her cardigan, trying to make mittens of the ends.

'But the man I worked for had other plans for me. He said …' She looked alarmed, her breath grew shallow and I wanted to still the trembling of her hands.

'What was it that he said to you?' I asked her, and immediately regretted it. Down her cheek trickled two tears, her voice choked, so that I had to lean closer to hear her. She exhaled before she spoke, a little cloud disappearing into the cool air. She began to shake and I wanted to comfort her, but I couldn't. My hands were as useless as stones. She looked at me then, her strange dark eyes, the darkest things in her face, measuring me. Her trust was a fragile thing, it hovered somewhere in the room between us.

Her voice was hardly audible, barely more than a whisper, the enormity of what she wanted to say wedged in her throat. Her voice gave out then, her mouth opened and closed but nothing came.

I didn't know what to say. Her silence stung my ears and I wanted nothing more than to blow away what troubled her like a dandelion clock. The parrot gave better comfort than I did, squeaking quietly into her ear, rocking on her shoulder. How can a man be jealous of a parrot, I thought helplessly.

'Ready to practise when you are,' she said quietly when she found her voice again, and I felt ashamed of my own speechlessness.

All day I felt I had let her down; a space gaped where my apology should have been. What had the man said to her? She wouldn't tell me now; I didn't blame her, for I was a fool who knew nothing about the ways of women. When we spoke we stayed to a strict script, though I desperately wanted to say something, anything to deserve her trust in me. Every time Lily brushed by, my nerves stood on end, in anticipation that there might be a conjunction of our fingertips.

Mr Clay had clapped at the end of our audition, a slow appreciative staccato. Lily and I had together stared out into the darkness, following the tip of his cigarette rise from the seats to the stage stairs until he was on the stage himself. He walked around us in a semicircle, his eyes on the birds, and they, as was their want, ignored him. Lily and I exchanged a tentative glance. Clay extracted his cigarette from his lip and stubbed it out on the sole of his shoe, before he stepped toward the parrot resting on Lily's shoulder. With an outstretched thumb he reached to caress the parrot, but received a decisive nip, a clear rejection of his advance. At the clack of the parrot's beak the lyrebird whipped his tail forward like a sail, sending the currawong back to the safety of her cage. 'Wonders never cease,' Clay said. 'You need a stand, or a prop tree, to give it that Garden of Eden feel – what do you think? How about a trial performance to see how the audience reacts? How does that sound to you?'

We had come so far, but in the shed, with my violin beneath my chin, watching the graceful arc of her arms, hearing her quavering voice, I knew I'd stepped too far. We practised until the sun reached the conclusion of its arc across the sky, the last of winter's chill slowly descending, the mauve shadows stretching towards us. She helped me usher the birds back inside their respective roosts around the shed, tenderly casting an eye over them before I walked her back up to the house, the proximity of her hand so close to mine that I could have reached out and held it.

'Night then,' she said, and I watched her as she mounted the back stoop.

'Lily,' I called to her, and she stopped and turned around to face me, my heart leaping in my chest.

'I'm sorry about what happened.' I'd said it. It was out. The weight of it lifted off me.

Her face crumpled for a moment and then she regained her composure with a tired smile. She took a step toward me and squeezed my hand. 'What do you have to be sorry for?' she said, standing a little straighter. 'Sleep well with the birds,' and then she was gone, swallowed into the house.

The lights turned on one by one and lit the back lawn. Tracking her movement through the house, I felt my eyes were trailing her like an astrolabe does the stars.

The birds turned to look at me as I entered the shed and one by one I stroked their feathers, filled their trays with water, replenished their seed bowls. Carefully I quartered an apple. The parrot swooped and sank his beak joyfully into the crisp fruit. His squawks and trills were louder than before, as though he were transmitting the unspoken things that had passed between Lily and me. The currawong clacked her beak as if she could speak, a low whistle muffled in her throat, and plunged her talons that bit deeper as I helped her to the perch.

The pricking of my skin made me think of the softness of her touch. The lyrebird had folded his feathers under himself and made a substitute bower out of some old rags that Miss du Maurier and I had used as drop sheets when I had helped her paint the house. The cat was suddenly at my feet, an apparition out of nowhere, eyeing up the birds with what I had thought was hunger. But as the lyrebird snapped and fanned out his imperious feathers, asserting his right over his kingdom, I realised that the cat watched them out of fear, three to one, the odds against him.

I looked at the cot in the corner, now heaped warm and welcoming with the blankets Miss du Maurier had loaned me. She had offered me a room in the house, but I felt I was trespassing enough, and was grateful that I would have more than the kangaroo skin to curl under later. I struck a match and lit the kindling in the old fireplace. The flames licked and curled around the few sticks I could find, the chimney's lungs inhaling it up into the sky. I put the grille in front and braced myself for what I had to do next.

It felt strange to knock on the door of a place I had only ever known as home. The handle would not give way to my grasp. I walked around to the side door, my hand pausing on the twist of the doorknob, hearing the low murmurs of voices next door in the synagogue. I remembered with a jolt. It was the start of Tisha B'Av. Next door my uncle would be leading his congregation, some sitting on the floor, others on low stools, while Lamentations was read in the solemnest of voices.

Tisha B'av marked the day that Nebuchadnezzar destroyed the first temple and the Romans the second, six hundred and fifty-six years apart on the very same day. On the ninth of Av, when the bricks fell and the offerings were covered with dust, the Shekinah, the feminine aspect of G-d, left. Every year on the ninth of Av we ate our bread dipped in ashes, we wore no shoes, we fasted, we read only from the book of Lamentations and did no work. But not this year for me. I turned the handle and walked silently up the stairs, cursing the creaks and moans of the steps that complained of my presence. As much as I loved my aunt and uncle, I didn't want to see them at this moment, as I sneaked up their stairs like an errant child.

The flat was quiet except for the clock ticking on the wall. My uncle's study door was closed. I pushed open the door to my old room and was shocked by its barrenness. It had been stripped of my presence. The mattress was bare of sheets, the blankets folded up in perfect rectangles. My few belongings and clothes were neatly piled in an old laundry basket. A label with my name was attached on the side with a piece of string, written in my uncle's deliberate cursive. I picked up the basket and was filled with the desire to empty out the contents all over the floor to make a wasteland of my room. This was not my doing. But it was too light; there was hardly anything in there, just a few sets of clothes neatly folded. Where had the rest of my belongings gone? I never asked to leave, never asked to lose my mother, never asked to be taken in by my aunt and uncle. I never asked to follow in his footsteps. I never asked for anything. All my life I lived in silence, listening to others' needs and never speaking of my own. And the first time I voiced a need, did he hear it? Did he think it a slight against him, at his gift of a life in a new country, at all the care and sacrifice given to a child of his sister's, father unknown?

I took the basket and walked out of my room and I couldn't shake the feeling that this might be the last time I took in the sight of what I knew as home. I turned in the doorway and looked around bitterly. There was nothing left of me already.

Then I looked up at the ceiling and saw that the attic hatch was slightly askew. Could the rest of my things be stored up there?

Because the synagogue had no attic, my uncle kept the old Torah scrolls, waiting to be buried, in the attic space between our flat and our roof. Words, he taught me, are living things and deserve to be treated with the same respect as the living. Usually the attic hatch was sealed tight as a tomb, its own mezuzah rarely kissed except for those occasions when the hatch was opened and something placed in there for safekeeping. I dragged a chair from the dining room and positioned it under the hole, stood up, pushed the cover to the side and I pulled myself up into the darkness.

A shaft of light shot upwards from the hall below, bleeding into the gloom. The space was dusty and dim, and I had to stoop to avoid brushing my head against the rafters of the roof. A large broken brass menorah caught a wink of light, two of its arms hanging by its sides, the candleholder having snapped off.

There was an old Torah scroll beneath it, the script of which must have been diminished in some way, and a dozen prayer books, spines peeling away. A large cardboard box sat at its base. It would have been fitting if my things had been in the box, destined for the ground, for burial. Kneeling, I reached into the box and felt not clothes but the scrolls of old parchment flake away beneath my touch. There was scroll after scroll, the print now faded and impotent, from the mezuzah and the tefillin, no longer useful. And one old out-of-place envelope. I pulled it out and stood, almost forgetting to stoop, tilting it to the available light. Could it have been from my mother?

It was addressed to my uncle in a perfect copperplate, each letter ringed with precision upon the now browning paper. Hurriedly, I shoved it in my pocket without thinking and stepped backwards, keen to be out of there before my aunt and uncle returned. My heel clipped something. As I moved, the light from below revealed my aunt and uncle's suitcase. I had almost missed it, tucked tight under the eave of the roof, disappearing into the shadows. I went over to it, the thick icing of dust working like a charm against my opening it. My fingerprints longed to open it. My curiosity burned, but I could not touch it; it was like disturbing the bones of the dead.

I pushed the envelope deeper into my pocket, my trespass burning cold through me. As I brushed past the menorah, an arm of it grabbed at my jumper, unravelling a thread, and with clumsy fingers I snapped the thread. The brass menorah, arms like branches, lonely for candles. I would do more than that, I would give it birds, just as Clay had suggested, winged things better than any tallow, winged things for my mother, Zipporah, a little bird herself.

I took the menorah and lowered it down the hole, its loosened arms swinging by its side. A candle holder dropped with a sickening thud on the floorboards below. I swung out into the hallway and slid back the cover as if it had not been moved at all, except for the faint marks of my smudgy fingerprints, which I did my best to wipe away.

Outside, the stars were surrounded by their own aureoles of frost, the moon absent. This time tomorrow, when Tisha B'Av was over, when the fast was done, my uncle would lead the blessings of *Rosh Chodesh*, consecrating the new moon, which seemed hardly the shadow of a shadow in the sky, a silver peephole partially open. A new start, though the path be dark. A new start, though the light comes slowly. A new start, nonetheless.

NINE

Billy

The clock struck the hour and I turned to the advertisements page. Lily would be home soon, she would not have gone far. Like me, Miss du Maurier was waiting, reading a novel by lamplight, the finished dress by her side on the sofa. The title glittered out, *Trilby* by George du Maurier. A fine tale. A relation of our dear landlady, perhaps? I didn't dare ask. In gold foil was the image of Trilby O'Ferrall, cropped hair and military coat, reminding me of Lily in her usherette's uniform. Mercifully Miss du Maurier was quiet. With the warmth from the fireplace I felt drowsy in an overstuffed armchair like a fat spider in its web, but I would not sleep, I was waiting to see the dress anew upon her limbs, glad of the Jew's absence.

After she had left me at the Red Rose I had sat and watched her cocoa steam just as I had watched my father's opium smoke when I was a boy. Within it coiled secrets I had no skill to read, not like Crisp, who was as cunning as smoke and just as elusive. I scanned the page, always on the lookout for an advertisement, a claxon call for *Doctor Cuthbert Crisp's Apothecary,* but thankfully the page was bare. Somewhere out in the street a door opened and closed and my eyes flew to the doorway, my senses alert, awaiting her arrival. Miss du Maurier looked at me but said nothing; her bangles jangled as she turned a page. Patience is a rare plant to cultivate in captivity.

Patience, a word I have wanted to find in every dictionary and strike out with a black pen. Bugger patience. I am sure I was born early, the taste of impatience incubated with me in the womb. Let me tell you, nothing is more abhorrent to me than a man who sloths about in his misery, like a duck puddling around in the same old shallow pond of muck. If things are miserable, it is in a man's interest to connive and manipulate, twist and confabulate his way out of his fate: anything is better than the self-indulgent snivel of a man who has accepted circumstances as they are. And I was impatient to spend time with Lily. She was spending a lot of time with the Jew. Nothing had happened between them, she was still as pure as the day I met her – I could tell by the blush that flared up her face like an emergency sign, her eyes always averted. She had not yet had the taste.

Oh, the lessons I would teach her. She would be the most willing of pupils, I'd see to that. She would be my treasure, my very own. I'd keep a gold band upon my finger for my bride, and a white picket fence around my kingdom and my baby in its cradle, my heir. Was this too much to dream of? She was no passing fancy: my love for her was as permanent and as true as my own heartbeat. She would make me lord of my own dominion. Just like Cuthbert Crisp, who owned everything he touched. Life for him was not something he fingered covetously and then put back down again, knowing he could not afford it. No, Crisp saw something, liked it, and took it, whether it was his to take or not. The thought of him consumed me, the desire for revenge burning hot as acid in my throat.

Crisp measured everything's worth in an instant and he seized what he wanted, just as he had decided my fate that first time he had turned to look at me.

I was caught in the flash and glare of the monocle signalling at me in the light, burning into my own retina, but I was transfixed by it, I could not look away.

* * *

'Why are you following me, what do you want?' His voice was a low command given to a disobedient dog. My mind went blank. There was no plausible answer. I had liked the way he had selected his books, the style with which he had taken them, the fruit he had plucked and sampled. Perhaps it was through his control that I had followed against my will, led by some invisible string.

'I am Billy Little, Esquire, and I want to know how you stole those books. Tell me and I will be on my way. And don't just tell me by sleight of hand.'

Cuthbert Crisp's face flared red, as if it was the first time anyone had dared ask him a question. 'Stolen? Are you accusing me of being a thief? I'll have you know, sir, that I was given those books by the librarian of her own free will.' He turned on his heel.

'But they weren't the librarian's to give, were they, Mr Cuthbert Crisp, sir? They belong to the people and, as I am a citizen of this fair city of Sydney, they belong to me.'

Cuthbert Crisp sniffed dismissively and turned and went deeper into his shop. I followed.

It took some moments for my eyes to adjust to the gloom, green and milky, as though I was at the bottom of the ocean. The room was strangely airless, an acrid smell filling the air. Soon I realised I was not alone. Cuthbert Crisp was nowhere in sight, but there was a dark-eyed girl behind the counter. There was something nocturnal about her, blinking in the gloaming. At her shoulder were shelves of apothecary jars, polished and shining, with dark fibrous contents that seemed to sprout upward in the dusk.

'Can I help you, sir?' she said, her voice flowing out to me like a lifebuoy on the tide.

'Why is it so infernally dark in here?' I asked, my voice a surprise to my own ears. I wanted to know where Cuthbert

Crisp had gone. I thought about pushing past her, through the door to the side covered with the same bleak curtains that hung in the windows. Would she have tried to stop me if I did? Stare me to death with her huge eyes until I drowned in her pupils?

'To keep the ingredients pure, sir.'

'I see. I see,' I muttered, stepping closer to the safety of her counter, which looked like the only solid thing in the room. I kept one eye on the side door, the other on the contents of the jars that seemed, in a trick of the light, to writhe.

'Can I help you with anything, sir? Are you looking for anything in particular?' She said the word *particular* in a strange way, as if there was a hoot somewhere in the middle of it. *Part-ic-hoo-lar*.

I needed to keep my wits about me. Who knew what sort of dark art this Cuthbert Crisp was pursuing, what foul pestilence he could be burning as a medicinal incense, what opiates he could be grinding down, dust filling the air? She blinked at me, her dark eyes fringed by eyelashes like feathers.

'What line are you in, exactly?' I asked, not sure if cures or curses were for sale here.

'Oh, all sorts, sir. Ointments for itches, scratches, dry bits, flaky bits, inflammation, irritations, rashes; elixirs for fatigue, sleeplessness, low spirits, youthfulness and vitality. Also Doctor Crisp can provide the laying on of hands – for healing purposes, mind you,' she added as an afterthought, as if I were somehow going to be misled by what she said. A doctor, my arse. Before I could reply, my words were lost in the drought of my mouth; so dry I was unable to swallow. Doctor Cuthbert Crisp stampeded out from the side door, a gust of heat of noxious heat coming with him.

'Merle, you know better than to talk so loudly with the patients while I am preparing my ingredients, it erodes their essence.' But when he saw me standing there surveying his kingdom, his face grew crooked with what I later learned was his smile. 'Still here?'

'Teach me.'

His tongue ran uneasily over his peeling lips. Perhaps one of his own salves or ointments could have remedied that.

'You?' he said, scoffing at me. 'Why you?'

I stood straighter and felt my fingers flinch into a pugilist's ready fists. In my mind I chanted, *Patience, patience*, though it was no virtue of mine.

'Although I suppose,' he said contemplatively, 'one is always in need of an acolyte, an apprentice, a mirror to reflect one's genius. What if I take you on a trial basis to see if that is you, sir?'

Ordinarily I would have had been all over him like a clump of spitfires on a gum tree, if not with my fists, with my words, telling him in no uncertain terms that William Little was nobody's acolyte and certainly nobody's fool. Yet perhaps, it occurred to me, I would be granted an opportunity to prove to him I was more than that and dance triumphant all over him.

'Yes,' I said, nodding my head, my keenness to absorb his knowledge overriding my common sense, for he had opened the mysterious side door and bid me follow.

My patience was its own reward.

The vibration as the door slammed behind her sent a thrill through me. On seeing me, Lily paused in the doorway as if her foot were caught in a snare.

'I have finished, my dear,' Miss du Maurier said, lifting up the gown so that it rose in the air like a spirit. 'Oh, and there is this,' she added, holding up a little silken cap. 'It is in the Pierrette style – what do you think? No, don't say anything until you have put it on.'

All I could think was that the cap looked like the one the Jew's uncle wore. And of how smoothly she would shimmy into that encasement of silk, my beautiful pale grub.

She took the stairs two by two while Miss du Maurier filled the air with her petty observations, persistent as flies, until Lily returned, transformed.

The bodice was tight as before, but flared at the hip, a ripple of tulle halting somewhere between her knee and thigh and a large V at her back where she hadn't been able to reach the buttons on her own. I imagined her twisting in front of the mirror like a dancing swan.

'What do you think, Lily dear?' Miss du Maurier asked. Lily moved from one foot to the other, the bareness of her legs making her uncomfortable, the cool air licking at her shoulderblades. There was an abrupt tug on the front door bell and it pealed loudly all around us. Lily moved to answer it, her silver shoes clacking like castanets, but Miss du Maurier stood in her way.

'I'll get it, my dear, you'll freeze,' Miss du Maurier interjected as she reached the door handle herself. As she opened it an icy gust pushed past her into the room, and a veil of goose flesh pimpled Lily's delectable skin as she peeped over Miss du Maurier's shoulder.

'Is my nephew here?' the Jew's uncle asked quietly at the door. I leaned forward in the chair to get a better view.

'Would you like to come in?' Miss du Maurier said, opening the door wider to let him pass, but he remained rooted where he was.

'Is my Ari here?' the rabbi repeated, his voice growing louder. He tried to peer down into the hall, but the puff of Lily's skirt caught his attention, his eyes slowly roving up and down and up again, from her naked legs to the tip of her little cap.

'You are that girl, the one who knocked Ari off his bicycle.'

She nodded. 'Lily Del Mar, nice to meet you.' She extended her hand to shake his, but his arms hung limp at his side.

'Can I help?' Miss du Maurier added smoothly, the calming oil for rough waters. 'Rabbi Pearl, do come in. Shall I pop the kettle on?'

'I'll not be coming into your house, Miss du Maurier. Not until my son comes out to face me like a man. Hiding behind ladies' skirts is shameful.'

'Hip hip hooray!' I whispered under my breath. Looking at Miss du Maurier and Lily, a feminine barricade, I couldn't help but agree with the rabbi. I crossed my legs and admired my freshly polished shoes. I didn't think anyone had heard me, Lily and Miss du Maurier were too preoccupied with their neighbours' affairs, but the Jew's uncle peered over Lily's shoulder at me.

The rabbi paused, his mouth open, spittle on his lip. I sat fascinated, waiting for what he would say next.

'You should watch your words,' the rabbi snarled and I was surprised, he had the hearing of a rabbit.

'He's not here, Rabbi Pearl. Have you tried the Red Rose? Have you tried the shed?' said Miss du Maurier. But he didn't acknowledge her; he was already walking away, her words wasted on his ears.

'Why didn't he shake my hand, was it my costume?' Lily asked, closing the door behind him.

'No dear. It is part of their faith not to touch any woman save for their wife. Don't take any offence at it.'

The more fool him. What a pity never to taste the fruits when they are in season.

'I hope you are happy with the dress?' said Miss du Maurier, packing away her threads and needles. A bobbin escaped beneath my seat and I bent to retrieve it, a chance to linger.

'Very much so, thank you so much, Miss du Maurier, although it'll take some getting used to,' Lily said, leaning down and giving her legs a little rub for warmth.

'I am glad you like it, dear, it wasn't serving anyone in a box.' Miss du Maurier smiled as I placed the thread in her palm. 'Night then, you two.' She walked up the stairs and I counted each step until I heard a door close. Here was my chance. I coughed politely in the chair, hand to my lips.

'Lily …'

Before I could continue, there was another knocking at the door, less frantic than before. She skipped to open it as if she was expecting someone. But it couldn't be the Pearl boy. He would have slunk through the back door as usual.

The door swung open and it was not the Jew or his uncle, but a swagman, blinking at her as if he had stared at the sun. He wore a stockman's hat and an oversized grey woollen coat that seemed to sweep close to the ground. A possum skin draped across his shoulders, the head of the animal near his own, the tail nearly touching the ground. On one shoulder he carried his swag, on the other sat a huge black glossy raven, so dark against the night that I almost didn't see it until its beak stretched open. I expected it would speak, a blue eye unblinking fixed on my own.

'Is young Pearl here? I have a favour to ask,' the man said.

'He's not here at the moment,' she said. 'Can I help you with anything?'

'You'll do,' he said.

'Do what?' she asked, confused. She shuddered in the cold. I was ready to stand up and slam the door off its hinges and into his face, to warm her and ward him off. There had been enough strange men cross our threshold, and I had other plans. But then her voice spoke in warm recognition. 'You are the man who speaks like a bird. Ari told me about you.' Lily opened the door wider and I thought for a moment she would invite him and the lice-ridden feather-sack inside.

'Beauty here needs a home for a while. I am heading to the mountains, men's business. She likes it better down here, closer to the coast, not as cold. Thought she may like to have a change of scene with you and the boy. I take it that you are the girl he is working with?'

Lily shifted uneasily on her feet.

The raven shifted on the swagman's shoulder. The swagman reached up and stroked the billowing feathers below the sharp beak. '*One for sorrow, two for joy, three for a girl, four for a boy.* Beauty is no trouble, really she isn't. She can say a couple of words already and do the odd trick. She's a loyal bird. Of course she sometimes heads off to the flock – place an egg in the nest I assume, though I've never seen her offspring – but she is a good bird, part human if you ask me. It will be spring soon enough, she will moult her wintry coat, but she will be good-humoured still.'

Lily shivered again, freezing, half-dressed in the gusty doorway.

'I am sure Ari won't mind,' she said. The raven let out an eerie gargle, its scaly lid lowered, before it placed its head beneath a big black wing. A bad omen with wings it was. It wanted to snuff out the light that spilled from the hallway.

'Lovely,' the swagman said and shrugged his shoulder, which seemed to wake the raven up, signalling to it to shuffle down his arm. 'Would you like something to wrap around your wrist for Beauty to rest upon? I don't want her to hurt you.'

I was afraid of the bird's claws on her delicate arm. Let it try and pierce her skin – I would pluck it like a chicken.

'Beauty and I will be fine, I think.'

The swagman ran his hand over the glossy dark of the feathers and whispered some things in its ear in a weird language, before the raven stepped over to her arm. The clutch of its claws made Lily wince but in an instant the bird settled, a blue eye watching hers until it lifted up its beak and shocked me by snapping it through her hair, close to the scalp. But the bird did not bite. Lily had been preened. The swagman tipped his hat and was gone.

As Lily walked back into the living room, the raven was already roosting up close to her face, its feathers brushing the skin of her neck, rustling like a turning page. It was truly the witching hour. I blinked, as if the raven were a black spot on my retina that I could blink away.

'Lily,' I murmured.

'It's a long story,' she said, already anticipating questions. She clucked at the bird, which fluffed its breast feathers and sat close to her cheek, giving her its warmth as the reptilian eyelids slid closed.

'It's not about the bird. I am growing used to strange deliveries of birds around here.' She was so charmed by it, she could barely look at anything else. 'It's ... well ... Maybe Miss du Maurier's sight is on the fritz, but ...' I paused and my fringe fell in my eyes as if to protect her modesty.

'Lily, it's just that when you lift up your arms like that, I can see,' there was no gentle way to phrase it, 'your knickers.'

The look on her face said it all – she didn't know whether to lower her arms immediately and disturb the bird into a black fury, or to bolt up the stairs herself, a silver streak. She flushed, violently, and with her free hand pulled at the hem of her costume. A clock chimed on the mantelpiece.

I stood up. It was the gentlemanly thing to do, though the secrets of her knickers were more glorious from below eye level. My hand rose toward the oily dark feathers of the raven, which woke immediately, its sharp beak angled towards my fingers. I pulled them away sharply, biting back an oath. But it would take more than an infernal bird to keep her from my touch.

TEN

Ari

I placed the menorah in the shed and rewired its swinging arms, the repairs invisible, and polished it until I could see my own tiny reflection in its curve. However, the letter I could not have mended even were I Houdini himself. I unfolded it from the envelope: it was miraculous that the paper held together for there were so many holes, words excised with the precise cut of the razor. The handwriting looked familiar, and then I remembered with a sickening feeling that I had seen the odd words, mainly Yiddish, stuck within the folds of my uncle's scrapbook.

Dear Israel

It is a cold day here, my friend. Not like where you are every day sunny as Eden, complete with snakes. Perhaps that is why you don't write so much; perhaps you are busy out there in the wilderness fighting them off with a stick, getting sunburned for your pains! Well I have almost finished my apprenticeship. You may have always been the better student, Israel, but you should know how I have caught up. Who knows, maybe you will require the services of a sofer, *someone to be a scribe for you over there?*

To think that when I first started as a scribe my letters looked fashioned by a finger in mud! Now I can use turkey feathers and with a stroke of a blade turn it into a quill that will be the servant to my hand. Press too hard and the quill pierces the parchment. The ink is made from gum arabic, gall nut, sulphates of iron and copper, which, when combined, make the ink turn black, like some sort of sorcerer's potion. Of course the letters rust after years, the copper sulphate shining through, so that the letters of the tefillin look like they have been written in ancient blood.

Each letter floats in its own little universe of parchment, no other character coming too close, each letter in sequence, each letter formed by writing, not scratching a globule of ink – all this precision to create the beauty of the word.

The parchment is made from the hide of calves. They are tethered together in the stable and though I know they are working for G_d as we are, their little brown eyes seem to know me, their tongues tickling my palms, in search of the salt of my perspiration from clutching the quill all day. They are still just babies; their bleating for their mothers is mournful when the butcher comes. We are all creatures serving G_d's will. Of course before we see the little fellows again, the tanner has them dried and lime washed and stretched, all waiting for me to say the blessing and sanctification of G_d's name.

How are yourself and your lovely wife Hephzibah? We all miss her here. For some reason when I think of you there in Sydney I imagine you two like Adam and Eve in the garden with no one but the animals to keep you company. That is foolish, I know – you are no more in a garden than the country is overrun with criminals! It is so far away I can barely imagine it. I think of those strange animals and the strange names given them.

The old village looks smaller upon returning to it, like looking at an old pair of children's shoes and wondering how one's feet ever fitted in them. I passed your sister __________ the other day, she is no longer a girl. It will soon be Tisha B'Av, I wonder if she will be there at synagogue? Maybe I shouldn't write such things to you, but I assure you my intentions are honourable. Would that be so bad, Izzy? I should send this letter for it will be old news by the time it reaches you. All the best my friend, next year in Jerusalem.

I turned the envelope over; the return address had been ripped off, so I looked for a date in the folds of the letter; if there had been one it had gone the way of the razor. Why had he been so angry he hadn't allowed her name to remain, Zipporah, my mother. Her name had been neatly snipped out as if scratched from the Book of Life. Who was this friend of my uncle's? He never mentioned anyone from his past, from before he came to Sydney. I had always thought that was why he was so angry with me when I arrived – my existence was final proof that his mother and sister had not survived. He held me accountable, weighed me down with his expectations, for had he not plucked me from the reeds of my fragile life, just as Pharaoh's daughter had Moses? I was my uncle's bargain with G_d, his covenant. If I didn't follow in his footsteps, the covenant would be broken. I was the one possibility he clung to. For to be born in shame, and raised dubiously, and then to follow his path, was proof of G_d's existence.

But how could I be his compass when I could not find my own? All I had, like the stranger in the letter, was the beauty of a word.

The lyrebird flicked his silken tail forward and over his head, the tigery feather standing up like an orange flame. I had taken to letting him scratch about the shed rather than putting him in a cage. It was what I had promised the Birdman. Every now and again he would break into song – a rosella or a parrot or the slow chuckle of the kookaburra. His song was so full of the sounds of others I wasn't quite sure which one was his own. Was that me, espousing a tune made up of others' thoughts? How could I live between my uncle's expectations and the vague associations made from ink ground into my skin? The lyrebird was singing for a mate to call his own. The currawong just rolled her eye in his direction.

I looked into the basket of my belongings from my room, to see what my aunt had included, looking for some sort of note of reassurance, a blessing, an offering of peace. To go into that theatre without it felt wrong. Yet if it wasn't the Sabbath, what did it really matter? Houdini's father was a rabbi and had taken him to magic shows. Houdini even performed on the Sabbath. I tipped the contents out onto the camp bed – my clothes tumbled out, as did the leather threads and box of a tefillin I'd not seen before, the lacquered box tangled with the web of leather cords. My aunt had packed it, but it made me feel my uncle wanted to tie them tight on me himself, his message clear. I weighed the tefillin in my palm. Reading the letter to my uncle from the scribe made me think of the tongues of parchment inside the boxes and the infinite care that had gone into their creation, the serifs of the letter, universes unto themselves.

I looked down at my hand, why *these* letters from the *aleph* to the *tav*, the Alpha to the Omega, the A to Z? There was a universe created in an alphabet. Why had my aunt put them in the basket? Or had it been my uncle? I turned them over in my hands. Were the leather boxes filled with parchment written by the scribe who had written the letter? Was his hair shiny black and slick with ink, from wiping the droplet heavy pen to save the page from the spill, just as Moses did? I put the tefillin on.

My uncle had showed me how when I was thirteen. He had tied the leather and I had followed his instruction as best I could. The tefillin on my forehead had slipped and his eyes had taken their measure of me and found me wanting, before helping me tie it right. Now I wrapped the cord leather around my finger, the black line of it crisscrossing the letters of my tattoo, erasing them. I felt a pricking at my eyes, a breath held prisoner in my throat.

'Ari?'

I spun around. Lily was standing there in the shed doorway, her trousers and a shirt billowed around her with the breeze. I tore the tefillin off quickly, the leather string knotting in my fingers as I threw them on the bed. The box rocked on the blanket, the tail bobbing, a strange tocking sound coming from within like trapped dice. I felt caught out, observed as if naked.

'I'm sorry to interrupt you,' she said. 'Is that something for our act?'

The shadow of a bird clutched at her shoulder – the raven I had seen before with the Birdman. Her blue eyes swivelled in a forest of dark feathers, taking us both in.

'No, it's a little box of vellum, we use them to pray with,' I said. 'As a reminder to keep the commandments.' I looked at the menorah and the letter still sitting on the bed and felt the shame of the thief I had become.

'The Birdman asked me if we could mind Beauty here.' As she said the bird's name, the raven butted her head up under her chin, then ran her beak through her hair like a comb. 'Isn't she beautiful?After all he has done for us I couldn't really say no. She lives up to her name to start with, don't you think?' The raven lifted up her head so Lily could scratch her shag of feathery beard. 'Also, your uncle came around.'

The way she said it made me uneasy. Had he found that I had not only come and collected my things, but had raided the attic also? The birds were ready, the stage awaited. Had my uncle renounced me or come with an apology?

'What did he say?'

Lily looked away from me and ran her hand down the slick feathers. He wouldn't come in, even after I asked him, and then Miss du Maurier tried, but he just wouldn't step over the threshold.' Lily looked at the menorah. The raven sprang from her shoulder, the movement of wings making her blink several times. The raven flapped once more, so that the parrot hopped anxiously from foot to foot and the lyrebird ran on his pencil legs to the safety of the stable wall, head low, his long tail barely hovering above the dirt. The currawong stood still, as if by doing so she could disappear. The raven raised her wings, and I could see the leathery black claws curled up beneath her feathered body like the tendril of a fern. She alighted on the upheld arm of the menorah, her claw scratching for a grip on the newly shined brass.

'Was it because of me that he wouldn't come into the house?' she asked, tucking her legs up under herself as she perched on the chair.

'It wasn't because of you,' I lied. Why should Lily wear the weight of his prejudice?

'I could feel the disapproval coming off him in waves.'

'I'm sure he is just angry with me. What could you have possibly done?'

Lily shifted in the chair and whistled to the parrot to come to her, but he was staying put, one eye drowsy, the other on the raven who at that moment cared for nothing more than to put her beak beneath her wing, in pursuit of sleep. 'There was something in his tone that reminded me of my mother.'

'How so?' I looked at her with curiosity. Surely there was only room on earth for one like my Uncle Israel.

'She has an anger that never passes.' Lily sighed, running a hand through her hair.

Lily twisted in the seat, her arms pulling at the sides of her shirt and I was afraid. Upon her back were darkened welts, a latticework of scars, as if waiting for a vine to grow upon it.

The raven let out a sorrowful *arc-arc-oh* and I wished I had words to offer or some other salve, but nothing but a jagged breath fluttered out of my mouth.

ELEVEN

Billy

The curtain rose and there was my Lily of the Valley, my Rose of Sharon, standing in that leg revealer, blinking, the lights bright in her eyes. I could tell she was resisting the urge to squint. The Jew stood beside her. The musicians killed the notes of their instruments one by one, and they were left alone in the light, a silence around them except for the breathing beast that was the audience, waiting, waiting, waiting.

The Jew struck the violin, a harsh series of loud notes, and Lily stood, the feathered fan at her buttocks poised like an exquisite tail. Behind them rose the brass candlestick, huge arms raised as if about to conduct an unseen orchestra. A series of birds sat on the brass holders, like winged creatures of the Gospel, minus one – partridges in a golden pear tree. A lyrebird, the largest of them all, flipped its feathered tail over its face. Lily did the same with the plumed fan, my beautiful white toreador.

From nowhere, suddenly lovely beyond imagining, the lyrebird sang, its song a second violin, a duet with the Jew. It flicked and shimmied its tail, then jumped from its golden pew to Lily's feet, the other birds shuffling aside to avoid the whip of its tail feathers. Lily stepped around the lyrebird, stately as the orbiting moon. The last notes of the violin faded, but the lyrebird kept going, the sound of strings blending into a strange treetop cacophony, imitating all the voices of sunrise – the screech of the parakeet and rosella, the chortle of the magpie, the disturbing laugh of the kookaburra, the strange dark sob of the lonely crow.

The audience sat in rapt silence, unsure of whether to clap or if there was more to come from its tiny throat. I myself felt a certain dread that the lyrebird might speak once more, its voice human. Whose voice would come chirping out? My father's? His accusations ripe for me? My top lip prickled with sweat and I drew a breath as Lily helped the lyrebird gently back onto its brass perch.

'Now,' the Jew boy's voice rang out across the waves of heads like a cymbal. 'Now we will have the currawong communicate.' A ripple of excitement set the heads nodding across the divide between him and me. Lily offered her finger to the currawong and it stepped eagerly onto it and shuffled up her arm. The Jew slipped a blindfold over her eyes. That he came so close to the soft nape of her neck made me vitriol impersonate. That should have been my right. If I had pried my little oyster open earlier I would have found the pearl of her secret. Perhaps then I would have been in the place where the Jew was now, close enough for her to feel my breath upon her tender neck.

'Who would like to test the bird's ability? You sir, in the third row, hold up the paper and the bird will whisper the word.' In my haste to get back to my seat I had dismissed the large pieces of paper the punters were scribbling words on. 'Hold it up to the audience, sir, so they may see it too.'

The house lights rose, an electric dawn. The man had written the word *Love* in large, clumsy letters. It was enough to make one sick. It was probably his sweetheart who sat so pertly next to him, her face burning red from the spotlight's embarrassing glare. The currawong twitched upon Lily's shoulder and she cried out, her voice slightly sibilant as the nervousness overtook her.

'Love!'

Love! The word sent my heart into a panicked beat.

The next audience member stood up, the word *Home* writ large on the white paper. The currawong warbled, and after a certain beat Lily called out the word and was correct. How I wished I had taken note of the paper in the foyer: what words I would have written – my declaration, my SOS, my warning flare – a sonnet would not have been as sweet. *MINE.*

I knew how Lily could tell the words on the pieces of paper; my apprenticeship with Doctor Cuthbert Professor Crisp had not been for nothing. I knew the difference between the power of the mind and the trick thereof. All Lily had to do was be aware of the Jew's subtle gestures. That they must have devised their own private language, their own little love code, made me twist in my chair. The memory of Crisp's ruse rose to my mind, the one that held Merle and I together: we too had had our own special code, or so I'd thought.

I concentrated on the Jew's movements, jealous of his proximity to her, the hours they had spent so close painfully obvious, heads bent together like two hands clasped in a prayer. Perhaps it was the creak of his foot on the floorboard, a scratch on the fabric of his collar, a clearing of his throat, or a sigh? The rules of their secret language were hidden to me, but she was directed by his clues as delicately and intimately as if he had taken her hand and led her to his lips. I banished the image from my mind.

Of course, it was possible to get it wrong, but the more it was done the more refined it could become. It was elegant in its simplicity, tricky in its complexity – but Lily, by God, stayed true. There were no tell-tale signs of their cipher. Her blindfold, made from a strip of Miss du Maurier's bridal dress, made her look like an innocent about to be executed. How I wanted to tear it from her face and liberate her from the darkness!

A middle-aged woman beside me stood up and flapped open her piece of paper. Minx, she had sat down with it between her ankles and I hadn't seen it. Oh, if I had I would have hijacked the page and written *my love* in one perfect action. I could stand on the red velvet chair and shout it to the theatre rafters. But if interrupted her act, disturbed the concentration, would my honey of the honeycomb, still be receptive to me? I was sat still and quiet with my constancy.

'Thank you, madam,' the Jew said. The currawong hopped up onto Lily's head, a black and white smudge of feathers, making the audience titter. 'What is the word, Miss Del Mar?'

'The word is *Vengeance*,' she replied.

Oh how sweet a word, how it warmed my cockles. The audience applauded but my heart was an ovation.

Lily removed the blindfold and led the currawong to the brass tree where she scooped up the green parrot, who babbled at the mere touch of her fingers, speaking in tongues. She placed it on the floor close to the footlights and stood behind it. The Jew walked in behind her, as if in a sacred procession. I watched close to make sure he didn't lay even a fingertip upon her. With a cloud of smoke the whole stage wavered and vanished and they were gone, the parrot left behind squawking:

abracadabra,

Abracadabra,

ABRACADABRA

as if it was surprised to find itself all alone. Then before the applause began, another little puff of smoke obscured the green blur of feathers, and it too was gone. Hands clapped, the curtain came down with a swish. Now I knew.

A new act appeared on the stage, I didn't wait to find out what the hell it was – the sight of their pasty makeup and the flimsy sparkle of their costumes sickened me. I skulked back to the box office and sat on the hard arse-numbing stool and let my hand swim through all the shillings, pennies and thruppences, reminding me of all the money that once was mine but had disappeared like a dream.

TWELVE

Ari

In the dressing room before our debut, her hands slid into my hair and I held my breath. Her fingers ran across my scalp, combing out curls, before starting up again, working the oil into subduing my hair. The scent of it, the feel of her touch, made my skin tingle.

I had helped her with her buttons and though I had been careful, had tried not to touch her skin, it was unavoidable. The filigree of the scars on her back had shocked me. Who could do such a thing to their own child? Up close I could see how the blows had pierced her skin, a spiderweb tattoo. The buttons were as small as seeds, the loops silk slippery, and my hands did a nervous flap, like two grey moths around the brightness of her flame. She was the first woman I had touched, as a man. I willed the buttons to their conclusion, but my fingers turned to fish, swimming between the silk of her dress and her skin, and for a moment I didn't care if the buttons were never done, my fingers electric in the current of her moonlit skin.

Yesterday I had seen my aunt's bescarfed head in the distance. The familiar figure made my heart swell. I hadn't realised I had missed her. I quickened my step, though I wondered whether, if she saw me, she would veer off the path to avoid me. As I approached, I could see she looked tired, her face wearing new creases, her eyes downcast, following the motion of her own feet.

'Aunt Hephzibah,' I called out to her, my voice sounding strange to my own ears.

She came to a standstill, the weight of a pumpkin in her string bag scraping the path. When she looked at me, her smile was weary, her eyes blinking back tears. She abandoned her shopping and threw her arms around me.

'Ari. Ari, are you coming home?'

When I didn't have an answer for her, she released me, her expression beginning to stiffen.

'I am debuting my magic act at the Bridge Theatre tomorrow night. Would you and Uncle Israel like to come? I can put your names on the door. You can come as my guests.' I felt the foolish hope radiate in my chest: would they come, my only family in all the world? In the book my aunt had given me, Houdini's rabbi father had taken him to the circus, sat beside him in the front row and marvelled. It didn't seem too much to ask, did it?

My aunt paused and lifted her bag of shopping again, careful to avoid my eye. 'I don't think so, *bubele* darling.'

'Why not? It is not the Sabbath,' I said, feeling the anger begin to pop with heat within me.

'No darling, I don't think it is a good idea.'

'Why? I am sure you would enjoy it, even if Uncle Israel can't. It's not as big as the Tivoli nor as grand, but it is a start.' My aunt knew how much I had wanted this, she had quietly encouraged me and clapped at my meagre tricks those times when my uncle was lost in the snip and cut of paper in his study.

'You could come by yourself, I could arrange a ticket.' I tried to suppress my exasperation but, as with fire, the smoke will out. I inhaled a gust through my nostrils, for my jaw was beginning to clamp.

'But it is not just you, is it, darling, there is that girl. She is a gentile. Your uncle ...'

'What did Uncle say?'

'It would just upset him Ari if I went, you know how he is.'

Alas, I knew all too well how he was. When Houdini came to Sydney when I was a child, I tried with all my might to persuade my uncle to take me, but he would not bend. My desperation was made more frantic by overhearing my uncle say that Houdini had once travelled to Russia to see the decimation caused by the pogrom's mad fist, and in my childish mind I wondered, had he come to find me, collect me? When I was a child, Miss du Maurier worked at the Tivoli, where Houdini was to perform. So when my uncle had me tag along to her house for philosophical discussions in her father's study, I rained upon her ear a hundred and one questions. Had she seen him? What was he like? Did he look as strong in real life as in the pictures? Had she spoken to him? How was the trick done? Could she tell while waiting in the chorus? Could Miss du Maurier tell if he was a good Jew?

Days after my failed attempt to persuade my uncle to take me, Miss du Maurier delivered an envelope to our door. I had never received a letter before; seeing my own name written on the front was a delightful novelty. My heart leaped just at that, but when I slit it open I got the thrill of my life. On the back of a printed flyer for his Tivoli performance was Houdini's signature. I couldn't believe it. My finger traced the letters, marvelling at each curl of ink that spelled his name, as if they were a thread, a line on a map that would lead me right to him. I flipped the page over and over, held it up to the light, peering at it, hoping against hope that there was a special message, an instruction, some guidance just for me. That night I slept with it on the floor next to my bed, every now and again staring at it to make sure it was still there, leaning over and tracing the letters with my fingers, his name so close to the magical letters printed on my hand. I felt an inexplicable link, and a growing resolve. Why else was I marked so? I lay awake, dreaming up a father of a different kind.

Eventually I slept and dreamed of a hundred doves flying upward, their wings applauding through my dreams, but when I woke there was only one lonely flapping pigeon on my windowsill. I pulled back the covers with a new sense of my direction. Everything made sense. I reached down for the autograph that Miss du Maurier had magicked up for me – my compass, my map and my direction all in one – but it was gone. I fell out of the bed and crawled, searching on all fours, thinking that perhaps a gust had swept it under the bed, but it wasn't there. I searched under the plaited rag rug, through the sheets, but it was nowhere. I opened the door and hopped down each stair, hoping to find it, my magical autograph, my paper escapist. My imagination ran away with me: if the owner of such a signature could break all bonds, escape all enclosures, then perhaps even his writing could elude the very page it was written upon. No matter where I looked I couldn't find it.

I burst into my aunt and uncle's room: my uncle was just lifting the *tallit* prayer shawl over his head, his tefillin already fixed, the morning prayer upon his lips. I heard my aunt's industrious movements in the kitchen.

'Where is it?' I shouted, surprised at the sound of rebellion in my own voice.

My uncle stopped, his eyes turning black with anger at the interruption, before he continued his morning ritual. I ran into the kitchen. I knew the punishment would come: not immediately, but it would come in time, if it had not come already. My aunt was there, leaning over the kitchen table, her back toward me, her hands industriously working away. She didn't lift her head when she heard my footsteps approach; instead her hands moved frantically. When I came around to her side I saw my Harry Houdini autograph torn to pieces. Aunt Hephzibah had been smoothing the fragmented pieces, joining them with pieces of tape. I wanted to scream, but swallowed it back.

I knew then I would have to hide what it was I wanted to be. I hated him then, for his narrowness, his wanton destruction of words, his flashing scissors, making peepholes to the world beyond, to a world of his own making. In his world there was only the book, never the magic. In destroying my autograph, my uncle may as well have struck off my finger or rubbed my hand with acid. This was my link to a world I felt I belonged to, the one thing that connected me to those faces I would never see.

Yes, I knew all too well how things were with my uncle. I had been deluded to hope at all.

My aunt patted my cheek gently. 'I'll pray for you, for HaShem to watch over you, for good luck,' she said before she gathered up her shopping. I watched her head back home, thought of her disappearing through that door I could not imagine ever going through again.

I was becoming someone my uncle wouldn't recognise, possibly the man I was supposed to be. More like Houdini. I watched Lily's hands in the mirror as she worked the oil through my hair, until I was someone else, my white shirt blending into the ivory silk of her dress, her head above mine like a guiding star. *Thou shall not approach a woman to uncover her nakedness. I am the LORD.* The words came to my mind unbidden, but I blanked them out as Lily smiled at me excitedly. Together we looked at ourselves transformed, an illusion of magicians, her tender hands, white as gloves, resting on my shoulders.

THIRTEEN

Billy

I had to go back to the house eventually, but every time I passed the front window and saw the glow of electric light in the sitting room windows, revealing their flushed faces, their animated gestures, as they relayed backstage tales to Miss du Maurier who clinked celebratory glasses in her hand, I couldn't go in.

Lily and the Jew were perched on the small red velvet settee, their knees not even a hand span apart. I had to circle around the block again. I had to let myself go from the boil to the simmer, until I could seem as innocuous as lukewarm water flowing meekly from the tap. If I had had my knife in my hand the first time I approached the front step, I would not have been able to ignore its hum for blood. The second lap around, my fist itched to feel the slam of flesh into his bone. A coiled snake in winter could not be as quietly deadly as my rage. Not since the time of my apprenticeship with Cuthbert Crisp had I felt it unwind so in the depths of my belly.

The first day of my apprenticeship I had learned that his Elixir du Jour was made up mostly of a cordial of urine, dispensed first through Crisp's bladder and then dispensed a second time by the fair hand of Crisp's assistant Merle. I had gone home that first night with a bottle of elixir, not for myself mind you, but for my father. It was crass, I knew, but I was curious. Did one have to have the messianic gaze from Crisp to believe wholeheartedly in the elixir's effects? Was it a scam, or was there a drop of truth in the matter? Piss du Crisp! It hadn't escaped my notice that in Crisp's antechamber there was a pamphlet from an Indian swami, printed at least fifty years earlier, about the health-giving benefits of the original amber liquid. My father would be none the wiser. If it shut him up, stopped him calling out the names of whores in the night, so be it. Anything for a bit of peace and quiet until I had enough to pay for my own room elsewhere.

I put the bottle in the middle of the table that night and in the morning it was empty: my father the sponge had soaked it all up. I watched him closely and, to my surprise, he was unusually chirpy and even asked after my own health. I didn't know whether to laugh or cry or throw my arms around him in an embrace. The only other time he claimed me as his son was when his drunken voice hollered at the bottom of the stairs when he was so pissed he couldn't make it up them by himself. I would go down in my underwear, hoping the neighbours wouldn't see me, and help the sweaty stink of himself up to our rooms, his bristly cheek pressing against mine, his arm wrapped serpent-tight around my neck. My father's loving embrace.

The second day at Crisp's was wildly different from the first. I may have learned the so-called secret of the elixir, but I still had no inkling as to what gave him his powers of his persuasion. If I knew that secret, the world would become a cornucopia of women, all ready to be plucked by me.

The bell jangled as I opened the door. Merle was at the front counter refilling the strange prehistoric jars with their dusty greenery. Her hair was pulled back in the same severe bun except for two little kiss curls that appeared over the scroll of each ear. It softened her face and added a little brightness to her cheeks.

'Morning, Mr Little,' she called out, her happy hum stopping for just a moment. 'How did your father go with the elixir? Did he find it to his liking?'

I had forgotten she had seen me take it. All at once I was concerned she would report my theft to our boss and my apprenticeship would be terminated quicker than a dandelion clock is dispersed with a breath.

'Well, I was sceptical about it, yet this morning I have to say that he seemed, well, improved from his usual malodorous self.'

'I am glad to hear it. Some would call what Father and I do a travesty, but I am sure you would agree there is a method in his madness.' Her father? Doctor Cuthbert Crisp her father – flesh of his flesh, blood of his blood? 'Go through. Father would like to see you. Shop doors open in a half-hour, so there is plenty of time. We prepared the elixir earlier.' The way she said *prepared* stunned me, her eyes lit up with the cheek of it. Far Eastern philosophy be damned, she knew the ruse, yet for a moment had me believing.

Crisp was sitting in his consulting room, which looked like a whore's parlour with him eagerly counting his money, pound notes heaped in piles on his table, which he covered with a copy of the *Herald* as I entered. The shillings that had been stacked as high as the Tower of Babel spilled onto the floor in a shining puddle as I closed the door. I waited for him say something, but he just watched me to see what I would do. Was I being tested already? I reached down to assist, but he swatted my hand and swept the coins into a small calico sack.

'Well, if it isn't the prodigal apprentice returned. I thought we would have seen the last of your pitiful hide yesterday. But, here, you prove me wrong.' My eyes must have lingered on the money for a moment, but it was moment enough for Crisp to register it. 'Well then, we haven't agreed on a price for your services have we? How does this sound?' He handed me the calico bag, the weight of it satisfying in my damp palm. That room of my own would come sooner than expected.

'I know you want to learn, but first you must observe, just as I will observe you to see if you are worthy. There are things in this business you must watch out for. The fool, for example, who would throw himself under the wheels of a passing cart if he thought it would please me. Not a problem in itself, but an inconvenience if the fool kept the address of my establishment in his pocket. I want no questions asked of me. I hope you are not one of those, Mr Little.'

I clamped my teeth down on my own tongue to stop it from shaping the words I wanted to throw back at him. Throw myself under a cart? To please *him*? Preposterous.

'Are you listening, Mr Little?' His eyes narrowed themselves upon me and I nodded my head, barely able to contain my aggravation, crossing my arms over my chest. Did a flicker of amusement pass across his face? He stood straighter and I felt my cocksure strength sapped from me.

'Another to watch for is the aggrieved family of a patient who comes demanding answers after someone crosses over – in that instant it is essential that one listen. Whatever they say, agree, unless it is to compromise yourself or the business. Money must never be mentioned. Their rage will dissipate with the healing process. However, if all one's listening and tender-hearted compassion is not performed in the sincerest fashion, then an odious creature from the Underworld may appear, and for him you need all your cunning, for God has cast him in a misshapen and twisted mould – the Journalist!' He said this with a bitter emphasis, lip twisting. 'Oh, he will come like a patient, a false ailment upon his lips, the details fleshed out with a storyteller's precision – that is the tell to his identity. The questions he asks, trying so hard, the clever little worm, to impale me on his hook, but alas, there is not much one can print in the newspaper to discredit me, when all that can be written is already printed on the elixir's label – *Results May Vary*. No man was ever sued for that.'

His voice rang in my ears with the timbre of someone who could not listen to himself with enough admiration, till Merle knocked on the door and his incessant babble ceased. The patients had arrived. I had not even heard the bell tinkle.

I followed her out into the reception area. Merle handed me a white physician's coat, just like hers, and as I took it, a blush spread up her throat and I grinned. My, we looked the part! Behind the counter with her, I was surprised at how little space there was. Her tidy little body was already making busy, crammed next to mine.

She showed me how to fill the bottles and I liked the artistic way the ingredients fell – a leaf of mint, a sprig of rosemary, petals of whatever flower Merle and her father had no doubt swiped from a neighbour's bush. I cast her enough sidewise glances to give her that infernal blush a hundred times over – just to check for the family resemblance. Between her obtuse plainness and his commanding obliqueness I started to see the sperm of their connection. Her mother must have been a pretty chameleon, to have a daughter who could change her colours so quickly before my eyes.

The customers flowed in and out with an easy rhythm until there were only two of them left to see the self-proclaimed doctor.

'Do you mind if I knock off early?' Merle said to me, her fingers patting down one of her newly acquired kiss curls.

I scrutinised her face, thinking she was teasing me, for I was working for her father and not the other way around, no matter how much my soul wished it. Not knowing what to say, I nodded and she slipped the white coat from her surprisingly shapely shoulders and sallied out through the preparation room door.

I wiped down the counter, refilled the bottles of herbs from bags below the counter, checked the caps of the bottles, counted the money, got the broom to sweep up the odd sprig that had fallen to the floor. Whatever patient was in with

Crisp, this one must be a chinwagger, talking his ear off with their tales of woe. The last two gents seemed well enough, impatient, but fine specimens of men, the likes of which I had fought beside in the trenches and seen blown to smithereens by their so-called bravery. There is not much bravery in being dead, I am sure of that.

I kept myself busy while the hands of the clock flew around half an hour. I walked over to Crisp's door and listened, hoping to catch a lull in the conversation so I could interrupt, but not even a murmur offered itself up to my ears. I pushed opened the door a chink, and then wider. The room was empty. Crisp had vanished like air under the door, undetectable. Puzzled, I spun on my heel, but the two gents who had been waiting ever so patiently for Crisp stood to block my way, their jackets gaping to show me their guns.

'Is your name Crisp?' they said.

To the astonishment of my own ears, I said yes. Where had that mad affirmation come from? How was that possible? *Little* my mind roared, but all that came out of my mouth was *Crisp*. What had he done to me? I was slow to catch on, the dupe that I was. I called out for Merle but there was no answer except for the sound of my boots scraping the floor as I pathetically tried to resist.

At the police station, the cell they locked me in smelled, ironically, of piss, which my own bladder ached to add to. All that flaming elixir gone to waste! What could I do but contribute to it, with the indignity of my fellow cellmate looking on. 'Good on you, mate,' he slurred as the golden arc hit the wall. I noticed then the splatters of blood congealing upon the floors and I retched over my shoes.

The first stars were almost out by the time they attempted to charge me for operating without a doctor's licence, but by then I was rage filled enough to spit out my own name in their faces. The police were thick as two small planks. How could I be Crisp? They put me back in the cell, my cellmate long gone. I thought the concrete slab would be my bed and the flea-infested blanket my cover, but who should stroll in but Professor Doctor Crisp himself, cool as can be. An icicle wouldn't have melted in his mouth.

'I have come for my son, William Little. I believe you have imprisoned him by mistake.'

The officer on duty looked through to me in the cell and to Crisp at the counter, but instead of laughing at the lack of family resemblance, nodded in absolute agreement without even asking Crisp for any identification. How he did it, again I didn't know. The hapless constable selected a large brass key from his jangling collection and gave me my liberty. I didn't know whether to punch Crisp or kiss him, for in the cell my fears had begun to creep, time had ceased and abstract shapes in the sandstone seemed to shift and reform into the faces of all those I had ever wronged.

'Come on, son,' he said as he slapped me on the back, hard enough to make me cough and splutter.

We were halfway down the street when Crisp spoke. I seethed with each step I took.

'That was lesson number two,' he said, as smug as a drunk with his lips around the bottle. 'I hope you learned it well.'

The lesson of being a fool I did not need to learn. I felt a bilious shiver and the desire to crush his windpipe.

'I can see it on your face, William, that you haven't learned it yet. You are so angry and consumed by your own rage, you are unable to see what the lesson was.'

I kicked the footpath, the stone grazing my shoe, heat threading its way tight up to my neck. He had called me William. No one ever, not any two-bit whore or sideshow salesman, ever used my full name. It was *my* name. The name I would use when I would hear it declared on the lips of the woman who would sanctify my honour, with love and obedience.

'What lesson is there in behaving as your fool?' I spat, my own spittle hitting my chin. Crisp laughed, the sound of it making me froth and fizz. Oh that I had my knife!

'Did you not say you were Crisp when you were asked?'

I nodded, ashamed. He must have been watching as I was arrested.

'Therein lies the lesson. Do you know why you said you were me? I will spare you the embarrassment of your ignorance. It was the power of suggestion, my boy, in the consulting room beforehand. Do you not recall? Can't quite remember it all? Blink and you missed it? That is the key.'

My mind swam. How had he suggested to me that I was someone else against my will? What a fool I was then, so easily gulled out of even my own name. But no more, I would learn my lessons as if they were tattooed on my heart. William Little. Nobody's Fool.

My rage still glowed in my guts even months later. It churned in me, a constant companion that would not go away. I couldn't wait any longer now, watching her from the window, smiling like a beacon. Quietly I leaned over a neighbour's fence and plucked some choice blooms, a bunch of red camellias and a branch of wattle that showered its pollen in the air like gold dust. I bounded up the stairs with my offering, turned the handle and entered. Was it the flowers or the sun-like smile upon my face that made them all stop and wait in silence for what I had to say?

'Congratulations,' I said. My words all for her and none for him. I thrust out my bouquet with one hand and pulled her up to me with the other. And in one smooth movement, as though sweeping her to me to dance, I planted the tender surprise of a kiss upon her snowy lips.

FOURTEEN

Ari

Miss du Maurier was waiting for us when we got in, a bottle of champagne sitting in the kitchen sink surrounded by ice. Her solo applause rang out for us as we came in the back door after settling the birds in the shed.

'Bravo,' she cried as she saw us and folded us both into her arms, Lily's arm encircling my waist, her hair caught in my mouth. We had walked the short distance home with the birds swinging in their cages, the air electric.

'Come, come,' Miss du Maurier said, ushering us into the sitting room, the dripping bottle in one hand and a trio of glasses in the other. 'This should be but the start of celebrations, dears, we should have a party.'

'A party?' Lily said. 'Why?' The fireplace had gone cold while Miss du Maurier had seen our act, but the room felt overly warm.

'In honour of your performance. A costume party,' said Miss du Maurier. 'You two are probably tired of costumes already, but the rest of us would love to dress up. It will be fun!' Miss du Maurier propped her thumbs against the cork and it shot through the air and landed obediently at her feet.

Lily laughed. She had been so full of the lights and applause and sheer wonder of pulling something magical out of the hat. All the way home we walked beneath the streetlights, the cold air swirling around us, but her cheeks roared with heat. She was animated, excited, the thrill of it all spilling out of her, but I felt strangely lost for words.

We had been a surprising success, but I couldn't shake the disappointment that I had had no family to share it with, just the applause of strangers. I'd known my uncle would consider the performance too much, but my aunt had not even tried to come. It was more than that, though; a greater absence gnawed at me. The loss of my parents, the incomplete fictions that they were. I couldn't even imagine their faces, for my father was a mystery to me, and my mother was fading in my memory, growing vaguer every year, mottled like the silver surface of an old mirror.

After I arrived here as a child, I tried so hard to remember who had inked my tattoo, the mysterious word that seemed to burn under my uncle's disapproving glare. Could it have been my father who pierced my skin with a needle over and over, rubbing in the stinging ink? Yet where my father's face should be was a vacancy, like the cut-out windows in my uncle's newspapers. But it didn't stop me creating my own portrait – false or not. In my imagination it was always the Master Mystifier, Harry Houdini, who took on the paternal role, his face revealed to me through a puff of smoke.

I had seen Houdini's face in a newspaper my uncle had discarded. The scissors had snipped a little into the photograph, but there he was, wavy haired, sparkly eyed, challenging the world to place him in bonds that no one else could escape from. Did I resemble him?

He was in Australia to fly his plane, the first to do so across this hot dry continent. My uncle had told me this country was desert at its heart, just like a knish is cheese in the middle. Houdini could not only break the shackles that held him, but he was brave and light enough to strap himself into his Voisin plane, which seemed as fragile as a moth, and fly with no fear of falling Lucifer-like to earth. That Houdini was going to fly across a landscape that was bigger than my imagining just made him larger in my estimation. He was not only a Jew, but he was a genius and a revered magician too, a fact that was lost on my uncle.

While he was in Sydney preparing for his flight, Houdini's name was splashed all over the streets. Day after day, challenges were published in the newspaper, tests that would seem impossible for any mere mortal. I would have done anything to have seen him in the flesh, hoping that his showman's face would look down to me with a father's acceptance. I did all sorts of things to sway my uncle – I tidied my room, spent hours practising my Hebrew, in the hope my uncle would acquiesce to my desire to see the Great Houdini at the Tivoli. All I could think of was Houdini's weightlessness, his freedom, treating the air as if he owned it. Patiently, Aunt Hephzibah listened to me chatter on about every lock and chain Houdini threw off, every challenge he rose to conquer, my childish opportunism injecting every conversation with a dose of Houdini.

The first challenge was issued in the *Herald*.

William Elphinstone lived, according to the advertisement, not five minutes away in Camperdown. The first opportunity I had, I was down there, looking through the windows, hoping to see what the carpenter had built, but there was no sign of it. Only a dog stirred that afternoon, his raspy tongue lapping at my salty hand. The box, I found out the next day, had been taken to the Tivoli so the public could inspect it before Houdini's arrival. The night of the challenge came and eleven minutes was all it took for Houdini to reverse the nails that had been pounded into the timber and driven through the rope, eleven minutes to step out to the audience, calm and unruffled. The box was left in the Tivoli foyer, a trophy to baffle everyone as to how he had done it.

The next challenge was posted five days later from a group of asylum attendants. I had to ask my aunt what the word meant, for the language was almost religious:

1. *They will bandage his hands to his sides.*
2. *They will roll him in a number of large sheets in mummy fashion.*
3. *They will fasten him down to an iron hospital bed with strong linen bandages.*
4. *They will pour from 10–15 buckets of water over his form, so as to cause all the materials and knots to shrink, holding him in a positively helpless condition.*
5. *The attempt to escape to take place in full view of the audience.*

The date of the challenge came and went and no mention was made of it in the *Herald*. Part of me despaired that he was still there trying to find release from his tortures, until my Aunt Hephzibah unwrapped a cabbage from a page of newspaper that contained a small paragraph from the *Town and Country Journal*. It reported that he had given them the slip after all, even though the challengers had objected to his blue swimming costume, thinking it part of his escape technique, and had given him the calico pants the insane were made to wear. Thirty-five minutes was all it took, from incarceration to freedom.

The third and last challenge was from a saddler at Rawson Place. Instead of the bag going over Houdini's head, it was made to fit around his shoulders and held into position by a broad leather strap encircling his back. He was to be strung up like a criminal on the way to the executioner – would he escape death?

This was my final chance to see him.

On the last day of all my hopes I rose early, ate my oatmeal, washed the bowl and put it away. I made my bed and helped my Aunt Hephzibah with the chores and swept the kitchen floor with a vigorous intention. Time came for the lessons my uncle gave to me and a couple of other Jewish boys who lived within walking distance. The other boys were older, readying themselves for their bar mitzvahs, and they kept to themselves, partly out of their sense of superiority that they would learn the ways of men before me, and partly because they associated me with my uncle. We were one and the same thing to them. I was his parrot, possibly transmitting all their petty adolescent secrets into his ear. Sometimes they would include me in their games in the small break we had, but more often than not I would stay inside at the table and shuffle a pack of cards that I had taken to carrying in my pocket, consoling myself with the flick of hearts and the retrieval of aces in my own attempts at card tricks. After the break we each had to tell part of the story of Moses.

One of the boys told how Moses was found in the reeds, by Batya the Pharaoh's daughter, the other told of how Moses parted the sea. I saw this as my chance. I could not ask my uncle outright; a *no* would come too swiftly to his lips. He had to know how I felt, what direction I wanted to head in. I would hint without saying it directly, impress him with the learning he had imparted to me. So I said:

'Moses, having had a stutter, commanded his brother to speak the eloquence of the Lord on his behalf, so Aaron became the first high priest. Aaron beheld a magic staff, a staff like no other. It was no ordinary rod, for on it was inscribed each letter of the name of the ten plagues and it was made from acacia wood studded with sapphire. HaShem created it in the quiet twilight of the sixth day of creation and bestowed it upon Adam when he and Eve were exiled from the Garden of Eden. It was a magical rod passed down generation after generation after generation to Adam's son Shem, then Enoch, Abraham, Isaac and Joshua. Until it fell into the hands of Jethro. Now the rod, being fond of the soil of Eden, whispered somehow to Jethro to plant it in the ground. He did, and it bloomed. He tried to draw it from the ground but he could not, the rod engraved with the Unspeakable name of G_d. Moses visited Jethro's house and it was Moses who read the Name, and the Rod released itself into his keeping. Jethro gave Moses his daughter Zipporah for marriage, for he had promised her hand to he who could ever withdraw the rod again.

'When Moses and Aaron faced the Pharaoh, the Pharaoh called his magicians to defeat them by casting their staffs upon the ground, upon which the staffs turned to snakes. Aaron threw down his rod and it turned into a great snake that consumed them all. Thus Moses and his brother Aaron were great magicians able to cast out the ten plagues, ride up the mountain on a cloud, receive the Ten Commandments and part the Red Sea, among other miracles. Because of his magic rod, Moses was a magician just like Houdini.'

The older boys barely suppressed their sniggers. My uncle's face was stony, not even the slightest expression rippled across it. At the time he said nothing, but moved on directly to the next task he had set for us. I knew his anger would come, just as the sun had to sink behind the horizon. The other boys left, their conversation fading to a whisper beyond the door.

'Ari, what was that?' He could barely contain the exasperation in his voice. I didn't want to speak it. My hopes of going to the Tivoli veered close to being dashed. 'Moses is our Patriarch, our Elder. Whatever power moved through him was not his, but HaShem's. He was not a magician.'

'I want to see Houdini. His final challenge of escape is tonight,' I pleaded, desperate.

My uncle's face softened for a moment, a mere break in the clouds, as if he could remember the senseless obsessions of children, having been a child himself an age ago.

'I don't know what that mark upon your hand has convinced you of,' he said, one of the rare times he spoke of it, 'but you know, Ari, that it is Friday, tonight is the start of the Sabbath, the day the Lord commanded as a day of rest, just as he rested on the seventh day. Tonight we will welcome the Sabbath as the bride she is. Your aunt will prepare the Sabbath meal and sweep our home from top to bottom as if to welcome the most of important of guests. You and I will attend *shul* as it is our mitzvah, regardless of whether you are a boy or a man. If he was a real Jew Houdini would do the same instead of participating in foolish parlour games to entertain the masses.'

And nothing more was said, though I willed it, dragging my feet from flat to synagogue and back again, but he would say no more.

'What do you say? Let me throw a party in your honour this Friday!' Miss du Maurier drew my attention back into the room. Friday. I wouldn't be making those familiar steps between the synagogue and flat this Friday. My place at the table would be empty. My aunt would light the candles before she covered her eyes and welcomed the Sabbath as was custom. Would they say a blessing for me? Lily looked at me. Why shouldn't we celebrate?

But before I could say anything, Mr Little strolled into the house as if he owned the place, a large bunch of freshly stolen flowers in his hand. I had seen them on the neighbours' bush, the comfort of bees.

'Congratulations,' he said and pulled Lily up from the sofa as lightly as if she had been a jacket he had discarded. He pulled her close, his hand in the small of her back, before pressing his mouth to hers. My heart pitched. Had I gravely misjudged things? Did they share more than just a house? How hadn't I seen it? I had been so focused on our act and my expulsion that my thoughts had not rested on much else. He liked her in a way I hadn't noticed until now. He had helped her to find a job. That time in the park when her hat had blown away, he had held it close to him rather than come any closer, waiting for her to come to him. I hadn't imagined his acid tone toward me made sense. But it was not because he was an anti-Semite; it was because I was the man in his way.

She broke the contact between them, her hands reaching up to his lapel and pushing him away. The flowers dropped their blown heads on the floor, a clutch of twisted brown stalks left in his hand.

She resumed her seat beside me, her legs trembling, subtle vibrations transmitting through the springs of the sofa. How could I have not noticed how drawn he was to her? Was she drawn to him in the same way? How could I speak? I cared for her in a way that I couldn't express: the words were locked down inside of me, where no pick could spring them open.

PART TWO

The Switch

FIFTEEN

Lily

His lips were a surprise, a warm wet press against mine. I was so confused I didn't know whether to twist away from them or to press my lips back with equal fervour. For there was something strangely alluring about Billy's lips demanding life from mine that caught me unawares. It was not just that he had plucked me from my chair. I knew he liked me. We shared a laugh, a house and a workplace. But with his kiss was it possible we shared something else? He was a handsome man with his piercing blue eyes and blond hair like risen bread. Every time he moved the forelock of it out of his eyes and looked at me I found myself reddening like a flare. His hands were large and muscular, and when I felt them rope around me into the small of my back I felt the power in them.

It was so different from my first kiss on that very hot day, the day I left home. A discarded newspaper sat on a chair, so I picked it up and lazily scanned the headlines, feeling my eyelids getting heavier with each line of print. The scent of petrol was like a dangerous hypnotic perfume. I am sure I only fell asleep for a moment, and I woke in an instant when my boss pressed down on me. His name I have banished from my mind, but still the touch of him lingers, malignant. I squirmed like a fish brought to land, twisting and turning under him, but I couldn't break free. The weight of him hurt my lungs, my breath ragged and nearly extinguished, my voice choked, as his lips roamed terribly all over mine. He used one hand to tug my braid as a rope to wind me in, the other struggled to undo my trousers fastenings, but the button stayed true.

A car honked wildly from out near the pump and he leaped up as if it were his mother calling his name. I rushed to the door first, so glad to see the driver even if he was just a stranger passing through, and went out to pump the petrol. I reached up to pull my cap down, but it was gone, only my braid escaping down my back, a trousered girl pumping petrol in disarray. The man raised his eyebrows, but paid me the money for his fuel without comment and went on his way. Without a glance backward, I tucked it in my pocket and ran. But it didn't stop that bastard's words coming thick and hard after me, and they followed me still, an echo in my ears even here in a boarding house far away.

Perspiration threaded down my neck as I reclaimed my seat, and Ari shifted to the edge as if he was only waiting for his chance to get away. Every time I tried to read him, he would not catch my eye. Billy perched on my end of the sofa, leaning too close. The evening's glow somehow seemed tarnished; I wanted to turn the clock hands back to before Billy entered, back before his lips struck a claim upon mine. All I could concentrate on were the fallen flower heads, their petals strewn on the floor. They were the colour of lambs' hearts, bleeding into the red pattern of the Turkish carpet. Red like the heart of Jesus.

At Sunday school sometimes, if we answered a question correctly, the teacher would give us little cards with a quote from the New Testament on one side and a picture on the other. A lamb with a staff, or an eagle, bull or angel, to represent the four gospels. A Virgin Mary, auburn hair framing a serene smile, was highly covetable when she was clothed in her blue robes of heaven. But if she pointed at the red cavity in her chest, she would be worth up to at least ten other cards. Even higher in value was the heart of Jesus – red and glittering like a jewel suspended in the middle of the card, so intense that the one child who had owned it before it had been swapped to me swore it had palpitated before his eyes. I stared at it until black spots crowded my eyes, but the red ink never stirred.

The card that was most coveted was the Holy Spirit, a highflying dove, gold rays radiating from it. I wondered, did other birds have the gift of the divine too? Was the bird singing at the window imparting a message? Could the birds themselves be the message?

I had that card for only a day. I was walking back from school clutching at my cardboard dove, squinting at it under the wide brim of my hat, the hat my father insisted I wear from the moment I left the house until the sun went down. The golden words were shaded, so I pulled off my hat and the sun blinded me. *My little sisters, the birds* was all I made out, before a huge gust tore the dove from my grasp. I chased it, holding my hat, the wind always teasing me, tumbling the card from my reach just when I thought it was mine again. Then it was gone, another gust blasting it once and for all into the never-never, winging its way back to the Lord as I lunged for it and went sprawling in the dirt.

Just then my father happened to walk past. He was always popping into the office to file a story or check with the typesetter that the headline was correct. He scooped me up, put me back on my feet and brushed off the gravel embedded in my knee. He picked up my sunhat, gave me a certain gentle look and pulled it down firmly on my head. I didn't want to tell him why I wasn't wearing it – he would have thought me silly running after one of the holy cards my mother took so seriously – but I was unable to keep any secrets from him.

'I lost my holy card,' I sobbed. 'The Holy Dove.'

'O Til, is just a bit o' paper!' he sighed. 'We can make one at home with some glitter and glue, will be just the same.' My father had a dancing voice, the ragged remnants of his Irish accent made everything he said sound like music.

'But it won't, Dad, it won't be the same at all.'

He crouched down close to my face, his blue eyes crinkled as he took his tender measure of me.

'We make our own way in this world, my darling, you don't need an invitation,' he said matter-of-factly.

I didn't understand. 'But it was the dove, Dad, the dove!' I felt the hot tears of my frustration track down my face and off my chin.

'I always thought the Holy Spirit should have been depicted as a swan, not a dove. A dove is just a pigeon. You can eat doves and pigeons, but you can't eat a swan, those necks can break a man's arm,' he said, his eyes twinkling.

'Dad!' I squealed.

'But a swan, there is something elegant in the idea,' he mused. 'In the old country a swan is holy bird. Aengus Óg loved a girl who was a swan in disguise, so to be with her he had to turn himself into one.'

'Who is Aengus Óg?' I asked curiously, my father's words replacing my petty loss with wonder. He was filled with stories; they leaked out of him and encircled me with his love like a cloak.

'He was the Irish god of love. He had a golden harp and every kiss he ever gave turned into a little bird.' And with that he erased my tears with a torrent of little kisses all over my face.

He took my hand, tingling from the gravel rash, and together we walked back to his office. His colleague wore a long black smudge on the side of his face where he had wiped at perspiration with inky fingers.

'Mike, you remember my daughter, Matilda, Tilly?'

Mike looked up from his case of letters and lifted the visor that shaded his eyes from the glare of the lamp, but still his eyes widened and I felt my difference, my whiteness. It made me squirm beneath my skin and I wanted to hide my face against my father's legs.

'Of course I do. Hello there,' he said, shaking my hand by daintily clasping the tips of my fingers with his blotchy hands, the fingernails black. When I looked at my hand again, it was christened with ink. My father led me off to his desk, picking me up and planting me on his chair before giving it a gentle spin, the thrill of a turn, my private merry-go-round. He pulled out his handkerchief, the smell of starch still freshly laundered upon it, dabbed it on his tongue and patted the wound on my knee.

'It's your birthday soon, Til the Lil, what would you like to do? Have a party?' He dabbed his tongue again and moved up to my fingers, finding ink more stubborn than blood. 'You could invite friends, have a cake, play some games.'

I had never hoped for a party before; it was something other families did but not mine. My mother had an aversion to guests.

'Maybe a magician?' Hope got the better of me, creeping out into my childish voice. I loved nothing more than my father's magic, a coin from the ear disappearing on dancing fingers.

'Why, I'd be happy to, but I may not be able to pull real doves from your ears ... though I possibly know someone who can. How about that?' I wanted to believe him, but even then I knew my mother's limitations.

'What about Mum?'

Dad cast a quick eye to Mike, whose head was down as he plucked the letters from the box and placed them on the composing stick.

'I'll talk to her, love, smooth things over. Why, even her beloved Jesus loved a bit of a party, water into wine and all that sort of thing. Was fond of a magic trick, too – making the dead rise, multiplying loaves and fishes, walking on water and doing that Houdini act at the finale, escaping from a tomb. He was a bloody magician all right!' my father teased, before his knelt down in front of me and cupped my face in his hand.

'What about the greatest magician of all time, Lil? What about that? What if we could get him to come to your birthday and invite the whole town too?' A thrilling wave washed over me. Mike stopped what he was doing and wiped his black fingers down the front of his apron. My father stood slowly and extracted a piece of paper from his pocket with a flourish and pressed it into Mike's hands.

'The Great Houdini will attempt flight here in New South Wales, this week. Can you believe it, a man flying in something that looks more like a kite?'

I sat up higher in my chair. Even I knew Houdini was no ordinary magician. His flight would be better than the flap of dove wings. He was going to fly.

'Did you get this date and places right, mate?' Mike asked. The letters he had held clattered back into the box.

'Of course. It's my darling daughter's birthday – I'd hardly not remember, now would I?' My father spun me again in the chair, all sting gone from my scraped knees.

'He's done Diggers Rest in Victoria and the few demonstration flights out at Rose Hill in Sydney. Now he plans to fly between stops as he makes his way to ship out at Brisbane. We are on that path, unless the map is wrong, and we're one of the few places with easily accessible fuel. My contact told me as much.' My father spun me another rotation of the chair and the room swirled to ribbons before my eyes.

'You bloody ripper! Just imagine it, an aeroplane flying over our sleepy little town. The air is the future! We could hold a civic reception, turn on the local hospitality. We could get the Oddfellows Hall set up with a decent spread, prepare a banner and the like. Keys to the town even. What do you reckon? The bloody cows in the fields and the cockatoos in the trees won't know what hit them, let alone the sleepyheads in this town. We got to get this sheet out, let everyone know. Give them time to wash their collars and polish the silver. Think of it, the tourists will flock in. A special meeting needs to be held. Can't let the Masons organise it – our Order of Druids will put on a reception and then some.' My father paused to catch his breath. His excitement made Mike's hands move faster over the trays of letters.

'Did you hear that, Til the Lil? The world's most famous magician will be flying over our town just in time for your birthday!'

My excitement ran across my skin in goose bumps, as the letters clacked into the compositing frame, waiting for the benediction of the ink, my father's story forming.

'Can you believe it? Harry Houdini flying over our bloody town!' He said it as if it was still not quite a possibility. We were giddy with the news.

That morning, as my father took me down to the bustling main street, a bundle under his arm, it felt as if the town were preparing for my birthday. The date of the guest's arrival had been ringed in every calendar in town; verandahs were swept, curtains bleached, laundry starched within a crisp of its life; cakes were baked, trees pruned, shoes spat upon and polished, dresses pressed. A banner was painted and strung across the Oddfellows Hall, the letters made large enough so they could be seen from the air.

As we entered the hall, a lady was spreading a tablecloth over a trestle table, weighing down the cloth with lamingtons and scones and cucumber sandwiches. As she placed a jug of homemade lemonade on the table, the liquid sloshed over the side and I heard her swear under her breath. My father looked at me and raised his eyebrows.

'Looks beaut, Rebecca,' he exclaimed, and the lady looked up shocked; she hadn't even noticed us.

'Mike, Stephen and his little girl are here,' she shouted, and it was then I looked up to see my father's workmate up a ladder, stretching a canopy to shade the table.

'Not a minute too soon. Hand her up, would you,' he called, his face red and hot, and for a moment I thought he was talking about me. My father mounted a chair and handed Mike the end of the bundle and, like a large skein of wool, they unwound it, the painted letters slowly appearing. *The Ancient Order of Druids Welcomes Houdini,* and beneath it, a star, a beehive, a pair of holding hands and a dove with a sprig, just like the one I had lost. My father looked down and smiled.

'See, I told you I could make another one, bigger and better. The dove for peace, the beehive for industry and the hand in hand for fraternity.'

He was right: the dove on the banner was radiant, with gold feathers painted on her breast.

After the banner was hung, my father dusted his palms on the back of his trousers and held my hand as we walked home singing 'I see the great mountains'.

The whole town could not have been shinier if the King had been coming. Most of the townspeople stayed outside watching the skies from their verandahs but some lined the main street. Waiting. In our house, my father fussed over the lint on his trilby, and my mother was quiet as if she was hoping the fuss would go way. I was in my Sunday best, a cake upon the table, the frosting slowly sliding onto the surrounding plate, a wire cage protecting it from the aerial assault of flies. Time moved sluggishly in the heat, the street turning to a shimmer as everyone stood outside, shading their eyes against the brightness. Except for me. I crouched in the window frame, protected from the sun's rays, scouring the sky like the rest of them, made jittery by the sight of a cloud or a bird or the sound of a passing motor.

Dusk fell and some of the townsfolk went inside, the wireless blaring news. But there was none. My mother ushered me in and we sat around the table. She served our dinner as the first stars came out. But still my father waited, his eye on the horizon, as much a child as I was, hoping against hope that Houdini would still come. He rivalled the apostles with his faith. He eventually came to join us, his disappointment blending with mine. The cake was cut, but the flavour was all gone.

I said my prayers and went to bed, my ears straining in the darkness for the possibility of my father's redemption, Houdini's arrival. My father had ignited the town with his story as if it was a bushfire, and now there was the strange quiet of it having passed us over. Before I went to bed, my mother came in and brushed my hair, releasing it from its tight braid, my hair a snowy veil wafting over my shoulders with the constant static from the brush. With each downward motion of the brush I could see the red threads of scars upon her arms and they unsettled me. After she had helped me into my nightgown and tucked me into bed, she smoothed the static from my hair as she said a prayer for my father, her words like a final curtain on his hopes, in the name of the Father, the Son and the Holy Spirit, Amen, before she kissed me goodnight.

In the morning he was already gone to the office, the broadsheet printed by the time I walked with my brother to school: *HOUDINI ABANDONS FLIGHT. TAKES TRAIN INSTEAD.*

As I walked past the Oddfellows Hall, a huge bin was stuffed with the streamers that were to have heralded a welcome. Something glinted atop the refuse and, magpie quick, I plucked it out. A brass key as big as my hand, ornately inscribed to *Mr H. Houdini, in honour of his visit to our town, 1910*. The key to the city in one hand and a world of disappointment in the other.

Ari absent-mindedly fondled a key hanging from a cord around his neck before he let it drop beneath his collar. All the while Billy's eyes never left my face.

'We could get a band,' Miss du Maurier said. 'Or maybe, Ari, you could play the old upright? Of course I'll have to have it tuned.'

Ari looked from her to me as if he were waiting for a sign I did not know how to give.

'It all sounds good,' I said on cue, not wanting to disappoint. Part of me wanted to agree to anything to bring this conversation to an end. 'Well then, it is decided.' I stood up and straightened my trousers. 'I'm bushed. See you all tomorrow.'

As I walked up the stairs, I felt their eyes prickle into me and I suppressed my desire to run. As I got to the top of the stairs, I wiped my mouth, trying to erase the pressure of Billy's kiss, my hand wiping back and forth again and again.

The raven blinked at me as I opened my bedroom door, as if she had been expecting me. How could I have so nearly forgotten about her? I chucked my fingers under her chin as one does a cat; a low grizzle of pleasure came from her throat. I was glad of her wordless company.

All night my lips hummed like a ghost wind on a telegraph wire. Who would have thought that two small parts of anatomy, the flesh of the lips, could stir up such a commotion? It felt as if Billy had been biding his time; all his kindnesses suddenly fell into line, his attentions little soldiers just waiting for the order. I'd felt his eyes upon me at the theatre, when we shared a shift, and I'd returned his smiles and rolled eyes, little jokes that made the shift go faster. It had never occurred to me that he had been scoping that chance moment when he could land a kiss upon my lips.

My first kiss had spurred me onwards, as far away from it and my mother's crippling grief as I could get. But as soon as I stepped off the train at Central Station, I was as stunned as a bird that has flown into a glass window. The city roared up at me. I didn't know which way to go. I stood on the platform, rooted in fear. What had I done? I had some money, but was it enough to pay for a room, for food? I looked down at my father's old shoes: I'd have to replace them too.

Light-headed, I took a wobbly step and a kindly nun asked me if I needed help. Was she thinking I was about to throw myself on the tracks? She suggested I find a boarding house run by a respectable matron, just the thing for a country girl like me starting work in the city. I couldn't correct her; what work did I know of, what work could I do? Pumping petrol, cleaning windscreens, selling maps and giving directions. How could she tell I was from the country? I hardly had a piece of grass hanging from my lip like a scarecrow's cigarillo. Then I realised the indicator board had given her the information. She bid me farewell and blessed me, her well-meaning words feeling like a shackle.

Pinned to a noticeboard at Central Station were advertisements for boarding hotels, pensiones, hostels, but how could I determine which were the ones run by respectable matrons and those that catered only to bachelors? I scribbled down a few addresses and made my way down City Road, the dust from the cars and carts blowing up into my mouth, a light rain turning the dirt to mud.

The first address was opposite a vast park across from the university, but I took one look at the young men lolling on the doorstep smoking and found my feet moving onwards of their own accord. The next address was a few blocks up, above a public house; the raucous singing from within pushed me onward. Mercifully the rain had stopped, but it had managed to soak me right through. I took a turn into a small side street, the footpath as wide as my forearm, the front of the houses crouched on the side of the road. As the sun burst through, the children of the street ran back outside and resumed their game of cricket, an old crate making their bat and stumps, a bundle of rags bound with rubber bands their ball. I was about to ask them directions but they stared at me slack-jawed, so I thought better of it and hurried on. A stone sallied through the air behind me and clipped my shoulder, spinning me onward through the maze of small tangled streets so I had no clue to where I was. In the distance I could hear trains rumble, and I walked in their direction as if they were my compass. When I found them, they ran parallel to a row of terraces, wet washing hanging limp across the balconies like a sodden parade, until the line of them broke and opened up into a small park, a green handkerchief of grass framed by large swaying figs.

The rain started up again and I ran for the shelter of the fig trees, crouching in between the cavernous roots, carefully sheltering my bag against the trunk. I curled into those canal-like tree roots as quietly as a secret. The rain pitter-pattered against the leaves and a magpie opened his agile beak and sang *too-ra-lie*. I felt so tired. My eyes closed only for an instant, or so it felt, and when I woke the sky had gone yellow, sunshine trapped in the silver clouds. Someone coughed.

'Are you all right there, miss?' a voice said and I squinted up into the light. A lady was looking at me from under a large spindly umbrella, her blonde hair escaping her beret, a voluminous black velvet coat nearly dragging in the mud. She reached out her hand to me, speckled with silver rings, and I took it. That was how I met Miss du Maurier.

She didn't ask me any questions and was happy to accept whatever rent I could pay her until I secured myself a job. She led me to her house, the both of us under her umbrella, the smell of her exotic perfume dazing my senses. 'You look like a lost thing,' she said. How close to the truth she was.

When she showed me to my new room, clean and bright, I took my father's magic book and placed it under my pillow, hoping I could dream him up. Instead I slept like the dead.

I pulled out that old book and placed it again under the pillow, my fingers running across the cracked spine until I resolved sleep was useless. Could I avoid facing Billy? I made myself get up, get dressed, close my bedroom door quietly behind me. Miss du Maurier was coming in from the letterbox, flicking through the mail; when she saw me on the stairs she stopped and waved an envelope in the air, white as surrender.

'One for you, my dear,' she called out to me and I panicked, almost flew down the remaining stairs. Had my letter been sent home after all, with the return address in Miss du Maurier's hand? Was this the reply? My hand flew to my pocket and patted the envelope, still reassuringly unsent. I didn't want any good Samaritan posting it for me, I wasn't sure I wanted to post it all.

'It's good news, I can feel it,' Miss du Maurier said and handed the letter into my keeping.

It was addressed to Lily del Mar and Ari Pearl, our names a sweet trill upon the paper. As I walked through the house, I tore it open, my eyes flicking across the page as I narrowly avoided bumping into things, including Billy who sat at the dining table, his eyes following me. I ignored him, even though he was waiting for me to say something, his mouth opening and closing. I dreaded the moment we would have to speak. I didn't stop; the words on the paper urged me forward.

Before my father left for the war, for the scoop of the century, he decided to teach me the one trick he knew. It was something he only ever did on special occasions – birthdays, Christmas, Easter. He knew the value of a trick's mystery, just as Houdini did – either do it rarely or make it so dazzlingly brilliant that it blinds everyone as to what is really going on. My father was no Houdini, so he stuck with the first option.

A fortnight earlier he had collected his uniform, the buttons as shiny as fresh minted coins. It hung on the outside of my parents' wardrobe like a guest too shy to go in and mingle with the other garments. The slouch hat sat lonely on my mother's dresser, the only masculine thing among the feminine paraphernalia: the ivory-handled brush, the silver-backed mirror, the photograph of my parents on their wedding day.

It was hot; flies sought the moisture from the corners of our lips, the rims of our nostrils, the ducts of our eyes. The house was made overly hot by the stove burning all night to roast the meat my mother had insisted on for Christmas, the eve of my father's departure. The Christmas pudding boiled in its pot, the tin lid like a drummer rat-a-tat-tat-ing, steam filling the house.

We took our places at the dinner table for the baked lunch, a halo of steam following my mother back and forth from the kitchen until our plates were filled with pork and turkey, baked carrots and potatoes. We said grace with one hand waving away the flies. Once our best plates were cleared, my mother placed the jug of custard on the table, the gentle clink of its beaded cover signalling the special time between the dinner and the dessert, the moment when my father would pull a penny from his pocket and proceed with his sole magic trick.

'See this penny, it is an ordinary penny.' He would pass it around and we would all good-naturedly tap it on the table or inspect it for strange markings, as we had many times before. I always gave it a tap on my teeth for good measure, convinced that the magic lay somewhere in the coin.

'Now I will proceed to make this coin disappear by rubbing it on my arm.' My father lifted his elbow theatrically and placed it on the table and the penny on the tilt of his forearm. With the constant friction, the coin fell to the table every now and again, spinning from his grasp. He would sigh and begin the determined rubbing again and again, the coin always making its bid for freedom. Until it vanished. We would each take turns to feel my father's skin, half-expecting the coin shape to be detectable beneath it. Again my father would start the furious rubbing of his fingers against the skin where the coin had last been seen, at first seeming to get frustrated with his lack of success, and then suddenly out of nowhere the coin fell, returned to the table. The smile upon my father's face was victorious. The pudding was served, and every silver shilling I found between my teeth would be placed on my own arm to see if it would disappear.

Late that evening when the shadows of the nearby gum trees fell on our roof and cooled the house, the tin roof ticking like a malfunctioning metronome, I sat on my bed flicking through the pages of my magic book. It had been my birthday gift the year Houdini never arrived. Then my father came in and sat on the edge of my bed and offered to teach me his secret.

'Til the Lil, it is all a matter of distracting your audience. The artifice is more important than the mechanics, the performance more important than the trick.' He looked at me so earnestly I felt he was trying to communicate something beyond his words. 'The coin, Tilly, does not get rubbed into the skin. It is the audience who is tricked into thinking this happens because of the repetition. The trick works because the magician feigns his frustration. As one watches one gets used to the release and fall of the coin, and thinks nothing of it. When the magician retrieves it with his hand and starts again, the rubbing continues, but lo and behold it has vanished. Where has it gone? It has been placed by the hand behind the neck, where it sticks with perspiration, the audience never questioning the moment when the magician rubs his neck in mock exasperation, while waiting for the impossible.'

My father handed me a coin and watched me rub it into the pale stretch of flesh on my forearm. The coin flew spectacularly across the room once or twice, but eventually I could move it onto my neck without risk of detection.

My father clapped loudly, as if I had accomplished something truly magnificent. The unusual sound was like a lure: my mother appeared at the door. When she saw it was my father teaching me his coin trick, she quietly retreated, her footsteps hushed on the floorboards. My father didn't even look up, but squeezed my hands in his.

'Now, Til the Lil, don't forget it. Someone has to do it at Christmas time while I am away. It is our own little O'Farrell tradition, small as it is.' The way he looked at me made me fearful. 'Just in case, darling,' he said in an attempt to reassure me, but all I could think about was the rest of the sentence: *in case I never come back.*

'But there is one more thing,' he said as he pushed back my hair and peered inside my ear, frowning. 'What on earth have you got in there?' He pretended to extract something out of my ear, his fingers dancing around a small shining thing, a little silver brooch the size of a coin which he placed in my palm.

'What does it say?' I asked, looking at the strange arrangement of letters.

'*Mizpah*,' he said. 'It means the Lord will watch over you when I cannot,' he said, kissing the top of my head.

'But I don't want the Lord, I want you,' I said, stifling a sob in my throat.

'I'll be right as rain. Every little bird you see will bring me word of you, you can be sure of that,' he said, a forced jollity in his voice.

The cold silver of the Mizpah brooch started to warm and I fumbled trying to fix it to my nightgown. It caught the light and winked at me. I had something for my father in return. I went to my cupboard and slid it out from where it had lain wrapped in a sheet of newspaper to shield it from the dust. My father's face lit up with curiosity as he peeled back the wrapping. It was the key to our town, meant for Houdini, which I had salvaged from the rubbish bin. I had read the tale of a bushranger who had taken a bullet through a locket and survived; perhaps this key could protect my father too.

My father looked at me in surprise, his face crowded with questions, then he reached out and crushed me to him, a shiver rippling through him. 'Take care of your mother,' he whispered.

He wore the key around his neck, a funny lucky charm, or so the letter from his mate said. But it was not returned with his watch and his wallet after he was laid to rest with the thousands beside the battlefields, where they said poppies now grew.

By the time my foot hit the back stoop I had already had a thought. It was risky, maybe even impossible, but it was worth a try. We had one card we hadn't played: our black spade, the raven. Not just a beauty, her midnight chrysanthemum feathers abloom beneath her chin, she was surely smarter than all the other birds too.

I hadn't expected to find Ari in bed. Perhaps I should have gone away and come back later, but the letter burned in my hand, the fire of an idea blazed in my head. He read it, his face growing darker with each passing moment, then he folded the letter until it was the size of a postage stamp and flicked it on top of the bed.

'I can't believe this. Is Clay asking what I think he is asking? I won't ask it of you!' Ari raised his voice vehemently, and the startled lyrebird swished his tail, sending dust motes falling through the air.

Couldn't Ari see what Clay was offering? It was more than just a contract, it was a real chance. Carefully I retrieved the paper, laid it on my thigh and smoothed out the creases with my palm.

'My father used to tell me a story,' I said, my voice sounding surer in my thoughts than out loud, 'about a girl who could turn into a swan by donning a swan-feather cloak. She caught the eye of the Irish god of love, Aengus.'

Ari sat up, pulling the blanket around his shoulders against the chill.

'That reminds me of something,' he said. He reached over to the stack of books on the crate, the blanket slipping to reveal the dark chest hair fanning out like a span of wings on his chest, before he pulled the blanket back. He flicked through the pages until he found what he was looking for. His voice was hesitant yet sonorous, as if they were words he had composed, but I knew they were not: I could see that the name Yeats was pressed into the spine.

'I made my song a coat
Covered with embroideries
Out of old mythologies
From heel to throat;
But the fools caught it,
Wore it in the world's eyes
As though they'd wrought it.
Song, let them take it,
For there's more enterprise
In walking naked.'

He looked up at me. I felt hot in my face, my mouth parched, and I could not swallow for wondering if I had enough courage to carry this through, our bold new enterprise.

SIXTEEN

Billy

The taste of Lily's kiss surpassed expectations – her lips plump cushions for my sting. I may have forced my lips upon hers, but her lips certainly pressed back – soft at first, but then with a greater pulse. She was not fiery, though her mercury would roar upwards at my command in time. I did not care that the Jew's eye was upon me; let him learn to savour disappointment, it would be his lot soon enough. Lily's kiss had the slight candied scent of camomile. My memory of Merle's was like the burn of mustard gas.

After my time in the holding cell I had risen enough in Crisp's opinion to become involved in patient consultations. I had obviously passed the first of the hurdles he had for me: little did I know how many there would be and how high they would become. I was sure he wanted me to take over in the consulting room eventually, so he could spend more time coercing the librarians into believing that their precious permanent collection actually belonged to him.

One day the shop front looked brighter and I hesitantly walked through the door, thinking fleetingly the shop had changed hands until Merle looked up at me from behind the counter, her eyes shining.

'You like it?' she asked. 'I cleaned the windows. Come up a treat.' She looked almost pretty, her voice a bright bubble of enthusiasm. Even the counter seemed to have an extra special gleam, the product no doubt of her elbow grease. 'Go right in. Father is expecting you.'

Crisp sat solemnly at his little table in the middle of the room, a sheaf of paper weighted down with his fancy fountain pen. He saw my eyes flutter along the gold spines arrayed behind him, but under such acute observation I could not let my gaze linger long enough to discern his recent additions. I would not be distracted this time.

'Today, Mr Little, is the day you see how I work my effects upon the patients. Today, you will be privileged to see working methods that very few have seen and survived! Ha ha, to see your face just now, worthy of a photograph. You must learn humour, Mr Little, it will make your face more handsome.' If he kept talking in this fashion, it would be my fists making a joke out of his face. 'Come, take a seat.' He pulled out the chair beside him and I eased into it gingerly, as if into an overly hot bath.

'Now, the patient will come and sit in the chair opposite us. I will introduce you as my son and fellow apothecary, as they are used to my company alone. You are to say nothing. Not even hello. To do so will disturb the confluence of healing taking place in the room.'

Healing, my arse – huckstering, confidence tricks, suggestion, mind manipulation and a good deal of persuasion to convince them that the elixir was more than the piss it was.

'The patient will pour out their concerns and ailments. Do not listen to these too closely; otherwise you will be distracted from your intentions. However, at all times you must ensure eye contact. If for some reason you break eye contact, nod your head thrice and meet their eyes again. In doing so, the healing will resume and you may continue looking intently. But do not, I repeat, listen too closely.'

I wanted not to listen too closely myself, as I felt my bile rise. So much waffle needed to cover up his secrets.

'The empathetic nod is your friend, the compassionate ear is not. If you start caring, you may as well move your sorry Catholic arse and go open your bleeding heart to your mate Jesus H. Fucking Christ. You will find none of that nonsense here, Mr Little.' His eyes held a determined gleam. 'I'll have you know that this is a legitimate business, regardless of what means and methods of healing we use. A business which, if you have the mind to pay attention, could earn you a tidy sum and time to pursue other fancies.'

As if on cue, there was a rap on the door and Merle poked her face around the corner, a strand of dark hair falling into her eyes. The effect was so fetching, it was as if she had stood behind the door and preened in a mirror to see exactly what alluring effect she could create.

'Doctor, your first patient is ready to see you,' Merle said, her voice almost breathy.

Crisp looked away from me then and I felt strangely released. Fatigue tugged at my eyelids.

The patient strutted through the door, a pretty if skinny thing, her teeth pressed into her lip as if she was frightened of what she was going to say. I sized her up: a delectable specimen. Oh, I could have made her press my flesh with those pointed teeth. It was clear at once what her problem was.

'Doctor,' she cried she took her seat, her pert bottom smacking the veneered wood, 'I am tormented by my thoughts. Every night and day I think of men ...'

Before my ears could absorb her salacious thoughts, I felt a sharp heel grinding into my foot as if extinguishing a cigarette butt. The pain seared hot and I willed my limbs to be still. All I wanted to do was shout out, an expletive hot on my tongue. I wanted to grind my heel into his foot as if it were a mincer and his foot only gristle. Instead my rage was interrupted by the nymphomaniac's rant.

Furiously I nodded my head, near breathless, wanting my ears to fill with her smut, but my head just nodded, in a complementary rhythm with Crisp's, his up, mine down. Hypnotically, the cap was free of Crisp's pen as he wrote a fantastical prescription, the paper folded authoritatively before he handed it to her. Her walk was primmer as she exited, her hips no longer swaying, as if with her confession she had folded up her desires like a nun. Crisp looked at me and opened his mouth, and instead of bracing myself in my seat for his rancid words, I stood to do the gentlemanly thing and let her out. Through the doorway then, a glimpse of the person I thought least likely to see. Was it some sort of joke? My heart did a sick twist in my chest and I looked back at Crisp, who offered me a curious smile.

'Is there a problem, Little?' Crisp asked as I stepped behind a medical screen, but I didn't have time to respond, for in came Merle, and hot on her skirt tails, the next patient. My surprise popping up behind her like a jack in the box: my father.

He was blank and bleary-eyed, his usual state after sipping turps or some other poisonous pickle juice. But his voice was startlingly sober, clear as an empty glass.

'Hello,' he said as he slid into the seat opposite, the sound of his voice a fresh insult as he waited for Crisp's cue to begin. Was it possible my father had read the label of the elixir I had left behind and found his staggering way here? My father's ability to read was negligible. Coincidence was surely an impossibility. He must have come of his own accord with the taste of elixir on his lips. He had asked someone to read him the address on the label, there could be no other explanation, but I couldn't shuck the creeping sensation that there was more at play, or was that my own paranoia? Crisp did not smirk or grin, there was no tell. If anything, he was all ears.

'Doctor Crisp, I recently tried your Elixir du Jour and found it very helpful. Calming, even. It put out a fire I've been trying to quench for some time. I was wondering if I could obtain another bottle. You see, I have an ailment, it shames me to say ...' Who was this man, talking cap in hand, bereft of all his dignity, whose unsuspecting seed helped form me? 'My ailment is, I am tired of life.'

For the merest of moments I felt sorry for him. He was a pitiful sight, always half-asleep, his eyelids drooping. His one suit was permanently crushed and stained; patchy whiskers peppered his face; white hair flared at his temples.

'Don't get me wrong, there is no risk of me flinging myself from the Gap, but since the arrival of that baby on my doorstep I haven't felt myself.'

That was a relief: the ringing self-concern that filled my ears from dawn to dusk remained unchanged. My pity began to evaporate.

'The thing that has haunted me, worn me to the bone, is that I have never been sure he is mine. There is nothing in his features that reflect me. I found him wrapped in a blanket, tucked inside a crate right at my own bloody front door! When I undid the swaddle I could see he was a little damaged, a tiny piece of him had been removed that could never be replaced. He was unlucky from the start.'

Any momentary sympathy I had had vanished. Blood swirled in my ears; I was desperate to strike out at him. My knife was strapped to my leg, I could have taken a little bit of him all right, but I was frozen, my ears straining. The photograph I had flicked from his pocket watch before handing it over to Golden Fortune loomed in my mind – would he say more of her?

'Oh, I could have handed him over to an orphanage or moved him along to the church step before he even opened his eyes and wailed for milk, but there was that odd chance, wasn't there, that he was my very own. My decision was sealed when he looked up at me, fixing me with those eyes of his, not a baby's faraway look at all, no, his gaze fixed me like ice fixes the water. Until he yowled. He always wanted more, he did. The more he had, the less I did, for as he grew, my luck began to dwindle, as if he were sucking it out of me. The day he spoke his first word, I lost all my winnings. The day he took his first step, I was struck with fever. But I never thought much of it, until the war began.

'Only when he went to war did my luck return. Every hand of cards I played came good. I found coins in the gutter, a gold watch left in the lavatory at the pub, a stolen wallet tossed in the street a hundred quid concealed in a secret pocket the thief had missed. But when my son returned, I stumbled backwards again. I throw myself at your mercy, Doctor. Give me some more of your elixir; help to bring my luck back.'

I became aware of a metallic taste: I had bitten my tongue so hard, blood filled my mouth.

Crisp uncapped his pen and swirled the ink across the page, looking up to catch my eye, no doubt still wondering why I had not come out from behind the screen. He handed the paper to my father and was none the wiser. My father clasped the paper in his hand as if he had just been given the code to a safe at the Commonwealth Bank in Martin Place and a promise of the bank tellers forming a guard of honour. Crisp looked at me, but I kept my face expressionless as a sphinx. Did he know this poor specimen of a man was my father? There was no twinkle in Crisp's eye. He did not know I was that unwanted, unlucky, misshapen child.

Crisp escorted my father out and I emerged from my hiding place and resumed my seat.

'I take it you know that gentleman, Little?' he said, and I nodded, my anger so raw I could not shape the words to reply. 'Who is he then?'

If Crisp was trying to crawl beneath my skin I would not let him; if he was going to be my itch I would resist the urge to scratch.

'Someone I thought I knew, that's all,' I replied, my voice a husk in my throat.

The next patient came in, a crease like a lightning crack etched into his forehead. He started speaking before his arse even slapped the chair. It was easy to keep the contact; I couldn't have listened even if I'd tried. Everything before me was a blur of rage. The son-of-a-bitch storytelling liar wouldn't know the truth if an angel came down and placed a wafer of it on his tongue. How many times had he spun this tale of woe? How many ears sopped up the spill of his self-inflicted tragedy? He blamed me for his loss of luck, did he, his fate. If he thought I was the face of misfortune, the bringer of his bad luck, it was time to reveal the full and mighty force of it to him.

SEVENTEEN

Ari

All that night, in my narrow camp bed, sleep eluded me. I couldn't get it out of my mind, the sight of his lips pressed against hers. The unsettled birds sang out, their strange nocturnal sounds puncturing my fitful dreams. The first sunlight splashed over me and I watched my breath rise out of me as if I had swallowed a cloud in my sleep. I felt my life being pulled out from under me, just as I had that night my mother made me run.

The previous night my mother had read out loud from the newspaper. A man had been set upon by bandits. A shop window had been smashed. Someone had left a dog turd on the synagogue steps. It was no accident, for in the latest incident a word had been smeared upon the door. My childish ears pricked up at my mother's angry tone, but when I looked up at her for reassurance she smiled softly and complimented me on the scribble of a house I had drawn. Until the words so upset her that she screwed up the newspaper and tossed it to the flames.

The night it began, the shattering of glass was like a hailstorm that would not stop. My mother opened the door, no coat across her shoulders, and I remembered thinking this was strange for the shouting was coming down the street towards us. My mother had me by the hand, her grip firm, as if she was angry with me. Together we flew through the streets, taking refuge in the old doorways, cramming ourselves into dark spaces as if we too could become insubstantial as shadow. With the first streak of dawn we came to a door and she kissed me roughly; she had no time for gentleness. I fell against the legs of whoever opened the door and it was closed almost as quickly, but not before I saw my mother claimed by the darkness of the street. The sound of shouting was accompanied by shrieks, glass shattering, sounds smothered by the stranger's hands, a woman's hands, cupped around my ears.

Why had my mother delivered me to strangers? We listened together, every hiss and spit of the fire making my new guardians sit fearfully still. The woman had a daughter, her hair in ragged ringlets, who buried her face in her mother's skirt. She also had a son, reed thin, who kept his eyes on the gun at his mother's feet, in case there came a time he too should need to aim it. From above we were watched by a painting of a mother and child: she clutched him close, just as my mother had held me. These were Christians hoping that they wouldn't be mistaken for Jews.

'Why is he here?' the boy whispered. 'He is a filthy Jew! He uses our blood for his bread. Saint Gavriil Belostoksky was six years old when they murdered him for their Passover –'

The woman's free hand swept through the air and stung his face with a loud cracking slap. The little girl peeked up from her mother's skirts and whimpered. I looked at the boy, his mouth open. I was younger than six. I was frightened that what he said was true, but I knew how bread was made, I had helped plait the challah bread, the egg sitting in the braid. Blood would have streaked the flour, I would have seen it, smelled it.

'You shall remember this boy in your prayers tonight,' she hissed. A rattle of stones was thrown across the roof and we were all hushed again. Somewhere out there in the muffled darkness my mother hurried back through the snowy slush to my grandmother, whom we had left alone in the house.

Eventually the sounds died down, a fresh fall of snow smothering and erasing as it went. The flickering from the fireplace was the only illumination. Silence fell again and I ran to the window, searching for my mother.

Before the woman could pull the curtain on my view, I saw what lay planted in the slush, grey with footprints blossoming black with blood. The snow was a blank canvas lit blue with the otherworldly light of a half-cracked moon. A body lay pierced and still, the legs and arms at uneasy angles. A dark serge skirt covered her face. Was it a long braid or a trickle of blood that trailed in the stained snow? It didn't look like my mother. On the other side of the street a house billowed with smoke, the suck and flick of the curtains in its windows an eerie kind of breathing.

I didn't sleep. I thought every footstep I heard was my mother's. Every knock upon the door was the possibility of her return. The stranger offered me food, but I could not eat it. She wiped my face with a damp cloth and removed the yarmulke from my head, then carefully took the scissors and cut the curls at my temples and tossed them into the fireplace. They sizzled with an acrid burn and were gone, the same curls my mother would wrap around her fingers as she sang me to sleep. She looked down at the letters tattooed on my hand and wiped at them with spit on her thumb, but they would not budge.

The streets were cleared by the time I was permitted to look out of the window again. The stranger's children slowly returned to their games. The woman ushered me over to them, her face kindly but distressed. I kneeled next to the children and watched them play, feeling a world away from them – why stack these dominoes, why watch them fall? I went to the front door and thought about tearing it open and running back wildly through the streets, but I did not know the way to the faces that knew me.

* * *

A knock at the shed door made me start. I took a deep breath and the past retreated.

I leaned up on my elbows, the blankets falling from me, the cold air pricking goose bumps at my skin. She let in a gust as she entered, propelled by some other force, and settled on the edge of the cot, the letter clasped in her hand as if she would not let it go. The springs of the bed murmured beneath her weight. I sat that bit higher to give her more space, my leg touching hers through the bedclothes.

'I hope you didn't mind me opening it, it was addressed to us both.'

I shook my head. I didn't mind: she and I, we were still in this together.

'Well, it seems Harry Clay likes our turn.' Her voice rose with excitement, her lips quivering. The same lips Billy Little had kissed last night, I remembered with a jolt. I felt a cold knot begin to twine itself in my chest. Did she really feel for him? Was I always to lose the ones I cared for?

'Well, that's good news.' I said, my own mouth moving mechanically. I could barely concentrate – had they kissed before? I rubbed at my eyes. I wanted the image to be gone.

'And he wants to give us a three-week contract.' She didn't look at me, yet I wanted nothing more in the world at that moment than for her eyes to rest upon mine. 'With one proviso.' She handed me the letter. My eyes ran over the words until I saw it myself.

> *To fit in with the new policy as we endeavour to compete with the talkies, all acts are being asked to diversify with novelty or controversy (within the laws of decency, but not to be completely constrained by them).*

As I passed her back the letter, her hand ran up her throat. What was he asking of us? *Within the laws of decency?* Above the stage manager's desk I had seen an image of a topless chorus girl from the Moulin Rouge. Was this what Clay was aiming at? How could I ask this of her?

I wanted to cut out the offending words with my uncle's scissors. What was magic but a diversion for children? But it wasn't Clay who had set these events in motion and neither was it Lily. I had kindled the idea of being a magician from the very first moment I understood *abracadabra*. The tattoo on my hand was a lie.

Lily stood on a chair and brought the raven down from the rafter where she perched to observe us. She was the colour of the very darkness; beautiful, self-possessed, the dark queen among the others. The parrot, the lyrebird, the currawong all shifted uneasily, their talons clutching and unclutching whatever it was they held. Why did she unsettle them so? I had seen ravens pursued by the angry cries of other birds, the raven winging itself away, black calligraphy in the blank expanse of sky. Were Noah's birds still trying to drive the poor raven away?

The blue-black bird so close to Lily's pale glowing skin would create a powerful effect. It would be like the black spot that hovers in the eye after staring at the sun, her tender skin at the mercy of the eyes of the world. To my own eyes. What were we doing? Was our act really worth exposing her so, like Eve after the fall? What kind of man was I even to let her entertain the idea? Certainly no gentleman and certainly no good Jew, 'pursuing the passions of my heart and straying after my eyes', breaking the commitments I had made at my bar mitzvah to become a son of the Law. Why couldn't we continue as we were? Surely there were other places that would have our act just as it was. But we had come so far here. Clay had offered us a contract; to go somewhere else would set us back to the beginning. Besides, Lily was adamant, though her cheeks had rouged up all on their own, that we could do it, that she wanted to do it, and I wanted to believe her.

She seemed nervous as she tied the end of an old sheet over her shoulder to see if the Raven could pluck it free and reveal her clothes underneath. Could we find a leotard to avoid her humiliation? She fumbled with the knot and I moved closer to help her, the fabric yielding to my fingers. She seemed to tremble, but as the knot tightened she straightened. The raven hopped onto her arm and turned a bright eye toward me, as if daring me to a greater challenge, and then, with a tug of her beak, released the knot as if she had only been playing with us. The creature was indeed as smart as the Birdman said.

'We may need to make it look more difficult than that, otherwise the audience will think the whole thing rigged,' she said, folding the sheet up and throwing herself and it into the armchair. 'It is not enough.' She was right – it was all very well to fixate on protecting her modesty, but to have a flash of her skin alone was not going to capture the audience's imagination. Lily twiddled her feet in the air as if they could manifest an answer.

'We could add a trunk trick, the Metamorphosis, like Bess and Harry,' she said. 'Where they swapped places in a blink. Could we pull it off?'

A trunk? The last time I had been in a trunk came back to me in a rush. I felt the pitch of failure in my throat, a kind of seasickness that tipped at the corners of the room and made the floor slant beneath my feet. I reached for the wall to steady myself, but the room seemed a carousel, Lily a figure spinning in my periphery. She called out to me but my dizziness conspired against me. I felt that if I opened my mouth the whole world would fall out.

How long did I live with that Christian woman and her family? I stayed until a stranger arrived at the door, a distant cousin with a telegram from my uncle in his hand. He had tracked my whereabouts and come to collect me; we were bound for another country, ripped from my mother and now ripped from my homeland.

We walked for the longest while, my cousin's hand in my back leading me onward. Was he leading me back to my mother? When I tired, he carried me on his shoulder. At one point we hitched a ride on the back of a cart that was rolling along the back roads; my cousin pulled a crust of challah bread out of his pocket and I nibbled at it, never wanting it to end. Eventually a port rose up ahead of us, the dockworkers like ants in the distance. I had never felt so small. At the dock itself, my cousin pulled me frantically through the crowds of people until he came to a group that parted for us and swallowed us in their cries and tears, their breath hot upon my face. But I was an icicle that nothing could warm.

The crowd started moving and my feet with it, though they barely seemed to touch the ground. I dug around in my pockets, empty but for a ball of soft red yarn – my grandmother must have put it there. I took the wool out of my pocket and knotted it to the railing, the metal so cold it bit my skin. The group of people slowly moved up the gangplank, their feet shuffling as one. Someone held me by the hand, moving me forward to who knew where. Crates and trunks bobbed above me, carried overhead. We were all of us so much baggage, flotsam and jetsam tossed up by a human wave. Yet the ball of yarn remained, unravelling in my hands. Sometimes it hit a snag, which a quick tug remedied, the wool creating a warm friction in my hands, spindling out like a thin taper of flame. The ball's red heart grew smaller as we shuffled on. A huge foghorn sounded and someone let out a cry beside me; an engine roared and the metal groaned, jarring my bones. We were off. The ball of thread dwindled in my tight-clasped fingers until all I held was one solitary thread and then at once, like the whoosh of a blown candle, it slipped from my fingers and was gone.

A pair of hands grasped me under the armpits and lifted me atop the trunks and perched me there for safekeeping while stranger jostled with stranger, searching for a little patch of ship to call their own. From that height I felt the world was a dizzy mess. I did not belong. I never would.

Lily repeated my name over and over, a weird chant as vertigo took a hold of my limbs. As if cast adrift, the room pitched. My body had no anchor. I felt Lily's hands tug at me and hold me down. I threw my arms around her and felt the flesh beneath the fabric of her dress, her body warm and real in my arms as she leaned into me, tethering me to the earth.

EIGHTEEN

Billy

Miss du Maurier was standing on a chair fixing paper streamers to the doorframes, swags of coloured crepe paper, a pastel waterfall. Of course I offered to hold the chair for her, the pleasure was all mine, for with every reach upwards she showed me the well-preserved shape of her legs, dancer's pins in remarkably fine form even for her vintage.

'Would you hand me the tinsel?' she asked and I became her lackey, though all in my own interests. This party she had insisted upon was surely a fine opportunity for me to step closer to my aim.

'Have you worked out what you are wearing, Mr Little? Do remember it is a costume party, no civilian clothes allowed!' She was as excited as a little girl. She stepped down from the chair, a fountain of gold tinsel in her arms.

'Like what?' I asked. Whenever I wore a uniform I felt like a clown, ready for the pratfall.

'Something literary would be good. Lancelot or Hamlet? You are handsome enough with your blond hair and blue eyes,' she said.

Handsome? Was she flirting with me? It was hard to suppress the guffaw at the back of my throat, which came spluttering out in a cough that I covered with the back of my hand. Miss du Maurier was obviously not impressed by my lack of interest in her suggestions and went back to dressing the mirror frame. It was a foolish individual that turned her back on me. My reflection was handsome? Perhaps to some, but all I could see was my white-hot desire to get what I wanted. Ah, Miss du Maurier was harmless enough, but my father, in turning away from me so neglectfully, had exposed his back to me – what else could I do but stick in the knife?

After my father's visit I watched Crisp closely all day, waiting for his guard to drop, for his tell, his twitch, the sign that he had somehow orchestrated my father's visit. But there was nothing, not even a flare of a nostril or a knowing glance. Merle dispensed as usual, a wisp of hair escaping from her bun, softening her face. Perhaps she knew? Yet there were no snickering glances between father and daughter.

A strand of hair hung over Merle's eye; I suspected a signal, some code as I waited for her to tuck the strand behind the whorl of her ear. But she left it alone, making no attempt to blow it away. It drove me to distraction, until I wanted to take the hair between my thumb and forefinger and do it myself.

I must have been staring for she turned those dark eyes upon me and smiled. And what a smile! At first in my paranoia I thought that too was a signal to her father, the proof of my duping, but the consulting room was closed and Crisp was nowhere to be seen. I looked over my shoulder to make sure she wasn't smiling at anyone else – it hadn't even occurred to me till now that she might have a beau – but there was no one there, unless she had a penchant for smiling at ghosts. No, that smile was directed at me, a smile so full and bright, it could have germinated a frozen seed! What wonders occurred on her face – the beakish nose softened, the myopic stare infused with intrigue – how could I not have noticed before? Merle was bordering on the beautiful. An acquired taste no doubt, but one that I could indeed acquire.

'Mr Little, would you pass me that jar?' she asked, her teeth grazing her bottom lip, as practised as a French coquette. I could have pinched her tender cheeks.

I leaned up to the jar, straining to reach it, but Merle did not step back. She stood so close I could smell the rosewater she had splashed under her armpits. I got the jar down, but before I could hand it to her, her hand was already overlapping mine as if she was greedy to touch me. I tried to step back but the cabinet was in my way and I had nowhere to go. My ears were pricked for Crisp's unexpected footstep. She stepped into my arms as if there was space cut out exactly for her and wrapped her whole hands around the jar before taking it into her clasp. She looked briefly up at me from under her lashes, a faint glimmer of moisture on her lip. From beneath the counter she pulled out a blue tincture bottle and loosened the lid: the faint sweetish smell of opium cloaked my nostrils. She let several drops fall into the elixir bottles. The label was hand-printed with Gothic script: *Tincture of Sleep*, as if inside was the very essence of closed lids, the soar and swoop of dreams.

This was the very thing my father needed to shut his trap! It was what he had sought all his life: why couldn't he have it, the pitiable bastard? It would cure him of me, surely; I who, in his own words, had turned his luck. Why else the pipe of delirium at Golden Fortune's father's opium den? Perhaps this was the very thing he needed now. It is a very hard thing for a son to learn that he is his father's disease.

Merle carried the bottles out into the storeroom. It was now or never – the moment her foot was swallowed by the green curtain, I swiped the small blue bottle and shoved it into my pocket. Merle came back, a bouquet of bottles in her grasp, and looked for a place to plant them on the counter, where the tincture had been moments before. I rushed to her aid and the concealment of my theft, and cupped my hands under the bottles. She had so many, a baker's dozen, that there would have been no way to put them on the counter without some skittling away. As I secured the glass, tricksy in my fingers, I overreached and found my fingers touching her breasts. She seemed as surprised as I, and for a moment we stood suspended, our arms full of empty bottles, an embrace brittle and as sharp as the glass between us. I could feel her nipple with my thumb, the slight rigidity of it beneath my touch. Was it my fault I had to feel it further? The bottles only had one place to go as she stepped back. They fell with such a spectacular smash, glittering shards a carpet for our feet, the greenish light from the curtains making them look like precious stones.

Now the bottles had been dispensed with in more ways than one, a vacuum was created between us. With my breath she was sucked right into me, her lips pressing into mine like a hungry fish, her tongue darting in and out of my mouth, an eel in sea coral, enticing my own tongue into her mouth. Where had she learned to kiss like that? I'd initially thought Merle have a heart like a shard of ice, a cool little suffragette who kissed the pictures of Emmeline Pankhurst before sleep, her toes frigid in damp winter sheets. But here she was, a firework, her tongue catherine-wheeling in my mouth, inciting a riot in my trousers. She wanted it as much as I did, and I hadn't even sought it, she had come to me – my powers of persuasion were more than Crisp realised.

I led her to her father's consulting room: the zebra rug looked like the perfect place to fall upon my prey. I was excited to think of her naked limbs stretched on the stripes, but Merle would have none of it. She tugged at my arm.

'What about your place?' she breathed hot in my ear. Usually I would have said no, but Merle's fingers danced across my skin and loosened my shirt tails. The Tincture of Sleep, which rolled in my pocket, would take care of my father.

We walked down Elizabeth Street, Merle cleaving to me, making it hard to walk without losing my balance, a ship with one mast tilted perilously close to the footpath. If people stopped and stared at Merle on heat, I didn't notice. I just wanted to get her home before the flame of her went out.

We walked through the backyard; a whirl of grimy washing was drying on the line. The outhouse door was closed, a pair of muddy boots visible beneath. I held her close up the stairs to our door. I had no need of a key. I just pushed and the door opened, and I led her inside. My father was sitting in his armchair, one we had dragged from the side of the street, the springs already bursting free beneath it, the arms threadbare, the seat worn. His head was lolling onto his chest. Merle paused as she surveyed my father, who embarrassed me with his dribble staining his collar, his gaping mouth, his nose a red cherry from the drink. The opium had been kinder to him. Now he was just a sad drunk. I pulled at Merle's hand, eager to get her into my room before she could change her mind.

Merle's breath was hot on my neck as I led her through to my excuse of a room, a balcony closed in with old wooden crates on both sides, a mattress on the floor. My clothes, such as they were, hung pitifully on the hook at one end of the balcony. Merle peeled off her coat and her blouse in one. I hadn't noticed her buttons had been undone, had she been undoing them all the way here? She slid out of her skirt and hung her discarded garments on the peg with mine, our clothes all over each other even before we were. She was the first girl I had brought back here; the others I had pursued and taken wherever I could.

She pulled off her shoes and sat on my lowly bed, her fingers drumming expectantly on the bare flesh of her knee. I slipped out with a quick excuse and an even quicker promise of a return. The bottle of Tincture of Sleep burned in my pocket. My father's breath was already shallow when I approached him, his eyelids barely fluttering. The half-empty bottle of Crisp's elixir sat in his lap, hardly a glowing advertisement, that was for sure. From piss it came, to piss it will return. I took the Tincture of Sleep and measured a good spill into the bottle. My father stirred in his sleep and an unexpected pity welled up in my chest: the poor bastard blaming me for his lack of luck when with one look at him anyone could tell he had never made any of his own, and never would.

'Is that you, Bill?' he mumbled.

'Yes, Dad, drink up, will you.' I guided his hand, feeling the tenderness, of a mother towards her child. There was a trail of dribble running from the corner of his mouth: I resisted the urge to wipe it away.

Miss du Maurier turned back to me, a sprig of tinsel caught in her hair. 'Do you know what Lily and Ari are coming as? In all the preparations I have forgotten to ask,' she piped up, her voice grating in my ears.

The gold and silver tinsel jarred against the arterial-red walls, and I thought suddenly of shrapnel burning into flesh. A sulphurous stench invaded my nostrils, making me want to gag. A poisonous taste bitter in my mouth. The old wound in my leg made itself known to me, turning itself inside out under my skin.

'For myself, I may come as a shepherdess, what do you think, Mr Little, am I too old to pull it off? Or maybe I could wear my apron and come as Bertha Mason from *Jane Eyre*.'

'Who?' I gasped. All I wanted was an end to the incessant noise that echoed through my ears.

'The madwoman in the attic,' she blathered on. 'Rochester's wife, the one who burns the house down and blinds him. The one bent on a perfect act of vengeance.'

Steadying myself against the wall, I felt the pain begin to ebb. Suddenly she seemed to be speaking a kind of sense. This was a game I would play to my own gain.

'Miss du Maurier, I shall need your assistance.' She blushed at my request. What if I could become the thing I wanted to wreak havoc upon, if I could inhabit my enemy's skin to show Lily just what she was sidling up to? It was what cannibals did: eat their enemies to cancel them out. Mine would be a metaphoric consumption: I would become the thing I hated, and satisfy my prodigious hunger. My words would become flesh.

NINETEEN

Lily

Spread over my bed was the sunset-pink dress Miss du Maurier had left for me to wear. 'Why let it be food for moths?' she had said. It felt as fragile as a dried petal, the fabric crackling under my fingers as I pulled it over my head. A shiver ran across my bare shoulders. The nape of my neck still felt strangely exposed, as if a cool hand were running across my burning skin.

On the train, in flight, I had taken a pair of nail scissors and fed the long strands to the metallic teeth, glad to be free of the weight of my hair. My face hovered in the glass, as the landscape unreeled like a banner, each mile freeing me, taking me further from home.

I tugged the suitcase out from under the bed and peeled back the loose lining. My fingers riffled through the fabric till I felt it – the slippery, silky threads of my own hair, which had once brushed the scars on my back. The plait was as long as my forearm: if it had been a tree each inch would have told the story of a year. I gathered some string and some pins and fixed it to the back of my head. As my plait fell over my shoulder, tickling my neck, all the memories of home came with it. Things I had thought tucked away, safe in my suitcase. My father's voice muted, as he rumpled dry my newly washed hair, the soft cloak of a towel cupping my ears.

'Aengus was beautiful and fair. He was the god of love who lived by the river in a valley in Boyne. Four little birds flew about his head, a feathered halo, each set of wings flapping so fast they were like an x for a kiss. Four little birds, four little kisses. One night he had a dream of a girl who stood at the end of his bed, but as he reached for her she vanished. From that day onward he could not eat or sleep. He searched for her for a year till he came to a lake where he saw maidens in the distance, each wearing a silver chain, except for the girl from his dreams, who stood a head taller, her hair dressed with golden bells, a gold chain around her neck. She was no ordinary girl, she was Caer Ibormeith, named for the Yew. She could disguise herself as a swan by means of the swan-down cloak she wore. As Aengus neared the water, a drift of swans floated by, without a maiden to be seen. He called her by her name. She glided to him and as he reached to embrace her, his arms turned to wings, and their long white necks intertwined. All the mortals who heard their singing lapsed into sleep for three days and three nights ...'

I wished I could stay in the drowsy spell of my memory, my father's voice disappearing as the noise rose from downstairs. Miss du Maurier laughed, too loudly, as if she had taken a swig of Dutch courage from the decanter while preparing the punch. My father's voice faded away. I looked in the mirror at my costume. Who was I supposed to be? Who were those people downstairs? Tiredness pulled at my limbs and I longed to climb into bed, to let a deep dreamless sleep claim me.

'Lily!' Miss du Maurier piped up the stairs. I stepped out the door, preparing excuses to escape the party. Just then I saw Ari coming down the attic ladder, his shaggy legs taking one step at a time backwards down the rungs. On his head were two little horns. Miss du Maurier had dressed him as a faun, but instead of going bare-chested he had left his shirt on. His eye caught mine, both of us uncomfortable reflections of each other, neither knowing what to say: a gasp would have been more satisfying than the silence. A feather of anxiety tickled in my gut.

'Your hair has grown,' Ari said at last. 'Miraculous!'

'Not like your horns,' I said. 'Diabolical!'

The laughter popped out of us, bursting into the hallway, until I felt squeezed of all air. We looked foolish and we knew it and we didn't care. Instead, we seemed closer; the walls of the hallway had narrowed, our breaths merging as we gathered ourselves. One of Ari's horns sagged to the side, a waning crescent moon. I itched to reach and straighten it, to see him as he should be, but the weight of my plait made me nervously finger the pins. All of a sudden I felt I would be naked if it fell, a lifeless rope, to the floor. How would I ever manage to stand on a stage in the altogether when the fear of losing a plait made me feel exposed? Whatever possessed me to think it – the sea air had addled my brain. In the end I could no longer resist: I reached across and pushed the horn back up onto his head, my finger catching in a spiral of his hair.

A door slammed behind us and the frames hanging from the picture rail danced. The hairs on the back of my neck stood to attention. Ari's features froze mid-laughter, his smile slowly dissolving into a grimace. I didn't want to turn around.

'Have you started the party without me? Tut, tut.'

I would have known that silken voice anywhere. Billy. I turned to look at him. His voice may have been recognisable but the rest of him was not. What was he dressed as? In the middle of his face was a huge nose made of theatrical wax. I had seen the makeup kit in Miss du Maurier's trunk. Billy's new nose was large and hooked. He had coloured in his fair eyebrows with a dark pencil. His wheat-blond hair had vanished beneath a long oily black wig. Hanging off his chin was a beard of biblical proportions, and he wore a crushed suit, the edges frayed.

'Well, I can see what you are, my boy, you are obviously a devil. But can either of you guess who I am? Can you? Go on, take a stab at it. You know you want to. Any ideas, any clues? Is the nose too much, do you think? If you prick me, do I not bleed? A touch of the Shylock but not quite so noble, I'm afraid. Still no idea? Shall I give you a clue?'

Whatever Billy thought he was, it was obviously a grotesque attempt to make Ari a victim of his spite. Was it some sort of perverse attempt to impress me?

'Haven't guessed it yet, friends?' he said the word *friends* as if it was sour. I looked at Ari, a frown carved into his face.

'I am that great wandering creation, the one who would not help Christ when he passed by, the greatest of all usurers, that circumcised originator wrapped up in a familiar nineteenth-century package. No idea yet? But surely you have both read your classics? I am that mind-controlling fiend, Svengali!'

Billy handed me a red velvet box, the one I had seen on Miss du Maurier's dresser when she had transformed her wedding dress into my costume. I had been curious as to what it contained but hadn't wanted to pry. I opened the lid and my stomach wheeled. Inside was a necklace, shimmering captured rainbows, four little hummingbird heads mounted in gold. Four little birds like kisses. I snapped the lid shut.

persuasion from me. When we left the room, she was purring like a cat, and my father was deep asleep, his snores barely puckering the air. Of course, back at the shop, one of us went ahead of the other. I was not foolish enough to flaunt my business with his daughter right under Crisp's nose: I still needed to learn his secret. Though as the days passed the chance of that seemed to recede from me like the outgoing tide.

I spent hours observing Crisp and fulfilling his tasks, cleaning bottles, standing next to Merle with invisible prescriptions, doling out the fragrant sprigs of herbs, hoping to catch Crisp's fleeting secret – while the night became mine. With a bottle of elixir spiked with Tincture of Sleep, my father cavorted with the clouds, while I unwound Merle's dark bun, a whirlpool that spilled all down the milk of her shoulders, and I dissolved her into me until the sunlight splashed over us.

Until the Day of my Judgement. I arrived at the shop, but there was a *To Let* sign swinging inside one of the windows. How could they have skipped town without me noticing? I peered in the glass, cupping my hands for a better view: nothing inside had been removed. I was frantic. Why hadn't Merle said anything? It wasn't as if she'd had no opportunity, with her teeth on my earlobe, her tongue down my throat. Had I been so close to understanding the mind-control mechanism but missed it? Had these weeks of subservience been nothing but a ritual humiliation by Crisp, an outlet for Merle's lasciviousness? I panicked, but perhaps that was what he had wanted all along. With Crisp the world was a test within a test. In my frustration, I pounded again on the door. There was no answer; my chances of being my own man were evaporating as the silence swelled in my ears. Then I walked around the back.

There I found Crisp and Merle with their belongings piled high in a cart. Crisp glowered down at me as if I had caused this exodus.

'Get in the cart, boy,' he growled.

TWENTY

Billy

The Jew's expression was more of a reward than I could have expected: like an egg thrown hard on a wall, his features were on the downward slide. But it was not his face I cared about. I looked to Lily, but she had her modest gaze cast aside. Whatever she was thinking or feeling, she kept it as veiled as a bride. Had she not wondered who she was, my little songbird? My Lily of the Valley, my dove, there is no spot in thee. She would know when I told her.

But she was an inventive squirrel, wasn't she? It was one thing to plant the seed in Miss du Maurier's head that we were coming as a pair, but my little well in the desert had added her own little flair, her touch of *je ne sais quoi*. Where had it been when I had shuffled through her things? She had kept it up her sleeve, a surprise for me, my little card sharp. Her beautiful long Rapunzel plait, a tail of rippling mercury. Oh, she was as slippery as the underside of a silver salmon. She was the soft mist that divided this world and the next; she almost made me believe I could put my hand through that waterfall and contact the dead. Perhaps with her trust I could make her believe it too. She could be transformed, just as Merle was transformed by my baptism.

Merle was the most accomplished virgin I had ever encountered, an eager sacrifice, offering herself up on my altar without

I hesitated; the spittle on his lip was like foam. Merle sat beside her father and would not meet my eye.

'Why should I?' I called, brazen as brass. I may have been his apprentice, but I was no idiot, I didn't need a keeper to instruct me like some dumb animal. The butcher from next door came out to the back step, his striped apron a bloody mess. He cupped his hand against the draught to light his cigarette and puffed slowly, observing us as if we were his own private circus.

'We are taking the miraculous and proven, the one and the only Cuthbert Crisp's Elixir du Jour to the masses on the high and holy road!' His voice echoed off the backs of the nearby buildings and craphouses, ringing like the crack of doom. If there was an audience, he had to be the whole bloody show. He reached out his hand to help me up. I thought of all my treasures, back in the flat my father and I shared. They were in an old box – the one my father said I arrived in, on his doorstep, the blanket long gone – my precious things covered with a pair of old trousers I had outgrown. I took Crisp's hand and was sure then that my treasures would be safe. Little did I know that I would soon be parted from them both – my box with its price above rubies, and my sodden father – for good.

Crisp hauled me up into the cart, his nails digging into the veins in my wrist. I saw the butcher grind the stub of his cigarette into the road with his heel, but still he watched every movement of our lips. Crisp pulled me closer, my ear perilously close to his rank mouth, my balance precarious. He was about to say something, but the butcher's eyes still followed us. Crisp gestured me to the back of the cart, a small space beyond the jumble of belongings, though there was room for me up front. It suited him to subjugate me so, a chattel. Had I thought I could squeeze between him and his precious daughter? Oh, no: I was just the boy in the back. My hand accidentally brushed the swathe of Merle's hair as I climbed past, but she didn't even give me the satisfaction of a twitch.

The road roared beneath the wheels, the dirt flew up in my face. We passed the ordinary Joes who had to toil for a living – a crapper straining under the weight of somebody else's shit; the iceman with his pick in a piece of igloo; some poor bastard sweeping up a poster onto a billboard, a glob of glue falling downwards like God hadn't bothered to use a handkerchief – all the poor bastards who never had enough imagination to put their faith in something else, to earn their bread without breaking their backs.

Merle sat stony-faced next to her father up front, not even turning her head to check I hadn't fallen off, not even a smile when her father looked the other way. There was only a small square for my arse, my legs hanging over the edge, the dirt and gravel running like a stream between my feet as I watched the city recede. Crisp kept up a blistering pace, the poor horse feeling the hot sear of a whip upon its back more for effect than purpose, for the animal could go no faster. When we slowed, caught behind some slower traveller, I turned and hoped Merle would look at me, but all I could see were her spidery fingers, saluting the incessant flies.

The Great Western Highway grew quieter; the buildings either side dribbled away and the sun was a well-aimed insult at my head. The rocking of the cart was a giant cradle and my eyes drooped, though I didn't dare sleep lest I fall off and be forgotten entirely. The sun wheeled further over the horizon, glaring into my face like the angry eye of the Lord, then it slipped beyond the lip of sky and was gone, a hush of dusky light descending. I was parched. Gum trees lined the road, fields lying fallow behind them. A star winked at me. The cart halted suddenly, and if it hadn't been for a large box of Crisp's sour Elixir du Jour wedging me in, I would have found my arse scraping along the road.

We had arrived at a pub in the middle of nowhere. I jumped off the cart, the hot rub of a blister forming on my left buttock, a powder of dust masking my face. Merle had already gone inside, her skirt swishing through the dirt, a halo of flies following her. Crisp waited for me and reluctantly offered me a drink from his canteen, the water like velvet in my mouth. We stood there a long time. The road had left a toll on him as well, a red stripe of sunburn down his nose. Did he expect me to go in and follow Merle, or help him unload the cart? The muscles in my legs wanted nothing more than to melt in a hot bath. But Crisp just stood there, his eyes boring into me like insects.

'Is there a problem, Doctor Crisp?' My legs ached and I longed to take a piss. I didn't want to play this game with him one moment longer.

Crisp's eyes narrowed and suddenly, a whip lashing from nowhere, he slapped me. Tears sprang to the drought of my face.

'My daughter is pregnant with your child.'

The words were so unexpected that I was almost at a loss as to what to say. 'No, no, not me, sir! I shoot blanks.' It was worth a try.

Crisp struck me again and I tumbled backwards, blood trickling through the dust on my face and spotting the ground. He turned and walked away, leaving me to the flies.

I thought about making a run for it, but out there in the middle of the bush I would have been food for bunyips, a pincushion for snake fangs, a less than heroic end for William Little, lost like a prophet in the desert. Instead I took my rest with the horse in the stable, the gusts and eddies of hay-scented breath sweetly lulling me to sleep. The morning was a distant shore I would find myself wrecked upon soon enough – as father, husband, indentured slave? It was a wonder I didn't take the whip and hook it into a noose and end it there. But I prevailed, unlike my father.

Ah, my father. Away from my measured dose, I later learned, he became befuddled from the elixir and the opium-laced Tincture of Sleep, until he stumbled over the balcony, convinced his arms had turned to giant feathers. This I discovered only when our time on the road had come to its end, only after I had learned Crisp's secret, but then that bloody victory was far from sweet. It stuck in my gullet like a fish bone, fine as a hair, which I could neither see nor pull out. The experience with Merle was like Eve after the expulsion – all hairshirt, shame and deprivation – but Lily would be Paradise.

Lily ran her fingers down the wig of her own hair; already she was transmuted by my attentions. When she was mine, she'd grow it again, a lush drift of falling snow, and let it cover me.

Miss du Maurier's party was in full swing, filled with her old cronies crammed into the living room. Miss du Maurier, her shepherdess outfit barely reaching to her knees, had already abandoned her crook. Her bonnet ribbons trailed behind her as she went round the room, punch ladle brimming, making sure everyone had a full glass in their hands. There was not a face I recognised, but even if I had, they were all in disguise. There were several Pierrot clowns and Columbines, but most of them looked like escapees from the Rozelle Hospital for the mad, streamers and face paint, tinsel and cellophane fixed to their costumes with flushed faces.

'To magic,' Miss du Maurier cried, and raised her glass before downing it in one swallow. 'Don't you three look a picture!'

My Lily of the Valley, the Jew and I were still clumped together like refugees from the human race, none of us getting swept into the throng of guests.

'Let me see, we have Trilby here who will sing perfectly under Svengali's enchantment. But Ari dear, I am not sure how you fit in the picture? A faun from Arcadia?' Miss du Maurier said quizzically, looking at me in confusion. I had given her instructions, which she had followed to the letter, but she had not asked me for a rationale and I had not offered her one.

A dish smashed somewhere in the kitchen. The doorbell pealed. A gramophone was cranked and out spilled the silky threads of ragtime. The Jew shifted uneasily on his feet.

'What say you, boyo, give it to us from the horse's mouth, who are you dressed as?' I pressed, revelling in his vexation. If the Jew had looked any more uncomfortable he would have stepped out of his own skin. How could he know what he was when it was I who had planned the whole thing, right down to the last dazzling detail? He was a cloven-hoofed beast, being prepared for the knife.

The Jew sat down at the piano stool, leaving the two of us standing together, my dove and I, the hummingbird heads brimming with opalescence around her long white throat. Their colour only accentuated her lunar skin. I envisaged Lily cleaving closer to me, for she was still to laugh at my little joke. The perfume of her rose up through my nostrils and made me dizzy with desire. I leaned closer to her, but she moved away, her hand resting lightly on the top of the piano as his fingers brushed the keys. I wanted to tug on that silver snake of a plait and pull her away from the lure of his music, twine it around my fingers and reel her in to feel the press of her lips again on mine.

The Jew played softly, the notes barely piercing the noise of the party, and cursedly Lily tilted closer to him, turning the pages of the sheet music. The room was overly warm, and they seemed bound together by the notes he played, their faces made rosy in unison. Then, as Lily turned the next page, her hand faltered.

'I know this song,' was all she said.

The Jew paused and then began to play the melody. And Lily took her cue: her voice rang through the room, pure and rich, belonging not in heaven but here on earth.

'Oh, I see the great mountains
Oh, I see the lofty mountains
Oh I see the corries
I see the peaks under the mist
I see right away the place of my birth
I will be welcomed in a language which I understand
I will receive hospitality and love when I reach there
That I would not trade for tons of gold.'

Oh, I would be her mountain! I would speak a language she would understand! Could she be any more beautiful? I did not think so. Her face was like an angel's carved from marble, her eyes cast heavenward as she searched her memory for the next line, her mouth a perfect little coral 'o'. Let me hear your voice, for your voice is sweet:

'That I would not trade for ... tons of gold...'

Her lip quivered. It seemed she was searching her memory for the next line but it would not come. The Jew slowed his playing to match her, and the notes seemed to hover in the air.

'That I would not trade ... for tons of gold...'

The noisy room had trickled slowly to silence, guests turning to look at her, my Lily-at-a-loss-for-words. Oh, I could have given her words to sing, like a ventriloquist's doll she would speak at my direction. A tear swelled in the curve of her eye, but it did not fall. However, her plait did; it fell from her shoulder to the piano keys, fluid as an eel, stopping his dancing fingers. I was glad. Why should he be the one to command the room, and her attention? He would not be her Pied Piper, I would. But before I could step in and be her comfort, she was off like a flickering moth through the dimly lit room, her foot swift upon the stairs, just the rustle of her ancient skirt behind her and she was gone.

The Jew sat there with the trophy in his fingers, looking at me as if somehow it was all my fault – her forgetfulness, her falling tresses, her flight. That look said it all. He suspected; he knew something. Yet he had had but a glimpse of it. He was going to be the Abel to my Cain.

TWENTY-ONE

Ari

I had worn the costume because I had thought Miss du Maurier had organised it. If I had known Billy Little had had a hand in it, I would never have put it on. I only stayed at the party to be with Lily. Yet when her hair fell into my fingers, the long cool silk cord of it, she was gone before I could fully comprehend what had happened.

I hadn't noticed how the room had filled up. As my fingers touched the ivory, as the hammer hit the wire, it threw out a net of notes to capture an audience. But when Lily sang, it was otherworldly and strange as the music from King David's harp that could play all on its own. Until she faltered and the listeners grew restless, then the song, elusive as a butterfly, was gone. It was *kol isha* to hear a woman sing, a type of nakedness, but I had heard her voice and felt it work upon me like a salve.

After Lily's flight, Miss du Maurier cranked the handle of the gramophone, the tinny notes spilled out and the party came back to life. I wanted to go after her, but Mr Little stood at the end of the piano like a bookend, hemming me in. The plaster holding his travesty of a nose in place was coming adrift. I wanted to squash that wax into his face and rub the darkened eyebrows from his forehead. What was he trying to prove, coming dressed like that? Was it a warning, a threat, or mere mockery? He leaned forward, fencing me in even further. I stood up, pushing the piano stool back with my legs.

'I'll take that,' Little said, his hand reaching to snatch the plait from me, but I had the advantage of height. 'Come, come, hand it over, my boy, no need to be childish about it.' Childish? He was the one trying to pluck it from me, like a schoolboy in a playground squabble.

'Don't worry, I'll return it to her,' I said, heading for the stairs, but he came and stood in my path.

'Come, tell me what's bothering you. Don't you like my costume? You can't find a piece of literature offensive, my boy, it is all just pretend. You know the difference between fact and fiction by now, don't you?'

I could feel the anger uncoil from my belly, slowly, like a snake from the shade. 'No, I don't find literature offensive. The only thing I find offensive, Mr Little, is you.' I pushed past him, my arm clipping his shoulder. He made a final lunge for Lily's plait, but he missed. As I walked away I could feel the anger spit out of him behind me, expletives hissing like oil in a hot pan.

At the top of the stairs was Miss du Maurier's costume trunk. I pulled off the headpiece and shoved it in, horns and all. The lid fell and nipped my fingers, but I was only too glad to be rid of the foolish costume, and the party.

The dark inside a trunk is different to all others: the last sliver of light, the pressure of the lid above, and then the abyss of the living tomb. At night at sea, while my mother's cousins slept on their bunks, I would sleep in a trunk atop a pile of stranger's clothes, the lid rigged so it would not fall down and smother me. Sometimes if one of the crew came down, I was whisked into the trunk, bundled in roughly as a foot creaked upon the stair. I would be able to make out only the strip of light, the cross-section of someone's trousers, a grease stain, the thumb of a disembodied hand. They had not had enough money for my passage; sending someone to find me had drained their meagre finances. I was a stowaway, a little Jonah in the belly of the whale. All I longed for was the ground beneath my feet, fresh air in my face, something green for my eyes to rest on. To my sea-struck mind, it was the flood all over again: I felt like Noah trapped in the ever-rising waters, no land in sight. The waves scared me, black obsidian, constantly moving, ceaseless in their roaring.

At night, rocked by a soft sea, I could hear them talking through the crack of the lid that had been propped open. 'The boy looks like her, doesn't he?' my cousin said. I squeezed my eyes closed and pretended I was asleep.

'Hephzibah will have the son she wanted then. Flesh of her flesh.'

'What is that supposed to mean? Zipporah is not related by blood to Hephzibah's family. Only through marriage to Israel ...' My mother's name was a bright little spark in the overwhelming gloom, one little word, a window. I would have given anything to be able to open it and find her.

'That is not what the sparrows told me.' I struggled to understand. Sparrows speaking? Could they?

'Well, Zipporah was very friendly with Hephzibah's brother.'

'Where did you hear that?'

'The sparrows.'

'The sparrows do a lot of talking, especially when they are supposed to migrate for the winter,' another muffled voice added. The air seemed to fizzle around me.

'Well, you should listen to them. You might hear a thing or two.'

'What happened to him, Hephzibah's brother?' The voice was full of curiosity.

'Isaiah was a newly trained scribe. He was friends with Israel, I hear, they had spent some time together at yeshiva.' The tangle of names, the threads of our family, were all twisted together like a challah bread.

'What happened? Why didn't he make good his promise? Why is the boy marked with that writing?'

The questions peppered the air but the ship's pitch and toss had claimed me; my eyelids were pressed together by the salt of my tears. I drowned in sleep and the trunk closed over me sometime in the night, a black thud.

The loud slam of the trunk snapping shut on my poor excuse for a costume must have disturbed Lily, for her door opened a crack and her tear-stained eye peered through to see who it was, before she opened the door wide to me. I held out the peace offering of her own hair. She reached for it tentatively, and then threw it onto the bed. The petal-coloured dress was abandoned on the bed too, the only colourful thing in her white room, that and the red splashes of frustration on her cheeks. She was dressed in a plain white shirt and her now-familiar trousers.

'I looked like an idiot,' she sobbed, tears falling, her nose running. A new wave of embarrassed blushes shot up her neck to join the ones in her cheeks as she wiped her face with the back of her hand. 'The words dried up in my mind.'

'No one noticed. Well, not much.'

She snorted, the incredulous beginnings of a laugh and the last remnants of her tears. Her whole face seemed to shimmer, painted pink, the tears like a glaze – she was as beautiful as a pearl. I took her face in my hands and wiped it slowly with my handkerchief. Her cloudy eyes stopped shifting and fixed on mine, her lower lip pinned by her teeth. My thumb grazed her lip, and it was soft as kid. A kiss – the possibility of it hung between us like a question mark. But the moment vanished as footsteps loudly passed the door and down the hall. With the slam of a door my hand fell away.

She stepped out into the hallway and I thought she had fled again, that I had already gone too far, offending her, my hand trespassing on her face. But she was calling to me and when I went to look she was pulling the trunk towards her room for all she was worth, the rope handles burning at the tender flesh of her palms. I didn't ask why, but took it from her and pulled, the feet of the trunk scraping the wooden floor, two black tracks left in its wake.

TWENTY-TWO

Lily

I felt my whole heartbeat fill the trunk.

Ari clapped three times and I pushed the lid and rose up, but clumsily, so before I could even get out the lid clanked down on me and shut me in. I had not been quick enough to brace it with my hands; how would I ever be quick enough? I pushed up the lid again and stood, a weird swan emerging from a battered wooden egg. Ari stood with his eyes glued to his watch.

'Forty seconds and counting,' he smiled, but I knew it was too long.

'Shall we try again?'

I crouched down again: if Bess Houdini could do it, so could I. With the lid down a second time it was stifling. The darkness grew and the sides of the trunk leaned closer somehow, the space seemed smaller. My face grew hot; my own breath turned the still air into a furnace, and I felt tears well at the familiar musty smell of old clothes.

After my father died I retreated to my parents' cupboard to avoid my mother. Tucked amidst his clothes, I felt close to him, the smell of his aftershave still lingering on the collar of his good suit.

While hiding in the cupboard one day I found a strange album filled with photographs of girls and women just like me, all of them as pale as I am, albinos each and every one. I pulled it out and listened for my mother, but I could only hear my own heartbeat. The girls in the photographs were posed on chairs, the frills of their dresses rippling down to the floor, corsets holding them in tight. They were made so thin I thought their bones would crack like wishbones. From each portrait a girl stared unsmilingly over my shoulder at something I couldn't see. Below each of the strangely eerie photographs were their names, *Astor Saint Clements, Daisy Sinclair, Xanthe Fitzroy* – each claimed to follow the tradition of Unzie the Great, the great white Aboriginal Albino, mind-readers every one.

'What are you doing, Matilda? Get out, get out at once,' my mother screamed, whiskey on her breath as she reached to pull at my ankle. I tried to draw my knees up further into the cupboard, dropping the album at her feet, but I was not quick enough. She pounced on it.

'What are you doing with that? You are not to have that! Who said you could touch things that don't belong to you?'

'Who are they, Ma? They look just like me. Are they relations?' At this she went quiet for a bit, then she sat on the edge of the bed, her fingers toying with the corners of the album, not daring to open it.

'Not likely. Your father bought me that at the carnival before we were married. He took me to see the Three Moon Maidens, who sat on the stage, their arms linked like they were doing the Pride of Erin.' Her voice caught in her throat and became hard to hear.

'What did they do?'

'They made predictions in otherworldly voices. We should never have gone, they were charlatans and it is blasphemy what they said.'

'But what did they say?' I pressed. Desperate to hear, I scooted out of the safety of the cupboard to listen.

'To your father they said he would work with words, which he laughed at of course, for he had just started at the local paper.'

'But what about you, Ma, what did they say to you?' Her look was steely then as she placed the album face-down on the bed as if it offended the Lord, but she would not speak.

'Ma, what did they say?' She pulled the rosary out of her pocket and fingered the beads, mouthing a row of Hail Marys.

'Ma?'

'That I should expect one like them,' she whispered as she lay the beads aside. I did not see her retrieve her stick from beneath the bed, I should have been quick enough, I should have known by then.

'I was expecting you before we were married and you were marked by my sin.'

Each stroke of it upon my back made me wince and writhe, but I would not cry out. I steeled myself inside the pain, each strike branding my skin with a bloody welt.

'Ready?' Ari's muted voice came from above. 'One, two, three!' He was counting words, not blows. I flipped the lid and sprang out: a jack-in-the-box could have done no better. But within three seconds the Houdinis would have first got out of a bag tied with rope, then out of a padlocked trunk *and* have swapped places too. *Three seconds*: Houdini had the power to make time elastic.

'Five seconds,' Ari said. He held out his hand to help me from the trunk, the touch of his skin on mine full of static. Surely he was going to lean closer; I felt the invisible hand on my back push me forward, the fingers of desire playing me like a harp.

'The hinge at the back needs altering, I think. There is a hammer in the shed, won't be a minute,' he said as left the room. I wasn't sure what he was meant to be dressed as – Pan, a faun? – but without the horns he reminded me, in his shaggy pants, of a cygnet, brown down to his feet.

Did Ari not kiss me because I was not of his faith? I thought about Harry and Bess and how they became the Houdinis. He was the son of a rabbi; she was the daughter of a woman who said the rosary every hour. Yet still they had found a third place, a place of their own.

When I was walking back from the theatre the night before last, a man was selling books on the side of the road, each coloured spine looking like a jewel on the blanket he had laid out along the shopfronts. The first book I picked up, red as a heart, sent a prickle of recognition up my neck. It was the biography of Houdini, based on the recollections of his wife Bess. Carefully I flicked through the pages, feeling as though there was a message between the lines just for me, admiring the gloss on their handsome faces in the photographs. According to the book, Bess and Harry met in three different ways and were three times married. Thrice like a fairy tale. Three times a charm. I was curious to read on and find out more, but could see from his stare that the bookseller, huffing impatiently with each page I turned, didn't want me to linger. Another passer-by stopped, picked up a book and drew the bookseller into conversation, which lent me the time to read on, uninterrupted.

In the first account of their meeting Harry was performing a magic show with his brother. Bess was there in the front row with her religious mother who, like my own, was deeply suspicious of anything magical lest it offend the Lord. In some twist of a bottle, acid spilled over the stage and onto Bess's dress, sizzling a keyhole in her skirt. Her mother indignantly swept her daughter out of the theatre, frightened that she would be burned up like a saint. A little accident. That could have been the end of it, but Harry had noticed her sitting beyond the glow of the footlights and he didn't give up that easily. He tracked down her address and appeared at the front door, begging for the ruined dress and a chance to redeem himself. Bess's mother reluctantly handed it over, not sure if she should, wondering if she should say the Lord's Prayer first in case he used it for strange rituals.

Harry's mother took a needle and a piece of fabric and a skein of thread and – *abracadabra* – she had made a new dress, even better than the old one, to the exact petite measurements of Miss Bess. And again, as in a puff of smoke, Harry appeared at Bess's door and would be not turned away by her Jesus-fearing mother until he saw that it fit snug as a glove on her doll-like limbs. When he saw her in his mother's hand-stitched dress, Harry asked her to step out, but did she dare? Her mother lay like a dragon across the threshold. 'Your mother wouldn't stop you if we were married,' he said. She took his hand and they ran down the stairs, their feet barely touching the ground, not stopping until Coney Island.

In the second account of their meeting, Harry and Bess were both in acts at Coney Island's sideshow alley. Bess, filled to the brim with the temptation of elsewhere, picked up her skirts and ran away from home to become part of the Floral Sisters song and dance act, singing their famous song 'Rosabelle'. Harry and his brother's act was after hers. Harry had the nightly study of her feet upon the floorboards, the stark white light on her face as she warbled like a little dawn bird at the sun. His brother Dash had pointed her out to him as the girl he wanted to ask out, but their eyes crashed into each other as they crossed places, between the wings and the stage, the light and the dark, their paths intertwining, never to be parted.

In the third account their meeting happened by way of Dash. He had eyes for the other Floral sister, so had invited them to meet him and his brother, to take an evening walk upon the beach, each the other's chaperone. They shook hands and enjoyed the fresh air along the Coney Island boardwalk, their lungs used to three stuffy shows a day, drinking deep the ocean breeze. They were halfway along when they were approached by a man who taunted Houdini and his brother, calling them and their act a fake. Houdini offered the man a hundred dollars if he could reveal the secret of the box, of the Metamorphosis, but they never heard from him again. Instead an article appeared in the *Coney Island Clipper*:

> *The Bros. Houdini who have mystified the world by their mysterious box mystery, are no more and the team will hereafter be known as the Houdinis. Houdini's new partner is Miss Bessie, the petite soubrette.*

They had known each other less than two weeks.

I looked at the bookseller, still deep in conversation. A tram rattled past and sent a warm dusty breeze up the back of my legs, a welcome warmth on the cold street. I raced through the words; I wanted to know if his family had accepted her, an outsider. A man wolf-whistled across the road, but I did not look up. They were married first by a ringmaster on Coney Island, a justice of the peace. Bess's distressed Catholic mother sprinkled holy water every time she passed their wedding photo, even splashing it in their eyes when they came to visit. So Harry and Bess decided on a second wedding, a Catholic wedding to appease her. The invitations went out, but she would not attend, for her daughter had damned herself, cleaving to a Jew and a magician. So to balance the seesaw of their life together, they got married a third time, this time by a rabbi.

Bess's mother would not yield for twelve years, not until Bess was dangerously ill and called out for her. Harry went to get her, but her mother would not come, not until he camped on her doorstep for three days and nights. Bess was afraid that Harry's mother would react the same way, appalled that her beloved boy had married a Catholic, but she opened her arms and blessed the Lord for another daughter. Ari's uncle would never do the same to me.

'Are you going to buy that book or just read the print off it?' the bookseller asked, taking a deep puff of his cigarette. I looked at the price and put it gingerly back down on the blanket. If Bess could do it, curl up and confine herself, knowing she would spring forth reborn, so could I.

Ari knocked on my door before he entered and I felt my face grow hot as he sat down on the bed and pulled out the nails from the back wall of the trunk, yanking like a mad dentist until the rusty tooth came free. There needed to be enough hold to stop the back flapping free, but enough give for us to push it out and swap places. The light danced over the heads of the hummingbirds back in their box on the mantelpiece, the most colourful things in the room. I didn't want to think of Billy and his provocation.

'This time, we can try to swap, you go out and I go in.' Ari readied himself in front of the trunk and I crouched down in the darkness made hot again by my own breath. I tried to concentrate and listen to the spiel that had begun, counting for my cue, to burst forth out of the wooden egg, but I couldn't shake off the sensation of his thumb on my lip. It had sent prickles up my neck. We were like bees hovering around the flower of each other.

My first kiss had been a curse, like a plague mark upon my door: it felt as if everyone knew that I had been sullied. But when Billy kissed me, his lips were so full of wanting, it was a strange persuasion; as if his lips had offered mine an answer and mine had questioned back. His kiss had set off a craving in me.

Ari clapped three times and I pushed out the back of the trunk, trying to be quick and elegant all at once, but the lid was weighted wrongly and it collapsed back down, folding me away like one of Miss du Maurier's old unwanted dresses. I waited for Ari to lift the lid and help me out, but all was quiet. Then a soft winnowing of air blew my hair across my face, for Ari had leaned close to the lid, his breath coming in the escutcheon, blowing me the breath of life as if to the drowned.

TWENTY-THREE

Billy

Without my playthings the party was too quiet for me, even though the gramophone needle burned hot through the music. He had the plait, the key to an invitation into her room. I went up to my room, livid, and cupped my ear to the wall between us, wishing I had brought my empty glass so I could have used it to extend the powers of my hearing. But the more I listened the more the room on the other side grew quiet. The silence grew like a drone in my ears as if I'd grown deaf. I held my hand up to the wall and wished I had the power to reach through and extract her from the Jew's malediction. Such was Crisp's reach that Merle didn't even look at me when I said my vows, but cast her eyes downwards as if in thrall to his merest suggestion, as if in Crisp she was in the presence of the Lord.

Merle stood beside me in a bedraggled lace dress, a straggly patch of purple Paterson's curse in her hand. I looked at her belly and wondered, could my child really be in there? I could see no swelling curve, but perhaps it was too early to tell; her face was certainly wan. In front of us, the courthouse official wrote out the marriage certificate like an infant learning his letters, while I waited impatiently for Merle to catch my eye, the gold band that Crisp had made me buy loose on her finger. It had nearly erased my resources: all I had left were two pennies to keep each other company in my pocket, their jingling friction more conversation than Merle and I had had since we had set out on the road. Now that I had got Merle knocked up there was no way to get on the good side of Crisp; every side of him was sour. And his daughter, the mother of my child-to-be, had turned, as if she were Lot's wife, to a pillar of salt.

Every town we rolled into, Crisp would drum up business on the main street, standing upon the wagon, a fat wedge of the Holy Bible in his hands. He would make a commandment's worth of claims to the elixir's benefit, so help us all. My God, he even smiled at the audiences that gathered, their careworn faces lifting up to him, the Father of Benevolence, an angel of mercy, convincing the poor fools that with his elixir, and his elixir alone, they would be healed. In between Crisp's oratories, I was to toss my knives at a target and Merle to do a psychic turn. If only I had had the foresight to lure Crisp to my cross of hay bales, to show him the promise of an accidental blade, then what hand would Fate have dealt me next?

Even though we had crossed the bridal threshold, Merle and I were still not permitted to share a bed. Crisp had made it very clear that I had broken his trust by seducing his only daughter, and though we were now married, it was for her respectability only. To gain my marital rights, I would have to scrape my way back to his good graces by only the very best of behaviours. Why did I obey, stupid bastard that I was, what stardust had been blown into my eyes?

We went together, black-weeded undercover mourners, to gather what dirt we could. It was a sick preparation but a necessary one, for how else could Crisp have the spirits speak through Merle to the townsfolk? In the smaller towns we would sometimes come across graveyards with no new occupants, or the graves of those so old when they were laid in the ground that there was no one left behind, no relatives to squeeze for facts. Often times Merle and I would get our information from the memorial in the centre of town, the gold lettering of the war dead baking in the sun. I would collect the names: lost to bullet, gas, mortar, the whole damn sacrifice to stupidity. The dates of their deaths could have been mine.

We would collect these names for use in the show, hoping some war widow or grieving parent would be still hungry for answers after all this time. I had had enough of the dead as a child when I worked with my father for a couple of bob out of Rookwood, digging the paupers' graves in that vast necropolis. Blisters ripened like fruit on my young hands as I laboured alongside him. Until he knocked off for a smoko and didn't come back – enticed to a game of cards in the stonemason's yard, or hitching a ride to the nearest hotel to coat his lips in a beer's cold foam while his son did the backbreaking work of a full-grown man.

Merle walked beside me, my eyes following the forward kick of her skirt to see what I thought could be the curve of a belly. But it was like a bellows; how could I tell the difference between the breath of her skirt and the growing life therein?

We would always look for the freshest soil, better still if dotted with splashes of flowers: these were the ones that were missed the most. Merle would kneel down and bow her head, reading out the details that could be gleaned from the headstone, freshly hewn from the stonemason's chisel, or sometimes still only a wooden cross with a name carved upon it. Any passer-by would see a mourning couple – she overcome, he standing supportively by. The worst were the little ones, those brief spans of life that lasted less than a year. Merle wouldn't falter as she read out the harrowingly brief inscriptions, and I wanted to shake her then, hear her teeth rattle in her head. How could we bring a child into this forsaken world?

I sometimes tried to grab her hand as it swung by her side, for I had had the taste of her now and I would have taken my fill where I could. I did not care about the dead, and the tombs would have shielded us from the eyes of the living. I didn't care about the nettles and the wild Scottish thorns. I would have laid my body down for her. I would be her blanket, her shelter, her new skin. The last time she pulled her hand away I slapped her. My hand ringing out like the bell of judgement.

'Why didn't you tell me, Merle, before you told your father? I could have sorted it out. There are people in Macquarie Street who for a fee will help girls out ...' Before I could continue, her spittle was running down my cheek. She had spat right into my face.

'Shows how much you know!' she said, wiping her chin. What did she know that I didn't? I wanted to take her then, drag her to the nearest sandstone tomb and show her in the biblical way all she didn't yet know about men. But there was no time: we couldn't be late, for Crisp's timetable was inscribed in stone.

At night we shared a plate of greasy chops, the vegetables boiled to mush. The locals whispered amongst themselves at our presence. Crisp took Merle up to their lodgings above and I was cast out to the stables where the horses whinnied in their hay-scented dreams. At the time I thought Crisp was just teaching me another of his veiled lessons, the riddle in the riddle. If only I could have blinked the haydust out of my eyes. With Merle I was but a man of dust and straw and bullshit. Lily was the snow water I would wash myself in, my hands would never be so clean.

I rapped my knuckles against my own skull to banish the silence and pulled off the nose and beard, glad to breathe without the fumes of theatre glue. There were no more sounds from her room. My mind swam with what they could be doing in there, and nothing gave my jealousy any respite. A better perspective would be had from outside, away from the whole damn lot.

The cold night air lapped up to me, like a cat in want of attention. The night air made me new and I inhaled it deeply. From outside I looked up to the windows; the light was on, but I could make nothing out in Lily's room, no shadow of a cooing embrace. The smoke from a neighbour's chimney drifted out slowly like the plume of a horse's breath; the shed windows were dark in front of me.

The shed. Why hadn't I turned my attention there before? I tried my luck with the handle and, as all handles do, it gave way to my persuasion.

It was bat-dim in there, and dusty, the ashes long since dead in the grate. The birds on their roosts hopped from one claw to the other, rearranging their feathers, as I entered, then settled. The crow flapped upwards and watched me from its rafter. The dark feathers caught the light as it turned its head with clockwork precision every time I moved.

Oh, the Jew had set it up all right, a meagre bed and a stack of books, a crate with odds and sods piled upon it. Here were objects even the most seasoned treasure hunter would pass to the rag and bone man without a blink. The crow cawed at me, so I picked up an old iron nail and threw it, but it didn't move: my aim was poor in the dim light.

My hands swept under the mattress, but there was nothing; behind the books, nothing; but then I went to that childhood hiding place, the pillow, the place where all innocents conceal their treasures. It took only a second before my hand hit upon them: a box and an envelope. I opened the letter, filled with holes, censored with scissors like in the war, unreadable. The box with threads I shook like dice in a cup, but what was inside would not come out, no matter how I rattled, for there was no opening. The crow hopped down at my feet and looked at me with its transparent white eye, the pupil staring right into me without apology, and I wanted to throw the whole blasted-to-buggery black box at it. The bird was Lucifer itself, waiting for me somehow, but for what?

I hastily returned the useless things to their hiding place and closed the door, still feeling the crow's cold pupil bearing down on me.

TWENTY-FOUR

Ari

We stood in the wings, the trunk at our feet. We had carried it from the house to the theatre between us, like a treasure chest. Around it the floor was all aglitter; someone's costume had cried a rain of little coloured jewels.

We had practised without pause, and slept only in short bursts. Beauty, the raven, had played her part, undoing the threads of the swan-feather cape. Lily had unpicked the seams, head bowed over each stitch. Stray feathers floated about the room, tickling our noses until they fell forgotten on the floor, only to be rediscovered clinging to my foot sole, trapped in a shirt sleeve, stuck in a curl of my hair. We had practised and practised, Lily bursting out of the trunk, Beauty flying from her perch on the menorah, but Lily had always remained clothed. It still sat uneasy with me that we were even contemplating such a thing, but she was adamant that it would be but a flicker of light's worth, a will o' the wisp, that the cloak would shield her mostly.

Lily caught my eye as she stroked the hackles of the raven. What did she have to be ashamed of? She was Eve in the Garden.

From the wings I took good measure of the audience, their faces caressed and softened by the overflow of stage light. This time I didn't hold any deluded expectations that my aunt and uncle would come, and for this I was glad: a sense of freedom trickled down my neck with the perspiration. For a moment I could feel that my life belonged to me and me alone, as it had before the night my mother and I fled.

I used to watch my mother readying herself to go out. She would hand me a patterned ivory comb and let me sink it into the silky water of her hair, the whiteness of the comb against her dark tresses like a candle against the night. She would braid it then, the strands solidifying it into one thick rope, ready for her fingers to twist into a bun, a firm seafaring knot.

Her white blouse was starched and heavy; the sleeves billowed while she strode down the hall in her purposeful boots looking for her gloves and muff. My grandfather's pocket watch hung from the belt that cinched her waist, appearing and disappearing in the folds of her skirt like the moon on a cloud-tossed night. She was heading out, even though the snow had started to ice the windowsills. My grandmother would be there, darning, her disquiet at my mother's venturing out unvoiced except for the occasional sharp suck of her teeth.

For my last birthday, my aunt bought me the biography of Houdini, based on the recollections of his wife. She wrapped it neatly in my laundered clothes folded at the end of my bed, hidden from my uncle's demanding stare and the flash of his scissors. When touring in Hungary, the land of his birth, Houdini had come upon a dress that had been stitched with the utmost care and was said to have been worn by Queen Victoria. But before the master dressmaker could send it, the monarch had passed away. So he had a dress fit for a queen but no queen to wear it. The dressmaker was reluctant to sell the last souvenir of his royal contract, but Houdini had the power of persuasion and he persuaded the dressmaker that none but his mother should wear it. He had it altered to fit her right away and sent a telegram and the money for his mother to come and meet him and Bess. While he waited for her ship to berth, he set about elevating his mother to the position she deserved.

He went to a fine hotel and persuaded them to let him use their Palm Garden for his private coronation, inviting all those old family friends and relatives who had snubbed his mother, turning up their refined noses at her for marrying a poor lonely rabbi many years her senior, rich in his learning and not much else, who had dreams of a life in a country he could call home.

She made her arrival in the splendid dress and was queen for an evening. How I would have loved to have done something like that for my own mother, to give her a new dress, make her a queen. I remembered the patches on her skirt, only visible from my child's eye level, the little thick caterpillar of stitches crawling across the once-fine fabric. How I would have loved to buy that queen's dress for her now.

When my mother rustled to the door, scooping me up in her arms and covering my face with her kisses before she left, I did not know where she was going.

My grandmother would call out to her, her voice ringing down the hallway. 'Why do you do this, Zipporah? What would your father have thought?'

'It has to be done,' was all she said, before she swept out into the dark. I was not enough to anchor her. All night I would listen to every footfall in the street below, the sound of the tree branches sharing their secrets, the sighing of my grandmother as she turned in her fretful sleep, hoping that my mother would return soon.

The applause for the previous act rang out, clapping me out of my reverie. I hadn't even taken in what their song had been about. The performers rushed off the stage, the flush hot upon their cheeks, a thin film of sweat glazing their faces. Lily smiled and nodded at them as they rushed past us, a breeze following in their wake, but they barely acknowledged her. Lily inspected her feet at their rebuttal, pushing at the stray sequin with the toe of her shoe. The curtain closed and a stagehand helped us shift the birdcages, the menorah and the trunk into position, while from the pit the theatre orchestra played, their notes barely covering the voices that rose and fell on the other side of the curtain, an impatient audience. Lily looked up at me, a sense of panic rippling off her which she tried to cover with a smile. She planted the feathered cloak behind the curtain; a sheet had been tied up as a makeshift screen and a girl had been enlisted to help with the puzzle of the buttons of Lily's dress.

We took our marks, the stage lights like the rim of dawn on the horizon. The currawong let out her morning song, and the raven replied. The lyrebird's eyelids blinked, his tail shimmering over his head like a shroud of mountain mist. The parrot ignored it all, running his beak through his plumage until each filament of feather stood apart from the next.

The curtain rose, and all I could see was the silhouette of the audience in the blinding light. My feet took root on the stage floor. Lily's hand rose to my back, her touch kindled me. I stepped into the light, my fiddle to my chin, my bow poised. I felt suddenly alive, tall, a green shoot responding to the sun of the expectant faces of the audience. Lily stood beside me, her feathered fan like a giant eyelash modestly lowered. The lyrebird flicked and clacked his tail and leaped from the stand, taking bold steps; from his beak came wild improvisations around my tune. Together they danced, the feathers from his tail and her fan quivering alertly at each other before fluttering to the ground like eiderdown. The music lit them up: Lily's hair fizzed around her face with each spin, her smile flashed and the lyrebird's eyes glittered; they courted each other with every step. Until Lily stamped her feet and the lyrebird flicked his tail, a waterfall of feathers dipping over his head in the air towards her, his chosen one.

The dance ended. Lily took her chair; I wrapped the blindfold over her eyes, my fingertips brushing against the soft flesh of her nape. The currawong was on her shoulder and the white pages audience members had scribbled on, wanting her to guess, were like flares in the darkness. The currawong nibbled at her ear and she cried out the words. I could hear her nervousness creep into them, but our code didn't falter and was right every time, to the audience's delight. The last word was still moist upon her lips when she got up from her chair and dashed to change, my violin filling in the void in her absence, though no note, no matter how tenderly the bow glided over the string, could match her.

Two stagehands positioned the trunk before me, another pair bringing out the screen. Lily appeared in the cape, the feathers floating up around her face: a fierce angelic beauty. She looked at me, her feelings unveiled, and I knew that the thing between us was not just birds and magic, but a tangible, living thing. Together we were more than just two performers working upon a stage. The heart in my chest sang for her.

Lily stepped in front of the screen the moment I stepped behind it. The raven took her cue and took wing across the stage, settling on the edge of the screen.

'Ladies and gentleman,' Lily chimed, 'the Metamorphosis invented by the Master Mystifier, the Grand Illusionist, Houdini himself!'

She opened the trunk and a little envelope of her flesh peeked out from the safety of her cloak. I stepped in and curled down; the trunk closed, the padlocks clicked and, all alone in the womb-dark, I listened for her voice, pushing back the rolling panic that made the ocean roar in my ears. I could hear the vibrations of the screen as it was dragged across in front of me. The raven let out a croaking caw that was my cue to kick quickly at the secret door I had made.

My back strained at the top of the trunk to tilt out the hinges and free myself. I could hear Lily's voice reassuringly through the wood, 'When I clap my hands,' she said with thrill in her tone, 'there will be a miracle, like in days of old, like with Osiris, Lazarus, Dionysus, Jesus ...'

She was buying me time with every syllable. I scrambled, disoriented in the black space, and struggled free. The hinges closed behind me and I was out, Lily's shadow falling across me. I could hear my cue as her hands went:

Clap

Clap

Clap

I appeared the instant she disappeared. I could barely hear the audience's applause, my heart was thumping so loud.

With a flourish, I pulled back the screen. The trunk appeared undisturbed, just as it should be, but I felt panic slow my movements, my tongue stuck to the roof of my mouth. I heard the audience breathe as I undid the trunk, the keys slicing through the locks. I didn't want her to be deprived of air for one moment more than necessary. The trunk lid flipped up and there, glorious, she rose, my Venus.

She was the magic.

I picked up my violin and plucked the notes, my fingers slippery. The heat of the lights belted down on the crown of my head like the harsh afternoon sun. Lily twirled her hand and the raven hopped to her shoulder, her beak pulling the first ribbon. The cloak fell to one side, but she was still hidden. The raven arched over her head to the other arm and released the second tie, and the cloak fell slowly to her knees like melting wax. The raven circled her head. For one brief moment she burned, the flesh of her body like a white flame.

She was white like the parchment before the Hebrew characters danced upon it, before the scribe fixed its destiny with ink. I looked away, but I had to return my eyes to the holy white curled flame of her, the lights flickering, hovering over her skin. She was a page fit only for God's hand. She was a pillar of cloud before the lights snapped to black. When they came back on, we were gone, except for the parrot that had settled in the middle of the stage. *Abracadabra, Abracadabra, Abracadabra*, he pealed, and with a puff of smoke he was gone too, the applause like the world's wild heartbeat in my ear.

TWENTY-FIVE

Lily

With a tenderness, the raven plucked at the ribbons that secured my own feathers, tugging at the ribbons as a mother ties bows. The feathered cape fell and for a moment I stood in the loneliest shaft of light in the whole world – my flaws, my imperfections, my failures, all visible. But within moments the brightness burned them away completely, so that I felt as new as if licked with a fresh coat of paint. My nakedness seemed a strange garment new-made by hundreds of amazed eyes.

When I had been attacked, when he had cursed me as I ran, I had distanced myself from the abomination of my skin, thinking it was somehow the reason for his strike, that worse would come my way, not just curious eyes and quiet sniggers. All my life my skin had made people stare with shock, then try to blink me away, but now it was something so bright, a flare, drawing eyes toward me. No one looked away. This was my skin and I belonged in it. When we had practised, I had not had the courage to show anything but my old trousers beneath the cloak. But before the lights flared up and faded to black, Ari saw *me*, not just my skin, and an arrow of understanding shot from his eye to mine. The smoke shot up from the floor and together we disappeared.

When the light rose again Ari and I were below the stage, underneath the trapdoor. The parrot held the stage alone, his singsong voice calling out. Ari reached up his hand and cradled the bird, the green feathers smeared against his chest. The applause roared in my ears, making me shiver, even though I pulled the feathered cloak around me. We stood on the platform and, as it rose upward, Ari took my hand and squeezed it. We took our bow, waves of sound filling my ears, until we were washed offstage, back into our regular clothes, Ari's hand still holding mine.

'We did it,' I gasped. The feel of the light on my bare skin, the sound of the audience's collective held breath, Ari's seeing me – the warmth of it curled around us and sliced through the cool night air. Ari twirled me under his arm, there on the footpath outside the theatre, in the puddle of the streetlight, before he pulled me closer.

'Let's celebrate. If we hurry we could make the last tram to Bondi,' he said, his feet already gathering speed and with them mine at the thrilling thought of it. I had never seen the sea. 'We can collect the birds in the morning.'

Quickly we filled the birds' water and seed trays and rushed out into the street. The night was cold but the scent of the wine-scented magnolias was a promise that this short winter would soon give way to spring.

The tram came to an incline and then went down a slight hill. For a moment I could see the ocean, the moon a fully veiled bride illuminating the white tips and ridges of the waves, then the tram dipped and we could see it no more. A gust of salty breeze rushed in. I didn't think my lungs could breathe so deep; I was a human sail ready to take the ocean and call it my own.

The tram slipped fast down to the beach, and for a moment I caught a teasing glimpse, a white crescent of sand in the moonlight, our descent seeming quicker than a slide down a slippery dip. As we crested another rise, Ari grinned and covered my eyes from the view, but I could hear the waves thrashing against the shore and my heart pounded in my chest. Slowly he unfurled his fingers from my face, offering to me the ocean, the big white curve of the beach and the galloping waves. I closed my eyes and opened them again, as if trying to fix my first sighting to memory.

I stood on the esplanade dumbfounded. I could not take it in.

'Take off your shoes,' Ari coaxed, steadying me as I balanced to slip them off, then putting them in his satchel. The sand squeezed up between my toes with each step down, but trickled like silk as my foot rose.

Ari laughed at my hesitant, cat-footed step. 'My uncle was the same when we first came down to the shore, as if somehow the sand was a trick someone was playing with him. He was casting sidewise glances to see if anyone was laughing at his expense. My aunt sat on the esplanade wall and watched us, hesitant to have her feet on show for all to see.'

There was no one foolish enough to be on the beach this late but ourselves.

'Me, I tore toward the waterline and splashed in it before I could feel the waves retreat back. For a moment I thought I could swim back home.'

'What happened to your parents that you ended up here?' I asked.

Ari's feet slowed, his toes dug into the sand, and the moonlight cast a blue tint over his face. 'I never met my father. I don't think my parents were married,' he said, his voice hesitant, the sea's pounding carrying the rest away.

'Well, they must have loved each other to have had you.'

'I like to think so.'

The spray blew up onto our faces. Ari grinned as he gathered up my hand in his and we moved forward to the ocean together.

The sea was upon us, its big dark tongue plunging at our feet, the spittle of the foam erasing the daylight's stamped footprints. The waters rushed towards us, a kiss from the mouth of life.

The waves flowed around my feet, my legs. The water was cold, but the salty swell made my feet tingle, and the wave tore past our legs and was away before coming right back at us again.

'To life!' I shouted.

The tide engulfed us again, the hem of my trousers dragging around my legs, a wet sail.

'L'chaim. *Remember us to Life, O King who desires Life, and inscribes us in the Book of Life, for Your sake O living G_d,*' said Ari as his hand wrapped around my waist and drew me in, his lips damp and salty against mine.

I ran my fingers up through his hair and I kissed him back. A catherine-wheel went off in my chest, illuminating the places where no light had ever dared fall. The wind began whispering at our clothes and tormenting the caps of the waves scudding across the beach and tossing sand like malicious confetti. We ran back to the safety of the promenade, the tide cold on our heels. I sat on the stone wall and Ari gently picked up each foot, knocked off the clinging sand and eased my shoes back on. A tram rattled down to the beach, the actual last tram to Bondi, but the driver happily agreed to take us to the interchange, as he had to go that way himself. It was good to be out of the wind as I sat close to Ari, his body my shelter. He opened his satchel and handed me something wrapped in newspaper with a ribbon rosette.

'For you,' he smiled and I held the present close to my chest, wanting to kiss Ari again, the salt from his lips mingling with mine, but I could feel the gaze of the tram driver upon us and held back. But Ari's hand still secretly encased mine.

By the time we got back to L'Avenue, the street was strangely quiet, as if the wind had blown everyone else indoors. Ari's eyes flicked up to his old room out of habit: all was dark, but Miss du Maurier's house opposite crackled with electricity. We walked inside and the wind slammed the door petulantly behind us. Every bulb was on. The voices reached us before I could see who they came from. Ari released my hand and it fell limp to my side. We walked into the sitting room, and there sat Miss du Maurier with Billy playing mother, pouring tea from a steaming pot. Next to him was the woman I knew to be Ari's aunt. She stood up shakily from her chair upon seeing Ari, her eyes puffed, her face still damp with tears.

'Ari. He's gone. Your uncle has gone,' was all she could say before she crumpled like a handkerchief into his arms.

TWENTY-SIX

Billy

The rumour ran through the theatre that my little neighbour, my Lily of the Valley, might just be, believe it or not, removing her clothes. I didn't believe it. I was an all-consuming fire, each added whisper that ran past the ticketing window just adding more fuel. I wanted to stop up my ears, it was surely a furphy.

Hurriedly, I put up the *Closed* sign, for I had calculated from the programme when their act would be. I ran to the auditorium, just in time. The Jew played his infernal violin and the satanic crow hopped onto Lily's outstretched arm. I wanted to ring its bloody neck. I wanted it all to stop. I could see it all unfolding and, as infuriated as I was, there was nothing I could do. All I could do was taste my own bile and wish time to stop. It was all his damned fault.

The bird's beak plucked at some bows on her garments and I could do nothing, I couldn't stop her defilement, all those eyes drinking her in as if she were some common whore. Then, for an instant, my rage faltered, for my Lily burned pure and naked before me and I struggled to take her all in, every last snowy part of her.

Her skin was like water for a man dying of thirst. The swell of her hip, the curve of her breast, the little patch of blossom between her thighs. I tried to moisten my mouth with my own tongue, but I was a desert to which she alone could bring the rains. I wanted to protect her, to cover her. She was in the altogether and all alone. I would have concealed her if I could, from all the eyes that burned her precious skin. Then Lily disappeared and the parrot spoke in its singsong scrape, warped words.

My rage consumed me again. The past roared in my ears and made me want to scream and tear my hair and rip my clothes. Merle's face loomed in my mind – I wanted to gouge out her eyes, cut out her deceptive tongue. Crisp too. I would have drawn and quartered him, cut his flesh into tiny pieces, made meat for dogs out of both of them.

'Ladies and gentlemen, welcome to Crisp's Elixir du Jour Medicine Show. If you have an ailment the Elixir du Jour is your remedy,' Crisp began his oratory to the country folk, revelling in their wide-eyed reverence of his knowledge from the big smoke. Merle and I would stand on either side of the charlatan healer, holding up the bottles, with only a mere example displayed on the table, so there would be a stampede for them later.

'Before I release the elixir for sale, at its more than affordable price, we shall hear testimony from those it has saved from the very pit of death. Step forth, William.' I felt my blood simmer. William, William – the only man who ever called me William was my father. 'William, when he first came to see me, was suffering from the effects of the war, which afflict so many of our brave boys. He was listless, depressed, seeing things that were not there, believing things that didn't exist. William approached me outside my healing establishment, his eyes bloodshot, his hands quivering. He couldn't even hold a pencil to write his name. Immediately I prescribed him a dose of Elixir du Jour and since then he has recovered his old talent with the blade, which soon, with his newly steady hand, he shall demonstrate.'

I felt my emotions buck within me. How easy it would be

to miss the red and white spiral painted on a bale of hay, have that knife sing into his bone. A simple accident, a tiny slip of the hand – who would blame me, survivor of shell-shock and the Battle of the Somme. But I threw a set of blades, each one arrow-true, to the target's painted heart, just as he bade me do.

'This is Merle, my adopted daughter. I found her wandering the water's edge, peering down to the swell of the ferries, looking for her mother who had drowned. She had nothing and no one. She put her little hand in mine and there it stayed.'

I didn't know whether to believe Crisp or not, for he had a way of taking a seed of fact and growing it into a tree of falsehood, and we were all charged with tending to it.

'Merle,' Crisp continued, 'displayed at an early age the rare and frightening ability to converse with those who have passed on.' At that a dozen hands shot up in the air.

Our research was ready. Most of the questions were pitifully easy to answer. When Merle was drawing her answers to a close, she would announce in her hoarse, otherworldly voice that with Crisp's Elixir du Jour they would be able to communicate with the dead in their dreams. Crisp's bottles of Elixir du Jour sold as fast as if they contained the tears of sweet baby Jesus, and Crisp grinned like a cat with a bird's fragile bones between his teeth.

In the last town, while Crisp went to see to the rooms, Merle drew me aside and kissed me with all her might. She pressed the span of my palm to the curve of her belly and whispered a surprising suggestive something in my ear. Then she smiled at me like I was the greenest of virgins, before she blinked demurely and waited for her father to escort her inside. After all this time, I was in thrall. Perhaps I had done my penance and the time had come when I could dip into her body again and be renewed. That first startling touch since we were back in Sydney gave me a fool's deluded hope, for it was just a means of keeping me blinkered.

The next day I woke at first light. The morning was clear, the blue spilling over the dry light of dawn, and despite the hay nesting in my hair, I felt as if the whole world was suddenly in my lap. All I need do was reach out and it would be mine. Merle would come to me where I lay, in kingly luxury with my coat over my shoulders, a piece of hay between my teeth, chewing it as if I had not a care in my kingdom. I waited for her footsteps on the gravel. But Merle didn't come.

I rose and splashed water on my face from the cracked enamel basin, then stepped out into the hotel courtyard. I went to the desk and lolled about, waiting for the clerk until I could stand it no longer, my finger hitting the bell with a staccato rhythm as urgent as Morse code. The smell of spitting bacon came unbidden, and then the clerk appeared, grease-stained napkin tucked around his neck, chewing before he spoke.

'Yes?' he said impatiently, not sure where to put his brandished fork.

'I am here to wake up Doctor Crisp and his daughter Merle.' The clerk looked at me like I was a madman. 'At their express request to be woken at this hour and for no other,' I added. Crisp had taught me well, or so I thought.

The clerk threw a cursory glance at his guestbook before he gave me a shrug, his hand reaching for the telephone. 'There is no one on the list of that name, sir,' he said to me.

What on earth did he mean? We had arrived all together; as usual I had carried their bags in. The same clerk had seen me do all this just yesterday. With the telephone clutched to his chest, he pressed down on the receiver, praying for the operator to speak.

'Don't you remember seeing me yesterday? I arrived with them.' His finger was caught in the dialling wheel, but I didn't care, I pulled the cord from the wall and watched as the wooden box of the phone splintered on the floor. That got his attention. He shrank back against the wall, his eyes wide at the trusty blade that I had strapped to my waistcoat. Now it had caught his eye, it was only fair that they should have an introduction.

'Please don't hurt me, please,' he whined.

I hopped over the counter. I had no intention of laying a finger on him; he was as pliable as a rubber band already. 'Where did they go?'

'I don't know who you are talking about!' He was snivelling now, snot erupting from his nostrils.

I pulled the register over and scanned the names. Of course Crisp would not use his own name: under last night's date were only two guests. The bloody clerk had been well and truly Crisped. There they were, brazen as day, Mr J. H. Christ and Mrs M. Magdalene. My cup fucking boileth over. It was time for a crucifixion. I ran up the stairs to the room that had been theirs, as if I would find some trace of them still. I kicked open the door. There was just a mauve chenille bedspread tumbled onto the floor. They had obviously shared this bed: there was the unmistakable onion-skin stain of dried semen on the sheet.

At first my mind leaped to the thought of incest and I wanted to slice Crisp's bollocks off for doing such a thing to his daughter, but then it all fell into place. That bed was a taunt. Merle had been Crisp's puppet; they had both played me as if I was nothing but a little lead soldier lined up before a marble cannon. Months of slavery and obedience, for what?

My knife vibrated in my hand, speaking its revenge before I could even form the thoughts. Oh, my steadfast blade, she hummed in my fingers as she pierced the mattress, slashing it until it oozed feathers. But she wanted more, my silver point, sharp as a star, and who was I to deny her? She sang her cutting song through the pillows, jagging down the curtains, plunging in and out of the space where Merle's heart would have rested, where Crisp's flaccid penis would have been spent. A snow of down fell through the air, blanketing everything, attempting to erase their crime against me. Then a little willy-willy spiralled over the wastepaper basket, circling and circling, until it drew my attention. It was surely a sign.

I plunged my hand into the bin and felt the touch of something slimy, and my stomach lurched. Piece by piece I pulled out the debris of Crisp and Merle: a half-eaten chicken leg, a broken bottle, a bundle of rags with a bloodstain – all curious enough. But it was the crumpled piece of newspaper that stuck to the side that drew my eye. I smoothed it, the black coming off on my hand. I scanned the page to find a clue, the broadsheet crammed with the news of the city. The suburbs' names read like the names of friends – Stanmore, Darlinghurst, Chippendale, Surry Hills, Haymarket.

> The Rocks: A Mysterious Death
> *The body of a man has been found outside his building from an apparent fall. It is not known at this stage whether the fall was an accident or suicide. The police have released the name of the deceased to the press in hope that his family may come forward, as he recently was the recipient of a deceased estate worth quite an estimable sum, which was deposited around his rented rooms. If anyone has any knowledge of the whereabouts of the son of Mr William Little, Senior, please contact the Argyle Street Police Station.*

He was dead and that was how I learned it. The words were smudged and dated the day after we left Sydney. Was this why Crisp had packed up shop and taken me hostage on the road? I'd been his captive and I hadn't known it. He had known my father's fate and had led me as if I had a ring in my nose, and I, compliant dumb beast that I had become, had followed. Now I was shipwrecked in the middle of dry nowhere with Buckley's chance of getting back, with only dust for currency, while Crisp and Merle would claim the money and make merry on what should have been my fortune. All this flashed through my mind before I could even dust off the feather down that had settled on my clothes.

If I had believed one could talk to the dead, I would have asked my father all those questions I longed to have answers for. Who was my mother? Had I really made his luck run out? Was he pushed or did he fly? And the thousand-pound question, how did he get so much money? Could the old bastard have been squirrelling it away for years, smug in the knowledge that now I was *apprenticed* it wouldn't be long until I flew the coop and he would be free to live like the lord he always presumed himself to be?

He was gone, my father was no more. I couldn't quite understand it – every time I thought of him it came with the fresh slap of remembering. I wanted to confront the son of a bitch for dying on me, cuff him about the ears and rain down every expletive upon his head. He may have not been the best of fathers, but he was mine.

There was a clatter of applause like gunfire and it snapped me back to myself, banishing them all, Crisp, Merle and my father, from my mind. My hurt was a thing that had been nursed enough. I returned to the ticket booth, a strategy taking shape in my mind, until finally the crowds dribbled out and old Clay came for the money, his eyes like saucers at the sight of the swollen till – traitor money, her flesh sold into slavery, for coin. I would liberate her yet.

I slid around the back to the stage door. There were more waiting there than usual, all stage-door johnnys for my Lily of the Valley. Let crows pluck out their eyes! They had the scent of her flesh and would not relinquish it. Blackbirds pluck off their noses!

I slipped back around to the entrance and made my way into the theatre where the usherettes were harvesting the sweets that had rolled down the aisles. A cleaner was sweeping the stage, the tiny feathers that had drifted from Lily's cape swirling into his dustpan. Where was she? Ducking behind the curtains, I found backstage deserted.

I knocked on the dressing room door, not wanting to catch her unawares, but there was only the sorrowful tone of a violin in reply. The bastard, I would give him a taste of what Billy Little could play. I flung open the door, but the room was void of human life. The tune stopped, the lyrebird snapped closed its beak and all was quiet, except for the crow, who preened its feathers, rustling each one as if to taunt me. The feathered cape, Lily's second skin, lay near its cage and I lunged for it, before the beast turned those eerily clear eyes at me. I alone knew how to save her from the clutches of that Godforsaken Jew.

I ran down King Street, my feet barely brushing the footpath; I was nearly airborne. I turned into L'Avenue and a fruit bat flapped low in the sky, so close I could feel the breeze from its webbed wings. Lily's cape soared over my shoulder, lending me the speed of air. The branches of the trees above pitched and tossed in a windy squall, sending a hail of gumnuts raining about me, but I did not blink. I was readying myself. My love was legion. Let my love for her be to him as all the plagues of Egypt!

Before me on the path a figure ambled, every gust of wind threatening to toss him off his feet. At first I thought it might have been an old drunk taking a piss in the wind. But as I neared I could see it was the Jewboy's uncle, wild-eyed, navigating the street as if it was an ocean. It didn't take me a second to realise he was cracked as he fell to his knees in front of me.

'*And it shall be on the day when ye shall pass over Jordan unto the land which the Lord thy G_d giveth thee, that thou shalt set thee up great stones, and plaster them with plaster,*' he squawked, his hands reaching out for mine as if for alms. I tried to shake him off, but he took no heed. '*And thou shalt write upon them all the words of this law, when thou art passed over, that thou mayest go in unto the land which the Lord thy G_d giveth thee, a land that floweth with milk and honey.*' His beard swung like a pendulum. '*Lord G_d of thy fathers hath promised ...*' he enunciated vehemently as I tried to shake him off, but his grip was strong.

The streetlights made a strange creature out of our shadows. I stepped backward and could see in my own shadow the undulating mass of Lily's swan feather cape rippling in the breeze. To the Jew's uncle I had become an angel. It was only right that I assist him with his mission, heavenly instructions spilling out of my mouth. I tingled with a conductor's energy, directing him with my will.

'Leave this place!' I boomed. 'It is His desire. Find the Promised Land.' I was lyrical, phantasmagorical; it would have been clear to any man with all his faculties that there was no such place in existence on this earth.

He tugged on my sleeve. 'Who are you?' he begged.

'Do you not see the face of an angel?'

He cowered before me as I crowed. The wind billowed through the swan's feathers, lifting my newfound wings, and he looked up at me as if my eyes flared with fire. Gone was the pillar of strength that had blanched with disdain when I said my hip hip hooray. His Jerusalem was destroyed, so I offered him a new one, his promised land, the idea spreading like a fungus in his mind. I ordered and he obeyed, until he repeated back my directions one by one. Jacob gave more resistance when he wrestled his angel. Let him live up to his name, let me be his blessing, let me give him his birth right. I was casting him out to a place where even a sane man could get lost; not even his shadow would be able to find him. If the uncle was the stick, then the nephew would be the dog scampering after him, and Lily and I would be free of both of them now banished to wander the wilderness.

I watched him walk toward the train station. I had forgotten my charity. I boomed at him to halt, my arm raised like a burning sword. His feet were lead. I pulled out a few quid and gave it to him for the train. I did not want him to come boomeranging back. He looked at the money in his hand, manna from heaven, and his fingers closed gratefully over the miraculous notes.

Let it be written, I shall blot him out. Long may he wander.

TWENTY-SEVEN

Ari

Lily's hand was in mine. With my thumb I stroked the skin of her palm, pale parchment, the lines a redefinition of our boundaries. Who would have thought one small hand could rewrite the map by which I had set my course?

When we walked into the sitting room, I had no further plans, just to continue – with the act and being with Lily. Her hand in mine was the promise of this. We had a pact, she and I; our kiss on the sand had sealed it. But when we walked into that room, the shock of seeing my aunt being tended to by Miss du Maurier and Mr Little came between us. I could not tell if Lily's hand fluttered away from me or if I dropped it. Lily stepped back as my aunt rushed towards me, her inconsolable sobs dampening my collar. Lily stood aside, pale and quiet. I tried to catch her eye, but her eyes were downcast. I should have introduced them, but the timing was wrong and I couldn't find the words.

'Are you sure he isn't visiting someone?' My uncle called on the elderly and immobile members of his congregation, even if they were out of his way, and read with them that week's Torah portion and the newspaper headlines. News from this world and the next.

'The police have been called but there can be no report until he has been missing twenty-four hours,' Miss du Maurier interjected. My aunt was struggling to find her voice; it was trapped in her throat.

'No, no. He is *nelm vern*, vanished.' She wiped at her eyes. 'You must come with me now. You have to see.'

I followed her out. I wanted to tell Lily I would be back, but I felt Mr Little's all-too-keen interest. I felt the heat of his glare prickle at the back of my neck and for a moment I was concerned to leave Lily alone with him. But he was just a man standing with a teapot in his hands. He had helped my aunt, and Miss du Maurier was there too, but still each step carried a sense of foreboding.

The flat was as silent as if a hundred years had passed. My aunt bustled ahead of me up the stairs, my shadow following her. I felt each step was a greater trespass than the one before, more than when I had come back to collect my belongings. Nothing had changed, yet the rooms were somehow smaller, or I taller; the world outside was the place for me now. I flicked on the lights.

In my uncle's study it had been snowing. Across every surface were scattered flakes of paper, their jagged edges crammed with print. All around us were the remnants of the scrapbook he had so painstakingly kept. For decades he had filled the pages, as if somehow all these articles could serve as a map, each inky headline a compass to the place he knew, to the place he dreamed of as home. But he was neither in Bessarabia nor the Holy Land. He was here, in Sydney, Australia, like I was, with only letters from a strange alphabet remaining to him. The only unripped paper was on the floor by his desk. I walked to it through the scrapbook snowdrift, shreds of old newsprint clinging to the soles of my shoes.

I picked the sheet out of the mess and it trembled with the weight of the weird confetti that burdened it. Gently, I blew off the debris so that I could see what remained, the only words he'd left untouched. The date was yesterday, the headline shrieking like a siren, *MASSACRE AT HEBRON, MANY JEWS KILLED*. My eyes tripped over the words. *Jerusalem indeed tonight is a city of the dead.* I didn't have the heart to read any more, the bile swirled in my throat. The cold rose up through my spine and I stamped my feet in my uncle's snow, willing my anger to heel. So much loss. Loss that we had shared.

He and I, we had both known my mother. From the start, we could have grieved together, both bereaved, both made orphans, even if on either side of the ocean. But instead he sat up in his study, hoping for a homeland and treating me only as his chance to remake someone in his own image. I felt he resented my very existence. Did he think it had been in my small child's power to stop what happened to my mother and my grandmother, or that I could replace them? When he looked at me, was all he saw a travesty, a living memorial of his loss, without seeing my own? Now his hope of the Promised Land was ringed in ink in my hands. The streets ran once more with the blood of the innocent, the same atrocities that I had witnessed and survived repeated.

My uncle in his storm had whipped through the pages of his scrapbook, shredding them like leaves, trying to erase the words, strip them of their power. But all he had done was find himself at the centre of a destroyed book, and the words still remained, dark proof. He could not undo them any more than he could undo the blows, erase the scars, revive the dead. Was there a message in all this from him? I could still feel Lily's touch from the tram, her fingers running over the words inscribed in my skin, tracing them with the velvet of her fingertip. I could tell in that touch she was curious, that she wanted to ask the letters' meaning, sensing that their story was bundled up with the story of my life.

It is said that King David's harp composed its own notes in the darkness; sometimes I wondered whether these letters talked amongst themselves in the pitch of night. I desperately wanted to know about my origins. But the tattoo was just a word, a remnant. I was like each and every one of these destroyed books, separated from the pages that told it who it was. What could Lily see in me?

My aunt was off making up my old bed before I had time to tell her I was going. She suddenly appeared older, frailer, without the presence of my uncle in the house, which now felt completely empty without him. His sadness and his rage had filled it. As she flicked the sheets over my old bed, I retrieved a broom from the kitchen and went into my uncle's study to sweep up the tatters of his life. With each brush of the broom against the paper tide, I knew what it was I had to do.

I woke with a jolt, the light already flitting through the curtain. A magpie chortled at the dawn and my mind shot like an arrow to Lily, the birds. I got up and dressed swiftly. I pulled my curtain open but hers was dark against me. The stairs were mercifully silent as I stepped down them. My aunt's whispered prayers came from her bedroom. I got to the door and was about to go to the shed, my own patch of earth, when the morning light washed the white paint of the synagogue gold, calling me in.

I stepped inside and closed the door. The mustiness of a hundred closed books rose up to me. I didn't know what I expected; surely not a snow drift of torn holy books here too? The morning light broke through the *magen* window, raining colours all over the floor. The ark curtains were closed, the Torah scrolls slept undisturbed. I thought of the letters on the parchment flickering with the life they had been given by the *sofer*'s hand. I thought of that letter I had taken. It belonged to my uncle; I had no right to touch it, let alone read it. If he knew I had done so, could that have made him lose his reason?

I walked up to the women's gallery. The benches had had a fresh lick of paint. I remembered how we had salvaged them from the seaside. When he dreamed of the synagogue, there were no funds for proper seats, so when he heard that some benches were being thrown out down by the beach, we borrowed old Mr du Maurier's horse and cart and made a day out of retrieving them. My uncle stepped out further into the salty waters than I that day, unconcerned with the water splashing up the length of his suit. He cried out. He opened his mouth as if he was about to say something, but then his jaw went rigid and his mouth turned into a painful grimace, as if he was forcing all sound back down, repelling the beginnings of his tears. So I said it for him under my breath, her name, stolen by a wave.

The first time I had seen the sea was on my long journey, when it had swallowed me up and spat me out here, on this land that we tried to call our own, erecting our buildings, praying to our G_d.

I heard the door open and turned, thinking Uncle Israel had come back, but it was just the men for the morning prayers looking back at me with the same curiosity, as if perhaps I knew where he had gone and would not say. They stood around me, but no words were exchanged. Nine faces all wondering if I would be their tenth, the magic number to form the minyan. They took their places in the pews and quietly gestured to each other, adjusting their *tallit* shawls, but not one stepped forward to the *bimah* platform to lead the service. The light grew stronger through the *magen* window and I did the one thing that would have pleased him, though I knew he wouldn't have done the same for me – I took his place. I stood upon the *bimah* and felt the expectation grow heavy as all the faces turned towards me, waiting for me to start.

In the balcony my aunt stood alone, her fingers gripping the balustrade. I called the first prayer. My eyes rolled over the Hebrew and I felt light-headed. My uncle had taught me all these letters; each letter drizzled in honey, which my finger would hurriedly follow, bringing the honey to my lips to lick. It was my uncle who had filled the place where a father should have stood, his stern gaze I saw where I imagined Houdini's glittering eyes smiling back at me. If his love was sometime harsh, perhaps I should have borne it with a greater measure of patience. For when I looked at him, he was everything that was unfamiliar, stern and new. But when he looked at me he must have seen the faces of those he had loved most in the world, the only family he had, now wiped clean from the page of the earth just to save me.

I knew before I had finished that first prayer that I would go and seek him, just as that cousin in Bessarabia had sought me out at my uncle's request, a blind hope. What did he know of me then to search for me, to save me? I was no more than a whisper on a gossip's breath. My uncle had given me a life, plucked me away from the carnage of my past as if he were a wind created by HaShem's mighty hand. I knew I would do all I could to find him, yet I felt the cold reality of his disappearance shake me to the core. What if he could not be found?

TWENTY-EIGHT

Lily

I watched the lights go on one by one across the road, burning throughout the night, shadows of movement behind the curtain. I waited for a while, thinking Ari would pull back the curtains of his old home and press his fingers to the glass as I did. But nothing happened. The street was still, not even a breath from another creature. A disquiet crept over me as I covered myself with the sheets. Why had he not introduced me to his aunt? Was he ashamed of me? She hadn't even looked at me. Was it because of her distress or because in her eyes I was invisible, alien, a blank? My whole body shivered; it was so cold and I could not get warm, except for the radiant spot upon my palm, where I could still feel the pressure of his hand on mine as sleep finally pressed my eyes closed.

When I woke, it was as if I hadn't slept at all. Every nerve ending hummed; my clothes from the day before were twisted tightly around my body. The curtains in the window opposite were blatantly wide now and I felt a maddening frustration. I ran to the shed, looking for signs of life, but as I pushed open the door, the emptiness made me feel sick. Outside a currawong let out its mountain cry, so solitary and lonely it resonated in my marrow. It felled me for a moment, so I sat there on the neatly made bed, the sheets cold to the touch, my knuckles gripping at the bed frame. I could not stop the memory of the soft flesh of his lip; his mouth still hummed on mine.

I went back into the house, unsure of where I should be. A pot of tea steamed on the kitchen table, so I poured a cup, but I hadn't even the will to sip, I just wanted something solid and warm in my hand. Then I felt his hand on my shoulder, and I turned, ready, but it was just Billy.

'Any news?' he said, giving my shoulders a reassuring squeeze, his thumb carelessly wandering to the scroll of my collarbone. It repulsed me and I stepped backward. I only could think about Ari – would he really have gone without saying a word? All colour seemed drained from the morning light, blotted up by clouds.

'No news,' I said, walking out through the front door. I let the wind slam it for me.

A gust swept up to my face, a pile of leaves chased each other in a circle. On the synagogue steps I saw Ari and the last of his uncle's congregation. He didn't see me, or perhaps he chose not to, embarrassed by my presence. He had already slipped into his uncle's shoes. I lifted up my arm to wave hesitantly, my hand a limp rag in the wind. He looked up, blinking, then waited on the threshold until the last of the faithful had departed before he crossed the road. I looked up at his face, but I didn't want to read it, I didn't want to see what I knew to be written there.

'Lily, come for a walk?'

Our footsteps sounded together, one falling and one rising, our bodies leaning closer with each step. The wind teased the circular tip of his cap and he pulled it off his head and slipped it into his back pocket. The fig trees shook their mane of leaves as if protesting. The sky was an angry canvas of bruises and I was waiting for the next strike.

'Lily ...'

My look slowed his words. I didn't want to hear it, but the lightning wrote it jaggedly in the distance, making me screw up my eyes. I wanted him to shut up, I wanted to run, but I knew the words would follow. I felt the beginning rumble of thunder and I remembered that curse, chanted at me like a spell across the rooftops, roads, rail tracks, where it had been spoken, right back to my home town.

'Lily. I'm going to go out looking for him. I'm worried. No one in the congregation has seen him. My aunt thinks the police won't help until it's too late. I don't even know where to start …' The branches rattled together overhead, but my mind was empty. '… but I have to try to find my uncle.'

A sparrow leaped up to the lintel of the doorway opposite. A low whistling sounded from down the street, the slow drip and fall of a currawong's song.

'You should have seen his study, Lily, something was not right. There was not a page left untouched, he had torn up every one, all the precious pages he saved over the years. He is not in his natural state. His mind is like a mirror cracked. I'm afraid I'll never find him.'

I was numb. Of course he should look for his uncle, and I wanted Ari to find him, safely, quickly, but his voice was so solemn and he spoke with such finality that I knew he hadn't said it all. He quivered agitatedly before me like a waiting lightning rod. I could sense that his defiance weighed as blame upon his shoulders, but was it because of what we had done in our act together, with the cloak and raven and the brief moment of my nakedness? The stage had seemed our place; together we were safe in those shining lights, it was our world.

But he would not meet my eye now. Had I gone too far? Was it regret that I heard in his voice? Did he regret everything, even our kiss? Questions jostled through my mind but I could not stop to ask even one. The lump in my throat made me mute.

'Lily? And if I find him, what then?' I didn't know how to answer him. Couldn't we just continue as we were? His voice was reduced to a rasp. 'My aunt spoke with me last night, she wants me to take over and fulfil my uncle's wishes for me to study overseas, to give up magic and follow in his footsteps. It has always been my uncle's wish.'

His aunt had looked past me, willing me not to be there, the obstacle to her husband's wish, the girl not like them. The uncle who wasn't even here still held sway, winding Ari back with a wish and wiping me away in one swipe. A kiss was not a promise, I realised.

'Or what if I find him dead?' The word hovered leaden and immovable between us. I could see him trying to rein in his emotions, but how could I console him, reassure him? All I wanted to do was reach out and touch his cheek, but I feared he would step away. There was nothing I could say, all the decisions had been made without me – whatever happened, he would be leaving and whatever was between us would disappear. My heart twisted like landed fish.

A raven tiptoed through the nearby gutter as if on a tightrope, before he plunged his beak down and pulled out something purple – fruit, a worm, a chick? The first sprig of lightning bloomed in the sky, sending the raven and his prize into a black swoop high up into the wind-tossed trees.

'Lily?'

There were more currawongs calling out to each other, each soaring and dipping, heralding the fat raindrops to come. I looked up the street; the trees were full of them. That is when I saw him, the whistle wet upon his lips. The Birdman had come. Perhaps he wanted his raven back? I felt the footpath sway beneath me.

'You are just the chap I'm after,' the Birdman said to Ari, his dark eyes glinting in his dusty face like baked currants. 'I saw your uncle boarding the train to the Blue Mountains, my country. A man can catch a train to wherever he likes, of course. But there was something not quite right, it was if a willy-willy had spun through his mind. When I whistled out to him he stopped suddenly, frightened. Of course I only wanted to introduce myself and hear how you two and Beauty were getting on, but he was completely bewildered and grabbed at my arm as if the world had gone topsy-turvy.'

'When was this?' Ari said urgently.

Raindrops fell but were blown away by a gust. The Birdman looked up into the sky to where the sun would have sat were it not obscured by the gathering momentum of clouds.

'Oh, I'd say the better part of the day and the best of the night. It would have been the first train of the day.'

Ari looked at me, his eyes dark. He knew as well as I did that those mountains were a wilderness. I had seen a poster hanging up in our school; they were blue, we were told, because of all the eucalyptus clouding the air, and they were a living sandstone wall, impenetrable.

'I know that country, friends. It is a place to get lost in. I'll be heading back that way soon, once I have had my sup at the Red Rose. Ah, a man would walk on water to have one of Jandy's milkshakes,' the Birdman said, wiping his mouth with the back of his hand as if he could already taste the sweetness. I could feel Ari's impatience, but the Birdman was not a man to be rushed.

'And I have come to collect Beauty, my crow, my raven, my *corvid australialis,* my little scrap of starless night. I've missed her, the smartest bird that ever was.' His words rang through the street and seemed to pierce the sky, sending fat raindrops splashing down my face. All we had worked for seemed to be slipping out of my grasp and I had no way to grab it back.

'Give me half an hour to get my things together and I'll meet you back here,' Ari said to the Birdman.

My mouth was not at my command, it would not open. *When will you be back?* It was the question I dreaded to ask because there would be no answer I wanted to hear.

The clouds broke then and rain fell in curtains, drenching us to our skin, and still neither of us moved. I wished he would pull me into his arms again, I wouldn't have cared if we never spoke – his fingers better than words, his touch softer than speech, his body the pages of everything I wanted him to say.

We walked to the theatre one more time together, a cleaner letting us in the back door. The spangling light from last night that had held us together was now dispersed and I longed for it. We collected the birds, joyous and blinking to be out in the rain, bathing in their cages in personal rivulets. Beauty, though, swooped out into the nearest signpost and gargled ominously, only for the lyrebird to mimic her cry like a lament all the way down the street.

PART THREE

The Metamorphosis

TWENTY-NINE

Billy

I knew the fates were on my side when the Jew's aunt showed up all a-sniffle at our front door. The old woman should have been thankful, praised her God: cut free of that old piece of dead wood, she could do and say whatever she liked now. Hip hip hurrah! Of course I popped the kettle on as quickly as I could and was wound tight with anticipation, frustrated that Miss du Maurier was taking her sweet time as she rummaged for a clean handkerchief in some chaotic drawer. The Jew's aunt's weeping grew louder as the kettle rose, until sobs and whistle formed a duet. My dear landlady came back waving the handkerchief like a white flag and it mopped up the tears all right, but all she could say was that her husband was missing. Then she was silent for a bit, mouthing words but nothing coming out. She blew her nose like a trumpet, three notes forming the devil's chord.

I can only remember one time that I cried. It wasn't as a child; it was on that slow trip back to Sydney, when I was like bloody deceived Hansel following a trail of crumbs. When all the time the crows were circling, ready to make their plunge. Those shameful tears evaporated with every dusty step that I took toward home. Crisp was carrion, I knew that. But Merle and I had been lovers; she carried my fruit in her womb. Or did she? And my father's fortune, how did Crisp find it? My mind swayed like a priest's censer, swinging between self-pity and desire for retribution.

With each step, I realised how far Crisp had taken me, blindly, into the bush, with the ruse of taking the Elixir du Jour on the road. It was only walking back for miles in the pounding heat that I could see how far he had led me from the city for his ambush. Occasionally I could cadge a ride, but mostly I preferred my own company, suspicious of everyone and wanting to be alone in my thoughts. It took me three weeks to get back to the Big Smoke, penniless and dusty. The sight of the Great Western Highway from the back of a chicken transport truck was like a drink to a thirsty man, though the birds heading for slaughter may have taken a different view. Their incessant shuffling and clucking were living reminder of all the two-bit hellholes I had traipsed through in this life – as a soldier, shearer, knife thrower and then Crisp's bleeding-hearted, easily duped apprentice. The stink of the chickens overwhelmed my senses, but I sat firm. The smell was my constant companion; it coated my nostrils, penetrated the fabric of my clothes and clung to my hair for days, but it was my covenant, never to leave the confines of the city and find myself up Shit Creek again.

The streets unspooled as we drove further into the city. The clock tower of Central Station was like a false moon in the darkening sky; the town hall steps were spilling with council workers, their fob watch chains swinging from their waistcoats. I wanted to take a chicken and hurl it – white feathers, red combs, green shit and all – at their self-important faces. And now I could smell the salty sea kiss come to me on the air: I knew I was back. The salt was astringent and it invigorated me, the sting of my vengeance sharpening my senses. The faces carved in the sandstone post office watched as I passed – an Indian, an African, a Chinaman, all bloody dagos each and every one of them, all spoils of Empire now made ornaments to peer down at us. Queen Victoria's bloated face loomed like a menacing fish, bulbous eyes just like Crisp's watching me as I passed.

It was time to throw off the shackles – what was the Empire except a machine that churned on soldiers' blood? What was Crisp but a balloon that needed to be popped? As we neared the Quay, I hopped off the cart. My city welcomed me with a bouquet of sea bilge and dog turd. The two ends of the newly constructed Harbour Bridge stretched towards each other like a metal spine. It looked a broken thing, a dragon's back that had not the power to span the distance. I knew that when I got to Argyle Street Police Station there would be no bells and whistles for me, no fanfare, for the race had already been run and I was not its victor. I was unsure of what wreckage awaited.

When I told the desk constable who I was, he stuck a finger in his ear and gave it a little jiggle as if to dislodge the deafening plug of wax that had formed there. He asked me to repeat my name and when I did the poor sod pulled a rosary from his pocket as if it was defence against the risen dead.

'I am alive and well, Constable,' I said.

'But, sir, your wife came a week or so back with her father. They were both dressed in mourning, she was crying, saying you had been killed in a freak accident. She had all the correct papers. She even showed me letters of condolence and a receipt from the funeral director for your funeral.'

What chance did the likes of me have against Crisp? The only accident here was my own stupidity. I had let myself be plucked up like a fiddle and my strings played to whatever jig Crisp commanded. Oh, he had been masterful, pimping his 'daughter', winding me up with the hook of a phantom pregnancy. I had been dangling from his reel far longer than I realised. I was lucky that I had not been gutted. They could have killed me for the money my father had secreted away. But they hadn't brought me so low that I couldn't reward them, with my own lack of mercy.

'I assure you I am William Little, and I believe you have my late father's effects and money. My father was William Hezekiah Little of Argyle Street, the Rocks.' She and he would have come, plucky as muck, but they would not have known his middle name.

'They took everything, sir, I'm sorry. They had the wedding and death certificates, what else could I do?'

'But there was a box – surely they left me a box?' Why had they need of my box of treasures? Wasn't the money enough?

'I am afraid Mrs Little expressed a request that she have the box to remember you by.'

'There has never been a Mrs Little, not even my mother,' I sneered.

The constable pulled out a receipt book and showed me her signature and an address. A splatter of bird shit would have been more legible. But the amount she had signed for seemed very high indeed, much higher than the newspaper had suggested. We had been richer than I could have ever imagined. The little petty policeman trembled as he tapped the ledger over and over again, but it would not bring that money back.

'We did a thorough search of the flat before returning it to the landlord, and found thousands of pounds stashed away, sewn into pillows, packed into books with their pages removed, in envelopes stuffed in the lining of your father's coat, slipped behind drawers. Wherever we looked, we seemed to find money.'

I felt the vomit rise. I had been a king in my own castle and had not known it. What had he been doing hoarding it, how long had he had it? We could have lived like men instead of swine rolling in the muck of derelict boarding houses, tormented by the attention of the fleas and the company of the rats who would steal the hair from our sleeping heads to line their nests. How long had he sat upon it, the wealth that could have transformed us both? It was impossible to know – it couldn't have just been the month it had taken for Crisp to fleece me, could it? He had got to my father earlier somehow and my father had become Crisp's cat's paw just as I had. Father and son duped by a crooked bloody spirit.

The constable was glassy-eyed, still caught in Crisp's hypnotic gaze. What secrets had my father squealed, trapped in thrall to that look? I could have kicked up a stink, I could have cried theft, demanded accountability, submitted a written complaint, but I knew nothing would come of it. I knew then Crisp was smoke. No man would ever come between me and what I wanted again.

From the kitchen window I watched the Jew hurrying from the shed, his overfull schoolboy's satchel bumping against his hip. He was mounting his search, and he could not move fast enough. Look at him go! The symmetry of my plan flooded me with sweetness. Let him look for the old man, let him search high and low, let him cooee over the treetops and down in the valleys, it would still be futile. He would be lucky if his own voice returned to him as an echo. To put so much faith in one's family was a mug's game.

A tidy wind stirred through the yard and with the vigour of a broom brushed the Jew out the gate. I stepped forward into the sunshine and let it wash over me, my spine straightening. I was a giver of help, a friend of the family, and soon to be more, much more, to my Lily of the Valley, lover to that pure bloom, with her lips like a thread of scarlet and her mouth comely. My love, my Lily of the Valley.

THIRTY

Lily

I went back inside, my feet swimming in my soaked shoes, my hair trickling water down my neck. I left my footprints all the way down the hall and up the stairs, but I could not bring myself to care. I felt the shadow of the mountain descend upon me, that deep sad coldness once the sun has disappeared. What was I going to do? I could ask Mr Clay if I could go back to ushering, or I could find another job. Ari had made it clear he would follow his uncle's wishes, whatever the outcome of his search. But I couldn't go home, could I? What was there for me now, except my mother's grief? In my pocket I still carried around the letter I had written to her, explaining and putting things to rights, but I hadn't yet found the forgiveness in me to post it to her.

I dried myself with a towel, wrapped myself in a blanket and just sat there. Ari's leaving was so unexpected.

I looked at the package Ari had given me last night, still wrapped in yesterday's news, a day that felt further away with each minute. What did it matter what I felt? He was gone and would go again. I tore off the paper and found a red bound book in my hands: it was a copy of the biography of Houdini that I had eyed on the roadside. I flipped open the front cover and saw an inscription to Ari from his aunt for an earlier birthday and then, below, yesterday's date and the words in a hurried hand.

My Shekinah.

What did it mean? I had no one to ask. Was it another magic word? It reminded me of the word emblazoned on the brooch my father had given me before he left for the war. I only could take comfort in the word *my* – two little letters that were a bridge between Ari and me. I closed the book and slid it back under my bed; I didn't have the heart to flick through any more pages. I listened to the sounds of the house: the water ticking through the drain, a branch squeaking against the cast-iron balcony, the creaks of the floorboards. Even though no one was home, the house was filled with its own life, so I was not alone.

A knock came, a hesitant rap upon the wood. I leaped up, thinking it might be Ari, but as I opened the door I saw it was Billy, a blond lock of hair falling across his eyes, which he brushed away with a smile.

'Care to go for a walk? Can't stay inside all day.'

'It's raining.'

'C'mon, Miss del Mar, bit of rain never hurt anyone. It's clearing up.' He pulled open the curtain and the sunlight slanted through the grey. He had come to try and make me feel better, and though I was still angry with him for his foolish costume, I grabbed my coat and followed him down the stairs.

A light rain fell soft as eyelashes over my skin, yet the sun still shone, making the sky a golden contradiction. Billy opened his umbrella and it arched over the both of us. Sap-sticky fig leaves clung tenaciously to the footpath as water coursed through the gutters. We walked in silence, and there seemed to be no need to break it, as Billy led me through the noisy rushing traffic of King Street, until we turned off into a small side street. There before us loomed a church spire, and Billy paused, his hand on the gate, before he swung it open. It surprised me, for I hadn't thought of Billy as a religious man. Then I saw the saint for whom the church was named. Saint Stephen. Stephen. My father's name.

When my father died, my mother retreated to her saints as if they were living, breathing people, more consolation to her than I could ever be. While she was lost one day in her prayers for him, I heard a muffled thump. Investigating, I found a superb fairy-wren stunned from the collision with the window, his brilliant blue body limp, a small flutter tickling my palm. I laid him in a shoebox lined with newspaper and old holey socks. My father had taught me once how to line a box for an injured lorikeet and put it in a warm, dark spot in the laundry.

'They are fragile things, Til the Lil, so many tiny bones, some fine as hairs. They've just knocked themselves senseless against the window, can't tell their head from their tail. When they are hurt they long to be back in the egg again, so best keep them warm and dark to mend.' The lorikeet opened his beak and let out an ear-splitting screech.

'All right now, feathered thing, you'll be right as rain in no time,' my father said as he carefully placed the poor green creature in the box and covered him lightly with an old tea towel. While we waited my father told me stories about the old country, where the rain was soft as a kiss, where music could be heard beneath the ground, and where birds could be women in disguise. When we went back, my father and I, and listened at the door, I marvelled, looking up at him quietly. The bird had recovered and was shuffling about, stretching his wings by the sound of it. My father let me do the honours and I held my breath as I slowly swung the laundry door open. The lorikeet paused before swooping out of the door, a bright green screeching exit. 'You have the knack, my darling. They can trust your gentle hands.'

Just like the wren, my mother had been knocked senseless by my father's death, but no warmth or quiet could rectify her. She'd always been superstitious, fragile, but my father had kept calm, speaking honeyed words, taking extra care when he found her sticking pins in her palms or making tracks of small cuts up her arm with a razor blade. My father had the powers to keep her darkness at bay, but without him she was without the light she needed to break through the darkness that consumed her.

When I went to liberate the wren from the laundry, the box and bird had gone. In the house, my mother was busy bending over the shoebox, carefully surrounding the bird with flowers and fern fronds, her fingers winding white ribbon to make a rosette.

'A little house for the wren,' was all she said as her hands worked away with an automaton's persistence. I leaned in closer to see if the wren was still alive, but its eye was a black full stop, its little neck floppy, broken.

'In Ireland they hunt the wren every Saint Stephen's day, the first day after Christmas, and carry it from door to door in its bower, its little house. To those who refuse the wren, no luck comes …'

'How about you lie down for a bit and I'll bring you in a nice cup of tea?' I coaxed, taking her by the elbow. There was her medicine in the cupboard, but I wasn't sure I could convince her to take it. At least if she could rest, in the quiet she might regain her senses. My mother shrugged off my grasp and clutched at my hands, holding them so tight that her nails left crescents on my skin.

Seeing my upset only enflamed her and her grip tightened. 'No, Tilly, the world still isn't free of its Judases. They will walk amongst us until the Last Day.'

She dropped my hands with a little sob, and I felt them tingle as the blood returned. She gently lifted her wren house and I dreaded the prospect that she would want to take it from house to house to show the neighbours. But it seemed the fire of her mission was gone from her eyes now and I ushered her down to her bedroom, carrying the box with her.

'Have to keep an eye on our little betrayer. You remember the story of Saint Stephen. He hid in the bushes from those that would martyr him, but this little Judas bird squeaked and hopped over the furze until they found him out. Their stones rained on him, yes, they killed him, they killed your father, pushed down in the mud.' The tears pricked at my eyes, for it was rare that she ever mentioned my father, his memory was for her alone.

I helped her place the box just so, on the pillow beside hers, where my father's head would have lain in sleep, once. This seemed to lend her peace for a time, for she lay there quietly, her eyes settling on nothing in particular, the doleful little bird in his funereal box beside her. I had heard different variations of this story before from my father. He used to tell of how the wren was sacrificed by the druids to call forth the spring. 'Poor bird,' he'd say, 'Spring will come anyway.'

'A penny for your thoughts?' Billy said, his footsteps cracking the twigs across the path between the headstones, bringing me back to myself.

'You'll need a whole pound.'

'See then, there's my quid …' Billy jested and pulled a pound note from his pocket and pressed it into my palm, wrapping my fingers over it tightly. I quickly pulled my hand away.

'I was just thinking of home, that's all.'

'Home, ha! What does it have that the city can't offer? Doesn't the city have it all?' He was playing with me, I could hear it in his voice, but this city never let anyone belong: it was spitting me out, even as I breathed here in this lonely place. I missed a place in the world where I belonged, had once belonged. That world was gone; it vanished the day the army telegram arrived.

'Do you ever wonder if the dead think of us when we think of them?' I spoke my thoughts aloud. Even though I had tried to evade Billy's questions, his joking attempt to pry me open with a pound, my thoughts were turning to my father. We never even knew where he lay. A magpie chortled somewhere high in the enormous fig tree. *Wardle-dardle-doodle-ardle* my father would always reply back. It stopped me in my tracks. 'Sometimes I just miss my father, that's all.'

Billy looked at me then and it unnerved me, for all the pluck had gone and was replaced by a sincerity I didn't know he possessed.

'None of us had much chance. It was Buckley's or none.' Billy had been in the war. We had spoken of it, but he had gone quiet then, and now I understood: there were some things that couldn't be spoken. Billy shifted his feet uneasily, batting a stone with the furled umbrella.

The wind gusted through the churchyard; I hadn't noticed but it had stopped raining. I pulled my coat tighter around myself and Billy, without taking his eyes from mine, put his hand on my neck as if to comfort me, shooting a shiver across my skin.

'So what are you going to do now your *friend* has gone off to find his uncle?' He cleared his throat, glad to change the subject.

I had the overwhelming sense that headstones were listening, seeming to lean in towards us. 'I honestly don't know.' The world seemed askew. If I had the least hint that my father was still alive, I would have crossed oceans. Ari could only do the same now, to find the man who was the only father he had. I understood that, but I had been too stunned to say so. But would Ari really leave his home and all who cared for him, at his uncle's command?

'Surely his uncle couldn't have got far?' Billy wondered. That is what I had hoped, but the Birdman's arrival had spelled otherwise. 'Ha, I wouldn't have looked for my father even if he was on the other side of the street! The boy's aunt said his wallet was on the bedside table, untouched, so he wouldn't have had two brass razoos to rub together.'

'Ari's friend, the Birdman, saw him board a train to the Blue Mountains, so he must have had enough for a train ticket.'

Billy arched his eyebrows then and a curious expression crept across his face. 'The Blue Mountains? Have you been there?' I shook my head. His face grew grave. 'Dangerous place to be stumbling about in. People go missing there every year and are never found. Perhaps the old man doesn't want to be found.'

The instinct to cross myself, just as my mother always did, was strong, but I pushed it down, folded it away in myself. A raven swooped into the long dry grasses between the headstones, taking up a small lizard in her beak, and I missed the pressure of those claws upon my shoulder. Beauty had gone too. How could there be any magic now?

Billy leaned close to my face, his breath upon my cheek, and whispered, 'Perhaps they can, perhaps the dead think of us when we think of them.'

I felt the prickling of my own need. Was my father thinking of me right now? I longed for his voice in my ear with its smiling cadence. If I could speak with him I could get the message my mother so wanted to hear, the message all her praying could never give her: that he was watching over us, close as a heartbeat.

Billy took my hand then, cupped in his, his long fingers engulfing mine. There was no shrinking away this time. I let my hand nest in his, grateful for the warmth of the living.

THIRTY-ONE

Billy

Together we walked in the soft washed world of the cemetery. She was close to bending, though she would not snap, for she was supple, a green willow sapling, pliable enough to be woven into whatever shape I chose. Unlike me, when Crisp and Merle nearly snapped me like kindling and put me in the fire. She was ready now. Ready to see a change in her fortunes.

Mine began when a twenty-quid note blew past me on the street on that dark day after I left the police station. With one step my foot claimed it. I thought about taking it down to the Quay to blow it away in a card game or inhale it through an opium pipe, a tribute to my father, but that thought vanished quicker than a smoke ring. How many of these notes had he stashed about him while we starved? My revenge burned quicker.

I took a room at a hotel and ran the bath water until it was hotter than a scald's tongue and immersed myself until my pores opened and released the bitter absorption of Crisp's influence. It was as if my nose had been pinched closed and my mouth pinned open against my will, the dry, sour pill going down my throat as I gagged. I swallowed a gulp of bath water, a strange brew, an antidote against the bitterness – Elixir du Little – and slowly, as the water began to cool, I felt myself return, the part that had been missing revealed to me. My face upon the surface of the water, in the transparent mercurial skin between the air and the liquid, my true mettle. I stood up, waterfalls trickling from my elbows, my shoulders, my knees. I was baptised: I would be my own salvation.

I dressed and returned to the police station, the air cold on my newly made skin. I could not call myself a man if I didn't at least try to get back what had been mine all along.

Of course the police sergeant had no fixed address for *Mrs Little,* I knew that, but I hadn't served my mock apprenticeship with Crisp without learning a thing or two, even if I myself had been the subject of the most recent lesson. People drop information without knowing it, like the stray hairs off one's head. I could see he was discomfited by even talking to me, pinpricks of sweat beading his upper lip, a tell if there was one. He was the one who had handed over my father's money and my possessions without hesitation, not even a breath between her request and his delivery, I reckoned. I bet his eyes barely skimmed the words of our certificate, the seal of our so-called marriage. She had softly breathed words that made his finger pluck at his damp collar. What light touch had she given him to turn him into such a compliant fool?

I would peel him like a fruit, with a question mark as my blade. But first, I had to appeal to his sense of justice: he was a police officer after all.

'You know what riles me?' I asked, taking my hat from my head and clasping it to my chest in the sincerest of fashions. 'It's not that she was tempted to leave me for the money – I can forgive that as I would have given it to her anyway.'

The desk sergeant's knuckles whitened as he gripped his pen, jotting incomprehensible characters on the blotter, as if channelling messages from the other side. He was but a fish, already sucking on my hook; all I had to do was reel him in.

'It is just that I want to know what I did wrong. If I knew that, I could make it up to her. To her and our little one on the way.'

The sergeant coughed, a surprise gulp of air sending his eyes skyward. 'What sort of woman takes a child from his father before it's even born?' Perhaps he had one of his own. Crisp's mesmeric hold on him was lessening. He cleared his throat and paused, as if trying to work out the most tactful thing to say without making me seem a dupe or him a gossip, but I knew what sort of woman Merle was now, nothing could come as a surprise.

'I did overhear her say something to her father about Australia Street ...'

I was just about out the door when he called behind me, another flake of information dislodging from his mind, a man now eager for my absolution.

'It has to be close to the city, as her father said it would only take half an hour at most for her to go back and get whatever it was she wanted. He was going to meet her back down here at the docks.' He had thrown the dart and it had landed so close. I knew where she was now. All I needed was to get my hands on her, lay them on her and squeeze.

Lily's marble-white hand was in mine; her skin was smooth like a shell. The tenderest expression formed across her face as she turned to make out the inscriptions on the gravestones, and it filled me with a new feeling. I had her hand in mine, but she did not struggle to reclaim it. She was the mouse surrendering to the paw. But even so, I held the kernel of desire that she would soon come to me of her own volition, that for all my defects she could see the better man in me, the man I could become, putting aside my past, my stash of objects, my pursuit of experiences, my gleanings from women who were but fickle examples of their sex when all the while she was the exemplary. Would it be too much to hope that Lily could, without my manipulations, find me already in her heart? Could she learn to love me of her own free will?

IN MEMORY OF
THE MANY HUMBLE, UNDISTINGUISHED,
UNKNOWN, UNREMEMBERED FOLK
BURIED IN THIS CEMETERY,
WHOSE NAMES ARE NOT WRITTEN
IN THE BOOK OF HISTORY
BUT ARE WRITTEN
IN THE BOOK OF LIFE

She read it aloud, leaning toward the monument, her hand withdrawing from mine. I wanted to snap her back, seal her fingers up in mine. It took all my control to resist. She looked at the monument for some time, a slight pink rising to her cheeks. I didn't need a crystal ball to tell she was thinking about the Jew. If only her thoughts of him were banished into the mountains. I knew how to wind her in and it wasn't by force.

'I once met Houdini. Have I told you that before? If I am repeating myself, forgive me.' I knew very well what I had and hadn't told her; this I had been saving for her ears alone. At the mention of the master magician, her face lit up expectantly.

'Not that I recall, I'm sure I would have remembered. Tell me!' There was a happy little skip in her voice. Our feet started moving again in unison as the playful breeze tossed the fallen fig leaves around us, little fox faces looking up at us, rustling as if trying to get our attention.

'Well, I was only a boy. It was when he was out here flying his plane and doing his escapes at the Tivoli.' The questions itched across her face, but she remained silent, her ears hungry for my voice. 'As a boy, I often worked with my father at Rookwood Necropolis. My father would be good for about an hour with a shovel, after I had scraped back the couch grass and dandelions with a hoe. The ground out there could be tough. Sometimes, beneath the grass, a bed of hard clay would make a mockery of his shovel, splintering the handle. These little obstacles would inspire my father's thirst; he would down tools and scan the horizon as if somehow there was a foaming pint of beer in the clouds. He was gone quicker than a raindrop evaporating in the three o'clock sun. For us to get the rest of the payment, I had to finish whatever it was my father had started, a boy doing the backbreaking work of a man. Don't think that I'm complaining. I knew I had to pull my weight and do my share.'

Lily walked even slower beside me, her step a metronome to the music of my word.

'Most things I could manage, except finishing the bottom – for that I would have to leap into the grave six foot deep. I would neaten off the corners, tossing the soil for all I was worth over the edge, some of it falling back down in my face like dirty rain. It was easy until I attempted to get out. I tried to make footholds in the clay and scramble out using the roots of the grass as my ropes to freedom, but not that day. When I met Harry Houdini, no siree, the soil was like sand. I tried to find somewhere to wedge my foot but the whole side of the grave seemed to shimmer as if it would fall like the wall of a sandcastle and drown me on land. I thought about calling for help but there was no one around for a mile. This was the quietest corner of the cemetery, only the sparrows bothered with their dive and burrow into the pools of dust. The sun swung higher into the sky, hot and blistering. I swallowed, my saliva not enough to wet my mouth. This was the view the dead had, the sky only a keyhole, before the dirt rained down, *rat-tat-tat*.'

Lily swallowed noisily beside me as I embellished my enchanting real-life tale with cock and bull tailored for her ears only.

'I didn't hear the sound of footsteps but I saw the hand thrust out. A hail of errant pebbles fell upon my head. Stretching up, I took it, thinking it may have been my father taking pity on me, but at the merest touch I felt that hand's strength, I knew it had to be someone else for it tingled where he touched my skin, like a light electric shock.'

'Was it *him*?' Lily said, her eyes searching my face, as if somehow she would find his name written there. She did not know her own name would be woven into my story before the afternoon was done.

'I was pulled out like a rabbit from a hat, a real little Lazarus. You can imagine my surprise when I saw who it was. I had read the papers, seen the photographs. It was none other than Houdini!'

Lily's feet stopped and she grabbed my arm of her own accord. 'Are you sure?' Her fingers were little trills upon my sleeve.

'He was shorter than I even then and that surprised me, for he was certainly strong to have pulled me up by one arm.

'"You were in a bit of a fix," he said, pinching a worm from my hair, contemplating it for a moment before gently setting it aside on the mound of soil that I had dug.

'"I know who you are," I said. I would have known those piercing eyes anywhere, for his face had been printed in the newspapers, his name splashed on every billboard. Back in the autumn of 1910 in Sydney there was no escaping the name Houdini, he was the master. A troupe of men marched down George Street; I had seen them and thought they looked suspicious when, at a certain beat, they lifted their homburgs one by one, each shaved bald as a convict, a letter painted on the back of each head. *H-O-U-D-I-N-I.*

'He thrust out his hand to shake mine and I was suddenly ashamed of my dirt-crusted nails and my patched trousers. I could see his suit was pressed with creases, the collar crisp and stiff with starch, his nails shapely and clean.

'"I am Billy Little," I said, shaking his hand and giving it a measure of my boyish bravado by squeezing extra hard to show my strength was equal to his, at least in my child's mind. "Is it true you always keep a key in your mouth?"

'Houdini guffawed and I was even more disturbed by those eyes that were sharper than a surgeon's blade. When he released my hand I noticed his two less glamorous companions behind him.

'"And I thought a thankyou was in order! No matter, curiosity is more important than manners in my book. I've done you a favour, now perhaps you can assist me?" I looked around, wondering what he was doing in the cemetery. "Come along, this is exactly the place where one does not want grass growing over one's feet!"

'I walked a little behind the great man, not because I showed any deference but because he set a cracking pace, nimbly leaping over the occasional rabbit hole. We walked deeper into the old part of the cemetery, moss speckling the names on the headstones, until Houdini called out for us to stop. One of his companions dropped a sack he had hauled, the clink of tools hitting stone. Houdini whipped off his jacket, though I didn't even see him undo the buttons. He hung it across the shoulders of the nearest marble angel and folded up his sleeves as if he was about to make a coin dance across his fingers. His companion handed each of us an implement and we all set to work on clearing the grass and muck that covered a particular grave. The writing on the stone was near illegible through the rippling grass blades. We worked for over an hour in the screaming heat, until the blisters on the palms of my hand had baby blisters of their own. Eventually the name was clear: William Davenport.

'William, like me.

'"*That,* my boy, is one of the first escapists, him and his brother Ira." Houdini bent down and flicked the lichen from the letters, but still it wouldn't budge, for it had been baked on by the sun. One of his assistants passed him a wire-bristled brush and then returned to lifting the weeds with a fork.

'"So how did they escape?" I asked.

'"Well, according to P. T. Barnum's *Humbugs of the World*, it was all in the knots. Though the Davenports claimed it was the spirits."

'With a grin, Houdini made the wire brush dance between his fingers, a weightless thing, till it vanished before my eyes.

'"Did the spirits just take that brush? Can you see their shadowy fingers, their muslin breath? No, it is the skill of a human being that made it disappear. Let me tell you this, my boy, my brain is the key that sets me free. I wouldn't want aspiring ghosts to claim my skill."'

Lily shivered beside me; the sun was brushed behind a cloud, a chill descended.

'"So are there spirits?" I asked. All this talk had made my curiosity tingle. Working in the cemetery I often felt eyes upon me. I didn't know if it was the human shape of the sculpted angels that gave a sense of an observing presence, or just the emptiness of the space, the high blue dome of the sky, making me feel like the most insignificant speck, easily blown away, unnoticed. Houdini fixed me then with his silver-eyed glare so that I could not blink even if I wanted to.

'"Let's hope so, boy, let's hope so."

'Houdini retrieved his coat from its angel guardian, which suddenly looked naked without the comfort of cloth. He shook my hand with all the courtesy of a gentleman, though I was but a step away from being a tramp's son. Before he walked away, he seemed to hesitate, and I thought for a moment he was going to tell me something so profound it could change my life and the life of anyone who crossed my path. I thought he would teach me the quicksilver power of his eyes. But he only stopped and picked up a stone and laid it atop the headstone of my namesake. I watched him walk away, acolytes in tow, unable to look away until he was just a flyspeck on the horizon.

'When I opened my hand from his handshake, a five-pound note was scrolled in there, folded over and smaller than a postage stamp. I wanted to put it somewhere safe, somewhere my father couldn't find it. With five quid I could find something to fill my belly when it roared like a fire that nothing could douse. I could pay a cobbler to mend the constant flap in my shoe. With five pounds I could begin to do something to raise myself up properly. I thought about swallowing it, the way I thought Houdini did with his key, or hiding it in the heel of my shoe, but I was frightened that with my sole's blabbering to the footpath I would lose it.

'I thought all these things as I made my way back to the grave my father should have been digging. The sides had collapsed in on themselves, destroying all my blistering work. A thought crept over me like the cold fingers of a shadow. I would have drowned in the dirt until I breathed soil. My lungs would have been stopped up with worms, I would have been buried, a coffin atop my head, if Houdini hadn't pulled me out. I would have been one of the spirits he thought we couldn't talk to but who watched over us. The hoe and the mattock, I realised, had also been swallowed by the grave's mouth. I thought about digging down in the dirt like a dog to try and retrieve them, but the sexton was already striding toward me, the dust ploughing up behind him. I knew my father and I were done for here anyway.'

Lily's eyes shone up at me as if she had seen me in a new light, as if –

Open Sesame! – I had rolled back the stone and been resurrected in her eyes.

'Did … did he say anything to you about his maiden flight?'

I looked at those eyes shining at me and I invented, if not quite the words he said to me, ones said freely to a journalist in a newspaper I had read in the lavatory once.

'I asked him what it was like to fly.' The word hung on my lip and she trembled as if I had all the answers to every question she might ever have.

'He leaned in close and said: "The plane is like a swan, she's a dandy. At first I was more timid than a bird. But it was different as soon as I was up. All my muscles relaxed and I sat back, feeling a sense of ease and freedom and exhilaration." Then a little black shadow caught his eye, twisting its little tail, its white breast bared, a willy wagtail listening to our conversation. The great man scratched at his head. "Funny thing is, when I landed and I threw my arms up posing for photographs and yelling, 'I can fly, I can fly,' a bird like that landed near my head, and chirruped." Houdini chuckled and said, "He was telling me that I couldn't fly a cuss."'

Lily laughed, the echo travelling through the churchyard, sending two crows flapping upward. One hovered around the cross of the steeple, each one driving the other off, great swooping glides, alighting only for a moment before his mate flapped closer, sending him dancing though the air, around and around and around – invisible threads joining them in their mating waltz.

I could read minds and she would speak my thoughts. If she believed in the spirits, why should I not to use them as a key to her door? Once she believed she could do it, then her heart would swing wide open. Lily was so pure she could make me cry. I knew I had sealed up the flaws in my self that Crisp's apprenticeship had exploited. I was no longer the gull. I deserved her. She was my reward in the world to come.

THIRTY-TWO

Ari

The scenery raced past the window quicker than my eyes could fix it, until I tried no longer, letting the shapes of the houses wash out to spills of green. Beside me the Birdman snored, his greasy hide hat just covering his eyes, his arms crossed over his chest. We had boarded the train and found ourselves in an empty carriage. And it was just as well, for Beauty made the carriage her own. She sat on the Birdman's shoulder, pinning us both with a blue intelligent eye, her claws clasping the Birdman's coat, until his snores disturbed even her and she fluttered upwards, curling her talons over the luggage rail above our heads. As the train inclined again the air pressure changed. I felt my ears cram with a thick fog that no amount of yawning would dislodge. I put my fingers to the glass and it was bitterly cold. A small flock of slow-winged black cockatoos seemed to hover on the other side of the window, suspended, before the train took a turn and they peeled away – swallowed by the fog as the train was by a tunnel.

When we came out, a huge gorge opened up, batter-coloured stone outcrops on either side of the gullies with massive drops down to the trees below. The woodland was so dense that I was sure the ground would seldom see more than a sliver of daylight. The train kept ascending, the view falling away with each curve, yet we were only at the foothills of the mountain range. As we climbed, the bush revealed itself to me like an inland ocean, one silvery green wave after the other. My heart plunged. Even if the Birdman had seen my uncle board this line, he could have alighted at any stop and be anywhere, drowning in a sea of trees.

Had Lily ever seen these mountains? There was something about them that spoke her name to me, in their breath gusting through the train's louvred windows, as if all the forgotten words from the song at the party were coming whistling through, eddies for bars, rattles for notes. I thought of her delight when she laughed at the sea making play at her toes. If only I could peel the world like an apple and give her every sweet slice.

The Birdman gulped on his last snore and woke himself, pushing his hat to the crown of his head.

'Not to worry, son, that's just the mountains making their introduction.'

Beauty clacked her beak as if she were adding something to the statement.

'What do you mean?' I asked.

'Some think a mountain is just a lump in the landscape, an obstacle to get over, something to get around. Little do they know the mountain can talk with its own spirit. Yet those that are trying so hard to get over and around, they probably have no time to listen.'

I raise my eyes to the mountains from whence my help comes. I could hear the psalm in my mind, the memory of my uncle's prayers.

'What does your tattoo mean?' The Birdman came right out with it. It shocked me. I was used to it being unmentionable, the mark that set me apart.

'I'm not exactly sure,' I replied.

'Did it hurt?' the Birdman said as he pulled up his shirt and showed me his chest. Below his ribs were several marks, each the width of a small branch. As I looked closer I could see there was no ink to speak of in his tattoos, only blood and scar tissue. 'These hurt like hell, though I didn't cry out, for they are what showed I was a man and no longer a boy, my father's idea, part of his Dreaming.'

The letters in my hand hurt in a different way. Even though I was in the city and had no experience of the bush like the Birdman, I had been part of my uncle's Dreaming, a rescued child. I was his chance of a son, someone to follow in his footsteps and become the family he had desperately wanted. But like my mother before, I had my own dreams and he could not control them.

Once, at the du Mauriers' house, my uncle and Mr du Maurier had been talking in the study; their slowly raising voices had drawn me in. I had caught a sneeze in my hand and they had not even heard me.

'Why did your boy have the mark upon his hand when he arrived? I know your people have their traditions and that it is forbidden.'

My uncle went silent and I felt goose bumps rise on my neck. While Mr du Maurier waited for an answer, a pigeon cooed on the windowsill, over and over like a motor that wouldn't quite start. Then my uncle spoke.

'You are right, Mr du Maurier, Leviticus states as much, for it is only the pagan that will rent his flesh and make markings in homage to false gods and fake messiahs. Like your Jesus you have hanging there on your neck upon his cross.'

I could hear Mr du Maurier's intake of breath, shocked at my uncle's personal tone, for their conversations were usually coated with the dust of formality. But my uncle couldn't stop there.

'Your Jesus, your saviour, was nothing but a charlatan who did small tricks to entertain the masses and called himself the Messiah. He knew how to, how do they say, work a crowd.'

'Israel, I didn't mean to cause offence. I was just curious, that's all,' Mr du Maurier spluttered, but my uncle could not stop, the flag had been waved at the bull.

'It is well known in the *Toldot Yeshu* that your Jesus was just a magician.'

'That is not the common assumption,' Mr du Maurier stiffened. 'Surely that is just apocryphal.'

But my uncle was angry now, and his voice rose and filled the room. 'He made a parchment written with the secret name of G_d, cut himself a tattoo and inserted it into the wound, like ink in my child's marking. Your Jesus chose to do so as a trick, my child did not. He is but an innocent, but we cannot say the same of your saviour – betrayer of his people, claimer of false titles, a mere man. There has been too much blood spilled in his name.'

Mr du Maurier went quiet and we left. As we walked home, I was unsure of exactly what had happened in the study, except that my uncle had come to my defence.

As we had crossed the road my uncle had reached down and taken my small hand in his, the hand with the tattoo, and enclosed it in his and I had felt the shelter of his love.

Instinctively I concealed the tattoo with my hand. The Birdman stretched in his chair and clicked his tongue to the top of his mouth, summoning Beauty. She dropped down to him, and his hands ran affectionately over the petrol-dark plumes. Noah had cursed the Raven for his disobedience; perhaps the same was my due. I was marked from the start. I did not know how to be like the Dove and bring back what was commanded of me. The Raven flew off and never returned; the Dove flew off and delivered a branch, but then it too flew off to find its own kind. What, in the end, was the difference between them? Didn't I have a right to find my own promised land?

The Birdman pulled out something from his pocket, a flash of a silver-bellied skink visible for the briefest of moments. Beauty seemed to smile and the lizard was gone.

'It is good Beauty is here. They are guardians of this area. If you do right by them, they will do right by you. *Wugan* like her have come from this country from the birth of time.'

'How did you find her?' I asked.

Beauty lowered her beak into her feathers and tidied the ones at her breast. She was a dapper bird; every feather had to be in its place. I had grown fond of her, though she belonged only to those she chose to. And part of me wished she had stayed behind and kept watch over the one I had left behind.

'There was a little boy who wandered away from the track into dense bush and me and some other fellas were on a search for him. Well, I came across the willy wagtail who was only too happy to tell me, little gossip, that he had seen the boy at dawn, asleep on a pile of twigs, but for the life of himself he couldn't remember where. I walked onward, my companions taking different directions. It was clear the boy had walked in circles, a dangerous sign, for who knew how far wide he had swung, and I knew that there were old mine shafts and gullies where none would expect them. I spoke a prayer to my ancestors and a flock of mountain-dwelling black cockatoos flew by, and behind them came Beauty, calling noisily. At first I thought she was trying to chase them off, but she was following them, shadowing them, blending into their flock, until for some reason she fell, her wing tips skyward, not flapping. I ran to where I guessed her descent, for she plummeted like a wounded thing, but when I got to that small patch of ground, there she was, her beak ripping apart the innards of a lizard she had spied. The little child was asleep, exhausted, the tracks of tears on his cheeks. I pulled him up into my arms and wrapped him up in my coat and he cried out for his mother, but I would have to do for now. I was about to leave when Beauty hopped up to my boots, thinking I had food, which I did. I gave her a scrap of bread I had kept in my pocket, and for that she adopted me there and then.'

The Birdman's tale was still circling in my head when the train halted and all the passengers tumbled out, including Beauty, the Birdman and I. The icy air stabbed into my lungs with each breath.

THIRTY-THREE

Lily

The rustle of the grasses brushed at our calves as I listened to the hum of Billy's stories. It felt peaceful. I read the monument, the names of so many ordinary, hopeful people inscribed in the Book of Life, and immediately my thoughts were back to the sand, our feet in the water, the salt passed between our lips, and our shout to life. But none of that could give me the answer to what I would do. My life had seemed a cup filled to the brim, but now I felt that with one false step I could tip and lose everything. My happiness was just water in my cupped palm, trickling through my fingers, until Billy mentioned his meeting with Houdini, and for a moment my hope held.

I was more than listening, I was *living* Billy's words, each one a spell, each one making me lean closer to hear them. His voice became quieter with each breath; he was the wind and I was the branch. Did Ari expect me to hold my breath until he returned? I could see now though I hadn't wanted to. He had been plain, he would go away, whether he found his uncle or not. A departure into the bush to be followed by an exile of duty later. When Ari left he took away our chance and the act, and the raven and left in their place a book with a word I didn't understand. But Billy was here. He always seemed to be nearby. When he spoke of Houdini it felt like a message from beyond.

My father's presence was close, I could hear his soul in Billy's words, disarming, enchanting, and it gave me hope, hope that I could find my place in this city yet.

'I could help you with the show if you like. I did a knife-throwing act a long time ago and once helped an old charlatan with his medicine show, so I am no stranger to illusions. But I can do something else, do something better,' Billy said. Knife throwing? I felt chilled, afraid of what he might suggest.

'But Clay said he wanted more flesh, more excitement ...'

'I can talk to Clay. I can give him all the excitement he can handle. But I don't want to see you made so low again, so bare, exposed to all those people that couldn't give a damn about you.'

Billy's vehemence surprised me; his voice was tinged with another emotion. I thought I had owned my skin when the cape fell, that there was daring and skill in it, but when Billy spoke to me, I saw in his eyes that I had presented myself as nothing but an offering to false gods, a misfit of nature in a tawdry display. What had I done? Perhaps my mother was right, perhaps I was tainted, a face turned away from the light. I shivered with my shame.

'What could we do?' My voice sounded desperate even to my own ears.

'You, my dear, will talk with the dead and they will talk back.'

It was as if all my mother's fears became my own. I thought of the album of albinos, those sideshow freaks: they had claimed my fate already once inside the womb, would they do it twice? Their words had followed me all my life like an eldritch hum. Could I speak it, such weird augury? Could I redeem all I had lost? Billy put his arm around me and led me from the cemetery, but I could feel the cold following me as if the dead were already tapping me on the shoulder with communiqués that only I could deliver. Was it possible? Billy seemed so sure, but should I trust in him?

* * *

When the telegram about my father's death arrived, my mother looked right through the postman, as if my father's spirit was right behind him, waiting to take shape and return to her. The door closed, and the telegram, still in its envelope, slid from her fingers to the hall table. My mother took to her bed, a low moan of prayer beginning like the wind whistling down a storm. I wanted to stuff my fists in my ears. She lay on the bed, her breathing laboured, her lips moving, speaking quietly. 'Mizpah, he said. The Lord watch between me and thee when we are absent one from another.' She had my brooch in her palm, squeezing it so tight the pin pricked her skin, a bead of blood in her palm. I snatched it out of her palm, it belonged to me.

My eyes skimmed the words, barely absorbing their meaning, before I let the telegram fall. All I wanted was to be free of my mother's pleas, but I could have told her that God wasn't listening.

I ran for as long as my feet could take me to the base of the hills my father had called his mountains, the hills that grew into the Brindabella Range that shaded our town.

I found a paper knife in my pinafore pocket that I didn't remember putting there. I must have used it to slice open the telegram. I was at the tree trunk scraping its blade into the bark. My mother was already sealing my father up and was drawing the curtains, rolling down the fog of memory, burying him with her prayers.

M

The last day we saw my father, my mother draped her arms around his neck and buried her face in his coat and I stood watching, my face puckered with tears. My father's kiss still pressed on my cheek.

I

My father patted his uniform, my key was in his pocket before he turned and walked away. A whistle on his lips.

Z

My mother and I stood watching him walk down the street towards the station, my mother running her hands down the length of my plait, her rhythmic prayer for his safety echoing the sounds of his footfall. 'God keep you, Stephen Aengus O'Farrell, and keep you safe.'

P

As soon as my father was out of sight, my mother turned and went inside, her prayer unbroken, one hand on her rosary, the other on the scapular she wore beneath her clothes.

A

And I shot out from under my mother's grasp, like one of my father's rescued birds and was after him down the street, the gravel spitting up at my legs as I ran. At the train station the familiar men from our town looked suddenly all the same as they milled around in their new uniforms. I saw my father hoisting his pack higher up on his shoulder and I called to him.

H

His eyes twinkled as he saw me. He swirled me up into the air and into his arms. 'Til the Lil,' he cried and I knew I didn't want to let him go, not then not ever.

'I don't want you to go, Dad,' I cried into his neck, my tears making his collar damp. 'I want you to come back.'

'I will, my darling fair girl, I wouldn't trade you for tons of gold,' he said and kissed my eyelashes and placed me carefully on the ground. 'Look after your mother,' he said before I watched him board the train. Amidst the future widows of our town, I kept watch until the train's steam billowed out in the cool morning air like a ghost.

Mizpah. I carved the word into the tree, but it didn't bring him back. The word was no more magic than I was; it had not kept him safe, it had not the power to keep watch. I furiously dug a small hole at the base of the tree and smothered the brooch in the dirt, turning to mud in the growing rain, and I stamped it down. A curious currawong swooped down to the lower branches of the tree and turned its orange eye on me before gargling out its rain-song. I shivered with the shock of its closeness. My father had said that birds would bring him messages of me, but would they bring me a message of him?

With Ari, I'd never felt the birds were anything other than themselves; they were not part angels or intermediaries between the living and the dead. But what if Billy was right, what if I was the instrument? If I could focus my mind, would I be able to get a message from my father? Just one word I could deliver home, and end the reign of my mother's dark grief. One word just for me?

What if my father had been trying to contact me all along, but I had stuffed my ears with the impossibility of it? *Believe*. The Houdinis' code. If Bess Houdini believed it was possible, couldn't I? Billy's suggestion was a rope thrown to me. I would be a fool not to take it, to keep me afloat. If he could teach me, I would learn.

THIRTY-FOUR

Billy

I blew her like a feather across my palm. It was so easy. I had my arm around her shoulders and she did not flinch. If she was the vessel I thought her to be, open to all I could give her – mind, body, spirit – what in the world would not be mine?

The Fates had smiled at me after my return to the city from my blinkered banishment in the bush – from the money that stopped beneath my heel to the hand that led me to the whereabouts of my box. I knew it was only a matter of time till they would grace me again. I sharpened my blades to a glisten on the stone. I picked up the most obedient and slid it through my waistcoat pocket, sheathed in its mons of leather. I spot-cleaned my one suit and used the steam from the hotel kettle in the breakfast room to reshape my hat. I would regather my strength and then all would see who was king of his kingdom here.

I walked the streets as if I owned them, patting children and dogs alike, taking old ladies by the elbow and giving them a quick foxtrot across the road while the traffic waited. I gave waitresses tips when I bought my cheap chops, as if I actually had in my pocket the money Crisp had taken. But this city was mine regardless. He could not take that. Only Merle's signature and smear of address haunted me: if only I could see through it, for the suburb to be legible, but that was a wild hope, for people like her and me, we have no fixed address. There were thirteen

Australia Streets in Sydney, several thirty minutes from the city. I would find which one. I dreamed it coming clear, the neatly swept front steps, the lace curtains hand-made by maidens in Brussels, a trellis of bee-fat roses nodding their perfumed heads in agreement with me. I was the font of all this generosity, all this rightfully belonged to me. When I caught up and made my mark, claimed what was mine, even the cicadas would sing out my name, from dusk until dawn.

It was morning when I found her. I had risen from the sheets of the hotel I was staying in, not a kink in my spine. I was as straight as a ruler. I shaved slowly with my sharpest knife; I would have used my razor but that was with the treasures that had been so cruelly pried from my possession. On the road I had let my whiskers grow until my face had a golden shadow, but now I scraped it all off with my knife, like the fur off a kill, until my face shone. I had three quid left in my pocket. I pressed my only set of clothes. As I stepped out onto the street, the summer humidity was already turning the sky sour.

I walked the length of George Street, up through the cake smell of the Brewery at Broadway, up the incline towards Redfern railway. My feet took a wild turn through the backstreets and lanes; the housewives hanging out their washing peered over their fences at my quiet step, my hat floating like a ghost over their eye line. The birds were silent, except for the crows that carolled me. It was an easy stone that glided from my hand in their direction, but they were too fast in their black glide. Up through Abercrombie Street and onto King I paced, walking into Newtown. My new town. Gliding past the ironmongers, the theatres, the haberdashers, the traffic rolling on beside me, horses kicking up dust with a military beat, their hoof-beats my accompaniment. I walked past the post office, wishing I had Mercury's winged feet instead of my own. I wanted to see Merle and Crisp so desperately that I started seeing their faces on strangers, their reflections in shop windows, hearing the sound of their voices in the traffic. But there is reward in wanting.

For I saw it then, burrowed into the blondest hair mere steps up ahead, like a golden sheaf in the sun. I squinted and blinked and felt the power of a swallow's first flight guide me, weaving me through the people. I followed close so I could see every detail – the jade insects, the coral leaves, the bloodstone blossoms, turquoise stamens, mother of pearl wings. It was my first treasure, the one I had fleeced from Golden Fortune in the opium den, worn in the hair of the woman who had taken everything from me. Though the crowd was thick with unfamiliar faces, I was only in search of one. I felt that familiar surge in my trousers, for I had vowed abstinence until justice served me.

I was right behind her, but not so near she would sense me, so I could observe her in every way. She cadged a choice cut from the butcher and he gave her a wink with it. She chose only the bruised fruit, to bargain for a lower price. She picked a loaf of yesterday's bread.

I followed her to the house on Australia Street, opposite the courthouse, watched her cross the road, open the door and disappear up the stairs, the door swinging closed behind her. Quietly, I turned the knob and followed, treading carefully on the stairs, but I needn't have for she was there, at the top – changed yet unchanged. It was Merle. Her dark hair bleached to the colour of sunshine, but her moth-fringed eyes the same, except no longer framed by her bottle-thick glasses. I blocked her only exit: unless feathers sprouted from her needle-sharp shoulder blades, she could not evade me this time.

'Billy. I think you had better come in,' she sighed, her voice quietly defeated as she anxiously fiddled the keys hung on a string around her neck. She turned her back to unlock her door and my knife blade itched. It would have to wait until I had back that which was mine.

The door to her room swung open and I knew then that Crisp had rolled over her with the force of a tidal wave as well, for the room was little more than a cell. She would not meet my gaze, but I sought hers in the mirror as she washed her hands in the washbasin in the corner of the room. She filled a dented kettle and put it on the gas ring and hung her head like a penitent. But I kept my eye on her, I who had been once an innocent, twice an idiot. There was but one window and it was nailed shut, so she could not jump out. There was a growing fug in the room as the kettle rumbled, spewing steam. I took the only seat available, the sunken edge of a single bed. The room was colourless except for the golden glints from my precious comb and the green bloom of mould sprouting in a moist corner. If she was living here, why hadn't she sold the comb? It was gold, after all. But I was blessed that she had not, for if she still had the comb perhaps she had the rest too, unless she had considered my treasures worthless and given them as alms to a rubbish bin.

She made me wait and wait we did, patiently, my blade and I. Her belly was far from round, not even a seam of her skirt puckered: if anything, she looked in need of a good meal. When she gathered herself to speak, she stood with her hands wrapped around her elbows, pressing up the curve of her bosom, offering it to me like a strutting dove. Ah, let her not underestimate me, I was steeled against her now, and I could have let the metal fly, target-true, without a thought. She was going to blame it all upon Crisp, I knew, and I waited for the jumble of excuses she would give in an attempt to save her own life. Let her splutter away, her time would come.

'If you have come for Crisp, you will not find him here, nor anywhere, I'll bet. As soon as the money was collected, he did to me what he did to you – disappearing with everything in his portmanteau, his steamer sailing through the Heads to Europe, no doubt with a new name already calculated at our expense.' She rubbed at her face then, before turning away.

My knife hummed in my waistcoat. Could she be telling the truth? If she had the money, then surely she would not subject herself to this squalor. She leaned on the window frame, her arms gripping the sill, the daylight catching my comb, but I let her continue, for I would not be satisfied with just a brief snippet of Crisp.

'I met Crisp six months before I met you. I was working nights on my back and he came along with a proposal that I couldn't refuse. Crisp had set up his apothecary shop and was fishing for the perfect catch.'

'And then he found me, the shapeable dunce?'

Merle cleared her throat. A dust mote pirouetted in a pool of light.

'No, it was your mother.'

My mother? I had no mother. The hairs on the back of my neck pricked.

'She came to Crisp seeking a cure, as they all did. She was suffering and had no one. I remember the first day she showed up, she had suede gloves that snaked up her wrist, every button a pearl.'

'What did she look like?' I remembered the photo I had pinched from my father's pocket watch the day I traded with Golden Fortune for my first treasure. It was in that box, wrapped safely in an envelope. Was that my mother?

'She was a fair thing, eyes just like yours. She had come to see Crisp because she was dying, but her heart was conflicted. With each session the truth cracked out of her like a nut. She told him that when she was sixteen she had an admirer, one of her father's staff who worked as an occasional labourer on their family's vast grounds. He would leave her flowers where she was sure to find them, notes stuck in tree bark along the paths where she would walk, and he would blush whenever she walked past him in his sweat-stained singlet. She would say good morning, but he stumbled with his words and would not talk, but his eyes would burn into her skin as she passed. Her father held her on a tight rein and, as you know, the horse bridled too hard will buck. So when he appeared in her bedroom she did not cry out. But when he put his hand upon her, her limbs turned to stone and she wished she could take back the shy glances she had offered him, will her voice to call out, for what he was about to take was not freely given. By the time her father found out, Billy, your father, was long gone and his daughter was to be a mother before she had the chance to call herself a woman. Her father was beside himself, his little girl was tainted and he hadn't seen it until the doctor came to see why she wouldn't get out of bed. In shame, he sent her away until you were born.'

I could barely keep up; I had more chance of catching a fly in my palm than grasping what she said. But she went on and I listened, against my will.

'Your mother never knew what happened to her child, she was not even permitted to hold you. She told Crisp that she knew the baby was a boy, but her father handled the adoption. He didn't know his daughter's resolve. She paid a sympathetic nurse a fine sum to make sure both your parents' names appeared on the birth certificate, so her child would not be a bastard. She paid extra to have it notarised quickly to skip the queue, so that the certificate was swaddled close to your skin before you were taken. Your mother did not know where you were going, but she wanted to leave you with a way back. The secret was hers alone, until she found Crisp and it all tumbled out.'

Birth certificate, there had never been a birth certificate. I would catch her in her own lie yet.

'Before her father died she asked him about the boy. All he would say was that the child had returned to whence he had come. His death left her a wealthy woman but without the knowledge she craved. Crisp was always swift to exploit the merest of opportunities. So he tracked you down through the registry of births, reading through the war enlisted, tracking your father's last known address and sniffing out your trail. Everything you did became known to him. He studied you better than any book, he knew you from inside out, cover to cover, until he memorised you.'

I wanted her to shut up; I could not hear my own thoughts.

'When Crisp told your mother that he had found you, he told her you were conflicted, not yet ready to see her, even though of course you never knew of such things because you were kept in the dark. She took a turn for the worse and it was at Crisp's encouragement that she made you and Crisp the only beneficiaries in her will. So when she took to her bed, it was Crisp who came and fed her remaining hope with little mouthfuls of you between spooning her broth – tales of your bravery, events that never happened, not a peep of your discharge for dishonourable behaviour – while he kept you close with the promise of learning the key to his great success.'

How could Crisp know of my cowardice? Who hadn't he sniffed at to find me?

'On her deathbed it was Crisp who held her hand and closed her eyes and shuffled through her drawers for an advance until the probate. But what she left him was never going to be enough; he wanted your share too.' Merle's hand wandered up to her neck and pulled at the errant hairs wisping from her bun. If what she was saying was true, my mother and I could have passed each other in the streets. We were sheltered by the same city, our lungs filled with the same air. Could we have met?

'Crisp knew your cheque would be sent to your father's address. He'd given the lawyer your address himself. All he needed in your absence was your namesake father to cash it. And under Crisp's persuasion, he did so. After that Crisp had no more use for him. The laudanum-laced elixir, spiked with arsenic, did the rest.'

The Tincture of Sleep. Merle had baited me with the bottle, letting me drug my father for my pleasure. But had the fatal dose been delivered by my own hand?

'He waited for you to leave your father's place the day we left Sydney. It didn't take much for him to convince your father he could fly. Crisp tailed you all the way back to the shop, ready to intercept if you turned around, while I wired the police anonymously of your father's suicide.'

'But the cart?'

'Packed the day before and kept out of sight. Crisp knew all he had to do was get you to come with us and leave you in the middle of nowhere like Hansel in the forest, then come back to collect the money, with your last name attached to mine, your ring upon my finger.

'I can see you don't believe me,' she said, the brazen tone returning. She was no more frightened of me than she would be a cat who had woven in and out between her legs and bared its teeth at her touch.

I rose from the bed, opened my jacket and took a step toward her. Her eyes flicked to the door but she had no chance of getting there. I heard the handle turn and I spun on my heel, for a moment convinced that the door had begun to open at her will. But in came an older woman with her hand on the shoulder of a little girl. Her dark curls flounced around her face as she ran towards Merle, her arms outstretched. I was seized with panic that the child was hers and mine, though of course the age was wrong. Could she be Crisp's? I could see her piteous ploy: she was going to try and milk me dry. She had been Crisp's attentive apprentice longer than I.

'See why I could not refuse Crisp? I was on my own and anything is better than earning a living on your back just to pay rent.' She held the child closely, cupping her head to her breast, stroking the dark hair. Just like my mother would have wanted to hold me. I had no choice but to believe her. All I wanted was what was my very own.

'Do you have my box of things at least?' I asked, stepping towards her and the child. She had shown me her weak spot now. I tangled my fingers through the child's fine dark hair and Merle lost all hesitation, finding a fleet quickness in her step. With the child in reach, she kneeled and pulled out my box from under the bed, pushing it toward my feet, a barrier between us. She leaned to scoop up the child, but with one tug I tore the comb from her ruined, bleached hair.

Wasting no time, I was out the door with the box in my hands, barely a moment to glance at the contents. By myself I was only half of what I could be. What I needed was the perfect helpmeet to complete me in my abilities. And I found her, in a house called Leda, my downy girl, my Lily of the Valley.

With the golden comb in my pocket I itched to crown her, she that was a price above rubies, my Lily among the thorns. On my own I was still only half of what I could be, but with her, who I had set as a seal upon my heart, I could be more than I dreamed. If Lily believed she could talk with the dead, then she would believe in me. She would be my Beginning and I would be her End.

THIRTY-FIVE

Ari

The smell of eucalyptus went right up through my sinuses and into my head, overwhelming my senses. The air was thick with it. Once we'd stepped off the train at Katoomba, the Birdman went to collect some of his belongings from a house not far from the station. A smattering of snow floated in the air as I waited. Could my Uncle Israel really be here in these mountains? His suit that he took so much pride in would be no match against this soul-chilling cold. The Birdman was not gone long, and he came back laden with a bulging pack, and a grey mass of fur that he threw in my direction. With a complaining caw, Beauty took wing.

'That should sort you out.' In my hands was a coat made of kangaroo fur and lined with wool, the collar trimmed with the fiery pelt of a fox. I pulled it on. The sleeves ended above the wrists, but it was warm and cut the cold before it could soak any further into my bones. I was glad of it, remembering with a jagged pain the last time I had felt cold like this, as the Angel of Death came close to my ear, as my mother ran with me through the snow. Again I felt the breeze of its wings against my cheek, the dark exhalations of the frozen earth beneath my feet, and I wanted to run – but to where? Away? Home? Home was a place as distant as the nearest star.

'I've seen better fits, but it will do you,' the Birdman said, tugging at the sleeve to see if it would give another few inches.

We walked off down the road and I tried to adjust to the heavy old coat that smelled of tobacco and must and pulled tight across my back. We were in the mountains but I couldn't see much, except for the small town we were walking through. Beauty flew along high up above us, and I wished I could see though her sharp eyes the span of the mountains and valleys, to spot from above a broken old man.

'Not long now, my boy, no use going into the belly of the beast without a blessing.' The supply of cans in the Birdman's pack knocked together and as we walked down the slope of the street I recited a prayer through my head, only barely noticing the people staring at the strange trio we made – Birdman, Beauty and I, with my weird coat flapping about my legs. *I will lift up mine eyes into the mountains: from whence shall my help come? My help comes from HaShem who made Heaven and earth …*

A mountain mist began to roll down, obscuring the street. It felt like we were scaling a cloud. Beauty flew in and out of view, and the houses that flanked us fell away until there seemed to be only the sage-coloured bush on either side. Still the Birdman kept up his whistling. Occasionally a parakeet, a red blur, would scream past in reply. He would stop and listen and then take up his tune again. A light whisper of rain began to fall, beading my coat. We walked onward, the sun pushing the clouds away, shooting rainbows through the slow-dispersing mist.

The view became clear. I didn't know the human eye could see so far: the mountains seemed like the rim of the world. Everywhere I looked they were insurmountable, a never-ending banner of trees, rock face and eucalypt-blue air. In the middle of this ocean of forest were three sandstone pillars bursting out of the valley, towering out of nowhere, making me realise how high up we were. The Birdman was singing something under his muffled breath, his beard tucked into his chest, fog escaping his lips. Vertigo made my legs sway. When he stopped, I asked him what this place was, this strange cradle that seemed to hold all the world.

'This, my son, is the womb of this country. Those three sandstone outcrops were once three sisters. Their father turned them into stone when a bunyip sought to eat them. Enraged, the bunyip chased him until he was cornered, so he took his wand and turned himself into a lyrebird, but in his efforts to escape, he lost his wand. To this day he wanders the valley floor looking for the wand he lost, his daughters waiting for the spell to be broken.'

'Do you believe that story? Is the bunyip real?' I asked.

Beauty flew off the ledge and it felt like part of me flew with her, the green falling away below us, as I peered over the edge.

'Well, son, I don't know. There is a bit of truth in every story, isn't there?' He laughed then, the sound echoing over the valley and sending a nearby pair of galahs off into the air complaining. 'But you are too scrawny and old for a bunyip, they like 'em young and juicy.' He chuckled all the way to the start of the track down to the valley.

'Where's Beauty?' I asked. She was nowhere to be seen; my one link to reality, to Lily, to the life lived on the other side of these mountains.

'Short cut. Don't worry, she'll be all right, she will have a full belly and be there the quicker for it.'

We zigzagged down into the valley. The earth was damp, and every now and again a step turned to a slide. It seemed endless, as if the valley floor would never rise up to meet us. Fern fronds brushed at my hair like fingers, and the familiar sound of the lyrebird filled me with the shame of all I had turned my back upon, on Lily and the birds cooped in the shed, poor creatures. If Beauty should have her freedom, so should all the rest. Would Lily think of this too, while I was gone, or would she wait? She was a constant presence in my mind. She had been almost silent when I left; I didn't blame her. I wondered if she had opened my gift. I was no wordsmith, but I hoped my inscription in the Houdini book would help her understand how I felt. It was my promise that I would return. She was my light.

I was unsure of the passing of time, only that the sun was no longer visible, the light diffuse, each shadow now falling heavier than the last. The further we went, the smaller I felt. When we reached the valley floor I was relieved at the first stripes of sunlight we had seen for miles. The Birdman would stop sometimes and I would pause too and look into the trees for the secret signs that I hoped he saw, but then he would just shrug his pack straight on his back and walk on without a word. If my uncle was here, we would need more than a miracle to find him.

Just before the light gave way completely, the Birdman struck a fire from some damp wood, a ribbon of smoke wending its way skyward. I don't know how the spark caught, but the Birdman had more knowledge about the ways of this wild world than I. When Beauty came fluttering in over our heads, a dark-winged familiar, I felt a little bit of calm descend. Perhaps this wilderness would not claim me, would return me and my uncle to the safety of home yet. By HaShem I hoped she waited there for me.

The Birdman opened a couple of cans of beans and sat them amidst the flames. I felt so pitifully unprepared. When I reached into my own bag, I had nothing to offer, but I felt something unfamiliar and jagged in my hand and pulled it out. The black leather box of the tefillin was cracked open like an egg. The Birdman poked a stick at the flames and they licked up in the night air. Tilting the leather box close to the flames, I was sure I could see something glinting inside, other than the parchment it should have contained, but it could have just been the firelight dancing off the lacquer. It must have crushed when I had slid in the mud on the descent. It was useless now the seal had been broken. I ran my fingers over the edges of the box; one part seemed tackier than the rest, as if it had been stopped up with glue. Something moved from one side to the other like a die in a cup. So I gently squeezed at the seam and shook the contents into my lap. The curled parchment came first, followed by the flash of a key. How had it got in there? Had my aunt tampered with the tefillin? She knew as well as I did that interfering with its seal made it invalid.

The Birdman whistled at the key in my hands but said nothing. He plucked out a couple of forks from his bag and vigorously shined them with the inside of his jumper.

I unfurled the parchment, hearing the words ring out in my uncle's quiet but rich voice. '*And Moses spoke to the People: Remember this day, in which you come out of Egypt, out of the house of bondage; for by strength of hand, the Lord brought out this place …*' I held it up to the light to read it, but behind the commandment, on the reverse, other letters sprung to life where none were meant to be. I turned it over.

> *By the angel of the hour and the star, in the name of the Lord, the great, mighty, and awesome G_d, HaShem is His name, and in Thy name, G_d of mercy, save me by this writing and by this amulet, written in the name of Israel. Help him, deliver him, save him, rescue him from evil men and evil speech, whether he be Jew or Gentile. Shake off the dust – arise! Wake up! Wake up! For your light has come, rise up and shine; Your G_d will rejoice over you like a groom's rejoicing over his bride! May the Shekinah rest upon you. Amen and Amen.*

Was it a message? Who had written these words? They were in a different hand. I ran my hand over the parchment. The words swirled in me and around me like a pair of arms, holding me close. They pressed on my face, warm as breath. The smell of the beans made my stomach roll with hunger, but these words were like manna in the wilderness. I put the case back in my bag and tucked the key and the parchment in the pocket of my shirt, safe beneath the patchwork fur coat. The Birdman gingerly plucked a can from the fire and handed it to me with a fork standing upright in it. The heat entered my body, bean by bean, and the hot can itself was better than a pair of gloves. When we had devoured every bean, the Birdman pulled a rope from his bag and drew some of the nearest shrubs together, bending them forward, stripping the lower foliage and attaching them to a branch that had fallen from a gum. From his bag he pulled a waxed canvas that would shield our backs from the bush as we faced toward the fire.

'It will keep the mist off us and the dew. They make a person feel the cold twice, then it sinks to the bones and chills the blood and there is no getting rid of it.'

I had never slept so close to the earth before, but at least we would be warm. Just outside the ring of firelight, I could make out the green-black sheen of Beauty's feathers as she too preened for sleep, her beak disappearing beneath her wing.

The Birdman's choking snores soon filled the night air, undisturbed by the possum's grunting among the treetops. I pulled out the parchment again and looked at it by the dying light of the flames. I prayed that the words on the amulet would throw the protection of HaShem over my uncle, wherever he was in this wilderness filled with a host of sounds foreign to our ears.

Sleep came and took me and in my dreams I could see my mother up ahead, turning back to me, the wind blowing her hair over her face. Stumbling to keep up with her, my small feet were caught in every rabbit hole, tripping on pebbles, leaves blowing in my face. But I never fell too far behind, and she was always there, just up ahead. Even if I couldn't see her face,

I could hear her laughter. As I followed, the snow turned to shoots of green, until the ground was a living carpet, the seasons spinning beneath my feet, until my feet were the size of a man's. But by then I could no longer see her. She had gone. All I could hear was the rustle of her skirts in the treetops, the sound of her laughter from the throat of a rook. When I stopped running I saw the tefillin in my hands, the leather cords trailing around my wrists, but I was not alone. I put the tefillin behind my back for before me stood a man demanding whatever it was that I held. With each step he took closer, I felt fear trickle like rain down my spine, until I could bear it no more. I held out the tefillin, but it was a black box no longer, they were two doves in my hands whose wings fluttered in the cage of my fingers.

I woke thinking I held them, but it was just the air trailing through my fingers, the parchment from the tefillin gone, lost in the night. The Birdman was already stoking the embers of the fire, the billycan in his hand, swinging it around and around in a strange ritual. I wanted to read the parchment again and scoured the nearby bushes, but it was nowhere. It had blown away, fluttered into the fire, or been scavenged by an animal. It had vanished. But it didn't matter, I still had the key, it must unlock something. And now I had read the parchment, the words were part of me, they had seeped into me like ink.

THIRTY-SIX

Lily

I was tired. I felt like a heavy sponge that had taken in all it could. Billy and I got back to the house, the long dark shadows of the afternoon already reaching through the shimmering windows. Billy supported my elbow and steered me up to my room like an attentive chaperone. He pushed open the door and sat me on my bed, then fell to his knees as if he was my own private apostle. He eased the shoes from my aching feet, his cold fingers pressing into the tired soles. He held each of my feet in turn, inspecting them with an antique dealer's air, his fingertips tracing the dips and variation between the skin, muscle and bone. With each caress I felt a little bit of tension disappear, until my feet no longer seemed my own.

Billy came to sit next to me, the mattress sagging, pushing us together as if in conspiracy. His thigh rolled closer to mine. In front of us, on the wardrobe, hung the magic act costumes, two ghosts, one black, the other white, the hems billowing with life, dancing in the draught from under the balcony door.

'Lily, I think the dead will talk through you. I feel it. I could teach you, if you were willing.'

'What makes you think I have a gift like that?' I asked.

Billy looked at me then as if he could see all those spirits behind my eyes, clamouring to speak. I desperately wanted to blink, but I could not, I could not look away from Billy.

'Because it is written all over you.' I felt overcome with the urge to scratch, as if somehow I had been imprinted with messages written in spidery ink, like having run into cobwebs that I could not pluck away. 'Just think of it, Lily, you could help others find the peace they have been craving. You could speak to those you have loved and lost. Not only be heard but be given a reply. Imagine.'

My breath was ragged. I could not stop imagining. I thought of the telegram, my mother's crippling loss, and that word I had carved into the trunk of a tree. *Mizpah*. Was it a bridge not just over distance, but from this world to the next? *Mizpah, the Lord watch between him and me when we are absent from each other.* Could I dare hope to make contact, have word from him, be reunited with my father in spirit?

Billy bounded up and tugged the clothes from their hangers, which clattered at the affront. He bundled my dress and Ari's suit together as if he was about to throw them out of the window, but I was up on my feet in an instant, gathering them from his arms. These were our costumes, given over in good keeping to us by Miss du Maurier; what right had he? But as my fingers brushed Billy's, a crack of pain ran between my eyes and snaked its way into my head, illuminating Billy's face for a moment, like a photographer's bright flash.

'You are worn out. Let me run you a bath to ease your mind and body and then we can begin.'

The thought of melting into the water, dissolving the panic, sloughing off my old skin in preparation for the new, was the only thing in the world I wanted. How did Billy know my wishes even before I did? The silky satin of Miss du Maurier's old wedding dress caressed my cheek, soft like a feather.

'Perhaps I will just put these in the shed first,' I said, my hand at the doorknob before Billy could say anything. He took a step toward me and watched me go down the stairs, then I heard his feet above and the rattle of the taps as the hot water struggled to come through.

The shed was cold, but it made me blink and draw breath. I had grown too hot, without even noticing, Billy's ideas filling my blood like mercury rising.

Abracadabra, screeched the parrot at the shock of the light. The shed had never seemed so bare. The cot bed was neatly made and I laid the costumes on it, our clothes entwined together in a way that made my heart lurch in my chest.

The currawong and lyrebird watched me dully as I filled their bowls with seed and water, not even curious about the half-opened door. They needed some more greenery, an apple or a lettuce, and I felt guilty for my recent neglect. I couldn't keep them caged for much longer in this old shed, they needed air and light. I coaxed the parrot onto my finger and he gingerly stepped up my arm. I loved brushing down those feathers; the beauty of them still awed me. He deserved better, he deserved his freedom. Next to Ari's bed were the old plane tree seedpods. I cracked one between my teeth, but the bounty was small; what there was I fed him from my lip.

Abracadabra, the parrot said again, the word caught in his throat. I coughed.

'Mizpah,' I said back to the parrot, half-expecting another voice to reply.

Mizpah, it croaked.

'Shekinah,' I said, the meaning still unknown.

Shekinah, it echoed me.

The lyrebird floated down to the floor, his feet scratching in the dirt for imaginary grubs.

Abracadabra, the lyrebird sang, then rolled into the thrill and fall of the currawong's song, imitating his companions. I didn't know the lyrebird could speak too.

I sprinkled some seed on the floor for him to scratch at, then heard Ari's violin come chortling through his throat. Each otherworldly note sent me stumbling backward until I found myself sitting on Ari's bed, listening to the thread of notes spilling from his beak as if nothing had changed. For a moment Ari's shadow fell across me, and I looked up, but it was just the last light navigating the smears of the window. I felt the tears roll out of me then, a useless waste of water that burned as it flowed down my face. I would let the tears fall. For my father, for Ari, for what had been; they were never coming back and neither would I. That was the vow I made myself the day I ran away.

After my boss tried to force himself upon me I ran and ran, leaving the outskirts of the town, and eventually I found myself upon the mountain where my father and I used to walk. It had grown smaller as I had grown bigger, just a glorified hill. It was up near Merlin's rocky chair that I looked for the tree where I had carved the word, but each tree trunk was bare and bushfire charred. I ran my hand across the bark, and in the end I found one remaining letter, barely making it out beneath my touch, an *A*, on a blackened stump. Even that word, that link between my father and me, was gone. I felt my loneliness open up beneath me and I was frightened of falling in headfirst. I dug for the brooch but it was gone.

The sun was low on the horizon when I made my way back home, walking through the surrounding paddocks rather than the main roads, afraid of passing cars in case in one was my boss. His words still rang in my ears. 'I will tell how you parted your legs in an instant. I will plaster your name and address on the toilet wall, so every blow-in from out of town will call in at your place thinking it the local knock shop.' Not only that, he called out with every step I took, 'I will say you do it every which way and that you do it for free. But most of all you slut,

I will tell them that you like it forced upon you, that when you say no you mean yes and then some.'

As I opened the screen door, my mother was upon me, her switch raining down the blows upon my head, slicing through the air with a *thwick-thwick-thwick*. After my father died she turned her affliction outward and aimed it squarely at me. I put my arms over my face to protect myself, and turned myself away, but still her blows rained down.

'How dare you wear your father's clothing,' she shouted at me. 'You are a thief, Matilda O'Farrell, and a whore too. The Lord help me!'

'It's not what you think, Ma,' I pleaded. My father had asked me before he went to war to look after her, but how could I? Without him she had been consumed by her saints and her prayers and her superstitions. 'Not what I think?' she screamed. 'I heard it from Mike. He came here and told me what he heard at the bar up at the Royal this afternoon. He wasn't sure whether to tell me or not, his hat in his hands, but he thought I had a right to know. Your father would be so ashamed.'

I flinched, I had done nothing wrong. How could she speak of my father being ashamed when he was dead? How dare she speak for him? It was because he wasn't here that she had become a martyr to her prayers and rosaries and saints, the woman schoolchildren laughed at in the street for crossing and recrossing herself fanatically, the one who arrived early for every service, claiming the first pew as her own.

She raised the switch against me but I caught it in my hand, wrenching it from her grasp, and snapped it, tossing it to the floor. She fell to her knees, weeping, as the cuts on my cheek stung.

'He wouldn't have gone to war, Ma, if it wasn't for you. It was because of you he went, to get away from your poison. There are more bleeding hearts in our home than an abattoir.'

I too could strike a blow. At this she collapsed, pressing her scapular to her lips.

'Ma!' I shouted, but she didn't hear me. Her eyes were squeezed shut, her prayers growing louder to shut me out. 'Ma?'

My belongings didn't fill much space in the suitcase I took from my parents' bedroom. My mother was still prostrate as I slammed the door. She did not even pause in her supplication.

My tears had dried by the time I reached the bathroom, where the taps had stopped running. Billy must have heard my footsteps and opened the door. Every surface in the bathroom was pearled with the heat, a welcoming steam enveloping me. Beside the bath were a fresh towel and a bottle next to a glass of cloudy liquid that Billy had poured. 'Something to help you relax,' he said, handing me the glass. Something, I hoped, to take away the thump of headache that had taken root in my mind and made it hard to think. Billy slipped the bottle into his pocket. I sipped at it as he left me in the misty room, to shed my clothes and scald my skin in the lapping waters of the bath.

THIRTY-SEVEN

Billy

I could have watched her through the keyhole, but I didn't need to. I was changing, I could feel it; her growing presence was life's pure elixir. I could feel all the irreparable things I had done in my life mend. The sour taste I had had in my mouth since Merle was growing sweeter, ripening in my mouth like a summer fruit. I could almost taste the flavour of our future, Lily's and mine – it was manna, it was the loaves and the fishes, it was water turned to wine – nothing short of miraculous.

In my box I had found the remainder of a bottle of Tincture of Sleep with only the merest of misgivings, but I only gave her a couple of drops. Just to help her on our way, to release the last strings that bound her to another, to let me be her air, to make space in her for me to fill.

Those infernal costumes had enraged me, rattling their spineless bodies against Lily's cupboard, black and white, flapping at my eye like a splash of bird shit on a bride. I did not want them to drag her mind back into the past, to that Jew, he who had tried to debase what was mine.

I called her name through the bathroom door, but there was no reply. So I called it again and again until I had visions of her face falling below the surface, her nostrils filling with the hot water, her lungs capsizing. My own lungs hurt at the thought, and I hurriedly thrust open the door, my heart a military drum.

She was asleep, the water cradling her face like a star. Her body was partially submerged except for the starfish of her nipples breaching the water. I walked over, closer until I was standing over her, seeing her breath sending ripples across the mirrored surface of the water. Her hair moved around her face with the currents of her breath; the hair between her pale legs swayed like a sea anemone's petals. She was the most transparent, most beautiful creation. She was proof that there was a God. She would give herself to me willingly yet. I sat on the edge of the bath, the steam wafting up to my face and drew her carefully up from her sleep.

'Lily, Lily can you hear me?' She opened her eyes sharply, but they had no focus. My lips moved near her ear and she blinked. She was the bride receiving the words of her bridegroom. The water entered her mouth and she coughed, her eyelashes fluttered. It was done. I was her holy wine. She was my Leda rising from the waves and stepping into my arms. I wrapped the towel around her, droplets from her hair kissing my collar, my lips, my shoes, and led her back to her room, her wet footsteps fading behind her. She had no one to guide her but me.

She shivered, her teeth clicked together like the beginning of a cicada's song. I bounded over to the fireplace and stoked the flames, their shadows, an offering, at her feet, that lent an even redder glow to Lily's bath-rosy skin. I took the towel and rumpled it across her hair, soaking up the excess water. Droplets hit the flames, hissing. Let them hiss! I ran the towel across Lily's skin, running the towel across her flanks, between her delicate toes and fingers, down to the ivory dip in her back and the softest skin below her breasts until she was fresh and dry. Her head drooped, and she moaned as I led her to the bed, curling her legs under the sheets, pulling the blankets up under her chin.

I kissed her forehead chastely – there would be time enough after my experiment had been proved a success, after Lily had placed her faith solely in me. I felt around under the bed and found the plait and put it in my pocket. Tomorrow I would come for the rest. I lay on the bed next to her, the sheets and blankets all that divided us, and began filling her with all the words she needed to know, all the secrets she would take as proof.

'Believe, Lily, believe,' I whispered, stroking the smooth skin of her brow. She would talk to the dead if I told her she could, just as I talked to her soul, until she came to understand who loved her most in all the world, until she woke to the truth that she was born for me.

THIRTY-EIGHT

Ari

A low drizzle fell slantwise over our faces, clinging light as dew to our hair. The Birdman whistled, imitating whatever song was called to him from the trees above. A pair of rosellas screeched their news about us, shooting through the metallic sky. We walked through the undergrowth, the ferns growing thicker as we moved through the valley. Beauty held a twig in her beak as she flew, dropping and swooping to catch it with a satisfying clack of her beak. I could see no reason why she did it, except for the pure love of it, her own midair magic show.

Occasionally the Birdman stopped and would listen to the hush, which after a moment would teem with sounds that our footsteps had disguised. He read the signs where I could see none. Sometimes there seemed to be a path, and sometimes the bush was thick with bottlebrushes and banksias which the Birdman would point out to me and name, as if he found my education in such matters lacking. Which it was. Was this a new Eden? Could this be my uncle's Promised Land? A strange, verdant place shaped by the Master Craftsman's hand.

The leaves here never dropped, no matter what the season. The leaves from my old home I remembered were so different – adrift with blossoms in the spring, bowed with snow in the winter, turning gold to red to brown in between, until they fell.

With a whistle, Beauty soared down to my outstretched

hand, the raven's strong dark claws wrapping around my fingers, talon over ink, puckering but not piercing my skin.

And then I remembered an autumn night long ago, when the leaves had been dark shapes hovering around the window frame, their shadows casting arcane markings on the floor.

Inside my mother's room, which I seldom entered, a lamp burned low on a table, but in its glow I could see that the room was in disarray. She must have run out of paper, otherwise why else would she practise her letters upon the wall?

'I won't get in trouble, my love, and I haven't lost my reason,' she said as she helped me clamber up onto her bed. My eyes trailed over the markings, failing to comprehend them. 'It is these words that keep the food on our table, it is my trade.'

I didn't know what she meant, but I didn't dare ask and risk ejection from my mother's room. The small table beside her bed held a tower of books that trembled as I touched them.

'Where did all those books come from?' I asked, my eyes flitting over the spines.

'They were your grandfather's, and then they were your Uncle Israel's, but he didn't take them when he went away, neither did he want much to do with them when he was here. He didn't think them fit for the likes of him.' Her small dressing table was the only clear space, and I could see she used it as a desk. Upon it was a bottle of ink, a metal stylus, a fine blade, brass nibs scattered across the surface, a pen, a *yad* pointer and rolls of parchment.

'Ari,' my mother said, her hand touching my cheek. 'Ari, my beautiful boy. I am going to tell you a secret.'

I sat very still, waiting for the secret to fill me.

She reached around her neck for a silver pod, unscrewed one end and drew out a rolled parchment. 'Ari, this is an amulet. It is time for you to have one of your own.'

I felt the excitement course through me. I couldn't sit still. She unfurled it in her palm, and I saw the letters unfold, losing a letter with each line.

A - B - R - A - C - A - D - A - B - R - A
A - B - R - A - C - A - D - A - B - R
A - B - R - A - C - A - D - A - B
A - B - R - A - C - A - D - A
A - B - R - A - C - A - D
A - B - R - A - C - A
A - B - R - A - C
A - B - R - A
A - B - R
A - B
A

'What does it mean?' I asked. I knew my letters, but not this word.

'It is a magic word,' she whispered, taking me by the hand and leading me to her dressing table, seating me on the stool and placing a towel on my lap. 'HaShem's magic,' she said laying my hands across a cloth. 'It can extend His protection over you.'

HaShem shall keep thee from all evil;
He shall keep thy soul.

Beauty hopped from my hand to my shoulder before flying back up to her vantage point amidst the treetops. Eucalyptus twigs crunched underfoot. Up ahead something fluttered in the undergrowth. I was barely aware of the landscape we were walking through, but the Birdman led me up an incline and I followed, my hand tingling as it had when my mother had run her cold fingertips over mine that day she had marked me. Her gentle face had smiled reassuringly in the circle of lamplight, a circle I had thought could never break.

'Your father of blessed memory had an amulet that I made for him, but he thought it foolishness.' She opened a bottle of ink and gave me a spoonful of strange-tasting honey that made my tongue numb, the dullness spreading down my limbs.

'Is that before he went away?' I asked, my tongue fat in my mouth.

'Yes, my *boychick*, before he died.'

'If he had taken it with him, would he have lived?'

My mother took the stylus and tested its point on an odd scrap of parchment, the line sharp and colourless. She looked at me but didn't answer my question.

'This amulet I am going to give you is one that you can never lose or forget. It will be with you always, whatever may come.' She held the stylus over the middle finger of my left hand.

'Like the *hamsa* hand that Bubbe wears under her blouse?'

'Yes, but better – your hand will be the *hamsa*, you won't even have to take it off for a bath.' She kissed me softly along the flesh of my hand and asked me to be brave as she made the first piercing marks upon my finger, my teeth clamping down. The pain roared in my ears and then was a quiet rumble after she spooned me some more strange honey. She filled them with stinging ink, her voice soothing and low like a lullaby. Slowly a word emerged, between the blood and the incision.

I had not known then that it was forbidden, that the word would set me apart, as I had been both bewildered and blessed by my mother's pen.

The Birdman up ahead whistled and turned to me, his eyes aglint with what he saw. When I caught up, I too could see what it was. A circle of ground had been cleared and patted down, round and shiny, carpeted with a litter of leaves. At its centre were two curved walls of twigs, leaning together but not quite meeting. Scattered around the central structure was a surprising cache of objects, familiar, but strange in this setting. And there in the middle was a fragment of blue-and white-fringed cloth, otherworldly, a scrap torn from my uncle's prayer shawl.

THIRTY-NINE

Lily

My mind swam around itself like a fish in a bowl. Everything was blurred. I remembered getting into the bath, those first few moments when I felt the hot water burn away the tension in my skin. But how I had arrived in my bed I did not know. I couldn't tell what was real and what was not; all I could remember was a warm breath on my face and odd words coming through the silence. I could not get my bearings. Had I always had the gift Billy claimed for me, but just not been still enough to hear it? *Believe, believe, believe. Answer pray tell now believe, believe, believe.* Where had I heard these words before? My mind spun around their ring and echo but could not settle. It sounded like a nursery rhyme. Was that my father's voice?

Points of light flickered around the room when I managed to pry open my eyelids, but my lids were made of a heavier stuff and fell against my will. I slid back into darkness. And then I was suddenly like the air, the rooftops running fast beneath me, until I was over vast stretches of water, between the patches of green. I was the dove that left the ark, flying higher and higher into the heart of a mountain, where the mist rolled off the mountains.

I reached out my arms and let the mist run over me, tickling my skin and drenching my face, surprisingly warm. I let it run down my cheeks unchecked like tears. I felt a rustle in my palm and saw a little blackbird making a nest in the cup of my outstretched hand, fluffing her feathers as she took shelter.

When I woke, Billy was asleep in the chair beside my bed, his chin lolling onto his chest, candlelight flickering across his blond hair. Why hadn't he slept in his own bed, it was only next door? His face was soft and boyish when he was asleep, yet he had mauve shadows beneath his eyes.

I eased myself upright, but realised with a shock that I was bare beneath my sheets. How had I made it from the bath to here if not with Billy's assistance? He slept on as I pulled the sheet around me and slipped from the bed. The door of the opened wardrobe shielded me as I pulled on yesterday's clothes, now hanging up neatly. Quickly I dressed. Perhaps hearing the latch as I closed the wardrobe door, Billy opened his eyes. As if on cue, so that I doubted he had been asleep at all.

'So what did you dream? Did the spirits come and whisper to you in your sleep? Did you see anyone you knew?'

I went over to the mirror to try to fix my mussed hair, but my fingers were clumsy. How could I answer that? Did spirits come as birds, did they speak in images and symbols and whistles? If that was the case, perhaps they had.

'I had strange dreams, if that is what you are asking,' I whispered, not wanting to share my dreams and break their fragile web.

Billy stood behind me, his eyes in the mirror dancing with excitement.

'What? What did you dream, what did you hear?' he demanded. He could hardly contain himself so I told him, I had no resistance. All I wanted was to be blanketed again in my dream, which clung to me and would not let me go.

I stepped away and crossed the room to make my bed, but Billy was in my way, ushering me into a chair, urging me to rest. Rest for what? I had just been asleep for who knew how long, what need had I for more rest? He shook the sheets and I felt my limbs grow heavy in the chair; my eyes began to close, but he snapped the sheets with a whip crack.

'Are you ready to try? I have spoken to Miss du Maurier, she is happy to assist in our experiment, to be the first receiver of your information from the other side.'

It was all rushing too fast, like the landscape of my dream, carrying me along with it. How could he be so confident? I had no proof, but what did he see that I couldn't? Together we were on the edge of something vast, and I didn't dare look down.

He slid his hand into the small of my spine and I found myself being led to the threshold of the door and down the stairs.

The velvet sitting room curtains were drawn, but as I looked at their hem I realised no light shone behind them. A line of candles stood lit on the mantelpiece, their doubles dancing in the mirror. A vase of roses exhaled their last scent, stray petals floating in the fetid water. Billy had a firm grasp of my elbow, steering me toward Miss du Maurier. She was already seated with her hands folded in her lap and her face turned expectantly in my direction. What had he told her? The candle flames bowed as I passed, two little rows of fire soldiers in their bright salute. I wanted to blow them out, to defy them, but they were too far away, tethered as I was to Billy, his hand now encircling my waist.

Billy settled me in a chair opposite Miss du Maurier. With the padded arms around me, the antimacassar cushioning my head, I felt sleep tap me on the shoulder and wind me in.

'Because of the nature of our experiment, I shall stand behind you, Miss du Maurier, for I am the conduit and the conductor,' Billy commanded and my eyelids lowered until the room became a mere slit between my eyelashes.

'Is she all right?' Miss du Maurier sat forward in the chair as my eyes completely closed. I could only hear their disembodied voices.

'She is entering her trance state to ready herself for your questions.'

The clock bell struck the hour. My eyelids flicked open and I found myself fixed by Billy's eyes, the brightest blue in his otherwise fathomless face. We had begun.

FORTY

Billy

She looked up to me like a flower to the sun: I knew she could not look away. Miss du Maurier's fingers shook, tense with waiting. She would wait until I was ready. Lily could no more speak to the spirits than I could, but I knew I could influence her. I had tuned her like a harp; the notes of her psyche were ready to be plucked at my direction.

All the time Lily had slept I had chanted to her, my words flowing through the perfect cockle of her ears, deep into her body, every cell filled with them till she was soaked through. When I had heard her breathing begin to echo the rhythms of my voice, I had known she was following as I willed it.

I had just been closing Lily's door and heading to my own room to prepare when Miss du Maurier had plodded up the stairs. If her suspicious eyebrows had been raised any higher, she would have lost them to the forest of her hair. If the old tart wanted to question why I was leaving Lily's room at an odd hour, I would let her serve my will at the same time.

'Just the person I was looking for,' I said, blitzing her with a smile so broad my face ached. I could not risk her bursting through Lily's door and disturbing the work of my words cycling through her dreams. 'Since the magic show is done with, Lily and I are working on a spiritualist demonstration.'

Miss du Maurier reached for the banister, steadying herself; it was her turn now to smile until it hurt. She was the perfect specimen. Desperate and unreconciled to her loss, her smile said as much. If she wanted to talk to the dead, all I would need to do was to read out what was written all over face and feed the prompts to Lily.

'I didn't know she had the gift,' Miss du Maurier said breathlessly, as if she had suddenly discovered she had a princess from an exiled kingdom living under her roof.

'Well, though it is early days, from what I have seen of her abilities, she is truly exceptional, but we need someone else to prove her on. Would you be interested in contacting a departed loved one through us?'

Her face took on an almost beatific glow at this news. I told her the hour Lily would be ready and she avidly agreed and hurried off down the stairs. I took a peek at Lily to ensure she was still sound asleep and then proceeded to my own room to prepare for her arrival. I stripped my sheets, for my bride must have clean ones. The blackened walls called out for words in praise of her, and the chalk in my hand sung an epistle of my devotion.

I took my box of treasures, removing them from the detritus of paper from reclaimed from Merle, and dusted each one, laying them out as an offering for her. The cut glass of the grenade shaped perfume bottle from France caught the light and sent diamonds dancing across the dark walls. My mother-of-pearl opera glasses glinted like the sea. I polished each of the knife blades until they were like fractured slivers of mirror, helping to throw the light around the room. In the centre I placed the golden comb, still untarnished after all this time, just like the purity of my Lily of the Valley. Soon I would weave it through her hair and lay her down next to me, skin upon skin, upon the downy soft nest of her swan-feather cape.

I hunted through the papers in the box for the photo of my mother that I had lifted from my father's watch, but it was nowhere to be found. What I did find was an envelope I had never noticed, my name in my father's hand, *Billy*, as if it was his voice in my ear. All I could think of was the wickedness of Merle's tale and the trampled innocence of my own poor mother. Lily whimpered, the sound faint through the wall that soon would no longer separate us. I would do everything in my power to show her *my* honour. With my body I will worship and with all my worldly goods I will endow. Lily sobbed loudly. There would be time to look at whatever my father had sealed up later when I had made Lily completely my own. I rushed to her, my arms soon to be her comfort.

Carefully I latched my door before I ducked back into Lily's room, where she was feverish and not far from waking. I pulled the blankets she had tossed off up around her again, drinking in the sight of her pure naked limbs, before sealing her up in a cocoon of fabric. The time was not yet quite ripe.

I ran down the first few stairs. Miss du Maurier had lit a trail of candles and had drawn the velvet curtain against the world. A curl of incense found its way up to my nostrils. God bless her, she was the perfect unwitting accomplice. She was sitting, fit to burst, on the sofa, her hand brushing the weave of the fabric back and forth restlessly.

I went back to Lily then and sat in the chair by her bed, resting my own eyes while keeping my ears pricked. My time was coming and I did not want to miss a moment when it came. Even with my eyes shut, I could sense her movements in the dark room. She was swimming up to the surface of her self through the last remnants of the opium. I opened my eyes as I heard her feet pause upon the floor as if to test their seaworthiness, but shut them again as she walked, unsteady on her feet, to retrieve her clothes. Her fingers must be finding the fixings tricksy.

'Lily,' I called to her and she blinked repeatedly, her eyes hazy, before she tilted. My arms were around her then and she took her support from me.

'What did you dream?' I breathed into her ear. She moved her lips but made no sound. I held the cup up for her to moisten her mouth, the tincture lending the water sweetness.

'An egg,' she stuttered. 'A blackbird laid an egg in my hand.'

An egg! Of all prophetic symbols – the most whole, most complete of things. What other proof did I need that she was the pure vessel of my desires, the pinnacle of feminine perfection?

'Anything else?'

Her voice was so quiet I had to lean my ear to her lip. 'I heard my father's whistling, but I could not see him, no matter how I looked around, until I realised it was coming from the throat of the little blackbird, whistling with all it had.' I caught a tear with my finger and helped her stand.

We walked down the stairs and she clung close to me, her white sail to my strong mast. I would keep her feet steady; every step was under my governance.

She was one step away from the belief that would tumble her forever into my safekeeping; she would be the prize, better than anything I had ever collected. With my arms around her, I arranged her in her seat, her pale palms resting upwards on her knee.

'Let us begin,' I said and Lily closed her eyes. There was nothing that she would say that I couldn't make fit the moment, for Miss du Maurier was no different to anyone else. Was the departed one safe, did they think of them, were the living forgiven? All the rest were just thrilling variations of the same theme. It didn't matter if they were a little bit off, as long as universal answers were given to obvious questions. With a beautiful pure flame like Lily, everyone would hold their breath to see which way she flickered.

'Open your eyes, Lily, for I am your conductor. I am the road to Lethe upon which the spirits will walk to talk to one as pure as you.'

Miss du Maurier had clapped her hands then; she was the cat lapping up the cream. Lily's had eyes flicked open, their shifting motion wild at first until she had met my reassuring gaze and was still.

'Lily is ready,' I said now. 'You may begin, flower amongst women. What do you hear? Who comes through?'

Miss du Maurier sat close to the edge of her seat, her hands clasped together, a desperate clutching of her fingers as if in prayer.

'Do you know anyone with the first name that begins with the letter W?' Lily said, her voice hardly more than a breath. 'A woman's name?' Lily's eyes wavered from mine, but a clearing of my throat brought them snapping back.

A little sound popped out of Miss du Maurier as she gulped. 'My name starts with W, my mother loved the colour of the flowers.' She tried to stop herself from giving it all away in a gush, but I already knew what it was. Lily made the connection as I cleaved my mind to hers, our gaze the channel.

'Wisteria?' Lily said. The vines grew up the side of the house and were half a season away from opening.

Miss du Maurier jumped to her feet but quickly sat down again, as her rational mind tried to keep order. 'Yes, that is it! That was the one compromise between my parents before I was born. My mother wanted to name me after a flower and my father wanted to name me after a man of science – so since Wisteria is named after Caspar Wistar, I am named after him.'

'And a last name that begins with L or a …' Miss du Maurier was motionless as Lily corrected herself, I threw my eyes open to her like a flare to steady her. 'An M? A last name that begins with M?'

'That has to be my last name, Morris. I changed it to du Maurier for the stage. My mother adored the novel *Trilby* by George du Maurier. I remembered it from her shelf, it sounded so French. I thought it would give me a foreign advantage.

The thing is the name stuck, even to my father. Rabbi Pearl called him Mr du Maurier, but my father never had the heart to correct him. No matter now.'

Lily blinked as she listened to Hysteria Wisteria Morris du Maurier pump our ears with the paltry details of her little life. Lily looked lucid for a moment, and I feared the breaking of her concentration in the reminder of he who should be forgotten forever. I sent the letter F between my mind and hers, my mouth making the echo of its shape. Lily plucked the letter out of the air, needing no other direction than the one that came from me.

'The letter F? No, the letter E – does that mean anything to you?' She rang almost true, her concentration slowly returning. She was a natural apprentice, she was learning quickly: let the subject fill in their gaps, let them be the authors of everything they want to hear. It was a kind of service, to help the answers find their questions.

Miss du Maurier could hold back no longer. 'The last word he ever said was *Elysium*.' The tears were a-trickle, silent tracks down her face. I pulled a handkerchief from my pocket and she accepted it, but did nothing to stem the flow of her tears. 'Oh my dear,' Miss du Maurier said between choked gulps, 'you have the gift.' Only then did she wipe her eyes and nose, clutching the damp keepsake in her hand. No matter, I had no need of having it; it was nothing compared to the treasure I was about to claim.

Lily sat in the chair opposite, her eyes falling from mine as the opium dragged at her eyelids.

'I have worn her out, the poor thing.' Miss du Maurier got up and approached Lily, but I was already by her side, my arm wrapped around her waist, leading her up the stairs to share with her what I had so carefully prepared. To share with her my humble self.

We took each step slowly, her hair spread across my arm, her head on my chest. She had done all I asked of her, so far. She was worn out, she deserved her rest, for she had been a pretty polly in parroting all that I bid her say. Ah, the credulous of the world! The letters of the alphabet that started her association could have held meaning for anyone who heard them, the gullible masses filling the hard theatre seats, buttocks clenched in excitement at the unfolding *truths*, without a brain between them to set them free, as Houdini had told me as child. Everyone found their little personal truths in the general signs and symbols. They could even have had meaning for me. W could be for William. L could be for Little. M could be for Me or Mine. E could be for? I had no idea.

I pushed open the door to my room. The gust of air that came with me up the stairs taunted the papers I had rammed under the bed. They fluttered as if I kept a dovecote there. I practically carried her over the threshold and slammed the door with the backward kick of my foot. The papers all took their roost and were still again.

She was wafer light as I laid her down upon my bed, her skin hot as I ran my fingers down her face. I had waited so long. Could I wait any longer? I took Golden Fortune's comb and twined it in Lily's hair, the gold of the metal and the silver of her hair a celestial pairing. *My dove, my undefiled.*

With reverence and a little awe, I placed all that I had around her, my own personal offering.

FORTY-ONE

Ari

The scrap of my uncle's prayer shawl was not the only strange thing arranged on the mound around the two curved walls of sticks. Several parrot feathers were fanned out there too, iridescent blue on one side, black on the other. It reminded me of our beautiful green parrot, left blinking in the shed. There were glossy purple berries plundered from a bush, snail shells, silver foil, a long piece of blue ribbon that might once have graced an expensive present or a girl's hair, a sweet wrapper and an enamel bluebird earring. It was such an odd arrangement that at first I thought my uncle had constructed it in his madness, a tabernacle for the birds. There was a curiously beautiful method to the arrangement of it all.

'Not bad, not bad at all,' the Birdman said as he circled the raised mound. 'See the paint? He has mixed it with his own saliva and some natural pigment on the side of the bower. All these things the satin bowerbird has spied and collected and rearranged, all to lure his lady. Makes a bunch of flowers look like chicken feed, don't you think?'

All I could think was that my uncle had to be somewhere near if his prayer shawl had been torn by a branch and collected for its blue. The sooner we found him, the quicker I could take my own meagre offering, all I had, myself, back to Lily to see if I could mend all that I had broken.

Something dashed through the undergrowth, making a startling buzz, like an angry wasp caught between the sashes of a window. Out burst the bowerbird, its feathers crow-black except for the lustrous jewel of its violet eye. Beauty had disappeared into the upper reaches of the trees. The bowerbird ran forward, its wings tilting like an aeroplane. It cried out – a parrot's screech, a raven's mournful cry, a currawong's rain-song, a lyrebird's theft and blend of notes – another mimic in the bush. All these sounds that had seemed so strange to my ears when I first arrived were now the songs of my homeland. Spotting us, the startled bird made his mad bolt back to the safety of the undergrowth.

'Not the visitor he was expecting. Well, we won't take it personally,' the Birdman said as he carefully stepped closer to the mound and fingered the fraying threads of my uncle's prayer shawl. Did the fringes blow the way we should follow? Were the cries of the birds some kind of direction? What augury could be read from cloth, what proof was there here of my uncle's life?

Through the dense scrub rushed the sound of wings. The Birdman and I stood still, thinking it was the bowerbird again, come to greet his bride, but it was Beauty, a black arrow bursting out above our heads, circling low, *arc-o,* back and forth again and again, bidding us follow.

What had Beauty found? I wanted to run. Could my uncle still be alive? The Birdman and I gathered pace, but Beauty was faster. When we lagged, she waited up ahead, beating her wings against the fathomless blue of the sky. The Birdman navigated the incline as we followed higher – the jagged edges of rocks, the perils of rabbit holes – through scrub where the branches were knitted together, thatched and impenetrable. Time ticked between the dip and rise of a raven's wings, until we found ourselves hugging the outline of a cliff, the very edge of the ranges, each step peeling back the vista for us, showing the wild plummet onto the giant grey-green thicket below.

Beauty slowed and looked down at me with her colourless, fickle, unreadable eye, then looked away, down the cliff. I followed her gaze. There on a sandstone ledge below was my uncle's prayer shawl, its fringe rippling out over the edge. Curled beneath it, as if it were a tent, was the shape of my uncle Israel.

I scrambled down the short space between us, with no time to acknowledge my vertigo. Some of the berries the bowerbird had used as decoration were in his hand; the remnants of a bottle of aspirin smashed nearby were littered about him, glinting. Was this all he had eaten? Was he even breathing? Was he dead? The questions collided as I pulled him into my arms: his breath was rasping and irregular like a baby's rattle.

I lifted him like a child and passed him up to the Birdman's waiting arms, and his eyes sprang open, just for a moment. He seemed not to recognise me, his dry cracked lips moving slowly, his voice inaudible. The prayer shawl would have been no defence against the elements or the mountain, but then my uncle had a wilderness in him that nothing could shield him from. I took one giddy glance over the edge of the cliff, the valley floor rushing up to meet me, before I scrambled up and clutched with relief at the Birdman's extended hand.

I took the patchwork fur coat, warmed by my body, and wrapped it around my uncle, grown fragile, feeding his arms into the holes and fixing the buttons as my grandmother had once done for me. The Birdman held a canteen up to his lips; the water partially trickled into his mouth, the rest made a winding trail through the dirt of his chin. He opened his eyes again, but they were looking at no one in particular, except perhaps Beauty.

'*Elijah it shall be, that thou shalt drink of the brook; and I have commanded the ravens to feed thee there,*' he whispered.

The Birdman scouted around for sturdy branches and broke them to size underfoot, before emptying his pack of the tarps we had used for shelter, the wind tearing at the edges.

'Elijah?' my uncle said, his voice hoarse, I shook my head at him. Who was I? He didn't know me. I was Zipporah's son, his nephew, but no words came out of my mouth. 'Isaiah?' he said, his eyes squinting against the blue like a newborn. Was he trying to name all the patriarchs and prophets of the Torah? I remembered then the letter I had taken from the attic. It had been from Isaiah. Another member of the family blotted out? Who was he? I had so many questions, but my uncle grew quiet again, drifting off to sleep, his breathing ragged.

The Birdman had made a makeshift stretcher, binding the tarp to the branches with rope. Together we raised his weakened body onto it and, carrying him between us, made our way back through the bush. We tramped through the ferny undergrowth of the valley floor, the bushes flicking droplets into our faces, with Beauty, our black-winged compass, again leading from above.

We moved into a mist, a low-lying cloud, which cloaked us, covering our limbs with fine beads of rain. The moisture dampened my uncle's face, a kiss from a cloud. Beauty swooped into a bush heavy with purplish-pink berries, pulling them off and admiring them in her beak before she swallowed them whole. The Birdman halted and together we carefully lowered my uncle to the ground.

'Tucker time,' the Birdman said. He took off his hat and tipped it over like a bowl before gathering a handful or so of the berries. Together we propped up my uncle and the Birdman crushed the berries between his palms and pushed the sweet flesh into my uncle's mouth. At first the pulp just sat in his mouth, but slowly he began to chew, the sweetness reviving him.

'Won't hurt you either,' said the Birdman, offering the upturned hat to me. 'Lilly pilly.' I took only one, not wanting to deny my uncle anything that would help him recover. It was sweet like jam. We fed my uncle another, the fruit making his lips purple. Colour rose in his cheeks. When I offered him the water this time he gulped it down. He opened his mouth and I bent to listen.

'She travels with me still, my Cloud of Glory, my Shekinah,' he whispered and I shivered. His words had an otherworldly holiness as he spoke the name I had inscribed to Lily. How I prayed too that she was at Miss du Maurier's still.

We walked on. The scrub grew less dense as the Birdman led me out of the gizzards of the mountain. If I had been on my own I would have spiralled around until the bush claimed not only my uncle but also myself: the last two generations would be lost, the last Pearls gone.

The mist grew thicker around us, binding us all in silence again. Occasionally the black tips of Beauty's wings pierced the fog, which bought an odd smile to my uncle's lips. The Birdman whistled to himself, the sound seeming to come from all directions, and the occasional reply rang out from the canopy. My feet stepped into the muddy footprints he had made, but the Birdman was not our only guide.

HaShem shall guard thy going out and thy coming in, from this time forth and for ever. The ending of the psalm came to my mind. HaShem moved the stars and HaShem governed the waters, but it was up to me to now guide myself when we found our way out of the mountains, to carve my own path.

'See the supernal letters dancing in my cloud?' My uncle's voice quavered from the stretcher, so surely that I looked up as though I might see the words in the mist. 'A cloud guided Moses to the top of Mount Sinai to receive the living words.' But the only living words I felt I knew were my mother's inked into my hand.

'Tell me about Isaiah,' I said gently, wanting to guide his thoughts away from the spirit of the mountains and back to reality. He looked at me fixedly then, the coals of his old fire burning in his eyes.

'Isaiah? Was it out of spite that he picked my sister without seeking my permission? Shouldn't he have told me, his oldest friend?' he muttered. 'Did he love her, or was it just another competition to him?' He broke the connection of our gaze and turned his head away.

For a moment I couldn't breathe. The mist drizzled down my neck and coated my burning muscles with ice. My eyes stung, and not because the branches of the impromptu stretcher had rubbed blisters into my hands. What had the wilderness set free in him? He was a prophet now of my past, speaking of my mother. All my life I had wanted to hear him speak of her, was this all he would say now?

The silence that followed seemed endless, as we trudged on with our burden. Minutes, half an hour, more? Till a wallaby bounded out into our path and blinked at us. A light rain started to fall in sheets, the sunlight diminishing. Time moved in its own circle here. The Birdman looked over his shoulder at me, signalling me to stop as the sky grew darker, from the storm or oncoming night, I could not tell.

Together we carried the stretcher to an overhang of sandstone that would be our shelter. The Birdman helped me lift my uncle off the tarp and we eased him into the dry leaf mulch. He groaned, calling for my aunt in his sleep. The Birdman gathered some larger branches and together we huddled beneath them while the rain lashed the valley, a chorus of currawongs' thrilling whistles coming from high in the treetops. I touched my hand to my uncle's forehead. The skin which had been so cold when we found him was now hot to the touch. The Birdman pulled up the collar of his coat and headed out into the rain, picking small leaves off certain bushes, trilling all the while, while Beauty hopped from one branch to the next as if it were a game. I crouched closer by my uncle's head and gently plucked out the tangled twigs and leaves that had found their way into his hair and beard, streaked with white. How had he grown so old?

At my touch his eyes flickered open and he clutched at my hand.

'Uncle Israel, tell me about your sister, tell me about Zipporah.' I spoke carefully, squeezing his callused hand in my own. I was afraid to say 'my mother' in case he fell silent, as he had so many times before. He coughed and I helped support him, cradling his head in my lap.

'I called her an inkblotter. She was always hungry for words and asked questions I struggled to answer.' I leaned closer, my ear at to his mouth. He gave the ghost of a smile, gone in an instant. 'What I read, she read also, until she had devoured all that was in my father's study, except for the volumes that would speak too loud to a woman's ears, their arcane wisdom too much without the yeshiva to discuss them.' The mention of yeshiva made me pause and I felt that old push and pull, his wanting for me to be his shadow. 'I hid those books before I left, too heavy for our suitcase. I wanted to take them, to keep them from her, but Hephzibah would not leave her samovar.'

The Birdman came back to us with a harvest of strange leaves and a pile of twigs and set to making a small fire, crushing the leaves into the billycan, his song turning to a drone. My uncle watched the Birdman and spoke as if in a dream.

'I told her she must stop. Her pursuit of knowledge belonged only to mystics and sages, but she would not heed my warning. I told her she was like the Moon, the light she thought was hers belonged to the Sun, but she laughed.'

He shuddered and went quiet, his eyes following the dance of flames, watching as the smoke slowly wound its way up through the sodden canopy of trees, mingling with the rain and making our eyes water.

The Birdman poured the brew he had made into a tin mug and swirled it around to cool, offering it up to my uncle's lips. My uncle slowly took a sip, his face twisted at the herbs' bitterness, but the Birdman clicked his tongue and my uncle did as he was bid and swallowed down more. Beauty cawed from a nearby tree and the Birdman cawed back. They understood each other, unlike my uncle and I: we shared a language but could not understand each other. The bush potion gave my uncle strength to speak, his voice becoming stronger, as if we were his congregation of three, the dusk falling as if he knew the time for prayer.

'And my sister was punished, just like Miriam, who challenged her brother. Struck white as snow. Exiled.' My uncle's voice grew louder, rising above the falling rain and the sounds of the valley, birdsong and wind echoing all around us. His old command of the story, his steadfast belief, rising out of his frail frame.

My uncle was raving, his voice growing, feverish and he shook as if the words were physical things he was expelling from his body. His stared down at his own hands as if they making an offering, the shadow of the flames flickering on the sandstone and on his face.

'It was I who uttered *el na refa na la,* oh Lord make her well, for she was with child outside of wedlock. *El na refa na la.* To me this child was like a sickness, a punishment. I didn't realise then, a child is nothing but a miracle. My sister was blessed with a child by my best friend, when my wife and I were not. I railed against it and against G_d. Her letters came, one after the other, but I would not open them. My ears would remain deaf to her pleas. I exiled her from my mind and excised her from my heart, as if G_d had afflicted her, and I cast her out. But it was I that was afflicted, burned up by my own bitterness.'

My uncle began to cry then, the tears streaming tracks of dirt on his face. He turned and looked at me. 'But when I heard of the violence, I knew I had to try and raise that child if he'd survived, the last of our family. Hephzibah urged me to hurry. It was my duty. I telegrammed our cousins to search and sent what money I could. It was miracle that the child was found, alive. But when the child arrived I took it as my duty to straighten him. I lashed him to the rod to correct whatever it was his mother had bent him with. I could see that her belief in amulets and magical remedies had found their way into him, into more than just the markings on his innocent skin.'

The Birdman leaned over with the mug again, clicking his tongue gently, as if to a bird or a wounded creature. 'There now, a bit more, mate, it'll do you wonders.'

My uncle drank again at the Birdman's encouragement, his eyes following Beauty's beak as she preened the Birdman's hair, knocking his hat off, before he steadied his eyes on me.

'But I was mistaken. As the child grew, he only proved more of what a blessing G_d had given my sister in him. I had banished the memory of my sister – but there was her child, my sister the bird's child, keen-eyed, blinking up at me.' His voice tapered away and he began to cry, his tears mingling with the mist that had been travelling with us all this way.

I held his hand until he slept, his breathing deep and regular. The Birdman cocked his hat back on his head, flipped open his pack and tossed me a blanket.

'Beans suit you?' I nodded and watched him open the cans and sit them in the flames. My hands glowed as I warmed them. Above me on the overhang, dark shapes loomed, following the flames. The sandstone glowed even in this minimal light, mica glinting in the ochre. When I saw a hand painted above me, I thought it a shadow of my own. Yet when I moved my fingers it remained still. Kneeling closer to take a look I could see many hands stencilled on the overhang of stone. I reached up and placed my own hand on the cold stone, on the nearest lowest one, small as a child's.

'What do they mean?' I asked the Birdman who was gingerly retrieving a can from the fire with a forked stick.

'They are those that have gone before and are not forgotten,' he said, tucking his fork into the tin. 'Thousands of years old they are. Made by blowing ochre and animal fat over the hand.'

I took my hand away then, feeling time slip beneath me, feeling as if I had held my own childish hand from long ago. An adult's hand sheltering the child's, just as my mother had sheltered me. But as I looked at those raised hands, a testimony to the past, so many tiny *hamsas*, I felt their protection fall over all those I loved, as profound as my uncle had felt the Shekinah in the depths of his wilderness. Those small stretching fingers, child-sized amulets, cast their own shadowed refuge over my lost grandmother and mother of blessed memory. If only I had as a child had the power to keep them safe, as they had done for me.

FORTY-TWO

Lily

I remembered my head melting into the pillow, the relief of it. Billy guided me through a fog of questions, with Miss du Maurier's face like the moon waxing close to mine. I could not make out her features, only the general light of her. With each word that came out of my mouth, she appeared to float up and orbit near the ceiling, out of reach. And then the world turned dark and everything was silent.

When I opened my eyes a sharp ache pained my head. I ran my fingers up to my hair and my fingers touched the smooth chill of metal, the sharp teeth of a comb planted in my scalp. I pulled it out, but my head still throbbed. It was a golden comb. I turned it over in my hands – so beautiful and intricate, with tiny leaves, insects and flowers twisted into the metal, inlaid with semiprecious stones. I held it up, eyes focusing on each stone – turquoise, jade, bloodstone, ivory ... As I blinked, my eyes adjusted. I was not in my own room – the walls here were nearly black, except for the spidery web of writing scrawled across the walls.

I struggled to sit up, but my head was an anchor. Desperately I wanted to read the words. Were they a spirit message from my father, had the experiment been a success? Again, I tried to sit up, but my elbow would not take my weight, forcing me back down. The bed felt like down beneath my hands, and I realised

I was lying on my swan-feathered cloak, the ribbons tied close round my throat. How did it get here?

My memory of last night's experiment was vague, a dream had more substance. I forced myself to sit up and the room whirled. The morning light crept from behind the drawn curtain and in the dimness my eyes rested on the words. They were scribbled in chalk, each white letter running into the next:

> *Who is she that looketh forth as the dawn, fair as the moon, clear as the sun ...O my dove. As a lily among thorns, O thou fairest among women ...*

Whatever did it mean? It reminded me of something from Sunday school. My eyes stung. The walls were filled with it. On the mantel sparkled several silver moons; when I blinked I could see they were sharp knives. As I swung my legs over the side of the bed and sat upright, a pair of opera glasses rolled into the hollow where I had lain, followed closely by a perfume bottle shaped like a grenade, the two clinking together in a toast. My bare feet tried to find purchase on the floorboards, and I frantically pushed up with my knees, but I could not stand up because suddenly, right before me, Billy barred my way.

'Up so soon, my little Jerusalem skylark?' He tilted my head up to look at him, a cool finger beneath my chin. 'Do rest some more. I can wait.' He gently pushed me back towards the feathers, but I did not want to lie back down. 'Or we can continue,' he said before placing his lips upon mine, kissing me, his mouth forcing mine open, his tongue searching the space in my mouth. I tried to push him off, but he was above me, his weight bearing down, as his knee hit the bed between my legs. I did not want this. Not him. His weight pinned my arm beneath my own body, crushing the breath out of me, something sharp pressing into my spine.

'Get off me!' I cried, but he just swallowed my words as if they were cries of love, his mouth sucking on mine. I could barely breathe. He pulled at my trousers and a button flew loose and hit the wall, before clattering away somewhere on the floor.

Fear had owned me before; it would not own me again. I could feel the metal prongs in my back as I tried to twist away from him. With all my strength, I bent my arm behind my arched back, which made him moan with the delusion of reciprocation. I pulled the comb out. I raised it into the air and brought it down with all the force I had upon his face, the teeth briefly piercing his skin, six pinpricks of blood. It was not a forceful blow, but it was a surprising one. His hand rushed to his cheek with the shock of it. I had bought myself a moment.

I pushed him back; his hands at his face, the blood on his fingers as he fell backwards, losing his balance. Rabbit-quick I sprang from the bed, and the comb, its teeth now bent, barely made a clink as it hit the floor. I ran out. But where to? My own room was not safe. Was he going to follow me? Miss du Maurier had to be somewhere in the house, but how would I explain to her when I myself had no clear idea what had happened? Should I call for her? But I didn't want to put her in Billy's way. I wanted to pull down the ladder of her attic room and fly up it, but what would I do then – sit and hold my breath? Why was I running even? It was Billy who should flee. But how could I protect myself against the edge of a knife? My foot caught on Miss du Maurier's Persian carpet and I fell. As I tried to get up, I could hear the creaking of the upstairs floorboards. Was Billy coming after me? Fear roared in my head, willing me on, to get up, move, move faster, to get to the only safe place I knew that remained, to get to the shed.

As soon I was in the safety of its walls, I slammed the door shut and secured the lock and wedged a chair beneath the handle just in case. If I'd had a knife in my grasp, would I have used it? Billy had set those objects around me, laid me in his bed like a wren in his house, a sacrifice to his desires. How long had he used me? How long had he planned his revolting seduction?

The lyrebird's eye peeked out from under his wing, glinting in the dim light before, with a swoosh of his tail, he returned to sleep. If Billy followed I would let him have more of what I had given him already, but in a greater dose. In the shed were rakes, hoes and shovels – if he touched me again I would do more than leave six little berries on his cheek.

What had I expected by trying to talk to the dead as if it was some sort of trick? My father was in my thoughts every day. I didn't need Billy or any man to tune me in. My father was in my blood, just like all my ancestors were, each travelling through my veins. The gift of my life had come through him. I didn't need to talk to the dead; they talked to me through every pulsation of my heart. I was the message. There was no question I needed anyone else to answer. There was no question I couldn't answer by looking to myself.

I sat down on the cold bed and the room spun around me. The tail of whatever poison Billy had given me still coursed through my system. I looked around me. At the bottom of the stack of Ari's things was a book I hadn't seen before. I pulled it out, the papers crackling with newspaper cuttings – Houdini's name stamped in black type across each one. I flicked through the dates 1910 to 1929. From Houdini's arrival to the Houdini hoax. I could barely believe my eyes. I blinked but the words remained. *HOUDINI SPEAKS* had been a hoax? I read the whole article, my eyes moving fast across the page, afraid to take a breath. Bess Houdini had confirmed that the medium must have known the code that she thought had been hers alone – Houdini had not spoken to her beyond the grave. Her grief had blinded her. Her longing for reunion had made her clutch at whatever remnant hope of him came close.

Bess had been pushed into the background as Houdini's star had risen. Did she miss the applause of her early days, when she had been more than just a wife or an assistant, her name sharing the headlines with the man she loved? Her name, after all, was shaped in the same lights, they shared the same stage and the same bed as they metamorphosed and merged into each other night after night. Perhaps all dear Bess wanted was to be the magician herself, to believe one more time that she could step through time and find things as they had been before he went away.

Somewhere in the house I heard a door slam, making me start to my feet. I grasped a metal rake and laid it across my lap and waited, but no other sounds followed. The currawong swivelled up her tail like a question mark. Sitting on Ari's bed I watched the shadows grow and lengthen as the sun crossed the sky. I listened, alert, but still Billy didn't come.

The parrot stepped from one foot to the next agitatedly and swooped down and landed on my shoulder, chattering in my ear. I took some seeds and offered them to him from my palm, but he kept leaning over to my mouth, preferring to nibble for them on my lip, a parrot's kiss.

With the parrot running his beak through my hair, a thought came to me. Here I had everything I needed. On Ari's bed were the costumes I had placed there what seemed days ago but what must have been just yesterday. Miss du Maurier's father's old morning suit, so similar to my father's wedding clothes, sat draped in the arms of the old bridal gown, a ghostly embrace. I peeled off my torn trousers and slid on the pair that belonged to Ari's costume. The cloth was an icy slip up my legs and I gasped as I shakily fastened the buttons. There was no time to lose. I didn't know what Billy had told Clay, but it was nothing I couldn't undo. If Billy showed his face again at the theatre I would have him named for what he was; there would be no escaping the power of my accusation. If I walked fast I could make it. I transferred the letter that I had written to my mother, but had failed to send from the old trousers to the new. It was no longer flat, but curved to the shape of my thigh, the print no longer fresh, but to my mother the news would be.

My father had asked me to take care of her, and I had tried. Working at the petrol service station to cover our expenses, making sure the cutlery drawers held only blunt butter knives. I tried to keep her angry Lord away. But leaving with no word? I owed her that. I would not be responsible for the chasm of her grief opening wider, but neither was I going to fall into the chasm that my father's death had created. He would have wanted me to fly, in any direction that I could.

I gathered up all I needed and hesitated at the door, peering through the window to make sure Billy was not waiting for me there. I rushed out into the late afternoon and slipped out through the back gate and into the lane, a birdcage in each hand, the swan cape streaming behind me. There was still time.

I went straight around to the side entrance; some of the performers were already arriving for the first show of the evening. Their eyes widened when they saw me. A cleaner walked up the red-carpeted aisle with the vacuum bellowing where my torch had shone. Mr Clay was running through the programme with his secretary when I entered. The cord caught in my feet and was liberated from the socket, the noise stopped and I had my first solo audience of three.

'I do apologise, Mr Clay, but there will be a change to the act tonight. I am not sure what Billy Little told you …'

Clay removed the cigarette from his lips, his bemused expression at my awkward entrance vanishing like smoke. 'If you left a message with Little I didn't get it and probably never will, since he no longer works here. He has missed too many shifts. Head along backstage, we'll fit you in.'

I did not have time to think through the machinations of Billy Little; all I knew was that I had found a hole in his net and I had been lucky to wriggle through.

The dressing room was empty except for the birds and me and my quickstep heart. I felt Ari's absence in its quiet. He would be back, I knew it now, but would he even consider staying? I let the birds out of their cages; the parrot flew to the dressing table and looked admiringly at his new mate in the mirror. The currawong flipped her tail and swooped to the rack of clothes, a note curdled in her throat. The lyrebird stepped daintily over the edge of the cage door, his tail sweeping around him. I pulled off my shirt and cape and put on the suit jacket, the tails dipping like my own wings, the cape my feathers. I heard voices come through the wall of the neighbouring dressing room; others were gathering.

'Thirty-minute call,' the stage manager called, knocking on each door along the cramped corridor, which sent the thrill of goose bumps up my spine. When he arrived at my dressing room, I called out to him, and he looked surprised to see me on my own. I explained the last-minute changes. 'Good luck, Miss del Mar,' he winked at me and I felt the boldness of my plan begin to unfold.

In the mirror, the parrot's chalky green tail grew white from brushing at a puddle of spilled face powder. I rubbed two blushes of rouge into my cheeks and ringed my lips with red. I was almost ready. The fifteen-minute call came, the stage manager's voice booming down the hallway, the audience already starting to fill the auditorium. My reflection in Ari's costume looked back at me blankly. Something was missing. I found the trunk and pulled it open. The top hat gleamed like the black shellac of a gramophone record. I set it atop my head with a tap. I lifted the lyrebird into my arms, his tail feathers melting into mine. Together we looked like a silky note, a treble clef, the herald of a new start. The parrot came at a whistle and sat on my shoulder, the currawong came at a click of my tongue.

When I stepped onto the stage, the audience was like a mountain in front of me, the curved mass of them on either side of the aisle leading up from the orchestra pit. The spotlight swelled like the sun and the lyrebird dropped from my arms and flicked down his tail – his notes and my voice a duet. When he swished his tail, I swirled my cape, a mirrored reflection of each other as we danced, his throat bobbing with the sound of Ari's violin, the tears in my eyes making prisms of light. The currawong sang her chortled prayer. The lyrebird chortled with the currawongs voice, a reply.

I asked for three volunteers, and all across the audience people rose up. The birds swooped over their heads, the currawong leading the way in her black and white glide. The lyrebird followed close behind, his tail hanging low, brushing the hair of the heads just below, a benediction of feathers. The parrot took his roost upon the plentiful nests of hair – the audience all achatter until I spoke.

'Please rise,' I motioned with hands to the trio that had the birds upon their heads. A man with the parrot atop of his head coughed and the parrot screeched. The lyrebird coughed and screeched in an echoed reply and the audience applauded. The lyrebird made the sound of a hundred hands clapping, reducing the audience to a superstitious hush. The currawong's whip and soar song bubbled out and the lyrebird matched it with unequalled joy. The woman whose head the lyrebird had landed upon quivered, feeling the trembling flick of those tail feathers creep from her back and radiate out in front of her face, a fern's fronds of feathers. The lyrebird sung out then, starting quietly with the tinny notes of the wireless, before falling into the first few bars of an ecstatic symphony.

'My little sisters, the birds, much bounden are ye unto God, your Creator, for He hath given you liberty to fly about everywhere,' the words rose out of me like smoke. The words on the back of the Sunday school card, Saint Francis's sermon to the birds, shivered through me.

I whistled and the parrot returned to my outstretched arm and together we vanished into the trunk, the light turning to a slit before it was gone beneath closed the lid. A stagehand pulled a screen across to conceal me and counted to three.

I had disappeared, but the parrot remained.

The stagehand opened the box and out flew the green blur to the rim of the trunk.

Abracadabra, Shekinah, Mizpah
Shekinah, Abracadabra, Mizpah
Mizpah, Shekinah, Abracadabra.

The parrot spoke then shot like a bullet over the audience and up above the stage, the spot man racing to follow, the light illuminating the bird like the Holy Spirit. Then the parrot flew with a swallow's speed into the trapdoor of the stage and was gone. There was only silence – and then the thunder started, or so it seemed, but it was the sound of one hand meeting another, a communion of applause. The curtain swelled and closed and then I was up on the stage among the birds, my feathered cape streaming behind me in the gush of air that the curtain made as it drew open. I took the top hat from my head and ran the satin brim through my fingers before I bowed. This, after all, was where I belonged. Before the curtain closed I heard my father's voice in my ears for me alone, the parrot on my shoulder covering me with his kisses.

As I exited the stage, my fellow performers were clapping for me in the wings, Mr Clay among them. He patted me on the back, his encouragement muffled by the changing of the set. I was not a mark of my mother's sin, I didn't feel strange or exposed or anything other than myself, but how I wished Ari could have been with me, even though I had proved that I could do this by myself. The longing I had to see him made my heart bloom. Where was he now?

The street was dark except for the glint of the quartz chips in the road, like shy stars in the Milky Way. As I walked home in my costume, the currawong and parrot on each shoulder, the lyrebird in my arms, I must have looked a strange sight, but it didn't matter, for those I passed were to my mind wearing stranger costumes than mine.

Walking towards the Oddfellows Hall in my direction were two rows of men, silent except for the crackle and flare of the scrub torches that lit up their green-tinged faces and their beards tied with ribbons and bells. Each of them held a staff. When we came to the point on the path where one party would have to give way, they lifted their torches, the heat from the fire blowing across my face and ruffling the birds' feathers. Alert, the birds sank their talons through the cloth of my jacket right into my flesh, uncertain as to what danger there was. The men lifted their staffs, each crossing the other until an arch was made for me to pass under, their eyes following me as I moved through. The birds' tails all fanned, ready to alight, but I was unafraid. After I had passed through, the men walked single file into the gate of the Oddfellows Hall, the firelight making the painted eye in the sun at the top window twinkle. All this time I had never noticed it, never having seen it lit. Shivers washed over me. Affixed to the wall was a sign – *Annual Meeting of the Ancient Order of Druids Friendly Society* – and I laughed.

I laughed until tears swelled in my eyes and the lyrebird let out his kookaburra imitation in response to my own. I felt in my pocket for the envelope that I had carried for so long and shot it into the mouth of a passing letterbox, my long overdue message to my mother.

FORTY-THREE

Billy

I froze at the sight of my own blood, afraid to touch my own skin, to feel the sticky damage the sharp teeth of the comb had done to my face. I hadn't thought her capable of such violence, or that the opium would prove so ineffective. I stood up from the bed, shuddering. I never could abide the sight of blood – why else had I fled the field of battle? – it revolted me, its red spurt and ooze, its stink of iron, its filthy spread.

I tore open the curtains to let in a mere trickle of dawn light and peered in the shaving mirror hung on a nail from the back of the door. The damage was minimal, a lovebite from a mouse, a pinprick, but still my stomach turned. She was less pliable, less chaste than I thought, the sharp-toothed little fox. I would catch her yet. Below, the street was quiet except for the screech of fruit bats gliding through the tops of the fig trees that lined the street, dropping their leaves and sap, making the street as sticky as a licked postage stamp. Where was she now? She had displeased me, I would seek her out. She couldn't have gone far; she would be reined in by the dose I had given her.

Outside the window, a dark shadow flapped close. Another bat? But then it swooped down again, drawing my eyes with it. I could not make it out against the sky, not until it alighted on the lace of the cast-iron balustrade, cocked its head and peered in through the glass to take a better look at me. Then it hopped down and pecked rapidly like a telegraph, three times upon the glass.

It was that infernal bird, the craven crow that would pluck out someone's eyes at the first opportunity. It was not going to have mine. I had seen them gorge themselves on the battlefield, supping on the slain, sending dread into the marrow of both sides. The stones we threw could not disturb them from their human feast. This bird would tear at me too. My fingers twitched. My knives were on the mantle, but with a quick swipe I had one back in my hand, the other a reassuring weight in my belt loop. The damnable creature might be quick, but surely my blades were quicker.

However, that bird was only a harbinger for my true target, for below, down the street, came the bloody Star of David, traipsing up to the steps of his old abode. How dare he return? I had expected the mountains to erase all trace of him and his uncle. Why the hell was he back? He wasn't going to have what was mine. The blood in my body hummed and the handle of the blade rattled in my hand, wanting to be free. He was the persistent stone in my shoe and I would shake him out. It was because of him that Lily harboured her resistance, that all my treasures now lay scattered and broken, all those precious things I had gathered and struggled so to retrieve – every one a little memory come to life, the thrill of sensation as each succumbed in her turn to my own particular and passionate persuasion.

It was the blue hour. I was grateful that there was still some cover of darkness as I opened the front door. I would seek Lily out soon enough; she could not be far away, she would not resist a second time, her punishment my pleasure. But first the Jewboy need to be hobbled. In my pocket I had her braid and I fingered it for luck. The infernal bird was nowhere to be seen, night-shade pestilence that it was, though I could feel its pale blue blink observe my every move. I would not chance a blade on its carrion skin now. The Jew had gone into the house; it was only a matter of time before he came out again, sniffing around for what I had already claimed, though he had no right to even breathe the same air as her, my Queen of Heaven.

The sky changed above me, black to the darkest blue; dawn would be flashing her wares soon enough. But the blanket of night was still my servant, and my fingers were ready to do their work without detection. I stepped back into the shadows.

I heard the door open, the complaint of the hinges in need of oil. I was ready, but the sound of the shoe as it struck the footpath rang wrong: it was the clack of a lady's heel. I let the shadows swallow me again.

'Will you be long, my *boychick?*' It was the aunt, her voice strained. The Jewboy was in the doorway; her body obscured my target.

'As long as it takes, Aunt Hephzibah,' her replied. My, how he stood firm! He had come back for Lily, that was clear. 'Uncle Israel is in the doctor's good hands. I'll be there as soon as I can.'

He had found his uncle and they had not perished as I had desired. My anger thrummed through me, the knife handle quivering in my palm. She turned and embraced him before she hurried on. Her staccato footsteps roused a neighbour's dog, barking and scratching at the wooden gate, wanting to be out, but it was silent again at a quick hiss from my lips.

Then the lights inside the house went out one by one. The click of the door was barely audible, but to me it was clamorous. In the barely lightening gloom the Jew was a mere outline. It was time for him to be Isaac, the sacrifice that his God had demanded of Abraham. He was the goat that would be cast out; his blood would be shed to cleanse me.

I threw the knife, my bright and shining shooting star, its handle like a comet. She whistled as she flew towards my target. I heard his muffled gasp as the blade came close but not close enough: my accuracy had been tainted by time, rust creeping over the exacting clockwork of my skill.

I stepped into the streetlight. My knife had pinned him, a moth to the board of the wooden door: the blade had flown straight through the flapping fabric of his mangy coat. He was tugging at the blade handle, but it was a loyal instrument and would not release itself to a hand that was not its master. Before he could register me, I struck him hard across the face. His head flipped back and hit the wall, a smear of blood across his cheek to match my own. His eyes rolled back into his head, and I struck him again. His hands grabbed at my hair, my face, trying to find purchase, but they swung wildly, meeting nothing but air. I pulled the other knife from my belt loop and brought down the handle hard on his temple, and then he was still, his hands hanging limp. His coat tore with a satisfying gash as he slumped to the ground.

To merely thrust my knife in his guts and twist it like a bayonet held no grace, no ritual and no satisfaction. So I pulled up a lock of his hair and slipped my blade between his scalp and the strands, a clump of brown curls in my hand. As I slashed, he was transformed before my eyes. Without his Samson locks he was weakened; without the vanity of Absalom, he was made meek. In no time at all I had shorn him like a convict ready for the gallows. When I had been a dab hand at shearing, no sheep had ever looked so well shorn. The effect was pleasing: there was a ramshackle artistry in my destruction.

My blade hovered at his throat, readying for the swipe to the jugular, when he opened his eyes and fixed his gaze to mine. He struck me then with a force I hadn't expected, sending me crashing backwards, my knife spilling onto the footpath, glinting between us, out of my reach. Using the wall, he propped himself up, the knife now closer to his feet than mine. How could I have hesitated? He reached over and levered the pinning blade from his coat with some remnant of strength, and weighed the knife in his palm. He was not afraid. I could see it in his eyes.

'I ran from Russia, but I'll not run here, not now and not from you.'

One of my knives in the space between us, the other in his hand; did he have the guts to wield it?

'Shut up, Jew.'

He lunged forward then, kicking the abandoned knife into the gutter, the mass of fig leaves hiding it in a sticky embrace. There was no way I was going to go down on my knees in the darkness, pathetic as a beggar. I readied myself. He took a step closer.

'I'll not be silent and I'll not take orders from the likes of you,' he spat.

How dare he threaten me! She was my Lily of the Valley, my Rose of Sharon, the finest creature in all creation. She had shown her faith in me and by it I had been made a better man. How could she think of choosing the likes of him? If the knife were in my hand, one fling and it would be but a flag in his heart. He spun the handle through his fingers and I counted silently in my head the moment when I would strike. His eyes were pinned on mine, but even so I didn't see the moment when the knife ceased to be, vanishing from his palms into nothing, my blade made air.

'Abracadabra!' he shouted and then he shoved me backwards, sending me sprawling, my arse scraping the footpath.

I searched desperately in the darkness for the knife amidst the leaves, while trying to keep one eye on him. He towered over me and I tried to scramble upright, but with a kick of his foot I was winded and the ground rushed up to me. But I couldn't see the other knife in his hand. Where had he smuggled that bloody knife? Was it slipped in his sleeve till he found the courage to use it? There was no telling. Panic pulsed through me.

'Fight like a man, Jewboy,' I taunted him. Let him show me his hand.

I waited for that magicked knife to reappear, singing for my blood, death by vermin, when he hit me so hard my brain wobbled, and the world turned black.

* * *

The sky was washed with shades of blue, the darkest high above me, near-black like the ocean deep, to the gradual blue of sapphire, every shade of blue like her eyes. How long had I been unconscious? My own blood trickled into my mouth, salty and disgusting. I spat it out. Lily had made the first blow, the Jewboy the second; what would be the fatal third? How could I have lost the upper hand, sitting in the gutter with my blood smeared on my own hands?

I looked over at the houses, all quiet, no one stirred at Miss du Maurier's, nor at the Jew's. But for how long? Time was against me. How long would it be before Lily or the Jewboy told the police? I'd not grace a prison cell again, that palace of piss, shit and blood. Where could I go? All the sacrifices I made, rejected. How could I preserve myself now? My love was no lily at all, she was just as feral as a weed. How could I have been so mistaken? *I sought she whom my soul loves; I sought her but found her not.*

Low in the sky hung something bright and shining, the morning star. I stared at it until my eyes blurred. I felt it communicate, in ripples of light, a language I could barely understand. It was calling to me. Calling me. *Arise!* Had I heard it from the star? Shakily I rose to my feet and began to walk in its direction. My feet led me down to the train tracks, towards the rail yards. Rail workers, black-clad beetles, walked across the yard, the machines, wheels and cogs all silently waiting for their touch. The blacksmith's hammer rang out against the iron. A whistle sounded and a train left the yard, steam billowing into the sky and disappearing into nothing. The first of the morning birds began their chant, waves of small twitters to my ears as if they were saying something to me over and over, but I could not understand. *Wee Lee Mee Eee.*

Wee Lee Mee Eee, the birds trilled. W L M E: letters caught between the notes in quick succession. The letters of the alphabet that Lily had plucked at my instigation. W for William. L for Little. M for mother. E for? The star in the sky seemed to be closer on the horizon, the dawn's fingers nearly touching it to chase it away, but still it shone out its starry language like Morse code in a fit of spits and spurts.

I looked over the rail yard, my fingers cold and turning purple. In my pocket I warmed my fingers between the fine threads of her hair like a silk tassel, the feel of it electric, but I felt even more chilled. What use did I have for it now? Carelessly, I dropped it on the footpath. Let it line the nest of the birds for all I cared. Between my fingers the minute snips of the Jew's hair itched. I blew them to the wind before jamming my hands back in my pockets. Another train left the yard, gaining momentum like a rocket with each clack along the rail line. I could see the driver, a cigarette a beacon on his lip. He was unaware of the star above, sending out her message, wink after twinkle. Whatever was she saying?

I walked onward in her direction, alongside the rail yard, the track like a whip stretching out. The trees with their low-slung branches were littered with birds that I could not see but only hear, little fragments of different songs; it would take a lifetime to decipher the individual notes.

Lily had been as corrupt as the rest, hadn't she? What else could one be if made from Adam's rib and not God's breath? Was it my fault she was made of clay? I had dreamed her up surely, my would-be bride, but now she was defiled, the corrupt deserved the corrupt. I ran my hand over the gash she had made in my cheek: the wound had opened anew, and the stickiness of my own blood repelled me. Reaching into my pocket to find a handkerchief, I touched the forgotten envelope, feeling it scratch the gravel rash on my palms and my nicked fingertips, catching on the ribboned lining of my pocket as I dragged it out. I tore it open. Inside was a birth certificate.

As I walked close to the weak glow of one of the street lamps, the birds' heralding grew steadily louder, their notes a xylophone up my back, and I trembled. The paper corners were chewed, by termites or mice; the page was pockmarked like the moon. I held it up, the words blurry before my eyes. It had my name upon it, my birthday and the name of my father and the name of the woman I had never met.

Esther. Esther. Esther.

The star seemed to throw its light with an added flare toward earth. I looked again. Father: William Little. No religion recorded. Mother: Esther Goldin. Religion. Jewish. There was a date and executor of a circumcision ceremony.

I was awash with revulsion and dry-retched over my shoes. I read the paper again and pierced the flesh of my own palm with my nail. Was this what my father had meant at Crisp's by 'misshapen'? What I had thought of as normal was nothing but a deformity, a disgusting covenant with the Hebrew's Lord. I was as tainted as the thing I hated; I had become my own target. My own blood revolted more than ever. Was there nothing I could do to erase it? Could I shuck off this old skin and grow another?

The sky wheeled above me. Merle's tale had had the ring of truth, it was I who had blinkered myself, for I could have verified her tale by looking in the box where my birthright had been used as a scrap to wrap a treasure in, my identity concealed in this fragile piece of a paper. Why had I collected all these things when all I wanted was one little remembrance, that little sweet-faced photograph I had lost. How could she possibly be corrupt? My poor mother who my father had forced himself upon; my mother who Crisp had seen as fruit from the money tree, ripe for the plucking; my mother who I had dishonoured by the example of my pitiful life.

Had I looked so long for the perfect woman, never thinking she would be the woman who had borne me?

I would not forsake her now, my mother, my Esther. Her blood ran in my veins. Surely she had watched over me my whole life, my guiding star? Was it her fault that she had no powers against my father's neglect and Crisp's malevolence? What stood between us now except an expanse of sky and my own blood, tainted by ignorance? I belonged with her and to her alone. I would reach her even if she lay beyond my grasp; I would follow her until my legs gave out; we would be reunited. See how she shines her light on me?

In the trench, I had been afraid to meet my maker, afraid to sacrifice my tender flesh and fragile heart, preferring to wound myself briefly than to slaughter myself upon the war's altar. Now I was unafraid of the grandest gesture.

The dawn is coming, the sky is spinning, its colour changing before my eyes, but still I see her, all a-glimmer, perfect and divine. The track as I step upon it looks like a ladder beneath my feet, stretching all the way into the blue distance. My eye never leaves her for an instant. I hear the shout of the blacksmith, his tools no longer singing their metallic throng; there is the sound of feet hurrying upon the gravel. Another train hurtles along the tracks; the clickety-clack vibration thrills up my legs, thunders in my heart. A whistle screams and I am deafened. The wheels make fireworks, sparks and catherine-wheels. They are no match for her radiance. Still she shines. The train strikes me a cataclysmic blow, as a match to a Roman candle.

Then light.

Only light.

FORTY-FOUR

Ari

Cramped beneath the sandstone and the tarp, my uncle slept through the rain-soaked night. Whatever the Birdman had given him, it had calmed him. The rain falling through the canopy lulled us, but I remained awake for a long while. My uncle's soft snores were punctuated by the odd mumble beside me, the Birdman speaking in a language I didn't recognise.

When I woke the Birdman was already coaxing flames over the billycan, a loaf turning black in the ashes, the smell of cooking bread bringing me to my senses. He leaned back on his haunches, pushed his hat back on his head and soaked in the warmth. Beauty sat in the morning light bashing a small lizard senseless before it disappeared down her throat. The whole bush glowed, the eucalypts turning golden and green by turns.

'Challah bread?' my uncle croaked. His face had regained some of its colour. Carefully I helped him sit up.

'Only the best damper you'll see this side of the mountains,' the Birdman said and picked up the hot damper, juggling it in his hands, blowing off the hot ashes. Beauty rose to his shoulder as he broke it into pieces for each of us, the steam billowing in our faces. My uncle just held it and inhaled the smell, burying his nose into it, the bread crumbling in his hands. I bit into it, watching him closely. Beauty hopped closer and stole a piece that had fallen to the ground. I tossed her another scrap until she hopped up on my hand and helped herself.

'It smells like your mother's bread, she had a knack,' he sighed. 'I think she talked to the bread, coaxed it to rise, used her secrets to make it light and sweet.' His eyes softened as he looked at me. His talk of my mother, which I had longed to hear since I was a child, came so sensibly and gently from his lips that tears pricked at my eyes. 'Your mother always loved words, in a different, powerful way. For her, the words of the Torah could protect newborn infants, guide women through labour, aid conception, assist G_d in casting out illness, and serve his children when they needed comfort to enter the World to Come – through her amulets, magic alphabets, *atbash* and hexagrams.'

I wiped my tears with the back of my hand. So these were the things my mother had been doing night after night, leaving against my grandmother's wishes. This was the meaning of the strange markings on the parchment, on my hand. Now I heard him speak it, I could barely take it all in. I was greedy for his words; they took me back to the home I had had before, when it had been just my grandmother, mother and me, before it had been crushed and destroyed in a single dark night. The weight of it felt as if it would crush me.

'Once I read of Hebron,' his voice faltered, 'I knew my scrapbook had become a false idol. None of these places suggested as a homeland could bring back those I loved. When I read of Hebron ...' His voice cracked and no sound came out. He covered his eyes, his hand shook and I knew then he thought of all those we had both loved now lost.

I looked around me at my uncle's promised land, the mist rising off the silvery scrub, rivulets running down the rock face, the dark blue shadow of the gorge itself, beautiful as Eden. What would my mother and grandmother have made of it here? Beautiful as this country was, it was unforgiving to strangers in its wildness. One wrong step and the scrub would fall in behind and keep you.

My uncle drew himself straighter and stuttered. He told me something had driven him; he had heard my mother's voice in the cries of the birds, an angel song out of the mouths of strangers, someone who pressed money into his hand, falling branches making Hebrew letters cast by G_d's hand for him to find his way. The Birdman looked at me and I thought the same thing: his mind had begun to wander again in his own wilderness. But my uncle's voice was his own, his eyes steady upon mine.

'Until you came, my boy, you whom I have raged against and tried to twist into a different shape. Yet it is you who come to find me, your hand guided by G_d.' He gripped my hand, his thumb grazing the letters of my tattoo. 'My heart's son.'

We carried my uncle out of the mountains to the nearest doctor's house we saw, his breathing steady as he dipped in and out of sleep. The doctor we delivered him to was wide-eyed at our strange arrival, but he did not turn us away. He checked my uncle's vital signs before donning his black coat and leading us out to his car to take us to the nearest hospital. We bundled my uncle into the back seat, where I supported him; as the Birdman climbed in the front seat the doctor eyed Beauty tentatively, so the Birdman tucked her under his arm, looking for all the world like a farmer with a prize chicken.

When we arrived at the hospital I carried my uncle in my arms and helped settle him in the bed the matron directed me to, the white of the sheets quickly darkened by the soil from our clothes. How light he had become. The doctor on duty promptly gave him a thorough examination before determining my uncle was suffering from exhaustion and needed bed rest.

'You found him just in time,' the doctor said. 'Not a month goes past as someone doesn't go missing in these mountains. Search parties don't always find them.'

My uncle's eyelids moved as if he was dreaming, and the relief of finding him alive suddenly hit me. How close had we come to losing him?

'They come to take the healing waters or to collect specimens, and the bush just takes them, their bones found years later right where the search party had walked by.'

The mountains would have taken his last breath to their cloudy eyries had it not been for the Birdman. How could I every repay him? He had already found himself a quiet corner, Beauty on his shoulder, his hat over his eyes, his quiet snores puckering the air.

The matron came in with a soapy bowl of water and a sponge, ready to wash the mountain away. Together we pulled off the Birdman's patchworked coat, my uncle's torn jacket and trousers, removed the boots, my uncle's feet raw with blisters – how far had he walked? – but it was I who insisted on bathing away the dirt, until the bowl ran black, seeing the scratches and cuts on his skin reveal themselves with each wipe of the sponge, tree runes. The hospital nightgown slid down over him and I lay his sleeping head on the pillow, abandoned in sleep like a child.

I left my uncle for a brief moment to make a quick telephone call from the nurse's station, to tell Miss du Maurier so she could let Aunt Hephzibah know that I had found him. My uncle had never wanted the telephone put on in case we were interrupted in the Sabbath. The phone rang out at the house. Why was there no one to answer it? I would have to go and tell my aunt myself. The Birdman agreed to stay until my aunt arrived, but Beauty didn't want to stay; she hopped up onto my shoulder, a black sentinel. I went to thank the Birdman for all he had done, but he wouldn't hear of it. The coat I tried to return, but he shook his head, 'It belongs to you now,' was all he said.

It was dark by the time the train rolled back into Sydney, the lights of the city twinkling like a fallen heaven – and all I wanted to do was get back to Miss du Maurier's and see Lily. Would she still be there? I wondered if after our parting she might have returned to the home she had run away from. I had given her no assurances, events had struck me blind. I had clumsily told her I would give all up to my aunt and uncle's wish to study overseas, as if it were not my choice at all. I had tried to tell her how I felt, tried to press her to see that she felt the same, but my speech was crippled. What did I have to offer her, after all? The affliction of the past? I would not be a curse to the girl I loved.

The new moon was like a silver trout in the sky as I walked down L'Avenue, the dim streetlights humming. I was so tired; I hadn't slept properly in days, the nights and days bleeding each into the other. I looked over to Miss du Maurier's house, the shadows from the fig trees spreading over it like wings. Only the light in Mr Little's window burned beneath the veil of the curtains, a strange light, not electric but the shimmering movement of candle flame.

Lily's window was dark against me. I turned the furry collar of my coat up around my ears. The chill of the valley still seemed to cling to me, though the wind was barely a puff. Beauty flapped from one fig tree to the next, before plummeting to a mound of sticky leaves piled up in the gutter. She pulled out a grub quicker than a blink and gulped it down into her throat, then flew up into the branches, sending a startled fruit bat flapping away.

Not wanting to creep like a thief up the stairs and startle my aunt, I knocked on the door like a visitor. My knocks echoed down the silent street. Aunt Hephzibah opened the door, her startled face asking a hundred questions without a word. She barely registered the sight of Beauty upon my shoulder, and I coaxed the raven to hop down onto the gate, knowing she would wait. My aunt led the way up the stairs to the kitchen and did not ask me anything, not a syllable, but filled the samovar with water and tea and waited for the brew to begin.

The kitchen was warm, the stove was still pulsing out its heat; the samovar steamed, and only then did my muscles begin to ache and the room recede as I felt my eyelids close. The key from the broken tefillin was still in my pocket, seeming to burn hot through my clothes and onto my skin. My aunt sat with her hands in her lap, composing herself. I wanted to speak, but she had bowed her head: her lips moved quietly, a prayer. I could not wait until she was done; the last of words of her prayer and my voice come out together.

'He's alive, Aunt Hephzibah. He is at the hospital up in the mountains. You can go to him. The first train is in a couple of hours. He's suffering exhaustion, but otherwise he's unharmed.' Whatever had been banking up her tears was now gone: they ran unhindered, her shoulders trembling with relief.

'G_d heard our prayers. What did your uncle say?' she said, wiping her face. What could I tell her, where could I begin? I was still trying to make sense of it myself. If was as though pages of his life and the Torah had become interwoven, as if the loose pages had been mismatched by a careless bookbinder's hands.

'He spoke of many things. And of my mother and Isaiah.' At hearing this name a fresh flood of tears found their way down the already wet tracks on her face. She was racked with a deep sadness.

'There is also this,' I said as I pulled out the key, heavy in my palm.

My aunt stared at it for a moment, speechless until she sighed deeply and stood up from the table, beckoning for me to follow.

'I put the key in the tefillin that Isaiah, my brother, made. He'd sent it to your uncle as a gift, to show him his skill. Isaiah was training to be a *sofer*, a ritual scribe. I knew your uncle had consigned it to the attic, having an inkling that his *kishef macher*, his magic-maker sister, had made an unwelcome addition with her amulets, rendering it invalid. Your Uncle Israel could not destroy it, as it was still filled with HaShem's words, so he consigned it to the attic to await its burial with the rest of the old mezuzah's scrolls and broken prayer books. I could see no harm in making my own contribution, nor putting it in with your things. It was a little bit of your mother and father joined together, a lot like you.'

She led me to the hallway and stopped beneath the hatch in the ceiling. Together we pulled the attic ladder down and she held it steady as my feet trod those rungs again.

'The suitcase, my *hartse*, you know the one.'

A square of light shot up into the darkness from the passage below, where my aunt waited. The suitcase was coated in dust like fur. I took it and backed my way down, the dust falling away with a sweep of my hand.

Carefully I carried it and placed it on the kitchen table between the still-steaming cups. The key was in my hand; it slid into the lock and the lid sprung free, but I didn't lift the lid. I had too many questions; the contents of the suitcase would only evoke more, until the room was crowded with them, like the ark teeming with animals. What could be in there? A willy-willy of hope rushed through my chest, loomed up in the child in me, that my mother would spring out, just as Bess had done out of Houdini's trunk, restored, returned, whole.

'At our wedding, I could see that Isaiah was enamoured of your mother. The only one who didn't seem to notice it was Israel. Your mother had helped me to put a sparrow's egg between my chest and dress as I walked up to the chuppah, a blessing of the children to come. She didn't know that it would be her firstborn she would bless me with. Isaiah had come back from his studies for the wedding, but Israel could only ever see Isaiah as his competitor and Zipporah as the little girl who was always sticking her nose into books that were not hers to peek into. He did not want to see how their faces grew rosy each time their eyes met, when the men danced in the men's circle and the women in theirs.

'Isaiah went back to his yeshiva to finish his studies, Zipporah went back home with her mother, and we left to come to Australia. When we arrived, a letter already waited for us from Isaiah declaring his intention to marry Zipporah. But Israel was against the match.'

'But why would he do that to his own sister, to his friend?'

'He felt Isaiah should have married a more traditional girl. He did not want Isaiah to be tainted. He knew Zipporah wouldn't put her 'arcane nonsense' behind her. Isaiah of course was angry, who could blame him. He expected your uncle to be happy for them. He loved your mother; he took no issue with her learning, with her being a *kishef macher*. For what were her amulets made of but the same holy words?

'A letter came from Zipporah, which your uncle couldn't bear to read. He started reading it out to me, but as the words progressed he stopped and the letter fell from his fingers. That was the last time either of their names was spoken in this house, it was as though we became only children then, our siblings' names forbidden. Israel took out his scissors and cut the letter into pieces and sealed himself up in his study.'

'What did it say?' I could feel the air change; the contents of the suitcase seemed to pulse beneath my hand and I felt my chest constrict.

'Painstakingly I pieced Zipporah's letter together in secret, and sentence by sentence I read the news your uncle wouldn't tell me. Isaiah was dead,' Aunt Hephzibah said, the words tangled with her tears, 'and Zipporah was pregnant and unmarried. He had gone to find a position in a town a week's journey away. She had begged him to take an egg, an amulet that she had inscribed with the first words of Genesis, but he would not take it, no matter how she pleaded with him. She hadn't told him of the life she carried within her; she was waiting until he had the good news that he had a position, so his refusal of her amulet made her despair. You can read as much yourself, it is all in there. Any other letters that came I intercepted before he saw them, I kept them all.' My aunt pointed at the suitcase. I rested my hand on the lid that been in the attic above my bed all along. My mother's voice captured in print. Her thoughts my comfort. If I had only known.

'What happened to my father?' My voice was not my own, husky, stuck in my throat.

'Isaiah was taken ill on his journey. Typhoid. His body came back to the village. Zipporah was pregnant and unmarried. She buried that egg by his graveside. He would take it with him then.' My aunt gripped the table, her face twisting with her own grief, for the brother she had not been able to mention for too long, the brother she had never been allowed to mourn. My father, who up to now had never been named, who'd been more mysterious than the Master Mystifier. How could I have lived my whole life so far without knowing anything about him? It pained me.

'What was he like, Aunt Hephzibah?'

Tears welled in her eyes then as he came vividly to her memory. 'He was tall like you, gangly even. He had smiling eyes and a soft heart, much like you, my darling boy,' she said, her familiar hand soft on my cheek.

'What is my name then? Isaiah's last name, your name before you were married?' Ari bar Isaiah, Ari son of Isaiah, Ari Pearl. Ari Who? Not Houdini, as I had dreamed as a boy, that I knew.

My aunt looked up at me, her hand wrapped around the curve of the cup, just for something to hold on to, for her tea had long since gone cold. 'Silver.'

Ari Silver. Ari Pearl. Ari Silver.

'All that you need to know is in here.'

My aunt opened the suitcase and the lid flipped back with a thunk upon the table-top. Inside, on the top of the suitcase, was a layer of little baby clothes, a little knitted bonnet, a pair of booties, a little blanket. The clothes for the longed-for child of my aunt's that never came. She carefully lifted them out and underneath was something familiar – the little coat I had worn tight around me as I had run that night with my mother. As she pulled it back, beneath it, I saw a bundle of letters, messages that my aunt had intercepted, kept from my uncle's eyes. Had she had snatched them from the postman's satchel before he could even put them in the letterbox? She'd kept so many things safe – the key, the tefillin, the bundle of letters. My aunt had saved my history from my uncle's scissors, just as my mother had saved my life.

My Aunt Hephzibah took my hand in her own and gave me a page stiff with tape, for my uncle's scissors had raged and done their worst after all: words not cut with his usual precision, but massacred, turned to ribbons. Aunt Hephzibah had patiently pieced together the scraps to form a whole, a gift through time, for me. My mother's voice shone through, my head rang with her words. Carefully I handed the letter back to my aunt and she put it back, safe in the archive, the tale of my mother.

'Your mother marked you to keep you safe. This tattoo on your hand is a living amulet, one that could never be lost or forgotten. Who is Israel to say it is superstition? They killed children in Kishinev, you know. But you came to us out of such a nightmare, all that way, unharmed. It was a miracle.'

I could not bear to meet her gaze; the gravity of what she said haunted me. My mother had saved me by sacrificing herself and her own mother. I felt the weight of my own life, her precious burden. She had read the signs, heard the danger coming, she knew the risk. She had flown me through the streets to the only safety that remained to her.

My aunt flicked through the yellowing pages, and I looked at my mother's handwriting, familiar and strange on paper rather than skin, thousands of dark strokes, links in a delicate chain between us.

My aunt's fingers rested on an envelope, she slid out a letter, thumbed through the pages and handed them to me.

He was born at the rising of the morning star. The first thing he did was not cry but yawn, his tongue darting like a pink bee in the lip of a flower, a yawn as wide as a lion's. I have called him Ari. I thought of calling him Ariel – a lion of G_d – but I have called him Ari – lion, just for himself, to be beholden to no one.

The words set a hot pulse in me. I could hear what she meant, a lion for myself. I had felt this sense quicken upon the mountain. My promised land was waiting. My mother's words were a map, my way forward. She had saved my life so I could live it, not to be as a memorial, as stone.

I have placed a mark upon his hand. I know it would enrage Israel if he was here, but we are already beyond the pale, he and I. We may as well make the best of it – what protection do any of us ever have but from HaShem and our own wits, deeds and words? Sometimes I think the whole world can be reduced to a word – in Genesis HaShem spoke and it was so. I know Isaiah would understand.

I could feel something writhe beneath my skin, an ever-so-slight palpitation in my chest. Inky butterfly wings danced over the page. My breath came in short, sharp bursts as I took in the words.

So I have marked his hand with the word Abracadabra, down the middle of his left hand, a word enough to guide him and not be lost or forgotten, just as the Shekinah can rest on us lightly like a breath yet have the power of the wind. Abracadabra from the Aramaic, avara kehdabra: I will create as I speak. Or the Hebrew abreq ad habra: Hurl your thunderbolt even unto death. The root of the three Hebrew words ab for Father, ben for son, ruach acadosch for Holy Spirit. Abracadabra. I will create as I speak.

All along I had had the key to my own life, inscribed on my hand. The gaps between the dark letters looked like the teeth of one of Houdini's skeleton keys, the ones he would carry in his hair, or curled under the sole of his foot. Yet I had had the means to set myself free all this time and had not known it.

'But who were the family that sheltered me, kept me safe?' Their faces blurred fleetingly through my mind and I recalled that picture on the wall, a mother and a child.

My aunt hesitated but she couldn't withhold anything more from me. 'That woman was the one who helped you into the world, my child, the only midwife that would attend when they turned their backs against your mother.'

My head was heavy in my hands. Her bravery sat in my chest singing. Zipporah. Zipporah. Zipporah. My mother named for a bird.

The clock chimed out in the hallway, it was only an hour before dawn and the first train. There would be time enough to read through my history in those letters later.

Abracadabra. I will create as I speak.

I turned to my aunt. 'The Birdman has agreed to meet you at the station. I'll come when I can.'

'The Birdman? Who is he?'

'The man Uncle Israel owes his life to. You can't fail to find him. He whistles like his namesake. I'll come when I can. There is someone I need to see.'

'It's that girl, isn't it?' I nodded and she stared at me for a time, trying to suppress her feelings, until they burst out of her. 'But Ari, she is a gentile.'

'I'll not give her up.' And I wouldn't, I was my own man, *beholden to no one*, no man, no rules, no religion. I knew that now. My mother's letters had given me my namesake's courage. I would not deny it now. My aunt nodded reluctantly.

She gathered a set of fresh clothes for my uncle, and his *tzitzit* fringes, his yarmulke, his second-best *tallit* shawl and his own amulets, for without them he would feel naked as I would without the mark upon my hand. My aunt handed the little coat to me. I had remembered it to be heavy when I was a child, but in my grown hand it felt just as weighty. As she embraced me I felt her whisper, hurried and warm, in my ear.

'Your grandmother lined the hem of your coat with coins. She's helping you even now.' She kissed both my cheeks, her own face damp, and was gone. I felt the raised shapes in the hem, tested the weight of them in my palm, and felt their gravity. My grandmother had provided me with a small inheritance, enough to build a new life with the one I loved.

I create as I speak.

I would go and find her now, not a moment to lose. I closed the door securely behind me and surveyed the street. A bitter wind hummed along the telephone wires, but I was warm. The Birdman's rag and taggle coat still covered my arms, and now the letters on my hand seemed to pulsate, radiant with their own heat. The last of the night's stars gleamed at me, one brighter than all the rest. The trees made a great rushing sound as if the sky were a great river. I felt goose bumps dance over my skin as if I was shedding something I no longer needed, like a chrysalis. Was that Beauty flapping above me? No, it was just the gathering ferocity of the wind.

Something whistled past my head, and before I could register it, I found I could not move. My coat was riveted to the door. I was pinned fast, then I was struck, a blinding pain across my jaw, and struck again, and then all was dark.

Slowly I grew aware of the pinch of my scalp as a blade scraped my hair away, the curve of the knife dragging across my skull, the cut and the sting of blood. The blow had made a bell ring in my head, my limbs tingle. When I came to, I was slumped against the door, but from beneath my eyelashes I watched, measuring my moment. Mr Little's face loomed over me, barber-close, his teeth digging into his bottom lip. A look of rapture. If he planned to kill me, the coward, why hadn't the blade already done its work?

I create as I speak. I didn't have to be a remnant of the past, the result of others' mistakes, a lost thread. I could begin anew. *I create as I think*. I steadied myself, opened my eyes and did not look away. I would not let another's will reduce me to dust.

My rage roared up in me then. All I had lost would not be in vain, I would not run, I would not be cowed by another's violence. If blood would be shed, it would not be mine. Then, with all I had, I lashed out at him, sending him reeling into the street. His knife rippled like mercury between us but I stood resolute. I reached up and yanked the blade from the door. I would not be swayed from what I had found. My roots were here, and here they would grow.

With a swift kick the knife on the ground was concealed in the gutter. Stepping closer to him, with the blade from the door in my hand, I approached him, letting the handle twirl and spin between my fingers. And then, with a conjuror's art, I made the knife vanish out of my hand into nowhere. I had no need of a coward's blade. I stood only a moment longer, seeing the desire for blood twist into panic. I struck him once more, my fist meeting his temple. He would not follow me now. It was done.

A sudden wind struck at the tops of the enormous fig trees, shaking a barrage of smaller branches to the ground. Twigs scattered behind me as I walked away.

Miss du Maurier's house was strangely silent. A lamp burned on a hall table, a small arc of light spilling on the floor. Before me in the mirror emerged a ghostly face and I realised as I moved toward it that it was mine. Flickering candles showed me to myself as my fingers crept over the shorn surface of my head. My hair was roughly cropped, my scalp grazed. It stung to the touch. The blow he had dealt me must have stilled me for some time for him to do such handiwork.

I got to her door and knocked but there was no answer. I called her by her name, but there was no reply. I carefully turned the handle, the light from the hallway flooding her room. She was not there. Her room was bare, anonymous.

I could see Mr Little's door wide open and I had to look. All the black walls had been used like a blackboard from a schoolroom, a mad scrawl of beautiful words, from the songs of Solomon. Scattered across the floor were the smashed remnants of glass, china, a curled ball of gold metal, the remains of a comb? Something had happened here. The room still bristled with violence.

Miss du Maurier appeared in the hallway wrapped against the morning cold in her dressing-gown, her bare feet in want of slippers. She looked at me and let out a startled cry.

'Ari?'

'Yes, Miss du Maurier, it's me.'

'Oh Ari dear, I didn't recognise you for a moment. Are you all right?' She instinctively reached to touch my head, the grazes stung beneath her touch. 'Your uncle?' she said, pulling her dressing-gown closer as a cool gust blew through an open window.

'I found him, he will recover,' I said hurriedly, peering over her shoulder to Lily's room, her absence yawning at me. Miss du Maurier turned to look at the room's emptiness and then to Mr Little's. The crazed mess of it alarmed me. Where could she be?

I raced down the stairs, out into the dawn light and over to the shed. She would be nowhere if not there.

Beauty sat in the window, her beak wiping the edge of the sill, a morning worm already in her belly. A loud chorus of sparrows lit up the old plane tree with life that seemed to surge with them, brown leaves amongst the freshly sprouted green. The wind steadily whipped at the branches, as the last of the night surrendered to the morning, a magic wind, a holy wind, whistling about my ears. Here I was – illegitimate, marked, shaved, set apart. But I would not be cast out. I was a blessing not a curse.

I will as I create. I speak as I will. I create as I speak.

I opened the shed door. Condensation beaded the windows and it was dark, but I could see her lying there in the gloaming. Her face glowed in the darkness as I moved closer to the bed. Beside it she had placed a shovel as if to arm herself.

I watched the breath from her tender mouth rise into the air. She was wrapped in the old kangaroo skin, underneath which she wore Mr du Maurier's wedding suit, the black plunge making a snowy V of her skin. The top hat was a new perch for the parrot: he shuffled sideways along the rim as if it were a circular tightrope, his feathers jade against the jet.

'Abracadabra, Shekinah, Mizpah,' the parrot whispered in his hoarse voice. Or had I imagined it? I listened for it again, but the bird was still.

'Lily,' I said, her name coming out of me like smoke, a whisper turning to mist in the air. 'Lily?' I wanted to wake her, to see those eyes upon my own, but I also wanted to let her sleep, untroubled. I could have stepped silently away, retraced my footsteps. Be gone and leave her be. But she opened her eyes to me, and they shone.

She was no glimmering girl; she was not going to vanish with the dawn. She reached out her arms and I felt her warm fingers brush the grazed skin of my neck as her arms encircled me. She was my Rosh Hashana, my New Year. I removed my coat before I slid in beside her. There was much to say. But there would be time enough to say it later. For now, it was enough to be close to her. Her body breathed warmth into mine.

'May you be written and sealed for a good and sweet year,' I spoke gently into her ear, and her hair caressed my face, soft as blossom.

She took my left hand, the petals of her lips pressing each and every letter until my skin tingled. She had written her name with kisses.

ACKNOWLEDGEMENTS

Thank you to Rabbi Chaim Rosenthal of Mikveh Yisra'el and the members the Sydney Jewish community who were kind enough to answer my many questions. All errors are mine. To Lauren Dawes, who shared her thoughts and experiences of albinism. To *Wet Ink* magazine, who published the first chapter under the title 'The First Seduction of Billy Little' in the June 2009 edition.

To early readers with gratitude: Rachel Cooley, Mary McCallum, Karen Ferris and Kate Menday, Ruth Richardson and Victoria Innell.

Thank you to my editors for their illumination and insight: Ali Lavau, Denise O'Dea and Julia Stiles. And to proof reader Nikki Lusk.

Thank you to Isobel Dixon and the team at Blake Friedmann, to HarperCollins Australia, and to my family for their love and support.

And special thanks to *kischef Macher* Catherine Milne.

Sandra Leigh Price lives in Sydney. She graduated from the Australian National University, Canberra, with a double major in English Literature and Drama, and co-established a small theatre company before moving to Sydney to pursue a career as an actor. She has written for both the theatre and the screen. *The Bird's Child* is her debut novel.

Printed by RR Donnelley at Glasgow, UK